THE DEAD DON'T BLEED

THE DEAD DON'T BLEED

A NOVEL

DAVID KRUGLER

PEGASUS CRIME

NEW YORK LONDON

THE DEAD DON'T BLEED

Pegasus Books Ltd.
80 Broad Street, 5th Floor
New York, NY 10004

First Pegasus Books cloth edition June 2016

Interior design by Maria Fernandez

Library of Congress Cataloging-in-Publication Data is available.

ISBN: 978-1-68177-139-7

10 9 8 7 6 5 4 3 2 1

Printed in the United States of America
Distributed by W. W. Norton & Company

To Amy

THE DEAD DON'T BLEED

CHAPTER 1

THE ALLEYS OF WASHINGTON, D.C., ARE UNLIKE THOSE OF ANY other city. Small carriage houses, one after another, abut the cobbled or clay backways. Within certain long, wide blocks, the alleys intersect, creating labyrinths as complex as a casbah. Here the two-story dwellings—woodframed and sorely in need of paint—pitch and lean, like a drunk who has stood up too fast. Stray cats slink along weed-choked walls, the stench of shit wafts from outhouses. Residents slump in rickety chairs and makeshift benches, drinking, throwing dice, sleeping. Here and there, scattered signs of neighborly pride. A vegetable garden tucked away, a whitewashed fence, a woman scrubbing her two-step stoop. Washingtonians who live streetside rarely venture into these slums pocketed dark and dank between the city and the capital. Why would they?

"Maybe rolled?" suggested Terrance. His listless tone could hardly hold up the question mark.

"Here?" I flicked my hand at the open windows of the dilapidated houses lining the alley south of M Street and west of Second Street, SE. Two young Negro boys watched us from a corner yard, thumbs hooked shyly at the corners of their mouths. Curtains fell back from an elderly Negro woman at a sill. Though it was 1 A.M., I doubted any of the alley dwellers were still asleep, but other than the two boys, no one had come outside.

"Maybe it happened in one of these houses. He fights back, the buck pulls a gun—he and the whore drag him out front and hightail it."

I turned to the Detective Sergeant from the Metropolitan Police Department. He stood a few feet away, his brim pulled low.

"Any prostitution here?" I asked. "Robberies?"

He exhaled cigarette smoke, shook his head.

Terrance and I looked down at the body.

"He didn't go easy," said Terrance.

On that he was right. Lieutenant junior grade Logan Skerrill, U.S.N., had fought hard. A deep scratch, congealed, swept down his cheek from his left eye. Blood matted his scalp and encrusted his nostrils, another cut slashed his chin. Torn shirt cuff, his pants smudged and scuffed. He had been a handsome man. Dark, curly hair, a little long in the front. Aquiline nose, jawline like a cutter's prow. Six feet tall, maybe. Slim, but strong. Would take an even stronger, or very reckless, man to bring down Skerrill.

"Why go to the trouble to beat up a man you're gonna shoot?"

I looked at the reddish brown stain across Skerrill's shirt.

"S'why we know this wasn't a two-bit con or robbery," I answered Terrance. "Someone wanted to hurt him first."

"Tough break. A month more, maybe, to this war, and he gets it back home in an alley."

The police photographer, a plump middle-aged man with a florid, sweat-slicked face, watched us expectantly. He had knotted his tie too high, his charcoal gray suit was wrinkled.

"How much longer you think?" I asked.

"Not long." He shifted the bulky Leica in his arms. "Ten more minutes, probably."

Terrance and I stepped back from the body. The photographer leaned slightly over Skerrill's feet and pointed the camera down, at the chest wound. *Ka-plunk.* The flash sounded like a billiard ball dropping fast and hard into a pocket. The light burst turned the body's face a brilliant white and, for an instant, lit every crack, crevice, and gap in the alley cobblestones. The failure of the eyelids to clench shut was unsettling, and one pupil was larger and rounder than the other. I walked over to the police detective, a man named Durkin. A few years older than me, gray eyes, ruddy face traced with acne scars, reddish brown hair.

"Takes a while," I commented, tipping my head at the photographer. Now he was standing close to the splayed fingers of Skerrill's left hand, which lay palm-side up.

"Yeah." Durkin seemed to give further reply careful consideration first. "He's good, though," he finally said.

"Maybe you could measure when he's done."

He shrugged. "Yeah, okay." Hands in his pockets, he walked slowly to the black Chrysler with the M.P.D. insignia on the door. Grit on the soles of his wingtips scraped audibly on the cobblestones. He leaned through the open passenger-side window to speak to the driver, a patrolman who hadn't yet left the vehicle. Two other patrolmen stood by their squad car, chatting—no gawking bystanders to keep away tonight.

Terrance ambled up, nodded toward Durkin. "How's our boy?"

"Unhappy. How much, hard to say."

He nodded absently. "We're gonna need to estimate time of death."

"Me or you?"

"I'll do it. You can do the blood."

"Thanks a lot." Grimacing.

He patted me on the shoulder. "Give you something to talk about at your high school reunion."

"Lieutenant . . . ?" The photographer's voice tapered off.

"Voigt," I answered. "Lieutenant Voigt."

"Yessir. I'm all through."

Terrance and I returned to the body. The photographer smiled nervously. "About the prints, Lieutenant Voigt, should I—"

"Two sets," I cut in. "Otherwise develop and log 'em like any other scene. We'll get our prints from Detective Sergeant Durkin."

"Thank you, sir." He nodded and walked back to the patrol car, passing Durkin. After the photographer loaded his gear into the back seat and got in, the car pulled away, the headlights reflecting off dark windows.

Durkin was all business now. He strode to the body's head and slipped a tape measure from his jacket pocket. He pointed to the alley dwelling behind me.

"We'll start there." He extended the tape end toward me. I tugged it with me to the house's front wall, pressed it to the bricks. Durkin snapped the tape taut and jotted the distance in his notebook. We repeated this routine, neither of us speaking, from the feet of the corpse and on the other side. Durkin took other measurements as well: length of the body, which lay crumpled on its right side, legs slightly bent, both arms extended; the width of the blood pool beneath the abdomen; the distance from the alley mouth, which he paced off, counting his steps. He returned, flipped his notebook to a new page, and started sketching the scene. Terrance, crouched beside Skerrill's left arm, shot me an annoyed look.

"We're turning him," he called loudly.

Durkin raised his head briefly, nodded, busied himself again with the notebook.

Terrance grasped Skerrill's left shoulder and pulled, gently but firmly, and the slack, pliable body fell onto its back. Terrance slipped his hand under the arm for a moment. "Still warm. No rigor mortis."

"So in the last few hours?"

He nodded and pointed to the dark pool of blood, now fully exposed. Looked at least twelve inches in diameter. "Try the pencil," he said.

Gingerly, I dragged a pencil tip through the blood while Terrance held his flashlight. The track of the pencil remained on the surface of the pool.

"See how it's dry around the edges?" he asked. "Been clotting two, three hours, I'd say."

"This a lotta blood?"

"Depends on how many times he was shot. One thing for sure, he didn't die right away."

"How do you know?"

Terrance gestured at the stain covering the bricks and filling the mortar lines. "Because the dead don't bleed."

Crouched beside my partner and the body, I surveyed the alley. The two young boys were gone. This close to the ground, the shadows cast by the lone streetlight spilled across the alley like ink blots. Weeds, garbage, slum—if Logan Skerrill had been conscious when he fell to the bricks, his last view of this world wasn't pretty.

I reached into the front left pocket of Skerrill's chino trousers, found only a few coins and a book of matches. The back pocket was empty. Terrance checked his right pockets. No wallet, just a silver clip of cash, and Skerrill's identification card.

"Traveling light," Terrance murmured.

"Could've had a satchel or briefcase with him," I suggested.

"Killed over it? Maybe." He quickly counted the bills in the clip. "Thirty-two bucks—so not a robbery."

Durkin leaned in. "What'd you find?"

Terrance showed him the clip and ID and said, "Change and matches, too."

Durkin scribbled this down. "So not a robbery."

"No kidding," Terrance replied flatly.

I stood up slowly. I had eight inches, easy, on Durkin—I gauged him at about five foot six. "How long till the wagon gets here?"

He peered past my left shoulder, as if the coroner was just now pulling into the alley. "I told them we'd be a while."

"Then let's start the canvass. Be sure to ask when they got home." I pointed to the north side of the alley. "You can take those houses."

He walked off, just slow enough to be noticeable. Terrance sighed heavily and rose to his feet, briskly swept dust from his trousers. "My clairvoyant powers have already told me what we'll get." He closed his eyes and rubbed his temples with his fore- and middle fingers. "Nah, suh, didn't see no' hear nothin'," he drawled.

He was right—we got nothing. No surprise. Half-a-dozen cops and two uniformed naval officers, all white, had descended on a Southeast alley in the middle of the night because a white man turned up dead. What'd we expect, a confession? Most of the Negroes muttered one- or two-word replies. *Did you hear men fighting?* "Nah." *Shots?* "Nah, suh." *When did you get home?* "Don' remember."

"Think a colored cop might get something?" Terrance asked, exasperated, when we reached First Street. I shook my head.

Durkin finished a few minutes after us. The residents had stonewalled him, too. "That it?" he asked me.

"Your men looked for casings, right?"

"Nothing. Too dark."

"So then we're just waiting for the coroner."

"Need me for that?"

Terrance suppressed a snort. "Hell, coroner shows up and there's a body and no M.P.D.—he'll think we did it."

Durkin failed to hide his annoyance at letting himself be shown up. "I'll check on the wagon." He strode back to the remaining police car.

Terrance grinned broadly. "If I'm not mistaken, he wanted to leave us out here by our lonesome."

"I'm sensing his spirit of wartime cooperation is fading as fast as the Nazis."

"Wait'll tomorrow when we ask for the photos. He's just getting started."

TERRANCE AND I WERE INVESTIGATORS FOR THE OFFICE OF NAVAL Intelligence, the O.N.I. A murder shouldn't have come our way—we worked in B-7, the Sabotage, Espionage, and Countersubversion section. Terrance had been a cop in Pittsburgh before the war but he'd only been a detective for a few months before getting his Navy commission. And this was no ordinary killing, as we had just learned. Commander Burton Paslett, our section chief, had called us to his office at the Main Navy Building an hour earlier.

"Know that alley on the west side of the Navy Yard, runs alongside M?" he asked.

"No, sir," I said. Terrance shook his head.

"You will soon." Paslett leaned back in his wooden chair, the steel swivel creaking loudly. He was about fifty-five, his close-cropped hair almost fully gray. The years had padded his cheeks, added a dewlap beneath his chin, but the lean face of his youth was still visible.

"Not till the morning, right, sir?" Terrance asked slyly.

"It is morning." He motioned us to sit. "Just got a call from the Chief of Detectives for D.C. Seems one of ours turned up dead there."

"If he's in an alley, he's theirs," I said.

"Any other alley, sure."

Terrance and I exchanged confused looks. Then my partner exhaled loudly, reached in his jacket for cigarettes. "Somehow this alley is part of the Navy Yard."

Nodding, Paslett said, "We bought the parcel between Second and First last year. All the homes are gone except the block along M and its alley houses. They're due to be razed but it hasn't happened yet."

"M.P.D. knew all that, sir?" I asked.

No answer, his impatient look my rebuke. I should've noticed the bound folio of Sanborn Insurance maps and the oversized diagram of the Navy Yard on the corner of the desk.

"So why do we want this murder, sir?" Trying to redeem myself.

"Because of the victim, Lieutenant j.g. Logan Skerrill." Paslett looked at me. "You knew him, didn't you, Voigt?" A statement, not a question.

I blinked, my mouth open—Skerrill was the victim? I sure had known him, not as a friend, but as a fellow recruit. "Yessir, we went through the Funhouse together," I answered Paslett. *The Funhouse. Coney Island. The Carnival.* All slang for the O.N.I.'s training program for undercover work. The facility, coincidentally located at the Navy Yard, was housed in an enormous aviation hangar and featured mock-ups of apartments, offices, and even a Hollywood-quality street stage to teach aspiring operatives how to pick locks, search rooms, and shadow marks.

Paslett asked, "How well did you get to know him?" Showing mild curiosity, but he must've studied my service jacket and Skerrill's before summoning Terrance and me. Which meant the commander knew precisely when Skerrill and I were at the Funhouse, who our training officers had been, how much contact we'd had.

"I didn't much care for him, sir, so I avoided him."

"Why didn't you like him?"

"He was too good, sir. A real natural. He coulda been a locksmith, the way he could get through doors, and he is—was—a natural-born actor. Put on covers as easily as hats."

"His ratings sure showed that."

"'Specially compared to Voigt's, huh?" Terrance chipped in, grinning crookedly.

The commander shot him a look, but my partner was right.

"Lotta men get tight in the Funhouse," Paslett said. A question, not a statement.

"Not us, sir. Sure, we'd end up in the mess together, we'd shoot the breeze there, maybe we went out with the boys a coupla nights."

"*Maybe?*" The commander squashed conditional answers like the rest of us smack cockroaches.

"*Did* go out with him and the boys, sir. To Borland's."

Terrance chortled—Borland's was a burlesque club off M Street, well known for serving bountiful cheesecake to bluejackets.

"Where you didn't spend much time talking, you and Skerrill."

"Nosir."

"When you shot the breeze at mess, what'd you talk about?"

"I guess—I recall once we talked about how we came to join the Navy, sir."

"And what do you recall about Skerrill's answers?"

"He made a joke. Said he ran away to sea to go whaling but they don't have whalers anymore. So he joined the Navy instead."

"Made a lotta jokes, Skerrill?"

"Yessir. Another reason I didn't like him. Everything came so easy to him, all seemed like a big joke to him."

"You felt like he was laughing at the rest of you."

I hadn't thought about it that way, but the commander had pegged it. Rest of us, all clowns, to Skerrill. "Yessir."

"Well, he sure ain't laughing now," Terrance remarked.

"Where was Skerrill assigned, sir?" I asked.

"OP-Sixteen-Z." The Special Activities Branch. "This last year he liaised with Army intelligence. To give you an idea of what the director thinks of him, he posted him with the Bermuda Special."

Terrance gave a low whistle. The "Bermuda Special" was the nickname for a cruise a destroyer had made from Newport News, Virginia, the previous October. Five officers from O.N.I., all Special Activities, had been detailed to the cruise, which the War Department had overseen. Usually when Army asks Navy to help carry its water, plenty spills along the way. Not this time. Word spread fast—gossip this, earn a long billet in the Aleutians. The vessel and crew, and whatever was aboard, had disappeared into the Atlantic and didn't return for several weeks.

Paslett continued, "Before that, Skerrill helped run the Mexican op that flushed out mercury smugglers for the Japs."

"What was he doing lately, sir?" I asked.

"Supposed to be running background on a couple of new Amtorg arrivals." Amtorg was the Soviet Union's trading company in the United States. Ever since we'd entered the war, the Soviets had seeded agents and spy contacts among Amtorg's staff.

"Supposed to?" This from Terrance.

"Seems our Lieutenant Skerrill wasn't his usual crackerjack self on this one. Spotty reports, no progress, kept raising doubts about his subjects."

"He didn't think they were spies," I said.

"Right. But I have it from a good source that these two Reds were in it deep. So why did Skerrill suddenly go soft?"

"Blackmail?" I suggested.

Terrance nodded vigorously. "Bet he was a fairy, Reds sussed him out."

Scowling, Paslett said, "Cross-checks usually found him tumbling out of some G-girl's bed the next morning. Doesn't sound like a swish to me."

"You think Amtorg's behind this, sir?" I asked.

Paslett thought for a moment. For the chief of an O.N.I. section, his office was modest. Had his share of citations, but none hung on the wall, just a photograph of him and his wife and daughters. His expansive desk was clean, orderly, polish reflecting the overhead light.

"Amtorg's got balls, but they're not stupid," the commander said. "Murdering an O.N.I. lieutenant, that's a shitstorm they don't want."

"So it's not the commies, sir," Terrance said carefully.

"I didn't say that—I just said I didn't think it was Amtorg." He paused, we waited. "I'm gonna share something with you boys you gotta keep to yourselves. The Reds aren't using Amtorg like they used to. Early on, sure, they shipped in spies like United Fruit brings in bananas. But it's too obvious to keep that up. The Russian embassy and the N.K.V.D."—Soviet secret police—"know we're tracking every single Russian who comes in with *Amtorg* stamped on his visa. Now, does that mean the Reds are winding down their ops here? War's about to end, they're just gonna close up shop and go home?"

We knew better than to answer—when the commander got going on the Reds, best you wind your watch and settle in.

"So how are the Reds doing it now, how are they infiltrating? I just had a confab with Army SigInt—they picked up a helluva spike in the Russians' cable traffic. They're working round-the-clock on the code, no luck yet. Now I don't think they'll ever break it, but that's not my point—fact that the cables are up fifty percent tells us something, doesn't it?"

We nodded dutifully.

"So forget Amtorg," Paslett finished. "Reds seeded new plants years ago, now they're reaping bumper crops."

"You think Skerrill was a Red spy, sir?" Terrance asked.

"I don't know—yet. But I think Skerrill getting killed after going soft on Amtorg isn't a coincidence. And you two are gonna find out if I'm right."

"Sir, if I may . . . ?"

Paslett nodded curtly at me.

"If Skerrill was a Russian plant, wouldn't him waffling on this Amtorg investigation be a dead giveaway? To keep his cover, he'd be gung-ho. Especially if Amtorg's no longer the espionage front it was. Like you said, sir."

Being a bright penny earned me a tight smile.

"Very good, lieutenant—guess you learned a thing or two at the Funhouse. Normally, yes, the plant would keep his cover at all costs. But I think something went wrong. Skerrill encountered someone he knew at Amtorg, and he panicked."

"Sir, that shouldn't happen," Terrance put in. "Cells are supposed to be isolated, and no one's better at that than the Russians."

Paslett's withering look caused my partner's shoulders to slump an inch or two. "I did say something went wrong, didn't I, Lieutenant Daley?"

"Yessir."

"And for the record, *we're* better at operational security than the Russians."

"But, sir, then who would want to murder Skerrill?" I put in.

"Jesus, you two—do I gotta fetch a towel so you can dry off behind your ears? If Skerrill panicked and exposed himself, the Reds would bump him off to keep all the other plants protected." He thumped his desk. "Fifty percent increase in cable traffic! They're not sending happy birthday wishes to Uncle Joe, goddammit. SigInt says most of that increase is outta the Russian embassy right here in D.C., and the consulate in New York's a close second. The Reds are on to something big in our yard, and we've gotta find out pronto—before the war's over."

"Yessir," we unisoned.

"Now, I want you to let the D.C. boys do their routine but never let 'em forget who's in charge. I want you turning Skerrill's life upside down for any connection to the Russians. If you don't find one—and you damn well better look long and hard—then we'll drop his murder back in the M.P.D.'s lap as fast as we snatched it away."

"Sir, what if what we find takes us to the Bermuda Special?" I asked.

"If there are holes you need filled, I'll fill them." He glanced at his watch. "You need to get to the scene. Take this." He slid Skerrill's service jacket across the desk.

We stood up, I picked up the file, we turned to go.

Paslett spoke before we opened the door. "Sixteen-Z raised holy hell about us taking this. I had to call in a marker the director's owed me for a while. A lot of fellas are going to be watching you close, sniffing around. But this needs to be our own little Bermuda Special, got it?"

We got it.

THE CORONER'S WAGON ARRIVED AT THE SCENE AT 3 A.M. I HELPED THE driver roll Skerrill onto a stretcher and load him up. Terrance told Durkin we'd call him later that day, after we got a little sleep and reviewed Skerrill's records. Night sky just paling, wrens and robins stirring as I went home. I had a basement flat in a row house on Caroline Street, just off Fourteenth Street, in Northwest Washington. A friend of my pop's, a sour German named Kleist, owned the house. Years ago, back in Chicago, Pop must have done something awful nice for Kleist, because he let me have the joint all to myself. In wartime Washington, your own place was as scarce as nylon stockings or copper pipes. Kleist glared at me every month when he collected the rent, like he was trying to eyeball me into three tenants and a lot more moolah.

A short set of cement stairs led to my door. Small front room, iron bars on the windows. Just one bedroom, long and narrow, parallel to a hallway leading to a galley kitchen and toilet with a shower stall. No stove, just a two-burner hotplate and a small icebox. Came with a fourth-hand sofa, battered easy chair, wobbly table, decent-enough bed.

Franklin D. barely lifted his head from his paws when I came in. A brown and white tabby, a stray I'd coaxed in from the alley colony to take care of the mice that scrabbled behind the walls at night. He was a decent mouser, though sometimes I had to leave his food bowl empty to motivate him. Tilted his head at my scratch, went back to sleep when I walked to the kitchen. I grabbed a beer from the icebox and double-popped the can with the opener dangling from a nail. After prying off my brogans, I stretched out on my mattress and stared at the roughly plastered ceiling.

Took a long pull of my beer. If I ran B-7, I'd let the M.P.D. keep this case lock, stock, and barrel. Hell, I'd never done police work. Just because the murder had occurred on property the Navy had a claim on didn't mean O.N.I. had to take the case, even with the victim being an officer. Paslett's instincts were good, but sometimes he got carried away. He saw Reds around every corner, and his paranoia had only deepened as the end of the war approached. There were a thousand and one reasons why Skerrill might have been killed on this particular night in late April 1945, and Paslett's hunch that Skerrill might be a Russian plant looked like awful weak tea to me. But then, Paslett had *Commander* in front of his name; Terrance and I just had *Lieutenant j.g.*

I drained my beer and set the can on the floor. I suppose anxiety over investigating a murder with barely a clue as to how to go about it should've kept me awake, but during war, when you're safely stateside, you don't sacrifice what precious time you have for sleep to fret about the dead.

CHAPTER 2

ERRANCE AND I MET AT 8 A.M. AT OUR SHARED OFFICE IN THE
Navy Building, one of the "tempos" lining the National Mall.
These three-story buildings had as much beauty as a hog shed and
only slightly more comfort. No conditioned air, only small casement
windows that took a lot of tugging to open. The heat failed to circulate
in winter, your toes went numb under your desk. (Not a few secretaries
and stenos switched out their flats and pumps for wool socks when they
had the night shift.) The bathrooms were cramped, the corridors dark.
Paint peeled from the ceilings and most of the fixtures—light casings,
door knobs, blinds—were loose. Seasonal change, a warm spring day
or a fall cold snap, brought shudders, creaks, and pops throughout the
building.

Terrance took a long drink of coffee, pulled on his cigarette. "Never
believe the dream I had last night."

"Lemme guess: You and Rita Hayworth were solving murders."

"Now, that would be a dream. But seeing as how you were there instead of her, it was more of a nightmare."

I grinned and lit a cigarette of my own, second of the day—the nicotine evaporated the sleepiness I hadn't been able to shake during the bus ride in. I picked up Skerrill's service jacket. "How d'you want to do this?"

"Split it up, I guess."

I slid the file across our facing desks. Terrance took the report on the Mexican operation that had busted up the Jap mercury smuggling ring, I read Skerrill's enlistment form. Tried to read, that is—I had trouble concentrating. I hadn't cared for Skerrill. Hell, I'd hated him. At the Funhouse he'd been cocky and arrogant, had never missed a chance to show off or razz the rest of us when we made a mistake. But he'd been one of us, had worn the same uniform, had served the same side. He deserved a full investigation. I had to find a way to give him a fair shake so I could do my job. *Let bygones be bygones*, I resolved.

Skerrill was nineteen when he got his ensign's commission in the fall of 1940. An only child, grew up in Philly. Pop was a department-store floorwalker, mom a window dresser. One year of college, chemistry major, University of Pennsylvania. First posting, D.C. Navy Yard, Oil Reclamation Lab. A year there, then promotion to lieutenant junior grade and a transfer to O.N.I., first stop the Funhouse.

Skerrill could have told me some or all of this when we met, but he hadn't. *Where ya from?* I'd asked at the mess, first week of our training. *Nowhere special*, he'd replied. I'd waited for him to ask me, but he'd taken a heaping mouthful of spaghetti, chewing noisily before saying something. *You, Voigt, you're from the Midwest. One of those 'I' states, right?* I'd nodded, told him I was from Chicago. *Shee-KAW-go*, he'd echoed. *Fun town, I hear, true?* So I told him a story or two about how a fellow could have a good time in Chicago. By the time we finished eating, he knew a lot about me, I didn't know anything about him.

Something to hide even then? I wondered now, but I kept that thought to myself, asking Terrance, "Whattya got?"

"Our boy had some real get-up-and-go."

"Yeah?"

Tilting back in his chair, he said, "So Sixteen-Z recruits him special for this Mexican thing, right after you and him got outta the Funhouse."

"Makes sense—he studied chemistry in college for a year."

"Yeah, he's there to run tests on the mercury this Mex businessman's going to sell to the Japs' agents. But this Mex, he's no good—keeps losing his nerve, can't keep his cover straight."

"Okay."

"So Skerrill convinces Commander Hughley—he's running the op—to send him in place of the Mex. Goes to the meeting posing as a pissed-off chemist from DuPont hungry for an early retirement in Veracruz. Even spoke enough Spanish to make it feel real."

"Japs bought it?"

"Their Mex contacts did. But it gets better. Skerrill—get this, he's going by 'Señor Corcoran,' how d'you like that?—he convinces these Mexes the mercury they got from their other sources is no good. Puts on a big show, acting like he's running this top-secret test created by DuPont, tells 'em they've been had. So they storm off to get even—lead Hughley's team right to the rest of the smugglers." Terrance snapped his fingers. "Bam! Just like that, Z's rolled up an op the Japs spent a year on at least."

"Not too shabby for his first time in the field." *Much better than me*, I thought. But I kept that to myself, too.

Terrance pointed to the enlistment form and asked, "Anything useful?"

"Not much. He did a year at the Yard in Oil Reclamation. Nothing unusual there. What'd he do after Mexico?"

"Let's find out," handing me half of the remaining documents.

What we got was, The Further Adventures of Boy Wonder. After Mexico, D.C. again, another false identity. Optician with a Kraut surname, fishing up at the Aberdeen Proving Ground for data on the Norden bombsight. Plan was, see if the Nazis had any sympathizers in the labs. They didn't, but his C.O. thought Skerrill was the cat's meow. "Born for Broadway," he wrote in his rating. Next, shortwave propaganda, writing scripts to demoralize U-Boat crews. Didn't even speak German, others translated; Skerrill reaped the praise: "quick study," "eye for detail," "exceptional creativity."

How about "Barrymore's bastard son"? That's what a Funhouse officer called him after watching him play a role during our training. Three of us—me, Skerrill, and an ensign named Lichtman—were acting out a bribery scene. Lichtman, crooked bidding agent for a defense contractor; me, his assistant; Skerrill, naval procurement officer. Lichtman and I: God-awful, grinning, mumbling. Skerrill: greedy, cunning, wary, all of it effortless. *You hams would get booted outta a fourth-grade pageant!* the officer shouted at me and Lichtman as he summoned replacements to try the scene with Skerrill.

Yet I turned the last page of my documents still not knowing who Skerrill was. He never visited his parents, never traveled, didn't belong to fraternal organizations or social clubs. No store accounts, no telephone, no car. Boarded cheaply in a house in Brookland, in Northeast Washington. No trace of hinky anywhere: debts, unexplained absences, expensive habits. On paper, Skerrill lived frugally, quietly, honestly.

"Too squeaky-clean, I think," said Terrance, lighting up.

"Yeah."

"So you didn't get to know him, huh? At the Funhouse?" Studying me through a plume of smoke.

"S'what I told Paslett, right?"

"But now it's me asking. Your old buddy, partner-o'-yours."

"All right, maybe I saw more'a Skerrill than I let on."

"*Maybe?*" Pitch-perfect imitation of Paslett; we both grinned.

"We went through a lotta training exercises together, me and Skerrill—I shoulda told the commander that. But were we pals? Uh-uh—nobody was pals with Skerrill."

"A lone wolf, huh." Terrance stubbed out his cigarette. "Maybe the old man's right. Christ, way he's always going on about the goddamned Reds, sometimes you gotta wonder if he's off his rocker, but there's something fishy about our boy Skerrill."

"Like he wanted everything to look perfect on the outside."

"Yeah, yeah. But what'd he do for kicks, who were his pals? Did he have a steady gal?"

"Never said anything about a girl."

"How was he that night you all went to Borland's? He let loose?"

"He hooped and hollered during the floor show, sure."

"I mean after the show. Help himself to dessert?"

As in, hire a prossy. I couldn't remember—I'd gotten drunk awful quick and had stumbled off to the shabby bungalows behind the club for a girl of my own right after the first strip tease.

"M'sure he did," I answered Terrance.

The telephone rang. I leaned across the desk to take the call; it was Durkin.

After listening for a moment, I said, "Sure, we'll come by," and hung up. "He's got the prints from the murder scene. So much for dragging his heels."

"Seems awful eager-beaver now, huh?"

Good point. Night before, Durkin was sullen, pissed off we'd snatched his case. On the phone just now, he'd been downright chatty. *See you here at the precinct in a little while, okay?* he'd said by way of goodbye. Like he wanted to make sure we were on our way.

"Shit, he's going to the coroner's without us," I said.

Terrance said, grinning, "Let's head him off at the pass."

THE OFFICE OF DR. MURRAY SPERBER, THE CORONER, WAS AT NINETEENTH and I, SE. We drove over in one of the O.N.I.'s dilapidated '38 Chevrolet sedans and presented our identification cards to the lobby clerk, who took us to the autopsy lab. I stared at Skerrill's pale, nude, gutted body laid out on a metal examining table. The sight made me queasy. Just the night before, I'd been crouched over this very same corpse. But Skerrill had been clothed then, lying crumpled and bloody on cobblestones, sure, but still recognizable as a man. Not so this naked, cut-up mannequin. I averted my eyes, scanned the lab. Fortunately, my partner didn't notice; he was trying to get the coroner's attention.

"Who the hell are you?" Sperber asked, finally looking up.

"Office of Naval Intelligence," Terrance replied. He flicked his hand toward the body. "He bought it on Navy Yard property, so it's our investigation."

"Durkin must love that," Sperber grunted, turning his attention back to the table. He looked to be about forty years old, stocky, with powerful forearms and hands. His bald head, fringed in gray hair clipped short, glistened with sweat beneath the hot glare of the overhead light.

"So how many times was he—" I began, but he cut me off.

"A moment, please."

Or several long minutes. Terrance and I drifted toward the door. The examining-room floor, decked in small white diagonal tiles, canted to a grated drain. Bell-shaped lamps dangled directly over each of the four metal tables mounted on cylindrical bases. Tall cabinets with glass-paned doors lined the opposite wall, medical instruments lay pell-mell on a broad wooden counter. A propaganda poster warned of the dangers of not car-pooling. *When you ride alone, you ride with Hitler!* Someone had taped a cutout from a photograph on the head of the driver. Looked like Sperber, but I wasn't about to walk across the lab to find out.

A metallic clatter, followed by a loud sigh, caught our attention.

"All right, that's the third one," Sperber said, more to the corpse than to us.

We took that as an invitation to return.

"Third bullet?" asked Terrance.

"Third wound."

"Shot three times—where?" I asked.

"See that gray ring?" Pointing to Skerrill's left thigh. "Your victim's first wound." We leaned forward warily. Faintly visible in the white flesh, a dingy circle, didn't look like anything more than a scratch.

"That's a bullet wound?" I exclaimed.

"You ever handled a homicide before?" Sperber asked.

Terrance saved me, quipping, "We're O.N.I., mostly we see drownings." No laugh, no smile.

"So your shooter plugs him in the thigh," Sperber went on matter-of-factly.

"How do you know that was the first bullet?" asked Terrance.

"Because of the angle of the second wound." He pointed to another grayish circle, this one just below the rib cage on the left side. "That's about midway on his torso, see?" We nodded. "Look where the bullet comes out." He lifted Skerrill by the shoulders and we peered at his back: the bullet's exit, ragged and much larger than its entry, was just above the buttocks.

"He was falling, or maybe was on his knees," I said.

"Yeah, probably on his knees. Then the fatal wound hits him in the chest, left of the heart. Bled out pretty quick after this shot."

"Took a beating before he was shot, right?" Terrance asked.

"Oh yeah."

"You get the bullet outta his chest?" I asked.

Sperber nodded and pointed to a metal tray on a cart next to the examining table. "It's beat up bad, though. Careened off his breastbone. The other two went clean through. Find 'em at the scene?"

We shook our heads.

"Did you look?" he mocked. Before we could retort, the lab door swung open. "Detective Sergeant Durkin, so good to see you."

"What the hell are you two doing here?" Durkin challenged Terrance and me. "I've been waiting for you at the Fifth Precinct House." Trying to sound indignant, as if he had actually been waiting on us.

"Navy's awful stingy with gas, thought we'd swing by here first," Terrance said, shrugging.

"You said you'd be right by." Durkin glared at me.

"I said we'd *come* by. Didn't say when."

He ticked his chin, his stare contemptuous. *All right then, gloves off.* I hoped Terrance could keep us one step ahead of him.

"Why don't you catch me up, Doc?" Durkin asked.

"Didn't miss much. Three bullet wounds: thigh, abdomen, chest. Last one fatal."

"Time of death?" Durkin had his notebook out, scribbling.

"Based on the liver temp, I'd say about ten P.M. Lividity's consistent with how you found the body." Sperber looked at me mischievously. "You do know what lividity is, right?"

"It's when the blood collects in the lowest part of the body." I pointed to Skerrill's lower right side, the color of mottled eggplant. "Looks just like the bruising the coroner might leave behind after he's had his way."

Terrance's guffaw echoed; even Durkin grinned. Sperber's expression didn't change, but he offered a trace of a nod, so I hoped he'd quit with the grammar lessons. He peered into the tray beside the table and picked up a tooth. "Quite a fist fight before the shooting. Knocked one of his molars loose."

My partner leaned in for a look at the corpse. "Flattened his nose but good, huh?"

"Killer had a sap," Sperber said, nodding. "Some added heft."

"How many punches did he get in?" Durkin asked.

"At least six." The coroner pantomimed a volley of blows. "First he goes for the solar plexus." He made a loud gasping noise. "Our body here, he's doubled over, trying to suck air." Now Sperber swung an uppercut, followed by a right roundhouse. "There's the broken nose." Two jabs, left-right, shot straight toward each cheek. "A ring opened this cut, which means your killer's right-handed." He pointed at the gash below Skerrill's left eye. "Same ring cut the chin—hard left hook."

Terrance looked respectfully at the coroner. "Some nice moves there, Doc."

"Used to box when I was younger. Golden Gloves."

"So was he still standing when he was shot?" Durkin interjected.

"Yeah, shot in the thigh while upright, shot in the abdomen while on his knees, then shot in the chest." He lifted the misshapen bullet from the tray. "This came from the third shot but I doubt you'll be able to match it to a weapon." He tossed the bullet to Durkin.

"Mind?" I reached to take the projectile, looked it over, handed it to Terrance.

"Any other bullets?" asked Durkin.

The coroner smiled. "Nope, still at the scene."

"Thanks, Doc," said Durkin. "You'll send the report to me in a few days?"

"I always do, don't I?"

Terrance and I nodded our good-byes to Sperber and followed Durkin to the lab's anteroom. I spoke first. "Durkin, d'you want to take charge of the search at the scene for those bullets?"

"You're not going to come?" Surprise, quickly turning to suspicion.

Terrance chimed in, "You've searched a lot more scenes than us."

"What're you gonna do?" Still slow to take the bait.

I said, "We got an O.N.I. case to wrap up."

"Another murder?" Smirking.

"Just the usual," Terrance said. "Spies, broads, state secrets." Returning the smirk.

"Well, I don't know how long it'll take to find those bullets."

"That's okay," I said. "We'll meet you back at the precinct house."

"All right." Sensing we were lying, not as yet knowing why. But he left, heels clipping on the tiled floor.

"So we don't want to know same time as him if we got a traceable bullet?" asked Terrance.

"What was that bullet we just looked at?" I asked.

"Thirty-eight, my guess."

"So we're looking for a strong joe, knows how to fight, owns a thirty-eight—how does having a traceable bullet help us find him?"

Terrance: "It'd prove he actually shot Skerrill."

Me: "Only if we can put him at the scene at the time of the shooting. Bullet won't help us do that."

Terrance: "We'd still need that evidence in court—" He broke off, grinned broadly. "But taking the case to trial isn't our problem."

"Bingo. We just gotta identify the shooter and figure out why he wanted Skerrill dead. Like Commander Paslett said, if it has nothing to do with Skerrill's O.N.I. work, Durkin and the M.P.D. can keep their traceable bullets—if they even find one—and ride this case all the way to California. But if Skerrill did turn, we're going to be holding his killer for a long time to see how deep the spying goes. Last thing Navy's gonna do is cut him loose for a trial in D.C. Superior Court."

"That's some devious thinking, partner," clapping me on the shoulder. "While our friend Durkin crawls around on his hands and knees in that alley, we get a jump on the interviews."

Now it was my turn for a big smile.

CHAPTER 3

L OGAN SKERRILL'S BOARDING HOUSE WAS A LARGE BRICK COLONIAL located a few blocks from Catholic University. Box elder on the front lawn, wooden deck chairs on the front porch. Close to noon when we rang the bell, everyone at work. The landlady, a Mrs. Sundstrom, answered the door, ushered us in, told us what a shock it was, what had happened to Skerrill. Of course, neither she nor her tenants could think of anyone who would want him dead.

"Clean, neat, friendly," she answered our first question.

"Always said hello," I said.

"More than that. He remembered names, what people had told him."

"He was talkative."

"He listened, and he told good stories. But he was no gabber."

"What kind of stories?" asked Terrance.

"About his travels. About growing up in New York."

Terrance and I exchanged looks.

"Do you remember any of the stories?" I asked.

Shaking her head, Mrs. Sundstrom said, "Not to tell like Logan did. He could do accents. Sounded just like an Italian waiter when he told us about being in Rome."

For sure, a trip to Italy would have been mentioned in Skerrill's jacket.

"Happen to say when he was in Rome?" Terrance asked as he studied a framed photograph on an end table.

She smiled as she looked at the photograph. "My eldest son, Richard. Army Signal Corps—he's in France now. No, he didn't say—Logan, I mean. Of course it had to be before the war."

"Signal Corps—important work." Terrance set the picture down and carefully realigned it. My cue.

"I've always envied those grand trips Logan took," I tried.

"Oh, yes," Mrs. Sundstrom said, now looking at me. "But if I might paraphrase F. Scott Fitzgerald, the rich are different from you and me."

"Yes, they send their children to Europe. If I might adapt Hemingway's answer."

"Very nice, lieutenant. My reference often goes unnoticed."

"Would you say Lieutenant Skerrill liked to boast about his family's wealth?" I asked.

"Oh no, quite the contrary. He was very discreet, I'm sure because he didn't want to make the other tenants feel uncomfortable."

Or get caught in a lie, I thought, looking at Terrance. He nodded knowingly.

"Could we see his room, ma'am?" my partner asked.

"Of course." She stood up briskly from her parlor chair and led us upstairs. A slim, tall woman, looked to be seventy or so, surprisingly spry. Gray hair fashionably set, looking smart in slacks and a checkered blouse. She told us her husband had been a professor at Catholic University until his death ten years before.

"I let the rooms to make my children anxious," she said, turning on the landing to face us. "That way they call more often."

We laughed obligingly. The hallway was narrow, the walls undecorated. She unlocked Skerrill's door and stepped aside so we could enter.

"You'll be quiet." A statement, not a question. "Mister Lombard below works nights."

"Quiet as mice, ma'am," said Terrance.

"Never say 'mice' to a landlady, young man. Bad luck." Pursing her lips in a smile, she pulled the door shut with the softest of clicks.

"Nice old bird, don't you think?" Terrance chuckled.

"Near-sighted, I'd say, calling you a young man."

"You're just jealous. So why'd Skerrill lie about his family?"

"From his jacket, looks like he never visited his parents. Maybe he hated 'em. Or was ashamed of his upbringing. More fun to be a rich man's son than a poor man's."

Terrance shook his head. "I'm thinking it's one'a two other reasons."

"All right."

"Maybe he loved field work so much, he practiced cover stories on strangers."

"Or?"

"He was a compulsive liar."

"No reason it couldn't be both," I said.

"Let's see what his quarters tell us." We turned our attention to the room. Mrs. Sundstrom was right—Skerrill was neat. Blanket on the single bed pulled straight and tucked, two pillows plumped against the headboard. On the nightstand, an alarm clock ticked.

"Mrs. Sundstrom seem the sort to come in and wind your alarm?" I asked.

"No."

I picked up the clock and turned the key, felt the slack. "It was last wound probably the night before." I showed Terrance the back. "Not set, either."

"Our boy planned to stay elsewhere."

"Guy like that, had to have a girl or two." I put the clock back. Books filled a small case within arm's reach of the bed. Margaret Leech, *Reveille in Washington*. W. Somerset Maugham, *The Razor's Edge*. Lots of novels, some history. Four titles from the library, a well-thumbed copy of the Federal Writers' Project guide to Washington, D.C. I leafed through it to see if Skerrill had marked any pages. He hadn't, but in the index there was an inked X next to the entry for Lafayette Square.

"Why would Skerrill be interested in Lafayette Square?" I held up the guide.

"Easy to enter and leave. Lots of foot traffic. Very public. Tourists always around."

People who sell their nation's secrets, they like to meet their contacts in public places, parks especially, where two people taking a stroll or sitting on a bench, chatting, don't look out of place. Lafayette Square was an ideal rendezvous, except—

"It's right across from the White House. Anyone who's lived in D.C. for more than a week knows where it is. Why would he have to mark a guidebook?"

"Maybe he did it when he first moved here."

"Maybe," I said doubtfully. The Skerrill I'd known at the Funhouse had often bragged about how well he knew Washington, though he was a recent arrival like the rest of us. Perhaps he'd used the guidebook to learn the city, but why just one mark in the index? Why was it so conspicuous? I couldn't help but think of the swashbuckler magazine stories I'd read as a kid. *X marks the spot.* I put the book back.

Terrance opened Skerrill's dresser and carefully examined the contents. Precisely folded T-shirts, square stacks of drawers, bundled socks. Slacks and sport shirts, arrayed as individual outfits, with one shirt atop each pair of pants.

"Jesus H. Christ, what kind of man lays his clothes out like this?"

"This place is like a model apartment," I said. "You show it, but no one lives in it." The dresser and bookcase were just the first signs that Skerrill prized order, structure, neatness. The small writing desk was devoid of papers, pens, torn envelopes, unfolded letters, magazines, scribbled notes—anything that might show it was regularly used. In the closet, a rack of shoes (polished), dress uniform, suit, and several blazers hanging side by side. No trunk, no footlocker, no boxes.

"No pictures," Terrance observed. "Not even of good old Mom and Dad."

I checked the pockets of the clothes on hangers, came up with a book of matches. *The Sand Bar.* "Heard of it?"

Terrance looked up with alarm from an inspection beneath the mattress. "Yeah—it's a swish joint. Local vice nets an officer there now and then."

"The commander said Cross-check saw Skerrill leaving girls' places early in the morning. So I doubt he was a fairy."

"Maybe he was throwing them off the scent."

Good point. OP-12-D, the tiny unit responsible for the O.N.I.'s internal security, was a dumping ground for retirement-ready officers and those who couldn't hack field work. Say Skerrill knows he's going to be followed on a certain night. He gets some gal he knows to pretend to be a date. But if he was smart enough to shake 12-D, how was he so careless as to keep the swish matchbook?

"Look at this." Terrance rose heavily from the floor, where he had been looking beneath the bed, and handed me a scrap of paper. *Chet, L.S., 10 P.M.*, it read in pencil.

"So he wrote a reminder about an appointment. Chet could be anyone."

"And L.S.?"

"Someone else."

"Or the place."

"Like Lafayette Square," I said, nodding slowly.

"Right. Local vice makes a lotta raids there, too. In the men's rooms."

Late at night, Lafayette Square was a notorious trysting spot for men, and men only.

"Might explain the lying about his background," I said. "Trying to be someone he's not."

"Would also explain why this room is so goddamned neat," Terrance said, laughing.

"Funny." I gave back the scrap, he slipped it into his notebook. "So whattya wanna do? See if they recognize his photo at the Sand Bar?"

"Sure." He brightened. "We'll bring Durkin along. We find out this is one homo killing another, I can't wait to see his face when we dump the case back on him."

WE DIDN'T WANT DURKIN TO KNOW ABOUT OUR SEARCH OF SKERRILL'S room, so we decided to tell him there were rumors about Skerrill being queer. After a quick lunch, we drove to the Fifth Precinct House, where we found Durkin at his desk, logging additional items collected in the alley: a shred of brown cloth that appeared blood-stained, two casings, and a bullet.

"Traceable?" Terrance asked.

"Our ballistics guy says I bring him the gun, yeah." Durkin carefully wound the string of the identifying tag round the clasp of a manila evidence envelope. His desk was a wreck: stacked wooden trays overflowing with papers, a black Underwood blanketed by a badly folded *Times-Herald*, an ashtray brimming with butts. Durkin lit up and blew smoke toward a giant wall map of D.C. He hadn't invited us to sit—no chairs in front of his desk anyway—so we stood. The detectives' squad room was on the second floor, its windows looking out over tiny Marion Park. I glimpsed an elderly man on a bench, feeding nuts or bread crumbs to a dervish of a squirrel, its tail bobbing as it chased the tossed morsels.

"Take care of your case?" Durkin asked.

"We did," I said. "And found out something interesting about Skerrill."

"Yeah?"

"Office scuttle has it he liked to hang his hat at the Sand Bar."

"The Sand Bar? Probably hung more than his hat there."

"What we're thinking." Terrance pulled out the glossy 3" by 5" head shot of a uniformed Skerrill and waggled it at Durkin. "Want to see if this pretty mug gets any double-takes over there?"

"Little early in the day, even for fairies."

"Bartender's probably setting up," I said.

Durkin stubbed his cigarette and tugged his jacket from the back of his chair. He started for the door, but we didn't follow.

"Durkin," I called after him.

"What?" Turning, annoyed.

"Can we have our scene prints?" I gestured at his desk.

"Oh, right." He returned, rummaged through the mess, and wordlessly handed me a thick envelope.

THE SAND BAR WAS ON FOURTEENTH STREET, JUST SOUTH OF THOMAS Circle. Easy to miss, on the ground floor of a red brick apartment building, no neon, just a small painted sign swinging from a bracket. Inside, black vinyl booths, black glossy tables, mirrors, and French café posters on the walls, bar veneered in framed maple panels. The bartender was uncorking a bottle of wine when we entered. He wore a pressed white shirt, black vest, and black tie. Brown hair combed back. Short but solidly built, with deepset eyes and a squared-off nose—even if he was a swish, he probably didn't have trouble handling drunks and troublemakers. *Plofft*—he finished pulling the cork and set the bottle down.

"You're supposed to raid right before we close, not right after we open." The bar's only two customers, two men in suits at a table, bristled.

"Don't get wise," Durkin said menacingly to the bartender.

We pulled stools out of our way and leaned in.

"Drinks, boys? On the house."

"No," I answered.

"Let me serve my paying customers. Then you can tell me who it is you want to know if he's been in here."

He didn't wait for our approval. Set the wine bottle and two glasses on a small tray, walked over to the table, no hurry. Gurgle of the wine being poured, no one spoke. With a practiced hand, the bartender swiped the lip of the bottle with a white napkin and returned.

"Hope you brought a photo. Tall, dark, and handsome describes a lot of our clientele."

"What's your name, sweetheart?" Terrance asked in a low voice.

"Ernest." He met my partner's glare with a cool look.

"Look, *Ernie*, we won't tell you again to button it. You speak when you're spoken to—got it?"

"Or what? You're gonna show me what a *real* man is like?"

"Listen, you homo, we can shut this place down and have you in jail faster than you broke your mother's heart when she found out what you are."

Ernest didn't flinch. "Yeah? You gonna take us in on Section Twenty-two charges? Two gentlemen enjoying a bottle of wine? How long you think that'll stick? Or maybe you think they're not of age. You're not vice, so don't try to play the game—the Sand Bar has a very good attorney. Two, actually."

Terrance clenched his fist, the tendons in his wrist tightened. I placed a steadying hand on his flexed bicep as Durkin watched us with an amused look.

"Let's show him the photo," I said.

Terrance grunted and slid Skerrill's photo across the bar. "Seen him here?"

Ernest picked up the glossy and took it underneath the cash register lamp. After a moment, he returned, shaking his head.

"Never?" I asked dubiously.

"Can't say never. But ours is a regular clientele. And a naval lieutenant would be popular here."

Terrance looked ready to explode, but I cut him off.

"You know the stripes." I gestured at the photo.

"Took enough orders, should know the rates. Sir."

"You were Navy?" Terrance snorted derisively. "That's rich."

"No one seemed to mind at Tarawa."

"Let me guess why you're out: you won the Congressional Medal of Honor, and now you tour the country selling war bonds. When you're not bartending here." Terrance flicked his hand dismissively.

He didn't answer, just kept up that level look. Not much we could say would get under his skin. A thought occurred to me.

"This isn't a field investigation because someone ratted on him," I said. "He was murdered, and we're trying to find his killer."

"I meant what I said: I've never seen him in here."

"If not here," I asked, "where might he have gone?"

"Try the Maystat. Sixteenth and L."

I nodded and picked up the photo. Outside we blinked in the bright sunshine.

"Jesus, Voigt, are we gonna have to go back there soon and ask about you?" Terrance said irritably.

"What?"

"Thought you were about to ask that swish to the prom, way you sweet-talked him."

I almost lost my temper, checked it. "Bad cop, good cop—isn't that our routine? Besides, your rough-trade act wasn't working."

For a second, his face flashed with anger. But then he grinned broadly. "Rough trade, funny." He patted me on the shoulder as Durkin smirked.

Who the hell got the answer we needed? I thought angrily. But I kept quiet, remembering Rule Number One of the O.N.I.: never quarrel in front of outsiders.

CHAPTER 4

WHEN I GOT HOME, A NOTE FLUTTERED FROM THE DOOR. *MEET ME AT the Palace for dinner? Be there till 7, Liv.* I yanked the paper free and let myself in. Franklin D. was at the threshold, back arched, brushing against me. I held the door open so he could go out, but he just stared up at me impassively, then turned effortlessly, like cats do, to rub my other leg. I crumpled the note and threw it down the hall, but he didn't feel like playing, probably just wanted to be fed. I hadn't seen any mice in a few days, so I opened some Spam and set the can on the floor. He settled into a crouch and tilted his head to get at the hash. I brought a beer in from the kitchen and dropped to my lone upholstered chair.

Terrance and I had called it a day after taking Durkin back to the Fifth Precinct. No point in visiting the Maystat, or any other swish joint, until we knew more about Skerrill's personal life. And that meant interviewing Skerrill's comrades in 16-Z in the morning. I wanted nothing more than to drink a beer, or three, and get some rack time.

Still could, if I ignored the note. Considered flipping a nickel, heads to stay, tails to go, but decided not to bother. If it came up heads, I knew I'd flip the coin again.

The Little Palace was on the corner of Fourteenth and U, the kind of diner where the counterman started pouring your coffee as soon as you came through the door and a well-timed nod caught you the daily special. Its counter and booth tops were wrapped in corrugated metal, and folded paper menus drooped, like neglected flowers, from brackets clipped to the table edges. The owner was a hulking immigrant with the improbable name of Gerald, his close-cropped hair the same texture and color as his griddle brush.

Liv sat in a corner booth, reading, a half-full coffee cup and a plate scattered with pie crumbs in front of her. White pleated blouse, herringbone-patterned slacks, matching jacket with padded shoulders. Jet-black curls, coiled like springs, brushing her shoulders, a forefinger absently teasing a curl. Even with her head tilted to the book, her smoothly planed cheekbones, demure nose, and wide round eyes were visible.

I slid into the facing seat, vinyl squeaking.

"You came." She didn't put the book down—just looked at me over the covers, and I had to guess she was smiling from her arched eyebrows. That, and the gleam in her eyes.

"Was in the neighborhood." Shrugging.

"You live in the neighborhood."

"Lately doesn't feel like it."

"Big case?"

"Vacation, actually."

"And how is the Riviera this time of year?"

"Cold. But at least they're speaking French again."

Liv laughed and finally lowered the book, set it to the side. She was smiling, and I was suddenly glad I hadn't wasted time flipping a coin. "Hungry?" she asked.

"Starving." Gerald was hovering in the vicinity, and I motioned him over.

"Yes, you want?"

"Steak, mashed potatoes, any vegetable."

He nodded—he never used a pad and pencil.

"How will you be?" Liv asked after Gerald had left.

Not, *how are you*, not *how have you been*, the question I asked her not long after we met. She'd shaken her head. *How will you be—ask me that.* Part of her personal philosophy, she'd explained. Always be interested in what's going to happen, not what already has.

"Good, hoping for better," I decided to say.

"You work too hard, El," smiling brightly. No one called me El but Liv. *Ellis from Chicago*, she'd said the night we met. *City of big shoulders, city with an el.*

"Maybe you should write me a doctor's note."

"Just a few weeks more, right?"

Shaking my head, I said, "I think this war's got some legs yet."

"What will you do? Whenever it's over?"

"Start going to church. Teach my cat to dance." Truth was, I was awful good at not thinking about what I was going to do when *it* was finally over. "How about you?"

"I'm going to the Pacific."

"Good God, why?" Laughing, certain she was kidding.

But she wasn't.

"Don't you read the papers? All those beautiful islands. Tropics, beaches, sun-drenched one minute, awash in rain the next. Papua New Guinea. The Solomons. Bikini. Did you even know these places existed before the war? I wanna pack a trunk of books, some clothes, and island-hop."

"Marines can send you tomorrow, all expenses paid."

"I think I'll start in San Francisco," she went on, ignoring my crack. "Work a while, save some more money. You could come visit."

"What if the Navy makes me an admiral?"

"You need to get out of the Navy after the war, El, at least promise me that."

"I thought you didn't believe in promises." Another part of her philosophy. *Promises are just preludes to disappointment.*

"You can believe in them, if it helps get you outta the Navy."

Gerald arrived with my food. Steam wafted from a dark puddle of gravy in the potatoes, buttered lima beans glistened.

"You had something, right?" I asked Liv.

THE DEAD DON'T BLEED

She nodded and said, "Eat, El—we'll talk when you're done." Without another word, she picked up her book and resumed reading. How inconsiderate, some might say, but that was Liv. Way she saw it, to keep talking while only one of us was eating was ruder than picking up her book. *Ever think how much effort we waste on unnecessary rituals?* she'd asked the night we met. *Guess I'll never send you a Christmas card*, I'd answered.

So I watched Liv read as I ate. *Ulysses.* Looked like she was about a hundred pages in. Last time we saw each other, she'd proudly told me that after being on the library's waiting list for months, she'd finally been able to check out a copy. Now that she had the book, nothing—not the clatter of dishes from the kitchen, the scrape and clink of my utensils, a gale of laughter from a nearby table—could distract her.

I crossed my knife and fork, pushed the plate to the side. "Due back soon?"

She lifted a finger, not taking her eyes off the page. A long moment, then she slipped the marker back in and put the book down. "Sorry, I wanted to finish that sentence."

"Helluva sentence."

"You have no idea. And it's due back in two weeks."

"So, Liv."

"Yes?" Smiling.

"How will you be?"

"Wonderful. It's spring—how could I not be?"

"Been awful cold and rainy."

She shook her head, curls swaying, as if shaking off that rain. "Never for very long, have you noticed?"

"Not really, no."

She reached across the table and took my hand. "Will you come with me to the cherry blossoms?"

"Now?"

She nodded brightly.

"But it's nighttime—you can't see anything."

"Which is why I'm gonna close my eyes when we get there."

I laughed, thinking she was joking. Then I noticed she wasn't laughing. "For real?" I asked.

"Don't they say your other senses are heightened when one is taken away?"

"You just wanna smell the blossoms, that's what you're saying?"

Now she smiled. And nodded.

I said, "Good way to end up awful wet."

"Not if we're careful."

"Oh Christ, Liv, you can't go strolling along the Tidal Basin with your eyes closed."

"El."

"What?"

"Live free."

"No."

"And the rest will follow." *Live free, and the rest will follow.* The heart of Liv's philosophy.

"Tonight's not good for freedom, Liv."

"If it wasn't, you wouldn't be here."

I shook my head and reached for my wallet.

WE TOOK A BUS TO THE MALL. THIS LATE IN THE WAR, ONLY THE memorials—Washington, Lincoln, Jefferson—remained dark. Scattered lights twinkled in the tempos, headlights flashed on Fourteenth Street, warning buoys bobbed and blinked red along the bridge abutments in the Potomac. Liv slipped off her flats to walk barefoot, dangling the shoes from her fingertips. A cloudless sky and three-quarters moon, its reflection rippling on the Basin and the river, softened the darkness. A stiff breeze chilled the air as we walked toward the pink crowns of the cherry trees.

"Did you read the book I gave you?" Liv asked.

"Yes."

"And?"

"Wilde's better."

"Not better. Different."

"Better. I like periods at the end of sentences. Also capitalization."

"But how else to tell us how Benjy sees the world?"

"Signifies nothing, so why bother?"

She pushed me playfully. "You just don't like writers who're still alive."

True enough. Liv had found me at the D.C. Public Library, reading a collection of Goethe's poems as she walked from the water fountain. *You can read Goethe in German?* she'd asked. I'd nodded. *Read me some.* So I read Goethe aloud, Liv leaning over my shoulder, her hair grazing my ear. A librarian shushed me, we both looked up, startled, then looked at one another; and Liv came into focus. Smattering of freckles across the bridge of her nose, lips glistening from her drink of water, eyes green-gray, color of the ocean catching sun on a wintry day. I turned back to the poem and resumed reading—silently. When she saw me moving my lips, she laughed so loud we both got kicked out. We spilled out onto K Street for proper introductions, the library's white marble walls tinged pink in the summer dusk, pigeons fretting at crumbs on the walkway, a young couple necking on a bench on the library's lawn.

Now we were upon the cherry trees, and Liv breathed in deeply. "Isn't it exquisite?"

The scent of the blossoms was faint, but I nodded anyway. I raised myself to perch on the iron railing of the path running alongside the trees. "I'll wait here till I hear a splash, then I'll call the Coast Guard," I said.

Liv pulled me off the railing. "We're not going to fall in."

"You're really gonna close your eyes and start walking?"

"Yep, and so are you. C'mon." She bent to slip on her shoes, then grabbed my hand, fingers of her other hand grazing the railing lightly, as if she was testing the keys of a piano. Ahead of us, the dome of the Jefferson Memorial was almost luminescent in the moonlight. Its columns looked like sentries on a remote picket. Mister Jefferson himself was lost within the shadows. Watching with a grin, I hoped—heard he was a *bon vivant.*

"Eyes closed?"

"Yes."

"Promise?"

"Yes." I blinked once, twice—the Memorial disappeared, as did the trusses of the Long Bridge. Liv quickened our pace. Gravel rasped underfoot, murmuring voices drifted across the Basin. Another couple—a trio?—approached, interrupted by our heedless charge. "What the hell—hey!" "Watch where you're going!" Scrape of shoes, rustle of clothes as they stepped swiftly aside. "Idiots," I heard over my shoulder. A low-hanging branch almost toppled my hat, and suddenly I realized Liv was right—the blossoms' aroma had intensified.

"Liv?"

"Yes?"

"Do you know when to stop?"

"Hope so!" And with that she halted and spun around, reached for my other hand, and pulled me close. We were near the base of the Memorial. "Wasn't that fun?"

I looked down into her eyes, her rushed breath caught between parted lips. "Yes."

"They really smell better that way, don't you think?"

I nodded. She sighed and settled against my chest, arms wrapped around me, head tucked beneath my chin. Neither of us spoke for a moment. In the distance, the dim bulk of the Lincoln Memorial was just visible, and the canopies of the Mall's trees were dark green, almost black. Overhead, the thrum of an airplane's engine.

"El?"

"Liv?"

"Take me home."

I AWOKE ABRUPTLY, GROGGY, EVICTED FROM MY SLUMBER BY AN unsettling dream. The one I'd been having every night lately, about the girl I'd known years ago in Chicago. Delphine. This time, I glimpsed her on Broadway, outside Goldblatt's, but the sidewalks were crowded, shoulder-to-shoulder, and it seemed an eternity before I'd pushed, bumped, and pressed my way to her, curses and threats trailing me like a foamy wake. *Delphine, Delphine*, I kept shouting before she finally turned. Bits of grass and dirt clung to her hair; her face was dirty. She took my hand—her grip was icy cold—and pressed her lips to my ears. *You shouldn't have come, Ellis.* As soon as I protested, she disappeared—and I awoke.

Franklin D. lifted his head, blinking, when he heard me stir, stretched his front paws out on the bedroom chair, and closed his eyes. Liv slept with her head on my chest, left leg draped over me. She stirred as I shifted but didn't wake. Dawn not long to arrive, I guessed, but I didn't look at the ticking alarm clock. If I was lucky, I'd ease back to sleep in a few moments, get at least another hour.

I wasn't lucky. As tired as I was, I lay awake remembering Liv's last visit, two, maybe three weeks prior. She had been lying next to me, naked, my palm resting on her hip, sweep of hair across my outstretched arm, breath warm on my bicep.

"Are you cold?" I'd asked.

"No."

"Do you have to go?"

She'd lifted her head and smiled. "Go where?"

"Home."

"Silly. This is home, right now."

"Welcome back. How was your trip?" An edge in my voice.

"El." Smile gone.

"Liv."

"What's wrong?"

"Nothing."

She hadn't answered, only waited.

"Okay, it's just that, well," I'd begun. Long pause. "Well, seems to me that you could. . . ." But I'd never finished the sentence.

She'd raised herself up, propped her chin in her hand to look at me. "Could what?" Asking inquisitively, no hint of concern.

"Tell me a little bit more about yourself?"

"Is that important to you, El?"

Good question. What I knew about Liv could be written on a postcard while leaving room for "Wish you were here." Came from Cleveland, or was it Cincinnati? Taught herself to type at the public library. Saw the government ad in a newspaper and bought a one-way ticket to Washington. These little bits I'd gleaned from rare, fleeting comments. But did it matter where Liv came from, did I need to know how many siblings she had, if she'd played the clarinet or the violin in high school, what her father did for a living? We had plenty to talk about when we saw each other—poetry, novels, music, ideas. Yesterday's Liv, a school girl, an awkward teenager, an adult striking out on her own, belonged to another time and place. Was I worried that Liv had secrets, had she run away from a drunkard of a husband, had she gotten pregnant at sixteen and given up the child? So what if she had, didn't we all have secrets? We also had *time*—we had the present, ours to savor or squander, depending on the choices we made. As she said so often, *live free and the rest will follow*. First time Liv had said that, I'd almost laughed, the adage sounded so hokey. But maybe I was catching on.

"No, it's not important, Liv," I'd finally answered. Then, repeating myself: "Welcome home." This time smiling. She'd burrowed closer, sighed happily, and we'd fallen asleep.

A good memory, I supposed. So why did I have so much trouble slipping back to sleep this night?

CHAPTER 5

L OGAN SKERRILL, LIKE THE REST OF US IN O.N.I., HAD MADE DO with a shared cubbyhole of an office. The lone window offered a view of the Washington Monument. On the desk, carefully arranged stacks of papers, tabbed folders lined up symmetrically. Familiar tempo clutter: Hulking steel safe for classified files; corkboard pinned with a messy quilt of maps, placards, graphs; jutting file cabinet drawers; dark glass jar of mucilage, cap off, its brush poking ruined bristles up toward the fluorescent light; colored onionskin carbons—orange, yellow, goldenrod, green— scattered like fallen leaves, the autumn of our paper war. Typewriters and telephones substituting for M1 carbines and hand grenades, Dictaphones for detonators, mimeographs for Mustangs; the smack of staplers serving as our rifles' reports, manila our combat green. Maybe I didn't know war firsthand, but I'd seen its wake—Pearl a watery cemetery, giants half-fallen in their graves—and sometimes, with the war drawing to a close, I looked around our offices and couldn't escape the thought that nothing we did here contributed to victory.

Skerrill's office mates, Lieutenant Samuel Warrington and Lieutenant Commander Dean Breit, were at their desks when Terrance and I came in. We didn't know them well. Warrington looked to be in his mid-thirties, medium height, paunch swelling his khaki shirt. Blowsy face, flat, wide nose, start of jowls. Breit was trim, with dark hair and brooding eyes behind wire-rim glasses.

Introductions didn't take long; they knew why we were there. Terrance sat at Skerrill's desk, I pulled up a chair.

"Helluva thing, isn't it?" Warrington said.

"Yessir," I said, and left it at that.

"Heard you took over from the locals," Breit commented.

"They're not too happy about it, sir," Terrance said.

"We've been going through Skerrill's Amtorg file since this morning. Here." Warrington plucked a sheet of notebook paper from his desk and leaned forward, swivel chair creaking.

"What's this?" I asked, taking the sheet.

"First two names, the Russians Skerrill was tracking. After that, their known contacts since arriving. About six, including three Russians attached to the embassy. Always a bad sign."

"He kept good notes, Skerrill did," added Breit.

"Thanks, sir." I handed the sheet to Terrance without looking at it.

"You don't want to go over it with us?" Warrington asked, irritated.

"Not yet, if you don't mind, sir," Terrance said. He folded the sheet in half and slid it to the side. We'd decided to be blunt and swift.

"Sir, what did you think of Skerrill being a fairy?" I asked.

Warrington's eyes flashed with anger. "What the fuck did you just say?"

"What is this?" Breit demanded.

"We don't like this any more than you do, sir, but this turned up at his place." Terrance tossed the matchbook to Breit.

"The Sand Bar? So what?" Breit handed the matches to his partner.

"Oughta be called the swish bar," I said. "Your boy Logan, sir, looks like he met men late at night in Lafayette Square."

"No, no, you're all wrong," Warrington said, shaking his head.

"How? How are we wrong, sir?" asked Terrance.

"Because we've seen Skerrill pick up girls. Many times." Breit spoke slowly but emphatically.

"So he put on a show, sir," I said. And if anyone was good at putting on a show, it was Skerrill.

"He did *not* put on shows," Warrington shot back. "He bagged these broads and took 'em into bathrooms or back hallways and they came back smiling, with their blouses and skirts not quite the way they were when they left."

"Also part of his act, sir," I said. "Probably some B girls who pretended to go along with him for a fiver." But what Warrington was saying about Skerrill and the girls rang true, sounded just like the Skerrill I'd known at the Funhouse. Skerrill had slept with scads of girls to cover up being a swish? That didn't make sense.

"Jesus Christ!" Breit exploded. "Some Red just murdered Skerrill and you're in here talking him up as a homo? What the hell kind of investigation is this?"

"Like Voigt said, we have evidence besides the matches, sir," Terrance tried.

"Fuck your evidence." This from Warrington.

"Look, sir, maybe we should come back later, after you've had some time to let this news sink in," I offered. But Warrington and Breit didn't need time to collect their thoughts—Terrance and I did.

"No," Breit said before Warrington could answer me, "we're finished with you two." He snatched up the list of Amtorg names. "And if we have anything to do about it, you two are finished fucking up this investigation. Get the hell out. You're dismissed."

We left, Breit slammed the door. An ensign from the Coastal Information section paused in the hallway to look at us. We ignored him and started back to our office. I shut the door, we dropped into our chairs.

"That was rough," Terrance said. "Guess you work close with a guy for a while—that kind of news has gotta be hard to take."

"They seemed awful sure."

He lit a cigarette, blew out a mouthful of smoke. "You tell me my wife's stepping out, even show me a mash note, what do I do?"

"Deny it. Get angry at me. Kill the messenger."

"Right. Let those two cool off, they'll come around."

"Something is off, for sure."

"Yeah, Skerrill was a swish," Terrance quipped, but neither of us chuckled.

"How do you explain the girls?"

"Putting on a show, like you said. Skerrill was a good actor, right? Played that part down in Mexico, fooled the landlady into thinking he was loaded."

"I'll give you that, he was a damned good actor."

"See? Plus we got the evidence from his room. That kinda stuff doesn't just appear by accident."

That's the problem, I thought, but before I could say anything, the telephone rang. I picked up the receiver to hear Paslett growl, "You two, my office, now." He hung up without waiting for a reply.

Terrance didn't bother to ask who had called. He stubbed out his cigarette, sighed, and followed me out the door.

PASLETT DIDN'T EVEN SPEAK, JUST GLOWERED, AS WE STOOD IN FRONT of his desk like two miscreant school boys.

"You were right, sir, Logan Skerrill was hiding something," I said.

The glower got worse.

"Sir, if you told me Voigt's a homo, I'd be awful upset, too," Terrance tried.

"Breit and Warrington went straight to the director after your little chat," Paslett finally said.

"We've got evidence, sir," Terrance said.

"Yeah? How about the evidence of what an asshole you two make me look like. Did you forget me telling you how steamed Sixteen-Z was that I took this investigation? But you two idiots barge in, tell them Skerrill's a homo, and what? They're gonna name off all his queer-os?"

We didn't answer. Paslett stood and walked to his lone window, back to us. Over his shoulder the reflecting pool was just visible, its shallow water glinting in the morning sun. "Why do you think he was a homo?"

We took turns describing what we'd found in Skerrill's apartment.

"Then how do you explain Cross-check finding him shacked up?"

"His cover, sir," Terrance promptly answered. "Lotta swishes, they live with women, right? Cross-check just never saw Skerrill's true sweetheart."

"More guesses."

"There's a pattern here, sir," Terrance continued. "We just need time to collect more evidence."

Two patterns, I realized, but I decided to keep that to myself for the moment. Before I said anything to Paslett, I needed to run my hunch by my partner and see what he thought. This wasn't *my* investigation—it was ours.

Paslett grunted and returned to his desk. "You get one more day. We took this case to see if Skerrill was a Red, not to investigate his love life. The director's made it awful clear that if I don't have evidence—and that means proof, not guesswork—by tomorrow of what Skerrill was into, he's kicking this case back to M.P.D. And if I have to do that, you two spend the rest of this war in A-Seven. Understood?"

Understood. A-7 oversaw the O.N.I.'s Central Files: rows of metal shelves; stacked, leaning boxes; legions of file cabinets; reams of blank Russell Index system forms. We'd be better off trudging guard paths at the Navy Yard.

"Sir, if I may?" I asked cautiously.

He nodded curtly.

"What makes you think Skerrill was a Red? Just his behavior on the Amtorg case?"

Terrance shot me a disapproving look—leading questions irritated Paslett as much as wishy-washy answers. But this time, the approach worked.

"It's not just Amtorg. The spike in the Russians' cable traffic occurred right after the Bermuda Special arrived in port."

We caught his drift. Whatever the Bermuda Special's mission, the Russians wanted to know about it—what if Skerrill had told all? But a spike in coded cables might just mean the Russians were shaking trees, trying to learn something. The traffic alone wasn't proof of a traitor. For Paslett to be so worried meant—

"What did the Bermuda Special do, sir?" I asked.

"Uh-uh, not yet," he said. "You two don't need to know anything about that to turn Skerrill's life upside down. I want you digging deep, to China if you have to—no more poking around his boarding house, sipping tea with his landlady, got it?"

And with that, he dismissed us and we returned to our office.

TERRANCE DROPPED HEAVILY INTO HIS CHAIR. HE WAS A SHORT, compact man. Massive hands, thumbs and palms as thick as drum legs. Wiry black hair cropped short, almost shaved; dark, unreadable eyes. To say his jaw was square was an exercise in understatement: you could shoe a horse on that chin. He had a wide smile, but his natural expression suggested a father who's just learned his youngest daughter is pregnant. Even when he tried to look emotionless, his lips tucked downward into a scowl.

"We could check out the houses listed in the Cross-check reports," he said. "See if a swish answers the door."

"Don't need to," I said firmly.

"Why not?"

"Breit and Warrington are right—Skerrill wasn't a swish."

Frowning, he said, "So how do we explain the matches, the note, the—"

"He wanted us to find them," I interrupted. "Think about it. First I come across the mark in the book about Lafayette Square. We wonder why it's there but not too much. Then I find the matches, you find the note. Suddenly we think we've got a pattern."

"It is a pattern," my partner said, but I could hear doubt creeping into his voice.

"What's the one consistent thing we know about Skerrill?" I pressed.

"He was neat, way too neat."

"Guy like that, say he wants to make it look like he's got a secret—how would he do that?"

Now Terrance saw where I was going. "He'd plant some clues. But he can't just leave them lying around, that's too obvious."

"Right. So he plants 'em where he knows they'll be found if someone gives his room a good going-over. Someone with investigative experience, who'll look for a pattern, even if it's not obvious at first. Someone like us."

"Sonofabitch, he set himself up to look like a homo. But why would he do that?"

"Because whatever Skerrill was hiding, he'd rather have everyone think he was a homo than know the real secret." I looked down at the photos of the murder scene, the 8" by 10" glossy prints strewn across my desk. In one, Logan Skerrill's battered face, eyes open, stared back at me. "Even if his secret got him killed."

"But if Skerrill wanted us to think he was a swish, why would he want Cross-check and Sixteen-Z to think he was a Casanova—another false front?"

"No, this is a joe who's gotta be in control and have everything perfect, right? Every *i* dotted and *t* crossed. Doesn't ring he'd put up two fronts."

After a pause, Terrance said, "Unless he had to."

"Right. I'm thinking—hoping—he made a mistake the first time they watched him."

"So Cross-check always following him to some broad's place, him not coming out till the morning—he was establishing another pattern. Making them think he was predictable. Uninteresting. Not a risk."

"And drawing their attention away from what he did the first time they followed him."

"Whatta you know, maybe the commander's right about ol' Logan Skerrill," Terrance said.

"Let's not get ahead of ourselves—we don't know if Cross-check got anything."

He stood up and said, "Let's find out."

CHAPTER 6

ARD NOT TO THINK OF CROSS-CHECK, OFFICIALLY OP-12-D, AS THE RAT squad. Any way you cut it, we were going to have a rough time with them. Not only had an investigation been taken away from them, but if I was right, then they had also missed something during a routine check.

Kirkendall, a lieutenant commander, smirked when Terrance and I appeared at their door.

"Look who found the first floor." He was bald and thin, with features—slanted brows, crooked smile, narrow eyes—that wear well behind a pawnshop counter.

Ray Brompton, the senior officer, looked up from his desk.

"Sir," Terrance said, addressing Brompton.

"Daley." Brompton was about forty-five, maybe older, a career officer who had weathered the interwar years only to see the best wartime assignments fall into the hands of the post-Pearl crowd who had cruised through Officer Candidate School in less time than it takes to shakedown a Liberty ship. But Brompton had only himself to blame. Terrance had told me he had been burning up the Special Activities Branch until he got caught colluding with a staffer on the Senate Appropriations Committee to fund an operation to find out if a steel mill in Indiana was illegally selling battleship-grade plate to Italy. Brompton's mistake was to let Indiana's senior senator, whose son-in-law ran the mill's export desk, trace the line item back to him. This same senator sat on the naval appropriations sub-committee—Brompton was lucky he was still in the O.N.I.

"We need your file on Logan Skerrill's cross-checks, sir," Terrance said.

"I bet you do." His tone was even, uninflected. Florid complexion, fleshy face, pouches under his eyes.

"On your way to the Sand Bar, boys?" a lieutenant j.g., Russell Ames, said mockingly.

"You know the way; why don't we follow you there," I said.

Ames just sneered—he knew they had us by the shorts.

"What're you looking for?" Kirkendall asked.

"We need your reports for Skerrill's last three cross-checks, sir," said Terrance. Anticipating a rough time, we'd decided to first ask for something other than the first file.

"And why is that?" This from the fourth officer, Freed, another lieutenant j.g. Young, sandy brown hair, pale eyes, skinny. Tapping a pencil against his desk, like a schoolboy anxious for geometry class to end.

"Seeing as how he got himself murdered, we'd like to find out who did it," I said.

"Oh, is that what you do now—solve murders?" Ames asked sarcastically.

I lit a cigarette, said nothing; Terrance, leaning against the door frame, also said nothing.

Brompton broke the silence. "Well, you know we'd like to help you, but we're still writing the field report."

As if a completed report mattered, with Skerrill dead. No point in saying that; Brompton would frostily remind us it was "for the files." One of the petty bureaucrat's many trump cards, that phrase.

"What about your search of his room?" Kirkendall feigned seriousness. "Surely that must have turned up all the evidence you need. For your *murder* investigation."

"Or did that lead you on a wild swish—I mean, *goose* chase?" Freed chortled. The others snickered.

"Maybe we could take the files you've already reported?" I asked. Nudging them toward what we really wanted.

"I don't know, we might need to look something up." Brompton waved his pen in the air, as if casting a spell. "To finish the current report, you know."

"How about just the sleeve for the first check?" Terrance asked quietly.

"I guess that's okay. Jim, get the folder," Brompton said to Freed.

Shaking his head in disgust, Freed walked over to a locked file cabinet, spun the combination lock, took out a folder, handed it to me. Brompton stood and plucked a softbound logbook from his cluttered desk. "Sign here," he said, motioning to me.

I scribbled my initials, we left. In the corridor, Terrance smiled wryly. "Starting to wonder how many ways we can fuck ourselves before we straighten this investigation out."

Holding up the folder, I said, "Let's hope this helps."

But neither of us made a move to open the folder back at our office. We fidgeted in our chairs, smoking, not speaking. A day wasn't much time to make things right.

"Want to do the honors?" I finally asked.

"No." Terrance watched his cigarette smoke drift toward the ceiling.

"Hell with it." I reached across and flipped the folder open. The report was brief, just two pages, didn't take long to read.

"Well?" Terrance asked when I finished.

"Nothing." I sighed heavily.

"Figures."

"Back to his rooming house by nine that night, didn't leave till the next morning."

"Probably played pinochle with Mrs. Sundstrom. Before his milk and cookies and beddie time."

Another lengthy silence ensued. I tried to envision myself in A-7. Learning the central decimal file prefixes, memorizing the row numbers. I'd been to A-7 just once, more than a year ago—we had three civilian clerks who retrieved files for us—and remembered only dim lights, low ceilings, endless metal shelves crammed with cartons.

"There is one thing," I said.

"Yeah?"

I read from the report: "Subject left Navy Building at nineteen thirty. Took Seventeenth Street bus to K, disembarked, walked two blocks east to thirteen twenty-one K. Time entered, nineteen forty-seven, exited at twenty twenty-five. Said address H & H Clipping Service."

"A clipping service?"

"It's not suspicious, but. . . ."

My partner shrugged. "Maybe he was using them for an investigation."

"Be a major breach of security if he was." To prevent tipping off foreign nations about O.N.I.'s areas of interest, we were forbidden from using clipping services, even to collect general information. Anyone who complained was icily reminded that the Japs had followed the comings and goings of the Pearl fleet in the local paper.

"Maybe he was just making time with a girl, then," Terrance mused. "Now that we know he wasn't a swish."

"Maybe."

"Doesn't look like we'll be getting the other reports anytime soon to see if he went back."

"No."

Terrance tapped his desk and said, "Guess we should ask the commander if he wants us to go down there."

"Well, hopefully he's done chewing us out."

"BACK ALREADY?" PASLETT GREETED US, NOT SMILING. BUT HE PERKED right up when we told him about Skerrill's visit to the clipping service.

"What did you say the name was?"

"H & H Clipping Service, sir," Terrance answered. "It's on K Street."

"Sonofabitch," Paslett said under his breath. "Sit," he ordered as he scraped his chair back. He went over to the filing cabinet against the wall. Terrance looked at me quizzically; I shrugged. We sat, lit up, smoked. Drawers rumbled open and clanked shut, hefty folders thudded on top of the cabinet as Paslett searched, and searched. Finally he returned, waving a sheet of paper like a little flag at a Fourth of July parade.

"Take a look at this," he announced, handing me the sheet.

It was a poorly mimeographed Federal Bureau of Investigation field report with the title *In re: Alleged Communist Affiliation of Washington Clipping Services*. I skipped the preamble—F.B.I. agents all but started every report they wrote with "In the beginning"—and read the text. At least, I read what I could, for I'd only been given the first page of what appeared to be a lengthy document. But what was there perked me right up, too. According to the Bureau, several clipping services in Washington were "fronts": otherwise legitimate businesses masking communist activity. Party meetings, recruitment, dues collection. And espionage. *The purported goal of most, if not all, of these clipping services is to recruit sympathetic followers in the Civil Service and the National Military Establishment in the capital region and to——*. Here the page ended.

"Jesus, Voigt, hurry up," Terrance grumbled.

"Yeah, yeah."

He snatched the sheet away as soon as I lowered it.

"Where's the rest of the report, sir?" I asked.

But the commander was deep in thought, his head bobbing slightly, and he didn't respond.

"Well, ain't that interesting," Terrance said, looking up.

"They shoulda flagged his visit," Paslett now said, shaking his head in disgust.

I assumed he meant Cross-check. But had they ever seen this report?

"Sir, is this"—Terrance held up the single sheet—"to be continued?"

"No, my source was only able to get me the first page."

We knew better than to ask who that source was. The rivalry between O.N.I. and F.B.I. hadn't prevented either intelligence agency from finding furtive ways to pilfer from each other's files. Paslett had "sources" all over D.C. Not just in the Bureau, but in the Office of Strategic Services, Army General Staff, Air Corps, and who knew where else.

"Does Cross-check know about this, sir?" I asked.

"Think I'd share a Bureau report with those clowns, lieutenant?"

"Nosir, but—"

"Doesn't matter if they know about this front business or not," he interrupted. "Nobody in this building, from the charwomen to the director, is allowed to use clipping services. Cross-check shoulda smelled fish right away."

"What else do we have on these services, sir?" Terrance asked.

"They make the perfect front, especially the ones that cover the international papers. Who's gonna think twice about that office place being chockful'a foreigners—they need 'em to read the foreign newspapers, right? All kinda mail coming and going—who's gonna raise an eyebrow over packages being posted overseas? If I wanted to set up a front, a clipping service would be my first choice."

I stole an uneasy glance at my partner. What the commander said made sense, but it wasn't exactly proof that H & H, or any other clipping service, was a commie front.

"Well, we should go down there now, right, sir?" Terrance asked.

Paslett shook his head firmly.

"No, I've got a much better idea," he said, a rare smile tugging at his lips.

CHAPTER 7

Y OU'RE GONNA GET A JOB THERE," PASLETT DECLARED, LOOKING
straight at me.

"Sir?!" Terrance and I, in unison.

"I know just how we're gonna do it, too. Daley, get me the city directory," he ordered, pointing to the bookcase behind us. Terrance retrieved
the fat volume, and Paslett eagerly flipped through the business section.

"Look here," planting his forefinger in the middle of a page, sliding the
directory around. "H & H Clipping Service, Offering Collections of Major
Newspaper and Periodical Coverage of Important and Timely Subjects.
All U.S. and English Language Publications Covered. Service for Polish,
German, Russian, Spanish, and French Publications Also Available."

"Just look at how many foreign newspapers they collect!" Paslett
exclaimed. "And Voigt, you speak and read German."

"But, sir, that doesn't mean I'm qualified to work there."

"How do we even know they're hiring, sir?" Terrance put in.

"Sir, even if they are, what if I don't get the job?"

"Voigt's damn lucky he ever got this job," Terrance cracked, but no one laughed.

"I've got a cover for you," Paslett said, ignoring our protests. "See, the thing is with these fronts, what they do is, they only take people they trust, so that means they're only gonna take another commie or a fellow traveler. But if you've been active in the party, if you've been out raising hell about the Scottsboro Boys or other such nonsense, that means you've come to the attention of the Bureau or the local Red squad, so they won't take you."

"But, sir, I can't pass myself off as a Red, I don't know anything—"

"Hold your horses," he said, irritated. Got up, went back to his file cabinets. More rattling, more clanking. I didn't dare look at Terrance. Lit a much-needed Lucky and inhaled greedily.

"From now on, this is you," the commander said, handing me a thick manila folder. "Look at the first endorsement," he added, referring to the signature page of the first link in the chain of command. Endorsements provide concise summaries for busy officers who don't have time to read complete reports, so three short paragraphs outlined who I now was:

Subject: Possible Use Deceased Prisoner Identities, Report on.

1. On January 21, 1943, a General Court Martial, Naval Barracks, N.O.B., Norfolk, Virginia, sentenced Shipfitter Second Class Theodore Barston to two years, four months confinement for Offenses against the Narcotic Law, Assaulting and Striking, Contempt of Superior Officer, and Conduct to the Prejudice of Good Order and Discipline (See 2135/KAF-wab, attached). While in confinement at the Naval Barracks awaiting transport to the Naval Brig, N.O.B., Charleston, South Carolina, Barston expired on February 4, 1943, of a self-administered dosage of narcotic (See 1435/KAF-dbr, attached).

2. Subsequent inquiry by O.N.I./B-7 determined that Barston died without heirs and dependents and no known living relatives.

3. It is the recommendation of O.N.I./B-7 that Enlistment and Fingerprint Records, Muster Roll Data, Court Martial Index and Proceeding, Dishonorable Discharge, Report of Death, and Disposition of Personal Effects of Shipfitter Second Class Theodore Barston be hereby removed and sealed per Circular Letter 1639, November 18, 1942, Secretary of the Navy to Director/O.N.I., for replacement with facsimiles per O.N.I./B-7 requirements.

I finished reading, swallowed a heavy sigh, and handed the endorsement to Terrance.

"Barston'll do nicely," Paslett announced, as if he'd just helped me pick out a tie.

You couldn't be more wrong, I wanted to say. Instead: "What is there in Barston's background that'll get me into H & H, sir?"

"You'll see—I had Seven-R work up a profile." Smiling.

Now I wanted to groan. B-7R was Paslett's own creation, a tiny sub-unit of three or four ensigns, all college boys who fancied themselves the next Hemingway or O'Neill. They spent their days dreaming up cover stories for those of us who actually did field work. Their reports read like a bad playwright's character sketches. *Edward Kensault is a man with few friends— at a party he is the guest lurking against the wall, drink in hand, watching the gaiety with intense interest yet engaging no one.* . . . I dreaded the thought of reading what their overwrought imaginations had concocted for Shipfitter Second Class Theodore Barston. *He was born to indifferent parents, raised in a rough, crime-ridden neighborhood in—*

"Why're we using a dead hophead for a cover, sir?" Terrance piped up, having finished reading the endorsement.

"When Voigt gets in, the Reds are gonna check him out but good. Was he in the Navy for real, did he get kicked out of P.S. Twenty-Two when he was fifteen like he says? All'a that's gotta be jake."

I asked, "But, sir, why would they even let a shipfitter with a dishonorable discharge in the door?"

"Believe me, once you tell them who your pop was, they're gonna be awful interested in talking to you."

"How's that, sir?"

"William Barston was the chief organizer for the International Long-shoremen's Association on the Jersey docks during the mid-thirties—he was a card-carrying Red and proud of it. The way the boys in Seven-R wrote it up, you learned the gospel of Marx and Lenin from an early age. Till Big Bill got flattened by a crate of machine parts one afternoon."

"Barston sure doesn't sound like a Kraut name," Terrance observed.

"And, sir, how's a guy like Barston learn German if he got kicked outta school at fifteen?"

"His mom was a Kraut for real, just like yours, Voigt. Seven-R even found her naturalization certificate when they were doing research. She died a few years after her husband. Liver cancer. The real Theodore Barston has no living relatives—no brothers and sisters, no cousins, no grandparents, nobody. You're even the same age as Barston. It's an airtight cover, and you're a perfect fit."

"Chances are, someone at H & H is gonna be from Jersey or at least have been there," I said. "Which I haven't, sir."

"Lucky for you, Ensign Wereford in Seven-R is from Hoboken. He's added all the local color you need to sell yourself as Barston."

That the commander had a quick and easy answer for every question didn't put me at ease. The raised-from-the-dead Barston might look good on paper, but I was the one who had to walk into H & H and get a job, and that was going to take a lot of moxie. And that was only the first impossible stunt I had to pull off. Once inside, I had to—

"Sir, what's Voigt s'posed to do as Barston?" Terrance asked.

Paslett gave us a peeved look. "Find out what these Reds are up to! The Bureau's on to something here, these clipping services have gotta be fronts. If they recruited Skerrill, I wanna know what he was giving them, and for how long, and what they did with it."

Have gotta be fronts. If Terrance or I had said this, Paslett would've chewed us out until his face was as red as a beet. But when it came to communists and the possibility of espionage, he often leap-frogged to conclusions before the evidence was in.

"So, sir, now we're not looking for who killed Skerrill?" Terrance asked cautiously.

"We gotta find out what H & H is up to first. A'course, we gotta make it look like we're working the murder, don't we, to keep Special Activities offa our backs?" He drummed his fingers on his desk. "All right, this is what we're gonna do. Voigt, you're getting into H & H as Barston to see what these commies are up to. I'll tell Special Activities and the director we got reason to suspect someone at the service killed Skerrill. Daley, you're gonna work the case from the outside. Like you two were already doing, I want you turning Skerrill's life upside down. You're gonna look hard at every friend, neighbor, and gal he ever had, you're gonna talk to every clerk and waitress he ever said two words to. If he turned Red, you're gonna find out how it happened and who got to him."

"What's the reason, sir?" I asked quietly.

"To suspect someone at H & H killed Skerrill? You're gonna gimme that reason, Voigt. Look, it might damn well turn out one of these Reds did kill him. Maybe Skerrill got cold feet, told 'em he's out—they killed him to keep him quiet. Wouldn't be the first time the commies ate their young."

"But, sir, what if this H & H turns out—what if it's on the level?" Terrance ventured.

"For all we know, sir, Skerrill had a gal down there and was just visiting her when Cross-check spotted him," I chimed in.

"Then prove it. Maybe we go to all this trouble to put you in as Barston and all you find out is that Skerrill was banging some broad who cuts up newspapers all day long. If that's the case, then we kick Skerrill's murder back to M.P.D. and let them solve it. At least we'll know Skerrill was clean and nothing hinky's going on at H & H."

"Yessir," we answered.

Easy for the commander to sum up the investigation so casually—he wasn't the one who had to go undercover. To become Theodore Barston, I'd have to spend hours poring over 7R's profile, memorizing biographical and behavioral details. I'd have to practice my answers in the mirror and start talking like a dishonorably discharged shipfitter who'd just served two years and four months in the brig. My hands were soft—I'd have to roughen them up, put on calluses. I needed to scar up my forearms to mimic healed needle marks. Barston was an addict, a dope fiend, and if I crossed paths with another hophead, I had to look like I knew how to shoot up.

I'd have to give up the comfort of sleeping in my cozy basement flat and rent a cot in a fleabag S.R.O., the only place that would rent to a deadbeat like Barston. It sure seemed like an awful lot of trouble for what might well turn out to be nothing. Of course, if I'd wanted to coast through this war, I could've kept my mouth shut when the Navy came looking for bright pennies for the O.N.I.

Paslett dismissed us, we stood to leave. He fixed me with a stern look. "Voigt, I don't have to say you gotta work this cover better than last time, right?"

"Nosir, you don't."

LAST JULY, PASLETT HAD ASSIGNED ME TO INFILTRATE A *KLATCH* OF German-Americans with suspect loyalties. The F.B.I. had already gutted the biggest Nazi front in the States, the German American Bund, by tossing its leaders into work camps in Iowa, seizing its assets, and arresting anyone who dared squeak *Heil Hitler* in public. Back in '42, a U-Boat had landed four saboteurs on Long Island, though those clowns hadn't even been able to evade the Coast Guard, let alone blow up any of the factories, dams, and bridges on their target list. There hadn't been a whiff of Nazi subversion in the States since, but that didn't matter to Paslett, who was convinced that a glory-seeking Hitler lover would plant a bomb in the Navy Yard, or one of the tempos, or a railroad trestle in the Potomac. Navy, and O.N.I. especially, had looked pretty bad after the U-Boat landing—we couldn't even keep Long Island safe?!—but both Terrance and I thought Paslett was seeing ghosts.

Working off a cover cooked up by 7R, I'd befriended an unemployed machinist named John Entemann who insisted I call him Hans. The fact that this skilled tool-and-die man didn't have a job when defense plants were operating round the clock suggested Entemann was a sad sack, not a foreign agent, but after a few beers, he loved to expound on "what the Nazis could do to us if they wanted to." After a rambling, almost-incoherent recitation of the vulnerabilities of all the factories he'd been fired from (including one that produced naval ordnance), Entemann would fantasize about being recruited by the Abwehr, Germany's military intelligence agency. His three drinking buddies were also of German descent, and every time Entemann started talking about the Abwehr, they started ranting about the Jews and how they wished "we" would take care of them like the Nazis were. Entemann would promptly forget about his wish to be an Abwehr agent and enthusiastically join in the Jew-bashing. On and on they'd rave, until finally they stumbled home to the Murphy beds in their by-the-week flats. Every night was just like the last, bleary and beer-soaked—never once did Entemann or his pals do more than talk.

Which is why I shouldn't have made the mistake I did. These souses wouldn't have recognized Gabriel if he'd floated down from heaven in front of them; but late one night during my third week of bending elbows in Seventh Street gutbuckets, the least pickled of the lot, a fat shipping clerk named Geider, squinted at me through bulbous eyelids and said, "Wait a minute here, just hold on—I thought you said you was from Baltimore. Union Square."

"I am. So what?"

"Then what's this Montrose Avenue? There ain't no Montrose Avenue in Baltimore."

No, there sure wasn't. I'd been telling a story about messing around in a cemetery with my friends as a teen—Entemann and his pals wasted a lot of hours swapping tales of how much fun they'd had as boys, how much better their lives were then, the usual tavern drivel. *Say no more than you must* is an ironclad rule of cover work, but to fit in I'd transplanted a true story from my youth to my fictional hometown, Baltimore, a city I didn't know well. I'd gotten the name of the cemetery right, Old Saint Pauls, but Montrose Avenue was in Chicago. I should have said Pratt or Lombard— hell, I shouldn't have said anything at all about the streets we walked down. Telling a tall tale to stay in the good graces of Entemann and Company didn't require fine-grained detail. And now Geider wouldn't let my slip go. *How can a joe not know the names'a the streets where's he from, huh?*, his pals nodding vigorously as they dog-eyed me. They peppered me with questions about where I'd gone to school, who the principal was, how many were in my class, on and on. I feigned anger and stormed out, protesting that I wasn't going to take the third degree from the likes of them. What else could I do? The real Herbert Paulreich would have stormed out, too. Of course, the real Herbert Paulreich wouldn't have mixed up the streets of

Baltimore and Chicago. I'd blown it—there was no way I could go back. I typed up my final report and slinked into Paslett's office to take my drubbing, the commander's parting line branded in my memory. *Thought you were better than this, Voigt.*

On the way out, I'd run into Skerrill. Word had already gotten out about my blunder, I was taking a lot of razzing, but it usually ended with a clap on the shoulder and a *Better luck next time.* Skerrill had smiled maliciously, slowly shaking his head and making clucking noises. *Maps, Voigt, maps. Oughta try reading one next time.* I'd brushed past, but he knew I'd heard the taunt.

Now I was getting my second and probably my last chance to do cover work—Paslett didn't keep screwups around. I wasn't going to dwell on the irony that Skerrill's murder made that possible. If I wasn't careful from the moment I became Barston, I might make a mistake—and some sort of mistake had cost Skerrill his life.

CHAPTER 8

STARTED WITH CLOTHES. I WAS NO DANDY, BUT THEODORE BARSTON wouldn't wear a stitch of anything I owned. The boxer shorts from Hecht's and socks from Woodies, my Guild Edge snap brim and Hylo worsted shirts—all of it had to stay in my closet with my uniform. My Harvel wristwatch, a present to myself when I got into the O.N.I., came off reluctantly. I put away my Gillette and the Murray and Lanman's Florida Water an old girlfriend had given me. From now on, I'd shave with disposable safety razors and splash myself with two-bits-a-bottle aftershave.

Secondhand shops and dime stores supplied a wardrobe. I was determined to think, act, talk, and spend as the real Barston would, which meant I had a budget of ten dollars. Prisoners leave the brig with only the clothes on their back and some scrip to spend at the cut-rate shops that grow like weeds outside army posts and naval bases. So from a Ben Franklin, socks and shorts; from "Sally," the thrift store of the Salvation Army, a pair of lightly worn dungarees, a flannel shirt, and a faded Van Heusen. From an old Jew's shop on D Street, I picked up worsted trousers, a scuffed leather belt, and a windbreaker. The owner expertly eyed the clothes I was wearing as he totted up my purchases, but he didn't ask why I was buying used clothes which, even new, had cost half as much as what I was wearing. A good reminder of why I needed to get every detail right. With the last two bucks, I bought a Timex watch at Woolworth's.

I went back to my flat and changed. Before finding a room, I wanted to study Barston's profile. As I read, I rolled a chunk of cobblestone from the alley around in my hands, to roughen them up. Franklin D. jumped up on the table and walked across the folder, mewling. I checked the urge to put him outside—soon he'd be spending even more time alone. Hoisted him to my shoulder, rubbed his belly, opened a can of Spam for him.

Like an actor practicing lines, I memorized every detail about Barston. The addresses of the flats he'd grown up in. His mother's maiden name, the city in Germany she'd emigrated from. What her father had done (bricklayer) and what had happened to her siblings (elder brother, killed at Verdun; younger sister, dead at thirty-four, leukemia). The elder Barston's scrapes with the law and his brawls with hired goons—union organizing on New Jersey's docks in the '30s was not for the meek or weak. Learned all about the activities of the Jersey communists, the rallies they staged for striking dockworkers, the fundraising for families whose husbands, brothers, and fathers had been jailed when the strikes got violent.

The file said nothing about William Barston being mixed up in communist espionage. *What the hell would dock workers spy on?* But if I'd learned one thing during the last eight years, it was: don't underestimate the Reds. Anyway, Big Bill, as he was known—and the lone photograph did show a bruiser of a man, shoulders as wide as a yoke, fists like hams—wouldn't have breathed a word about espionage to his son. *So what the hell am I gonna say about my pop to get into H & H?* A question I couldn't ignore. Paslett seemed to think I could just sashay into the clipping service and bask in huzzahs and hugs after I proclaimed myself to be the only son of Big Bill Barston, martyr of the '38 Hoboken strike. Paslett had a keen eye for what the Reds were up to, but what he saw, he saw from the bridge—he didn't know how workaday communists walked, talked, or blew their noses. And if I didn't hit the perfect note when I stepped into H & H, I wouldn't even get the time of day from those folks.

Memorizing Ted Barston's life story brought forth unwanted thoughts of my own family, of my boyhood. Unwanted only because I couldn't afford the distraction, couldn't afford mixing up my experiences with those of Barston. Yet I couldn't shake the realization that I hadn't thought about my folks and brother in a while, couldn't remember the date of Mom's last letter. I didn't keep her letters. Read them twice, then tore them up. Wasn't sure why, maybe I didn't want a stack of letters around reminding me of how long it'd been since I'd seen my family.

I wondered how Pop was doing at the print shop, if Mom still loved her job at the jeweler's. My brother, Eddie, my only sibling, was working as a house dick at the Sheridan Plaza Hotel in our Chicago neighborhood of Uptown. Eddie had been 4-F'd—he was partially deaf in one ear from a fall when we were kids. My fault, that accident. When I was fifteen and Eddie was twelve, we'd scaled the light tower on the breakwater at Montrose Harbor, in Lake Michigan. The rungs were slick with rain that had just ended, I should've warned Eddie to be careful. I was almost to the crow's nest when I heard a thunderous clang. His right hand had slipped, he was dangling. *Ellis, help.* I scrambled down, too late. Eddie dropped at least twenty feet to the concrete deck. A fisherman ran over, we broke every rule of first aid. Turned Eddie onto his back, lifted his head by the neck, wiped blood from a cut with a dirty rag. The fall broke his left arm, sprained his wrist, burst his left eardrum. Much of his hearing came back, but not enough to put him in uniform. Climbing that tower was my idea, and recalling that Eddie had needed no coaxing, that he was eager to follow his older brother up those treacherous rungs, didn't let me off the hook. *But maybe I saved his life*, I thought. Drafted, Eddie could've been one of the first to splash ashore at Omaha Beach, could've been at Guadalcanal.

"Barston, Barston," I muttered to myself. Had to remind myself that for the foreseeable future, Ellis Voigt had no childhood, no family, no past. Had to become Ted Barston, had to carry his history, his stories, his secrets. What was it like to be someone who kept part of his life hidden? I wondered if Barston had confided in any of his shipmates, if he'd found like-minded Reds in the Navy. If he'd been smart, he'd kept his mouth shut. Like me, like everyone in uniform, he'd taken an oath to defend and protect the Constitution, and the Communist Party wanted to overthrow our government—being caught as a member was an awful good way to earn a dishonorable discharge or worse. Was that why Barston had turned to dope, to deal with the pressure of his secret?

I closed the folder, scratched the now-dozing Franklin D. behind his ears, and set out to find a flop. Wore the dungarees and flannel shirt, carried the rest of Barston's clothes in a battered rucksack I dug out of the closet. D.C. didn't have a Bowery, not officially, but you wouldn't know that if you strolled Ninth Street south of Mt. Vernon Square. Got a taste for celluloid cheesecake? That afternoon, the Leader Theater featured a double bill: Julie Jericho (for real!) in *Jungle Drums*, Leslie Dey in *Hard and Fast*. Prefer the real thing? The Gayety Theater offered hourly burleycue. If you wanted to skip the tease and get straight down to ten-bucks-a-pop business, the pimps, touts, and girls would find you pronto. Pawnshops, gutbuckets, and taverns masquerading as "lounges" were wedged between fifteen-cent lunchrooms, "souvenir" shacks selling sanitary rubber goods, and two-bit flops.

The Jefferson Club Hotel for Men looked no worse than any other option, so I went in. Threadbare carpet and *Positively No Loitering!* signs greeted me in the lobby. The clerk, a squat, swarthy man with a frizzle of steel-gray curls wreathing a weathered pate, listed from his stool, an elbow propped on the counter. Studying the *Star* crossword, a pencil stub jutting from his fingers. Smoke drifted from a soggy cigar in a tray stuccoed with gray-black ash. I stood for a moment; he didn't look up.

"How 'bout 'Seeks Room,' five letters," I said.

"How 'bout 'Annoys Clerk,' seven letters?" Still not looking up.

"S'long as you got a bed, I can be a wiseguy or a guest, take yer pick."

He picked up the cigar and puffed fiercely, sending up more exhaust than a broken-down truck. "This being a classy joint, wiseguy, you pay the week ahead, no refunds for an early departure. One-seventy-five, plus a buck deposit if you don't got your own bedroll."

"I don't got."

"Two-seventy-five, then. Plus whatever you wanna give to guarantee prompt service in the future."

"I got nuttin' ta be prompt for," I answered, trying out my Hoboken accent.

He rolled off the stool and padded off to collect my sheet, pillow, and blanket. "You're in Four-D," he said as I tucked the bedding under my arm. "You wanna rent a lock, it's a dime-a-week."

"I'll get my own."

He shrugged and turned back to the puzzle. I left to buy a lock. "Classy joints" like the Jefferson didn't have rooms like real hotels. Instead, you got a 4' by 8' stall with a metal cot frame, a lumpy mattress, and a fly-specked bulb that worked if you were lucky. The walls were warped plywood boards that went up six feet—instead of a ceiling, chicken wire drooped from stall to stall, like a tarpaulin. It was supposed to keep tenants—inmates?—from stealing from one another. So was the lock you put on the door hasp when you went out.

I bought a cheap lock at a variety store, then trudged up the creaky staircase to the fourth floor. Plaster walls, dingy and cracked. Moldings thick with ancient brown paint, smell of unwashed feet and dirty laundry in the air. I had to stoop to clear the chicken wire over my stall. Pulled the light chain; at least the bulb worked. A roach scrabbled away. Dried bloodspots dotted the gray mattress, which meant the Jefferson also had bedbugs—lots of them. So many that when a man rolled over in his sleep, his weight crushed the pests who had just helped themselves to his blood. We'd had bedbugs when I was a kid. Hell to get rid of. They lay eggs in mattresses, burrow into cracks in the floorboards and walls—takes months for the powder to kill all of them. Pop finally succeeded, but Eddie didn't believe him, kept insisting he could feel them biting him while he was sleeping. He had nightmares every night and got hysterical when Pop angrily told him he was imagining it. One night I promised Eddie I'd stay awake till morning, keeping guard, making sure no bugs crawled on him. But I fell asleep in the chair in our shared room—has any child ever stayed awake through an entire night, no matter how strong his willpower? Fortunately, I awoke before Eddie. *Did you see them?* he'd asked as soon as his eyes opened. He'd smiled when I shook my head.

I sighed, shook off the memory—Barston, be Barston!—and made up the bed. Tucked the rucksack under the cot, reminding myself that I'd have to throw it away when my undercover stint was done—if the roaches didn't move in, the bedbugs would. At the lunchroom next door I counted out fifteen cents in nickels and pennies for a bologna and cheese sandwich, a mealy apple, and a cup of coffee that was somehow both weak and bitter. I wedged onto a stool between a fat man who huffed as he slurped soup and a white-haired bum who appeared to be wearing all the clothing he owned, including his winter coat. I gulped down the tasteless sandwich and lit up, tapping out an Old Gold—Barston's brand—for the bum before he even asked.

"Kind of you, friend, kind of you," he muttered, drawing eagerly.

What else did I need to do before I walked into H & H? Picturing myself reaching for the door handle and entering the office made my heart race, my mouth dry. Was this how actors felt right before the curtain went up? For all the memorization and rehearsal, did they dread the moment when they actually had to speak, did they fear that their first line wouldn't pass their lips, that they'd freeze under the light, paralyzed and terrified, exposed as frauds?

I forced myself to focus on my tasks. Visit the Red Cross and persuade the nurse to take blood from both arms and to put the needle in hard, to mark up my forearm. Go over Barston's file one more time, make sure I hadn't overlooked anything. Meet with Terrance for an inspection and a shakedown cruise, to make sure I could pass for Barston. Put out two cans of Spam for Franklin D. And, though I knew I shouldn't, leave a message for Liv to tell her I was free to see her that night. I knew I should sleep at the Jefferson Club, but one more night as Ellis Voigt, one more night with Liv—didn't I deserve at least that before I gave myself over to the bedbugs, roaches, and Reds?

I CALLED TERRANCE AND ARRANGED TO MEET HIM FOR LUNCH THE NEXT day at a place we both knew, Margie's. With Barston's last nickel, I called Liv's rooming house and left a message. *I'm free, will meet you at 6:30, El.* Then I walked down to Pennsylvania Avenue, to the Red Cross station, to give blood and get some needle marks.

Of course I couldn't tell the nurse, a round-cheeked cherub of a gal, why I needed marks, so I played nasty, goosing her hard and plastering on a leer.

Dressed as I was, wafting *Eau de Jefferson*, that did the trick—she jammed the needle in but good. Since I was out of money, I had to walk home, and I was pretty light-headed by the time I got there. I stripped down to skivvies and fell on my bed. Supposed to be a short nap, but I didn't awake for two hours. My sleep was fitful, unsettled by another dream about Delphine. We were walking endlessly down badly lit, desolate streets. *We're almost there*, she kept saying, but it seemed like we were on the same block, no matter how far we walked.

I got up, washed my face, changed clothes, left for my date with Liv. Or as she'd called it, our "surprise." *What kind of surprise?* I'd asked the morning after our visit to the Tidal Basin. She'd just woken up, was stretching her arms out, fingers clasped, smiling sleepily.

"You gotta say yes or no first."

"What if I'm on duty?" I'd asked.

"Then you'll miss it."

"No rain check?"

"For a surprise?"

"Okay, I'll see what I can do."

So at 6:30, I was standing at Fourteenth and P, as agreed. No sign of Liv. I smoked, bought and drank a Coke, tried hard not to look like a joe waiting on a girl. Whoever said surprises arrived on time?

At ten to seven, Liv walked up. White knee-length dress with vermilion stripes, a plum-colored hat, small clutch in her hand. Smiled when she saw me. I tossed my cigarette to the curb.

"How will you be?" she asked.

I leaned to kiss her, parting with the taste of her lipstick. "Good to see you, Liv."

"So, El."

"Yes."

"What do you know about classical music?"

"Other than that Mozart was deaf and Beethoven died young, not much."

Her mouth opened in surprise, she began a correction—then saw my smile. "Wise guy." She punched me playfully on the shoulder. "What do you know about Arnold Schoenberg?"

"Absolutely nothing."

"Good."

"Am I about to get a lesson?"

"Might say that—we're going to a recital of some of his compositions. The pianist is very promising."

"Promising to be good in ten years?"

She pulled a face. "Don't be cynical—I mean he's very talented."

The recital was in a Methodist church with an airy sanctuary. A gleaming black grand piano had been wheeled in front of the altar. Mixed crowd, scattered throughout the pews. A few pensioners, some students, a middle-aged woman knitting a scarf, two men quietly arguing about the merits of Social Realism in American art. Not my kind of crowd, but better than my new neighbors at the Jefferson Club Hotel.

Schoenberg's work was unlike any music I'd ever heard. The pianist, a chubby young man in an ill-fitting suit, sat on the bench and leaned precipitously to the left, like a man caught in a nor'easter. First, a few soft, random notes, his left ear cocked to the keys. Then, suddenly, a dissonant cascade, a jumble of notes; if a musical composition could be spilled, I thought, it must sound like this. The erratic volume, soft, barely audible passages followed by loud bursts, continued, as did the unpredictable tempo.

I didn't much care for it, although parts of the *Suite for Piano*, the first selection, reminded me of a choppy sea roiling outside a harbor, waves rolling in to break in unexpected ways against the seawall. My mom loved classical music. Back home, the shelves of a parlor cabinet bowed under the weight of her 78-rpm records. Featured, the usual suspects: Brahms, Handel, and, of course, Beethoven—no household of German immigrants was complete without the master's works. She also had a fondness for Russian composers such as Glière, Borodin, Glazunov. Not long before I left home for the Navy, she'd discovered Prokofiev and Shostakovich. I grew up hearing those records—as Mom did housework, as Eddie and I did our homework in the parlor, as a prelude to the family listening to radio serials on Sunday nights—so I thought I knew all about classical music, thought I liked it, too.

"What'd you think?" I asked Liv as we left.

"Think?" she answered lightly. "S'that what we're supposed to do when we listen to classical music? Think?"

"Funny girl. What'd you feel?"

"Ooh, much better question. Okay, at first I felt unsettled, off kilter. Then what I saw was, what I realized, is that I was resisting the music, that I wasn't giving myself over to the composer and his vision."

"Is that what we're supposed to do with classical music, *see* a vision?"

"Okay, I deserved that. Now, what I most loved was the second piece, when. . . ."

I smiled like a happy idiot, listening to Liv. She didn't even notice, she was so caught up in her recitation. I'd responded similarly to Delphine, the girl I'd loved in Chicago, hearing not her words, only her exuberance as she enthused about Shakespeare, Whitman, Austen. That memory—the comparison, across time—wiped away my grin. Seeing Delphine in Liv was an indulgence I couldn't risk, a way of thinking that wouldn't just spoil what I had with Liv but would also—

"El?"

"Sorry, what?"

"I asked what you felt."

I didn't admit I hadn't liked Schoenberg much, instead telling her how the *Suite for Piano* reminded me of a windswept sea. She liked that metaphor, urged me to go on. So I did, telling her about the kinds of seas I'd seen when I was assigned to the USS *Saratoga* and how the music reminded me of them. That, at least, was a harmless memory.

We were walking north on Fourteenth, dusky sunlight slanting between well-kept row houses. Canopies of wide-trunked elms, riffled by a light breeze, cast shifting shadows across the sidewalk. I held Liv's hand, our gait leisurely.

"Ice cream?" I asked.

"That'd be wonderful."

We went into a drugstore, sat at the fountain. Liv studied my face in the mirror behind a shelf of phosphate bottles, smiled brightly when I caught her looking.

"Book your ticket yet?" I asked.

"To where?"

"The Pacific. 'All those beautiful islands,' remember?"

"I remember, all right. But I'm not gonna book a ticket."

"No?"

She shook her head, still watching my reflection. "I'm just gonna go."

"Just like that? Wake up one day and say, 'This is it, this is D-Day'?"

"Not quite."

"So how?"

"D-Day will wake me up with a whisper and say 'Go,' that's how."

I almost made the mistake of asking if she'd call or send a note before she left. I knew the answer, we were having a good time, why spoil it?

Liv turned from our reflections to look at me. "You look tired, El."

"Rotten case."

"Aren't they all?"

"Yeah, but some are easy-rotten, some are not-so-easy-rotten. Guess which one this is?"

"Easy, hard—it's all work, and you can't—"

"I know, I know, we can't live to work."

She looked down, dipped her spoon into the ice cream of her root beer float but didn't take a bite.

"Hey, I'm sorry, Liv, I didn't mean to sound short, it's just that, well, I've got—"

"Why don't you tell me what you'll do when you're not on duty?" she asked.

"Are we allowed to have fun while the war's still on?" Studying her reflection in the mirror.

"For real, El."

"Maybe I'll become someone else for a while."

"Like who?"

"How about a dark, brooding poet?"

"A Shelley for our century."

"Or a young Werther."

"Remember the ending?"

"Right, maybe someone else. How about an actor?"

"Ooh, I think you'd be a great actor, El."

"Yeah?"

"I know people in theater! Remember that script reading I took you to? I could talk to Emmett, he was the director for that play, and see—"

"Liv, hold on, I was just kidding. I can't audition for a play—I couldn't promise to make it to the rehearsals." I'd already landed my big part and had just finished rehearsal, though of course I couldn't tell Liv that.

"El, don't talk about all the things you can't do, okay?"

"All right, Liv, I promise: when I'm not on duty, I'll find something to do to enjoy myself." An empty promise, that. Once I was undercover, I'd always be *on duty*, even when I didn't have to pretend to be Barston. Trying to separate my lives, thinking I could flick a switch between Voigt and my new identity, was dangerous. I might—no, would—make a mistake, might end up like Skerrill. But hadn't I been trained to be two men at once, hadn't that been the goal of the Funhouse and all my work so far? Barston was in me at that moment, and I was still Liv's El.

"You don't have to promise, El."

"Okay, I don't promise."

"But don't use the war as an excuse to wait."

I couldn't help but laugh heartily.

"What?"

"I've heard this war called a lotta things, but an 'excuse'? Never."

Liv sighed. "I don't know why everyone makes such a big deal over the war. It's gonna end soon, but we'll never get these years back."

"So live free now, right?"

"Right." She raised an eyebrow. "So?"

"Follow me."

CHAPTER 9

I TOOK LIV TO THE LOTUS, A BALLROOM ON FOURTEENTH WITH A FAR
Eastern décor the owners had hurriedly updated on December 8, 1941,
to eradicate all things Japanese. Well, sort of—the brocaded wallpaper
featuring silver-edged lotuses remained, as did the enormous *ersatz* flower
floating in the lobby fountain, but a framed placard now proclaimed the lotus
to be an import from "India, Our Ally in the Fight Against the Japs!" Before
the war, the cigarette girls and cocktail waitresses had worn tight-fitting silk
kimonos and ingeniously tied sashes that offered exposure just shy of violating
the District's law defining burlesque performances; now they wore flared
black trousers and red and gold Chinese tunics. The menu featured "Did
You Know?" facts about China ("Our Ally in the Fight Against the Japs!")
and cocktails like the Shanghai Sweetheart and Canton Clipper.

Not that Liv and I were at the Lotus to drink. We went straight to
the dance floor—thankfully, the Lotus hadn't changed its house band, the
Dexter Pierce Orchestra. The first few sets, you could count on Pierce and

his boys to deliver middle-of-the-road standards like "On the Sunny Side of the Street" and "My Funny Valentine"; but as the night wore on, and as the early-to-bed crowd tippled away the two-drink minimum and headed home, Pierce, a whippet of a man who preferred a waggling forefinger to a baton, would let the boys loose. The trombones and clarinets would take a break, and a quintet of drums, piano, bass, saxophone, and trumpet would take over. Pierce would sit down at the piano, they'd improvise. *Bebop*, a head-bobbing corporal had called it the first night I heard it. That *Kansas City sound*, someone else had said. Liv and I danced for an hour to the full orchestra, then listened to bebop as we drank Gibsons and talked. Then back to the dance floor, staying until the band packed up and a girl in a red and gold tunic took away our drinks, finally time to go home, foreheads damp from dancing, smiles bright, no worries of tomorrow to break the spell.

I WOKE UP WITH FINELY ETCHED MEMORIES OF THE TILL-DAWN TUMBLE I'd had with Liv, the dim yellow nightstand light catching the sheen on our chests, every kiss delicious, hands clasped as we both closed in on climaxes, a squeaky bedspring keeping time like a metronome. Liv heard me stir and smiled without opening her eyes.

"Still dreaming?" I asked. Traced a finger down her spine and over the swell of her hips, just covered by the tousled sheet.

"Always," she murmured, eyes still closed.

"Nice night?"

"Yes. You?" Finally opening her eyes, still smiling.

"A'course. We should do it again sometime."

"Thought you didn't like the Schoenberg."

"I wasn't talking about Schoenberg."

"The bebop, then."

"That's a word for it, sure."

She punched me lightly on the shoulder. "S'that what you'll tell the boys at the Navy Building today?"

"I'm not the kiss-and-tell type."

"That's because you're learning to live free."

"Think of all the followers you'd have, if everyone knew how much fun living free is."

"I don't want followers." Laughing.

"Admirers enough, huh?"

"You know I don't care about that kinda stuff."

True. Liv was the least self-conscious person I'd ever met, also the least egotistical. She had other lovers, I knew I wasn't her steady; but that didn't matter to me as much as it once had. A night with Liv, tomorrow's worries forgotten—why get greedy and demand more? Maybe I really was learning to live free.

As we were getting dressed, Liv asked, "Who's Delphine?"

So now I'm calling her name out in my sleep? I thought, annoyed. Didn't even remember the dream.

"My first girlfriend," I answered.

"Back in Chicago."

"Yeah. We started going together in high school." I never talked about Delphine, not anymore, but maybe sharing a bit of that history would get her out of my head.

"She left you."

"She left all of us."

"You mean she died."

I nodded.

How? Inevitably, the next question everyone asked, but not Liv. "Are they happy or haunting?"

"What?"

"Your memories of Delphine. The dreams."

"Does it matter?"

"Yes, El, it does."

HAUNTING. EVERY MORNING, THE DREAMS OVERTOOK WHATEVER HAPPY memories remained. Delphine at Montrose Beach on a July afternoon, sun on her face, treading water, grinning devilishly, wagging her finger for me to dive in. The two of us at Goldblatt's on Christmas Eve a half hour before closing, so caught up in our conversation about the Wordsworth we were reading in English class that we forgot we were there to buy presents for our parents.

Liv was trying to tell me I could replace the nightmares with my memories, if I tried hard enough—she was a fervent believer in willpower.

What Liv didn't realize is that the Delphine I recalled was unchanging, unaging, a life prisoner of the places we'd been, words shared, deeds done. I'd tried reading Proust, that didn't work; the memories were as fixed as a film's images. But the Delphine who visited my dreams was always different, always unsettling, the outcome of our encounter not known to me until I awoke. Liv would probably tell me it would take time, but that I could, eventually, conjure up a joyful Delphine in my dreams. Yet I didn't want advice or encouragement. Already I regretted telling Liv about her. Besides (and I wasn't about to tell Liv this), the dreams weren't really about Delphine. She was a totem, a stand-in for someone else, as the persistent shadowy figures who stalk our night worlds always are. All I had to do, if the Austrian dream guru was right, was figure out who that stand-in was.

But I had no time for such noodling, not that day. After walking Liv to the bus stop so she could get to work, I pulled out the Barston file and pored over it, yet again. Roughened up my hands some more. Downed four fingers of bonded whiskey and jabbed the scabs on my forearms with a sewing needle to perfect my track marks. At noon, closed the file. Made sure Franklin D. had lots of food and that the hatch in the back door for him was opening. Then off to meet Terrance.

We were eating lunch at Margie's, an ancient saloon on Seventh Street that had survived Prohibition by billing itself as an amusement parlor. Depending on who you asked, the now-dead Margie had been a bootlegger's moll, a senator's mistress, a retired madame—whoever she'd been, everybody knew her joint still served the city's finest breaded pork tenderloin sandwich. Sagging tin ceiling, high-backed wooden booths. Bar like a beached shipwreck, a massive hull of paneled oak set at an angle. So dark newcomers came through the door blinking like cattle pushed into a slaughterhouse, the barflies shirking the bright stabs of sunlight that disappeared when the heavy, windowless door swung shut.

"How you doing, Teddy-boy?" Terrance greeted me, smiling.

"Hangin' in dare."

"That yer *Joisey* accent, Teddy-boy?"

"So far. And stop calling me Teddy-boy."

"Okay, Teddy." Still smiling.

We took a booth, ordered sandwiches and Schlitzes.

"All set to go under?" Terrance asked, all business now.

"Think so."

I reviewed my preparations so far, the clothes, the flop, the track marks.

"Lemme see your arms."

I rolled up my sleeves. Terrance scrutinized my forearms like a doctor. "That one's too far from a vein."

"Yeah, well, when you're jabbing a sewing needle into your arm, maybe you don't wanna hit a vein."

"Try to keep 'em covered for now, till they heal some more and look older."

"S'why I bought long-sleeve shirts, Pops."

"Don't call me Pops."

"Okay, Poppy-boy."

We laughed and took long draughts of our beers, which had just arrived in mugs with ice chips gliding down the sides.

"Ready for your quiz?" Terrance asked.

"Hit me."

He peppered me with questions about Theodore Barston, mixing it up, just like a batting coach tossing pitches. Where had I gone to school, what was my grandfather's name, who was my homeroom teacher sophomore year, where had I enlisted, what did my recruiter look like? Also trick questions, like how old was my sister (I didn't have one, remember?). I didn't stumble once.

"You're sounding a little more *Joisey*, too," Terrance said.

"Gee, thanks."

We tucked into our sandwiches, chewing happily, and ordered two more beers. Terrance devoured his pork tenderloin, but I savored mine, enjoying every bite.

"The real Barston's not gonna eat that slow," he observed, pointing with his last french fry.

"I know. But the real Ellis Voigt wants to."

"Kinda your last meal, ain't it?" Crooked smile.

"Gonna hang me high tomorrow, sure."

He pushed his platter to the side and lit up, even though I wasn't finished. No matter—where I was going, manners were the least of my problems.

"So whatta you think?" he asked, exhaling.

"I'm ready, I'm not gonna mess up like I—"

"I don't mean you; I mean this whole undercover business."

"You mean, do I think the commander's seeing Red again?"

"Comes to the commies, he's always been a little batty."

"You brought it up, you tell me." Neither of us had to promise to keep the conversation to ourselves—unnecessary with a solid partner.

"I think he's off the mark," Terrance answered. "Way wide, even."

"Why?"

He tapped ash into the tray as I wiped my mouth and lit up. "Awright, the first thing is, we got no evidence this H & H clipping service is queer. The commander reads part of a report saying clipping services are commie fronts, Logan Skerrill went to this H & H once, so that means he was a Red and got murdered because'a it? Tea's so weak you can see through it."

"And the second thing?"

"It's way too soon to go deep like this. Dontcha think we oughta be coming at this clipping service the usual way? Pull their business records, check with the P.O. about their shipments, maybe sit up on them for a few days and see who comes and goes?"

I did, actually. I didn't think much of Paslett's boys in 7R, but they'd put umpteen man-hours into the Barston identity, which couldn't be used again, ever—if I went into H & H tomorrow to learn that Skerrill only had a girlfriend there, well, that was it, end of story. All that work and effort, mine included, would be squandered. But I didn't tell Terrance that. Truth was, I was thrilled to be going undercover. Had to prove myself, no mistakes, not one.

So what I said was, "If I'm gonna pull this off, I can't let myself think about that. It'll distract me, I'll make a mistake."

"Yeah, I didn't think about that," he said, nodding.

I told him about my room at the Jefferson Club Hotel, and we went over how I'd get ahold of him while I was undercover.

As we left, Terrance asked, "So how're you gonna go in?"

Meaning H & H.

"I got no idea," I lied.

CHAPTER 10

W E PARTED WAYS AND I WENT HOME, SHUCKED OFF MY UNIFORM, and put on Barston's clothes. Then I walked to Logan Circle, to the home of Griffin Crieve. A risky move, which is why I didn't tell Terrance. He didn't know about Crieve—it was a fluke I did. If I told my partner what I was going to do, he'd tell Paslett, and I knew the commander would order me to stay away. But it wasn't Ellis Voigt who was calling on Crieve, it was Ted Barston.

For a man who lived alone, Crieve had plenty of house. The roof of his two-story Victorian pitched steeply into a glut of yellow clapboard gables. A broad veranda stretched the width of the house. The lawn had been reseeded with bluegrass, which made the lot appear abandoned. Passersby were apt to overlook the unusual yard in favor of the home's distinguishing feature: Crieve had removed the original windows and replaced them with colored glass. Orange, red, vermilion, blue, green, purple. The porch was piled high with empty window frames, some bent at crazy angles, as if they had popped right out of a collapsing house; broken sills, sashes, and chains; twisted metal bars; and jagged wood strips. All this, the detritus resulting from Crieve's monomaniacal collection of colored glass. Every week he pored over the finds of his legion of peddlers and junkmen who, like lawyers on fat retainers, scoured the city in zealous pursuit of their client's interest. Crieve paid handsomely and asked no pesky questions about provenance. Even before his mercenaries had pocketed their money, Crieve began extracting the desired panes from their mountings, wielding tools with the precision of a surgeon. The shriek of cut metal, the echoing clatter of falling boards, and the groan of dovetailed frame corners being pried apart were just a few of the reasons why Crieve's neighbors had filed many nuisance complaints against him. But, as rumor had it, Crieve's largesse also extended to the city's building inspector.

Crieve was the youngest son of a pedigreed New England family whose fortune had taken root deep in the holds of colonial ships carrying rum, molasses, slaves; in the 1850s, a great-grandfather had invested in railroads. Crieve, brilliant and restless, finished Dartmouth in 1930 at age twenty, when the Institute of International Education selected him to pursue postgraduate study in Paris. Arriving just as the Depression was biting hard into Europe and America, he embraced communism with the fervor of first love. Back in the States, he happily slummed in a coldwater flat on the Lower East Side of Manhattan, where he taught at the Communist Workers School. In the mid-thirties, he quietly disappeared from the city's thriving communist scene, a telltale sign he had been recruited for clandestine work. What, exactly, the Soviet handlers of the Communist Party of the United States of America thought Crieve could do for them was never quite clear to our intelligence agencies. Crieve failed to blossom as a spy, but he excelled at recruitment. The party sent him to Washington, where he circulated in the higher social circles, casting for his kind and fellow travelers, the "pinks" who fancied communism but could never quite bring themselves to pay dues.

A year ago, he had suffered a breakdown and started imagining all sorts of conspiracies, assassins tailing him, the F.B.I. bugging him, the Kremlin sending him coded messages via shortwave radio. His paranoia—caused by schizophrenia—put a lot of people at risk; the party expelled him. Using hoarded trust-fund payments (and the party thought he was turning the full amount over to them!), he bought the dilapidated Victorian and turned his obsession with communism toward colored glass. By all odds, Crieve should have been killed, liquidated by the N.K.V.D., the Soviet secret police, but he had reputedly made extra copies of stolen documents and entrusted them with an unknown third party who would go to the F.B.I. and the press should he go missing.

I knocked vigorously for five minutes before Crieve finally came to the door. He peered through a side panel (leaded glass, Prairie Style).

"Who're you and what do you want?" he demanded.

"Ted Barston," I said, slowly and loudly. "I need yer help."

"Who?"

"Ted, Ted Barston. I just got outta da service, Navy."

He didn't respond, just stared.

"Can I come in?" I persisted.

Long moment, then clink of a chain, thud of a turned bolt. I stepped in, he swung the door shut and locked it. Wordlessly beckoned me to follow him, through the parlor and dining room to an add-on constructed entirely of colored glass fitted to a skein of delicate narrow metal bars.

I sat in a frayed wicker chair; he stretched out on a wooden bench and gazed up at his roof of rainbows. Another agonizing silence.

"Big Bill's son?" he finally said.

"Yeah, yeah, dat's right."

Now he looked right at me. "And you're in the Navy?"

"Naw. I just got out."

"I wouldn't think the United States Navy would discharge an able-bodied seaman during wartime, would you, Ted Barston?"

"Who said I was able-bodied?"

That crack got me a snort of laughter, but he kept staring, expecting a straight answer. Difficult to look back, he was so filthy. Grime blackened his denim dungarees, the dirt on his bare feet was so engrained it could pass for a tattoo; he stank. Only his nose, arched and delicately equestrian, matched the handsome face in the photograph in Paslett's file that I had once taken a long, stealthy look at.

"I got a dishonorable discharge, okay?" I said defiantly.

"For?"

I told him.

"Opiates, tsk, tsk, young Barston. What would your father think?"

"He's dead, he don't care."

"Still accepting visits from Morpheus?"

"Huh?" He meant was I still shooting drugs, but I didn't think Ted Barston would get the reference to the God of Dreams.

"Let me see your arms."

I rolled up my sleeves and showed him, trying to keep steady. The marks hadn't fooled Terrance, would Crieve get—

"These look fresh."

"Yeah, okay, maybe I took a shot last week. Whattya want—I just got outta da brig."

"How did you find me?"

"I remember you."

"From?"

"Da nineteen thirty-four strike, in Hoboken. You came and spoke ta da boys." So Paslett's file on Crieve had told me.

"One of my better speeches, too. My thinking on the class struggle was still callow—I was reading Kropotkin at the time, I recall, in what unfortunately proved to be a futile endeavor to link his early social theories to American industrial strife—but on that occasion I was able to rouse the workers by eschewing jargon and simply denouncing the bosses with parasitic imagery and metaphor. Very persuasive, didn't you think?"

"How da hell would I know—I was just a kid."

He laughed and said, "So you were. I vaguely recall you at your father's side, enrapt by the scene—the ranks of strikers, the bob of their pickets, the police wielding truncheons, odor of oil and brackish water in the air—quite a lot for a young boy to experience, no?"

"If you say so." Shrugging.

"I see you didn't inherit your father's rough-hewn eloquence. Rather like Lincoln, Big Bill was, with the autodidact's predilection for brief declarative sentences. He was a useful interlocutor between the workers and the leader-thinkers such as myself."

The real Ted Barston wouldn't say anything to that, and neither did I.

"But you failed to directly answer my question, Barston. I asked how you *found* me, not how you knew about me."

"Dis house, it ain't exactly hard ta find."

"That's a dodge, not an answer."

"Paul Thiel," I promptly said.

"Who?"

"Lester Thiel's son. We grew up together, in Hoboken. His pop was da field secretary for da New Joisey—"

"I know who Lester Thiel is. Was. But I don't know his son."

"Sure you do. But you knew him as Ken Jenkins. What Paulie told me, just before he got drafted, was dat his Pop wanted him ta work for da party, but underground, so he got sent ta you, dis was in I wanna say forty-one, but Paulie didn't like dat kinda work, so he quit and went back ta da docks."

So the Barston file had told me, without mentioning Griffin Crieve, whose file Paslett wouldn't trust to even his pets in 7R. I was making a big leap, guessing that Paul Thiel/Ken Jenkins *would have* trained with Crieve, who *supposedly* had been the primary recruiter for the party in New York and New Jersey before being sent to Washington. If I was wrong, Crieve would throw me out.

But I had guessed right.

"Is that what young Thiel told you, Barston? That he didn't like learning clandestine work?"

"Yeah, dat's right."

"More like the work didn't like Thiel. The poor boy couldn't even remember to answer to his new name when called. Even a puppy cocks his ear at his master's voice. So I sent him home, to the docks, on the second day of training." Now a wary look. "Why would that bumbler send you to me four years later?"

"He didn't. Last I heard, Paulie was in da Solomons. But da thing is, see, what Paulie told me was, cuz he knew I knew who you were, is dat you seemed ta know everybody on da Coast, I mean in da party, and—"

"Stop rambling—what do you want?"

"I need yer help, dat's why I'm here."

"You want money, you mean. To pay your debt to Morpheus. You can leave now, Barston." He straightened up and reached into his shirt, toward the bulge under his left arm I'd noticed right away. My guess, not much of a gat, probably a thirty-eight snubnose, but iron enough to decommission Ted Barston and Ellis Voigt.

"I don't need money, Crieve, I got a lead on work. But I was hoping you could help me get dat job."

Job. The word seemed to amuse him. Rich folk like Crieve, even after they betray their class and fight for the working man, never get past their fascination with paid labor.

"A character reference, is that what you need?" He laughed. "*To Whom It May Concern,*" he intoned, "I hereby declare Theodore Barston to have been an attentive young lad in nineteen thirty-four, on the one and only occasion that I met him—"

"You know what goes on at H & H, dontcha?" I interrupted.

"What, what did you say?"

"Dat clipping service on K Street."

"What about it?"

"Dat's where I'm gonna ask for work."

"You? Is that what you learned in the Navy, how to wield scissors?" He gestured at my forearm. "Given your other skill with needles, Barston, perhaps you should consider a career as a tailor."

"I speak German," I said hotly. In German.

That got his attention.

"How ever did you learn German?" he asked. In German.

I told him about my mother teaching me the language as a toddler. Not a difficult tale to tell—that's how I had learned.

"The working class never fail to surprise me," Crieve said, switching back to English. "But how does your facility with high German help you at a clipping service?"

"What I hear is, dey clip a lotta foreign newspapers. What with da services taking any joe who speaks German, I figger I got a skill dey need."

"*What I hear is,*" he repeated mockingly. "You hear many interesting things, don't you, Barston?"

I took the jibe as a warning. "It's no secret, huh? Ad in da directory says dat's dare line."

"How could I possibly help you obtain a position there, Barston?"

"See, da thing is, Paulie told me sometin' else before da Marines got him. He told me da party was setting up clipping services ta, you know, help out." Hard not to shirk from his stare. Or the stench that was getting worse in the airless room.

"Is that what you want to do, Barston? Help the party?"

I shifted uncomfortably, as I imagined Barston would have. "I never got mixed up in all'a dat, but I was just thinking, well, if dis H & H, if de're doing what Paulie was talking about, den maybe dey could help out da son'a somebody who was loyal ta da party all his life. I was hoping, I guess, dat because'a how important you used ta be, you maybe could tell me how ta go in dare and talk ta 'em."

Crieve startled me by slapping the bench he was sitting on with his palm. "I just knew this conversation would lead back to Big Bill. You do realize what you've just done? Of course you don't, otherwise you wouldn't have asked. We see here the incipient bourgeois tendencies of an ignorant peasantry, or proletariat, in your case, asserting, however clumsily, familial ties for purposes of advancement. Fascinating, absolutely fascinating."

As much as Barston and I both wanted to punch Crieve in the face, I checked the anger and smiled awkwardly. The puppy cocking his ear at his master's voice.

"Very well, Barston, out of admiration for your brazenness in coming here, as well as out of pity for your rough manners, I'll help you. But understand, and never forget this: I *am* important to the party. Not was, am. *Verstehen?*"

I nodded dutifully and, with that, Crieve lurched up from the bench and began pacing the stone tile floor of his solarium, speaking so rapidly that I had difficulty following every word. No matter, because what I did catch was plenty.

H & H (I learned) was a not-so-clever rendering of the monogram of the owner, one Henry Himmel, who had opened the clipping service in the mid-thirties. Himmel's real name, though, was Pavel Nevelskoi, a Russian émigré who had come to the United States right after Roosevelt established diplomatic relations with the Soviet Union. Just as Commander Paslett had guessed, based on the F.B.I.'s intelligence, the clipping service was a front. Most of its employees were legitimate—as far as they knew, they worked for a modestly profitable business—but accounts manager Nadine Silva and office manager Philip Greene were bred-in-the-bone Reds who worked closely with Himmel. Crieve claimed he had even trained Silva how to set up dead drops, run couriers, and carry out other basic tasks of espionage. Unfortunately, Crieve was less coherent in relating details of the spy ring itself.

" . . . who cloaks himself in clippings, cuttings, and scraps," he was saying about Himmel. "Entirely without original ideas of his own, he slices up others' thoughts and deeds. An ink-stained vulture."

"But d'you think he'll help me?" I interjected.

Crieve asked, with a withering look, "Have you been listening to a word of what I've said?"

"Well, yeah, a'course, you was saying how you was really da one who found all'a da spies for Himmel and dose others, how dey didn't know a thing about—"

"Which means Himmel has accomplished little, if not nothing. Without my direction, one strains to imagine how these three—Greene, especially, is a fool, overly eager and painfully clumsy—could ever have guided their minions to gather anything of note for the party. As I was saying," he added acidly.

I kept quiet.

"Indeed, Barston, it's a wonder they haven't descended upon Himmel's klatch already and swept it away."

"Dey?"

"The Bureau, of course."

"What Bureau?" I played dumb.

"My God, have the opiates permanently addled your brain? The F.B.I."

"The F.B.I.'s on to H & H?"

"I should think so."

"But how?"

"Obviously, high-frequency transmissions are easily captured. I, for one, strenuously argued for sole use of couriers, but I was rebuked. Harshly, I will add. Although no reasons were given, they weren't difficult to deduce: the Soviets' complete trust in their cryptography and their inherent suspicion of human couriers. Let the Americans collect all our codings, they seemed to think, for the lot shall remain secure *ad infinitum*." He stopped pacing and fixed me with an unsettling stare. "The Bureau's been listening to me for years. They're listening right now, of course. I've been bugged for years. They send messages, too, laughably awkward propaganda aimed at cracking me up."

They're doing a damned good job of it, I thought, then said, "So I shouldn't try ta get a job dare?"

Crieve, now staring up at his glass roof, said, "It's your risk, Barston. I believe the sky will soon fall on Himmel et al. Whether you want to be there when that happens is up to you. But if you decide you still want a job with those vultures, my advice is to stride into their storefront like you own it. Himmel, fool that he is, has a peculiar admiration for the strutting rooster."

Which had been my gut instinct all along. Kicked out of the Navy, broke, friendless, without family—was Ted Barston the kind of man who'd go hangdog or spit into the wind? Wasn't a meek man who had beaten an officer senseless, wouldn't be a meek man who asked—no, demanded—a job at H & H. For all his quirks, Crieve appeared to be a tough bird to hoodwink, but he'd bought me as Barston. And if I could fool Crieve, I could fool Himmel and his two helpers, Silva and Greene.

I hoped. Told myself that I wouldn't freeze on the stage, that I'd just finished Act 1 without flubbing a line or missing a cue. I was Barston, to my bones, and Lieutenant j.g. Ellis Voigt was merely the last role I'd filled, a likable enough character but nobody Barston would know. Or like, or respect, or obey. Strangely, voiding my real identity was exciting. All those fears of making a mistake belonged to Voigt, not Barston, who had no self-doubts, who didn't care what anyone thought, who didn't swerve out of others' way.

"Showtime," Barston said with a grin.

CHAPTER 11

H & H WAS ON THE FIRST FLOOR OF A NARROW THREE-STORY BRICK building on K Street. A wide counter divided a small waiting area from the work space: long wooden tables brightly lit by hanging lamps, wire carts stacked with newspapers, file cabinets lining the walls. If not for the whisk and whir of scissor blades slicing through one daily after another, you might think you were at the library. The clippers at the tables didn't even glance up at the jangling bell that announced my entrance; their gazes remained fixed on the newspapers spread out like leaves on a forest floor.

"Yeah, I wanna see Mister Himmel."

The girl at the reception desk gave me a look of annoyance and curiosity. She was young, probably six months out of school, with blond curls hooking under delicate ears. Eyebrows plucked into perfect half-circles set off her bright blue eyes. She was just on the wrong side of plump, but carried the weight well, in high, round breasts.

"Who're you?"

"Ted Barston, and I'm here ta see him about a job."

She wet a stamp with a quick turn of her tongue and pressed it onto an envelope. "Mister Himmel doesn't handle hiring, Miss Silva does. Anyways, we're not hiring at the present moment."

"He'll see me, honey," I said breezily, "so stop wasting both a'our's time and tell Mister Himmel Ted Barston's here."

"Is he expecting you, Mister Barston? Does Mister Himmel even know you?" Her tone had turned playful. Not yet nineteen, I guessed, but she had probably already encountered a hundred men trying to impress her, flaunting their ranks and rates, pouncing with pick-up lines, turning her head with whistles.

"He ain't expecting me, he don't know me, but here I am. So just pick up yer telephone, girlie, and give him a jingle back in his office—"

"Miriam, everything okay?"

The question came from a woman who had come over from the cutting area. She looked to be in her late twenties, slim and tall, with sharp features: tapered nose, narrow chin, flat cheeks. Her chestnut-brown hair was cut short and coiffed into tight curls. Her once-over was quick and expert, taking in my faded dungarees, scuffed brogans, wrinkled shirt. Thanks to my cheap razor, my shave was uneven. I gave her a lopsided smile that immediately bounced off her rock-cliff expression.

"He wants to see Mister Himmel," Miriam said.

"What about?"

"A job."

"Are you Miss Silva?" I asked. "I'm Ted Barston."

The woman ignored me. "Tell him we're not hiring."

"We're not hiring, Mister Barston," Miriam dutifully announced, trying hard not to grin. However this turned out, at least she'd have a story to tell during her lunch break.

Turning my smile on her, I said, "Could you tell yer boss who I am? I don't think she caught my name."

"Miss Silva, he says his name is Ted—"

"Don't be such a stupid cow, Miriam," Silva snapped with such ferocity that I almost flinched. "I heard him the first time."

The receptionist bowed her head. Her hands fluttered over the stack of envelopes she was stamping, then fell to her lap, her shoulders slumping. All work had ceased. The clippers had set down their scissors to watch us, low murmur of gossip replacing the rustle of turned pages.

Silva turned her icy glare on me. I expected a preamble before she told me to leave, something about how this was a place of business and I was wasting her time, but no:

"Get out."

"Uh-uh. Get Himmel or call da cops."

That threw her—threatening to call the cops was her trump card. In the rear, a man behind a metal desk stood and walked to the front. He was short, maybe five feet, six inches tall, his black hair combed forward to conceal, poorly, a bald spot. Tortoiseshell glasses perched low on a puggish nose. A mustache wedged between plump cheeks looked out of place, like a dime-store disguise. At first he looked overweight, but as he came close I could see that his baggy clothes—uncreased khaki slacks, white oxford shirt, and brown jacket—concealed a broad torso and muscular arms. This was Greene, Philip Greene, I guessed, Himmel's other faithful commie.

"Trouble, Nadine?" His voice was surprisingly hoarse and indistinct, like a hungover man croaking the first words of the morning.

"No," Silva answered tersely.

"Because I can toss this guy out—"

"Everything's fine," she interjected.

"Oh yes, of course. Everything's fine," he repeated dumbly.

"Are you Mister Himmel?" I asked him.

"Me? Why no, of course not, I'm—"

"Philip." Silva cracked his name like a whip, and he fell silent. Not once had she looked at him; she kept her eyes on me. "Miriam, ask the operator to get the police on the line. Tell her we have a disturbance."

As Miriam picked up the telephone, I pressed my lips into the tightest of smiles and ticked my chin up. *I know all about H & H, honey. Sure you want the coppers here?* But if my hint worried Silva, she didn't show it, her Arctic gaze still a thousand yards long. My bluff wasn't all that strong—if the cops did come, I sure as hell couldn't tell them H & H was a commie front. The cops would toss me out the door, I'd have to slink back to Paslett and admit I'd flopped. *Barston doesn't slink, he doesn't flinch*, I told myself. So I stared right back at Silva.

"Operator, Metropolitan Police, please," Miriam said. She spoke quietly, her voice shaky. "Yes, yes, it's an emergency—we have a disturbance at thirteen twenty-one K Street."

She held the line as the operator connected her to the police dispatcher. Silva and I continued to stare at each other, like Western gunslingers itching to draw.

"Nadine, perhaps it's best if I just show him to the door so we can—"

"Shut up, Philip. Let me handle this."

I was sweating it now. I'd gone after the woman, figuring she'd give in easier than a man, but Silva obviously wore the pants at H & H, not Greene. I only had one play left, and that was to blurt out who my pop was and pray that Big Bill's name rang a bell.

"Hello, police? Yes, this is H & H clipping service, we're on K Street, thirteen twenty-one, and we've got a man here who won't leave." Miriam paused, listening to the dispatcher's questions. "Well, he's not being violent or nothing, but he says he's here for a job and we told him we're not hiring and to leave but he won't, so my boss—"

"Nadine! Send him back."

The booming voice carried from the back and whipped all our heads around. An older man, his graying hair worn a bit long, stood in the doorway of an office in the rear. He had a broad, flat nose and a gap between his front teeth. His suit, a gray pinstripe, did not fit him well, and he reached to pull the right coat sleeve down to his shirt cuff. *This is Himmel?* I wondered. Trying to keep my composure.

Silva's fury at being undercut in front of the entire staff was obvious: slit eyes, scowl, knuckles white on the folder she was gripping. The smart thing to do was to ignore her and head straight back to Himmel. But Ted Barston wasn't smart, he didn't know when to leave well enough alone. I shot her a smirk, gave Miriam a hearty *Thanks, girlie*, and walked to the rear office.

Himmel was already seated behind a desk when I reached the doorway. "Come in. Sit." He motioned to a wooden chair.

I sat and said, "Thanks for seeing me, Mister Himmel."

"How do you know I am Himmel?"

"I figger only da boss coulda stopped dat gal up front from siccing da coppers on me."

"Siccing?"

"You know, getting after. Letting da dogs out on."

"I see. *Siccing*." He savored the word like a hard candy, rolling it on his tongue. His accent was surprisingly faint—I'd expected a Russian inflection as tangy as borscht. I should have known better. Paslett was always going on about the Soviets' language schools and how good they were.

"It is a job you want, yes?" Himmel asked.

"Yessir. Clipping newspapers, deliveries, sweeping up, filing—whatever you need."

"Why is it you are here? There are many jobs in this city for a strong young man. Especially in the Army."

"Funny you should say dat, cuz I just got outta da Navy. Ahead'a schedule, you might say. So when I found myself here in Washington, I remembered sometin' my pop told me when I was a kid, about how if you had da right kinda friends, you could always count on 'em ta take care'a you."

He nodded slowly, his face blank. I badly wanted to light a cigarette, but I left the Old Golds in my pocket.

"I see. Is someone here your father's friend?"

"Yessir."

"Who?"

"You, Mister Himmel." Letting my words hang in the air. My heart was pounding, I clenched my thighs to keep my hands from trembling. Everything rode on how he responded to those three words. *You, Mister Himmel.* Would he take the hook, was he curious enough to ask, or would he tell me to get out? Had I—had Barston—gone too far, been too cocky? Himmel's expression remained neutral, but his gaze, boring down, was unsettling. Did he expect me to say more? Fighting every instinct, I kept quiet. Work had resumed on the main floor, I could hear metal file drawers clanking shut.

"Who is your father?" Himmel finally asked.

"William Barston. Big Bill, dey called him. Chief organizer a'da long-shoremen's union. He led most'a da dock strikes in Joisey in da thirties, til da bosses had him killed. Made it look like an accident, like da cable snapped when he just happened ta be standing under da crate." *Just let Barston talk*, I told myself—couldn't let my exhilaration show. Just because my ploy had worked didn't mean I was in, not yet.

"Never heard of him."

"Doesn't mean yer not friends, Mister Himmel."

"I don't see how that could be. This is an information service. All our customers are right here, in Washington. We have nothing to do with anything or anyone in New Jersey."

"If you checked yer files, Mister Himmel, I think you'd see I'm right. Big Bill, my pop, was a friend in kind."

"In kind?"

"Both a'youse had lotsa common interests."

"Such as?"

"Finding friends and allies. And keeping track'a enemies."

"I see. Your father sounds like quite a *fellow*."

As in traveler, fellow traveler; parlor pink.

"Helluva lot more dan a good fellah, my pop."

"Tell me, Ted Barston, did your father ever tell you what he did with strangers who came to the dock claiming to be 'friends in kind'?"

"Yep."

"And?"

"Dey worked 'em over but good. Figgered dey were company stooges or G-men."

"And even if they were not?"

"Better safe than sorry."

"Yes, excellent advice. *Better safe than sorry*. Is it not advisable I should follow such advice?"

I shrugged and said, "That fellah up front—what's his name, Philip? He already told yer gal he's ready ta give me da heave-ho."

"He is stronger than he looks, Philip."

"Sure, everybody is."

Himmel picked up a pencil, upended it, tapped the eraser on the desk. "Leave, and give us an hour to check our files on your father. Then come back."

I shook my head vigorously.

"Due respect and all'a dat, Mister Himmel, dat's just a cheap way ta get rid'a me. So I tell you what: I'll wait up front, quiet like a church mouse, while you do yer homework, and if after dat, you don't think dare's an opening for me, I'll leave pronto and never darken yer doorstep again. Deal?"

"This is not a negotiation, Barston," Himmel said coldly.

"Den consider it a favor. For my pop. Who gave his life for our common interests."

Himmel played with the pencil. Tap, tap. Tap-tap-tap. He pointed the tip at me. "All right, you may wait in the front."

So I did, taking a seat on the wooden bench facing the receptionist's counter. Silva shot daggers at me as she strode to Himmel's office, Greene on her heels like a puppy. The door clicked shut, but the muted sound of raised voices was still audible.

I smiled at Miriam. "Got anything ta read 'round here?"

"Gosh, no, Mister Barston, sorry—oh, you're making a joke!" She giggled nervously. "You mean all the newspapers, dontcha?"

Nodding, I lit an Old Gold and inhaled greedily. "Thanks for being nice ta me, Miriam."

"You're welcome," she said, though uncertainly. Was I going to get her in trouble again?

I stood and came over, propping my elbows on the counter. "Worked here long?"

"Since last fall. Why d'you wanna know?"

"Hey, I'm not trying ta be nosy or nuttin'. It's just, well, never mind." I made like I was going to sit back down, but Miriam stopped me.

"No, it's okay, go ahead."

I took a long drag, blew the smoke at the ceiling fan overhead. "Well, just seems ta me, a pretty girl like you could work anywhere." I lowered my voice to a whisper. "For someone who's nice, know what I mean?" I cast a look toward the back.

Flustered, Miriam looked down at her typewriter and gave the roller a twist. "Oh, Miss Silva, she's . . . she's just particular, s'all, and anyways—"

Himmel's door opened and slammed, Silva exiting huffily, Greene behind her. They were making for a row of file cabinets on the far wall, behind the cutting tables, but Silva detoured when she saw me talking to Miriam. I straightened up and plastered on the crooked smile.

"Don't you have those invoices to finish, Miriam?" Silva said tersely, ignoring me.

"Yes, Miss Silva."

"So finish them. Without distraction."

Silva pivoted on the spike of her high heel and joined Greene at the cabinets. He had a drawer open and was riffling through the folders.

"Don't let her get ta you, dat was meant for me," I whispered.

"Thanks," she murmured.

I sat down, stubbed my smoke in the brass ashtray next to the bench, and waited dutifully, like a schoolboy waiting to see the principal. Hoping fervently that his two minions were about to find everything they needed to.

Which, to Ted Barston's delight, they did.

CHAPTER 12

WHATEVER SILVA AND GREENE FOUND IN H & H'S FILES ABOUT BIG Bill Barston persuaded Himmel to give me a job. Not that I was in the clear—far from it. A stranger struts in, flaunting his pop's name like he's John D. Rockefeller, Jr.; of course he's going to have a cover story that checks out. So even if Himmel didn't believe I was Ted Barston, he'd want to know who I was for real and why I'd showed up on his doorstep. Stalin had once said keep your friends close and your enemies closer. That was the Russian way of life, and I was certain that Himmel would keep digging even as he pretended to accept me as Ted Barston. I just had to hope—pray?—that Paslett's pets in 7R had dotted the i's and crossed the t's.

Himmel said he had all the readers and clippers he needed, even if I did speak German, so he took me on as a part-time delivery boy, responsible for taking boxes packed tight with folders of clippings to various clients. Part-time was good, part-time was perfect; it gave me lots of time to be away from H & H, and I had to stop myself from calculating how I could spend as many of those absent hours as possible with Liv. When I told Himmel I didn't have a car, he shrugged and said I could use Greene's. I said okay. He told me to come back at eight the next morning. *Okay.* I didn't say thanks as I left. *Gotta stay brash,* I told myself, so I sauntered out of H & H like I owned it. Too bad I couldn't send Griffin Crieve a thank-you note—he deserved one.

If my dime-store watch was keeping the right time, then it was almost five when I left. A long walk around the block to buy cigarettes put me up on the hour. As I pulled on an Old Gold and made like I was trying to figure out a bus schedule, Miriam exited 1321 K Street and headed my way, the heels of her pumps adding to the staccato clicks and taps of the office girls' quitting-time chorus line. I gave my attention back to the schedule, fished for a nickel in my dungarees. If she saw me, great; if not, I'd wait another day or two, because—

"Hi there."

I looked up and acted surprised. Miriam had wrapped a colorful scarf around her head, tucking the end into her bright yellow spring jacket. To my pleasant surprise, she had slender legs, though her knee-length skirt also showed ample hips and a wide, corset-defying waistline.

"Hey, Miriam. All done for da day?"

"Yeah. So you got the job."

"Yeah, how 'bout dat?"

"You musta impressed Mister Himmel or something, 'cause I've never seen him hire someone on the spot like that."

"My lucky day, hey, Miriam?"

"I'd say so!" she said pertly. "Is this your stop?" She motioned at the sign, at the growing swarm of office drones waiting for the bus.

"Naw, I was just thinkin' a'maybe taking a bus down ta see da sights, some a'them memorials. I only just moved here, see." I smiled sheepishly while silently cursing myself. For real, the memorials? Was Barston the kind of fellow who'd spend his free time staring up at old Abe's face or gaze slack-jawed at the pinnacle of the Washington Monument? I needed to be more careful, to think my stories through first. Silva, not to mention Himmel, would sniff the air like a bloodhound if I blurted out another oddity like that one.

"Oh! That sounds like fun," she said unconvincingly.

I laughed loudly. "I'm just joshing, kiddo! Naw, I was gonna treat myself ta a drink—wanna join me?"

"Well, I don't know, I'm s'posed to meet a girlfriend at Woodies, she wants me to help her—"

"Some'udder time, den," I interrupted breezily. "See you tomorrow, hey, Miriam?"

"Um, okay." Her hands dropped to her clutch and played with the metal clasp. "Is it far, where you're going?"

"Naw, just around da corner. Nice place, classy and all a'dat. Sure you can't join me for one, Miriam?"

"Well, maybe just one."

"Dat's da spirit, kiddo!"

I crooked and extended my arm in an exaggerated gesture. Giggling, Miriam hooked her arm around me and we walked west on K Street. There were a lot of law firms around, which meant finding a cocktail lounge wouldn't be difficult. We turned north on Seventeenth Street. Sure enough, right next to the Blackstone Hotel, was a swank place called the Excelsior. Awning above the door, settees and marble-topped tables dimly visible through the smoked-glass windows.

"Gee, I don't know," she said doubtfully when I steered us toward the door.

"Are you suggesting my attire may not be suitable for this establishment, madame?" I said in a British accent. A very bad British accent, but Miriam still giggled.

"Yeah, kinda."

"Well, let's find out, hey?"

I unhooked our arms before we entered. I nodded curtly at the maître d', barely looking at him as I scanned the room.

"Sir."

Ignoring him, I pointed to a table in the corner and said to Miriam, in my normal voice, "That'll do."

"Sir!"

"The table in the corner, please," I told the maître d', finally looking at him.

He responded with a deprecating chuckle and head-shake. He was whippet-thin, with quick dark eyes that scanned Miriam and me like searchlights. His suit fit him well, but it was off-the-rack, and the diamond in his tie tack was so small it barely reflected the overhead light.

"Is there a problem?" I asked coldly.

"The Excelsior has a dress code, sir. Jackets and ties are *de rigueur* for gentlemen."

"Not when I'm on assignment, they're not."

"Pardon? Assignment?"

"I'm in Washington from the New York office of Finnegan, Anderson, and Wake, and my inquiry into fraudulent workmen's compensation claims requires me to pose as a supervising architect at a construction site—look, I'm not going to stand here and argue with you about my obviously uncustomary attire. If my assistant and I aren't welcome here, then we'll go elsewhere and I'll pass on the details of our shabby treatment to Mister Finnegan."

Just as I wanted, a second reference to the law firm we'd just passed on K Street grabbed his attention.

"You're with Finnegan, Anderson, and Wake?"

"Didn't I just say that?" I snapped.

"I suppose I could make an exception this one time, sir. The attorneys at Finnegan, Anderson, and Wake are good friends of the Excelsior, and while our dress requirements are—"

"Just take us to our table, will you?"

His wind-up for a tip having been swatted away, he huffed, "Right away, sir," and took us to the corner.

"Goddamned swish," I muttered to Miriam after we were seated.

"Gosh, that was awful impressive," she said. "How'd you learn to do stuff like that?"

"Stuffed shirts like dat, it's easy-breezy to fool 'em—you just gotta act like you own da place."

She looked around trepidatiously. "Gosh, I don't even know what to order in a place like this."

"Don't worry, I'll order for you. Remember, yer my assistant."

"I am?"

"Ain't I a lawyer? Who's treating his girl Friday ta a drink for distracting all dose construction workers with her pretty legs while I investigated fraud and all'a dat. Whatever it is shysters do, right?"

"You think I have pretty legs?" With a coy smile.

I smiled back and said, "You heard all dem boys whistling, didn't you?"

She giggled. "I applied to work in a law office before I started at H & H, but they didn't hire me."

"Dare loss is our gain, hey, Miriam?"

The cocktail waitress came up, decked out in a tight-fitting black skirt, bolero jacket with silvery piping, and a white blouse. The maître d' had obviously told her to push us along, to get us out of there as soon as she could. Fine by me—pretty soon, an actual lawyer from Finnegan, Anderson, and Wake would stroll in, and the maître d' would check on my story pronto. I ordered myself a scotch, Miriam a Singapore Sling.

"I've never had one!" she exclaimed.

"Yer gonna love it," I said.

The drinks came fast.

"Here's mud in yer eye," I toasted.

"Boy, you sure did stand up to Nadine today," Miriam said after we drank, looking at me over the tiny umbrella in her tapered glass.

"I hate bullies," I said emphatically. "All my life, it's just been one god-damned know-it-all after anudder, shoving me around, telling me what ta do." *Too strong*, I rebuked myself. *Easy does it.*

Fortunately, Miriam didn't notice. "I know eggsactly what you mean."

"You wanna know sometin', Miriam, just between you and me?"

She nodded enthusiastically.

"I was just gonna walk outta dare today, after Silva said dey wasn't hiring, but when I heard her push you around like dat, I had ta do sometin', you know?"

"For real?"

"You bet. Can't let bullies like Silva trample all over you. Say, is she butch or what?"

"Nadine? Oh no, not at all."

"She sure acts like it. But hey, maybe dat's because she don't like da competition."

"Whattya mean?"

"Her boyfriends come in, see a dish like you, suddenly she don't look so dreamy."

She giggled. Again. "Aw, now you're teasing me."

"Yeah, but it's fun, ain't it?"

I had pegged Miriam as nice, but available—second-date score, easy. Boy, was I wrong. *Let's get outta here*, I said around six, expecting her to say she needed to get home, or still try to meet her friend at Woodies; but no, she wanted to get another drink. *Some place more our style, dontcha think?* she said. *Sure, you bet.* I hinted I was pretty much tapped out, till I got paid at H & H; she hinted that was no problem. So I shrugged and off we went, jumping on a bus to Southwest D.C., where she lived. Southwest, tucked along the docks and warehouses of the city's industrial waterfront, was a part of town I didn't know well, but it was definitely Ted Barston's kind of neighborhood, all ramshackle woodframe houses with leaning porches, corner taverns, secondhand stores, and rooming houses. Even the worst-looking flops—paint peeling from the clapboards, hand-wrung laundry hanging in the windows, privies out back—had *No Lets* signs nailed to the front doors. Till this war ended, D.C. was packed to the gills.

We hit a couple different places, Miriam paying the whole way. Around eleven, we ended up at her local watering hole, Mavens, a sleepy joint with spindly wooden tables scattered across rough-hewn floorboards and a bartop ringed with stains. The mirror behind the cash register had silvered—our reflection looked like two people stepping out of a dense fog. The bartender was an impressive stump of a man with a head as big—and as weathered—as a Halloween pumpkin, his skin pitted and creased, his heavy lids giving him a sleepy look, a graying crew cut lost in the rolls of his nape. He nodded slowly when Miriam greeted him with a hearty *Hiya, Leo!* and immediately set us up with Old Grand-Dad and beer backs.

We hadn't had any dinner, but Miriam never once asked if I wanted to get a bite. Since we were riding on her dime, I chain-smoked to kill my gnawing hunger. The booze—bourbon and beer backs at every stop—was getting to me, though I was able to spit a few shots back into my mostly empty beer bottle. The alcohol hardly showed on Miriam, who could put it away like the sailor I was supposed to be and still prattle on about her life, such as she had had one so far. She was a native, two years out of Roosevelt High, her pop some kind of clerk for the Weather Bureau, her mom never out of an apron or the kitchen. She did let slip that she was their only natural-born, and that her mom, who loved kids *(jus' loves 'em to death, you know what I mean, Ted?)*, had taken in a succession of foster children. Interesting that Miriam was now living with one of these strays—Kenny, she called him. *Like a brother, jus' like a brother, love him to death.* Kenny and his friends rented a house up the street, Miriam informed me, adding that her folks would never have let her move out except to live with Kenny.

"Wanna meet him?" she asked.

"Sure," I said, eager to get out of there without pouring any more liquor into my very empty, and very unhappy, stomach. Leo was the kind of bartender who'd notice a joe dodging shots like I'd done at the other taverns, and I didn't want him telling Miriam there was something fishy about me next time she was in.

Kenny wasn't around when Miriam led me through the unlocked front door of a two-story house that hadn't been painted since the Harding administration. She flicked on a parlor light to expose a messy room with broken or improvised furniture: Sagging sofa with a brick for one leg, wooden chairs missing slats, apple crates for endtables. Dirty carpet, patches showing through to the boards. A skinny, disheveled young man was slumped in a chair with padding tufting from tears. He blinked at the sudden light—he'd been asleep—and ran a hand through tousled blond hair in need of a cut.

"Oh, it's you," Miriam said.

He didn't reply, just stared at us vacantly.

"Is Kenny home?"

His head shake was barely noticeable, and Miriam looked away suddenly, as if he had disappeared. She fixed me with a big smile. "Kenny's not here."

"Maybe anudder time."

She swayed slightly—finally, the booze was showing—and I steadied her, drawing close.

"Wanna see my room?" she murmured.

"You bet."

But for the next hour, Ted Barston didn't see much of her room, not with a stub of a candle the only light, and Miriam reaching up to press her lips to his, pulling at his belt and pressing her hips into his hands as he groped for her skirt's zipper.

CHAPTER 13

I FOUGHT THE URGE TO FALL ASLEEP, AS MIRIAM DID, AS SOON AS WE were done. The second time. The dim glow of my watch read 1:30. She seemed like a nice enough kid, Miriam—what the hell did she see in a loser like Barston? Some girls only had eyes for men who never treated them right. Barston had called Miriam "girlie" all night, ogled other women when he should have been listening to her, and he'd prodded her to keep paying for drinks even as he saw her cash dwindle away. I remembered how Logan Skerrill had boasted of spurning girls after he'd had them. Was that how Barston would turn out? *S'all just an act*, I reminded myself. I needed a source, had to know what went on behind the scenes at H & H, and Miriam was my best shot. Barston was a roughneck, I had to play that part, right down to the *Joisey* accent. Maybe, when it came time for me to resurface as Ellis Voigt, I could do something nice for Miriam, something unBarstonlike. Treat her to a classy night on the town, or get her a real nice present. I liked the last idea—I could have Hecht's or Woodie's or wherever

I bought the gift wrap it up in expensive paper and mail it. With a note, something about how I had to leave town suddenly, about how a buddy from the Navy had called to offer me a job on the other side of the country. Enough noodling—I had a helluva lot to do before I put Barston out to pasture. I needed to wash up and change clothes, needed to wake up in my cot at the Jefferson Club Hotel. Silva was careful, Silva was suspicious; and she already hated my guts. If she was checking up on me, then I must look and live like Ted Barston. Which meant I couldn't go back to Ellis Voigt's flat for a hot shower, a sandwich, and a few hours sleep with Franklin D. nestled at my feet.

I snuffed the flickering candle and crept down the stairs, leaving Miriam snoring gently, flat on her back. The mute housemate was nowhere to be seen. I caught a Mall-bound bus just a few blocks away. With so many tempos open around-the-clock, the buses ran all night. My last dime bought me a bologna sandwich and a banana at a brightly lit luncheonette. I was bone-tired, but my mind raced. What if I garbled some detail of Barston's background, and Silva caught on? What if Greene had the party check up on me, and they caught something that Paslett's boys in 7R had missed? How the hell was I supposed to determine if Logan Skerrill had been part of H & H's communist cell *and* figure out if someone in it had wanted him dead? How reliable of a source would Miriam prove to be? She talked too much, which is why I needed her, but that also could be a big liability. Could I carry on an affair with this receptionist without losing my attraction for Liv? Vivid images of how much I'd enjoyed that night's roll in the hay sure didn't help answer this last question.

I kept the banana for breakfast and dragged myself to the Jefferson. The clerk was rousting a joe trying to cadge a free flop in a lobby chair. The bum was pretending he couldn't wake up, his eyes squinched shut as he twisted and shimmied to escape the clerk's grip. I bypassed the struggle and climbed the stairs. Figuring there'd be a line to use the toilet come daylight, I washed up as best I could without a towel or comb. I would have paid a buck that very moment for a shot of Listerine. Or an alarm clock. Lacking both, I had no choice but to sleep light and ignore the ashy taste in my mouth.

I DIDN'T HAVE TO WORRY ABOUT OVERSLEEPING. A LOUD ARGUMENT over a debt—a whopping fifty or seventy cents, depending on who you believed—woke me up at seven. I dressed and sat down on the cot to collect my thoughts. Even seated, the toes of my brogans touched the partition. My next-door neighbor was whistling off-key, but at least the debt discussion had moved on. Thankfully, the worries and anxieties that had vexed me the night before didn't loom as large. They were Ellis Voigt's problems, I realized. Today, and tomorrow, and the day after, I was just Ted Barston. As long as I played the part, as long as I kept my cover, all was well. Barston was no worrier, and neither the past nor the future concerned him. I smiled. *Live free, and the rest will follow.* Ellis Voigt hadn't yet taken Liv's wisdom to heart, but Ted Barston had. For all the danger, maybe being Barston would do me some good.

I got some money out of my rucksack and locked the door, whistling. Ted Barston was one happy joe. A few weeks ago, he'd been in the brig. Just a day ago, he'd been broke, jobless, homeless. Now he had work and a place to rest his head. Hell, he'd even gotten a swell lay, and if he figured out how to tell Miriam why he'd skedaddled, he could probably help himself to more.

Silva was waiting for me at the door of H & H, didn't even let me greet Miriam. To judge by Miriam's hangdog expression, she'd already gotten a dressing-down. It was too early for her to have made a mistake, but I had a feeling you didn't have to do anything wrong to earn Silva's wrath. I shot Miriam a warm smile and mouthed *Hello!* She brightened, a bit, and I ticked my chin to let her know we'd talk later. I followed Silva back to her office, a cubbyhole next to Himmel's.

"Have a seat, Ted," she said briskly, smoothing her skirt as she sat behind a small desk piled high with papers. She was pretty, no doubt about it, but her beauty had a sharp edge. Shapely legs, but they whisked like scissor blades when she walked. (And where the hell did she get black nylons—the real McCoy, not paint-ons—during wartime?) A rear end you could imagine cupping in your hands, until you noticed it didn't roll easily, like it does on most lookers. Taut, sure, but coiled like a panther's haunches. Her eyes—darting, watching, taking everything in—gave her otherwise attractive face a sinister cast. Her brilliantly white blouse perfectly complemented a midnight blue jacket with padded shoulders, her coiffed hair curling above the collar. A long silver necklace lay flat against her neck, and I resisted the urge to follow it down, into her blouse—she'd notice, for sure. *A triple-A ball-buster*, Terrance would have called her.

"I'm going to go over your duties," she announced.

"Awright."

She picked up a silver case and tapped out a Viceroy, lit it with a slender gold lighter with crosshatched etching. She took a long drag and exhaled the smoke over the desk, letting it drift my way.

"You may smoke, if you want."

"No, thanks."

Obvious ploys, on both our parts, but the game had to be played.

"How well do you know Washington, Ted?"

"Whattya mean?" I played dumb.

"Do you know how to get around? Do you know the streets, the addresses, how the quadrants work?"

"You mean like da difference between Northwest and Northeast?"

"Yes, that's what I mean." Getting exasperated.

"Well sure, any mope's gonna know dat. But I gotta say, I don't know my way around all dat good."

"You do understand why I'm asking you this question, don't you, Ted?"

Was she baiting me? Had she already learned why Ted Barston had spent the last two years in a naval brig? Was she hoping I'd lose my temper so she could fire me? If so, I had to admire her courage—if the real Ted Barston lost it, he could do some real damage to that pretty face before someone pulled him off her.

"Sure, Miss Silva. M'gonna make deliveries, I gotta know where I'm going, don't I?" I offered the same lopsided smile I'd given her the day before.

No reaction.

"We have deliveries that must be made this afternoon, Ted."

"Gimme a map, I'll know it like da back'a my hand in a hour, easy. Scout's honor."

She didn't look at my raised two fingers, just rolled ash off her cigarette. "I certainly hope so, Ted. Otherwise your employment here will end, immediately."

Her way of telling me I wasn't iron-clad, that Himmel wasn't my guardian angel.

"Nobody's gonna be disappointed," I answered.

"Let's hope that's true."

Nothing to say to that, so I waited for her to go on. For the next ten minutes, she briskly lectured me on the purposes and practices of a "respectable" clipping service, about how we did more than just gather information on various subjects of stated interest to our clients. According to Silva, we also "intuited and anticipated" our clients' needs. Attentive "collectors" (her word for the clippers) also recognized related topics, collected news about them, and then the "account representatives" (her and Philip Greene) recommended that the client add them to their "portfolio" of subjects. The first time, this material was provided for free, but the fee increased if the client wanted to continue to get the additional coverage. For a Bolshevik, she sure talked like Jay Gould. She also sounded like a college professor, spinning long, convoluted sentences like so much yarn. But I grinned like an idiot, ignored the fancy phrasing, and committed the important details to memory. The last task wasn't hard, thanks to my training at the Funhouse, where we'd been forced to listen to canned lectures on all sorts of topics—botany, lithography, Greek drama—and then take written tests. I'd been seated next to Logan Skerrill during one lecture. He'd made a show of closing his eyes and tilting his head back, claiming it helped sharpen his attention. To the immense satisfaction of the rest of us, our minder had slapped him on his noggin and ordered him to sit up straight, eyes forward.

"Any questions, Ted?" Silva finished.

"No, ma'am."

"Very good. Philip will give you a map and show you where you can study it."

As I stood and turned to leave, desperate to light an Old Gold, she asked, "Why'd you leave the Navy, Ted?"

An old, old interrogator's trick, that, springing a seemingly innocent question after the interview ends. And Ted Barston didn't need Ellis Voigt's help to see through it.

"Warn't my choice," I said.

"I see. But you were discharged, correct?"

"A'course. I got my papers, you wanna see 'em."

"Perhaps I should. We wouldn't want to employ a man who was absent without leave, would we?"

She was prodding me again—why? Just to show she was in charge or because she didn't believe I was Ted Barston for real?

"Unauthorized Absence," I replied.

"What?"

"Dat's what da Navy calls it. A.W.O.L.—dat's an Army name."

She bristled and said, "Well, whatever it's called, we want to make sure it doesn't apply to you."

"Awright, I'll bring my certificate tomorrow."

"Make sure that you do."

I left, lighting up as I looked for Philip Greene. He frowned when I found him talking to a clipper—er, "collector"—at a long table.

"We disapprove of smoking in the materials area," he said.

"Sorry 'bout dat." I hustled over to the reception, giving Miriam a big wink as I took a long drag and stubbed my Old Gold out in the ashtray on the coffee table. She gave me a furtive smile. At least she didn't appear upset that I'd ducked out on her the night before.

"Miss Silva said you got a map I could study," I announced to Greene when I returned.

"A map? Of what?"

"Da city, Washington. So's I can make deliveries. Gotta know where I'm going, hey?"

"You mean you don't know your way around?"

"Just moved here." Shrugging.

A clipper, a rotund middle-aged man with a graying brush cut, smiled and started to chuckle until a glare from Greene turned his attention back to a dismembered edition of the Cleveland *Plain Dealer*.

"Well, all right, follow me," Greene said peevishly. He took me to a map cabinet set against the wall, pulled out a drawer, and poked through the contents. Handing me a worn copy of the Rand McNally Standard Map of Washington, 1941 edition, he pointed to a table in the "materials area" that was only partially occupied.

"You can study it at the end of that table."

"Okay."

"No smoking, remember."

"Gotcha."

"We've got a lot of deliveries scheduled for this afternoon, so you need to memorize that map, not just pretend to look at it."

"You bet."

"What sort of vehicle do you drive, Barston?"

I checked the urge to smile. "You better ask Mister Himmel 'bout dat."

He frowned, not understanding. It would have been fun to tell him I'd be driving his "vehicle," but I didn't need to needlessly antagonize him. At least not yet.

AS THE MUTED SOUNDS OF GREENE'S PROTESTS CARRIED FROM HIMMEL'S closed office, I pored over the map. I knew the city better than Ted Barston did, but there were parts of D.C. I'd never been to, so the geography lesson was helpful. I hadn't known there was an Alaska Avenue, let alone how to get there. (Appropriately, it was way north.) Knowing how jammed Rhode Island Avenue got during peak times, I was pleased to learn I could take New York Avenue to Bladensburg Road instead, should I need to get to far Northeast D.C. After forty-five minutes, I jotted down five addresses scattered across the city, closed the map, and wrote down the best routes to get to these sites. This was an exercise we'd done many times at the Funhouse, often under stressful circumstances—using torn maps, say, or working in the dark. Figuring I deserved a smoke break, I wandered over to the reception and lit up.

"How's the homework going?" Miriam asked. She was wearing a plum-colored blouse with a pale blue scarf tucked around her neck. Her ruby red lipstick went well with her outfit, and I wondered what kind of skirt she was wearing. Black, with matching cotton stockings? We were having a chilly spring, and office girls were still wearing stockings.

"Dandy. And how're you, Miss Miriam?"

"I'm good, thank you."

"So, Miriam, I never thanked you for dose directions last night."

"Directions?"

"Yeah, you know. At the bus stop, when we ran into each other. You were very helpful."

Now she caught on, and smiled. "Glad I could be so helpful, Mister Barston."

"Maybe I could repay da favor sometime, Miss Miriam."

"I'd like that, Mister—"

"Miriam, do you have those invoices ready?"

Silva's sharp-toned query preceded her swift crossing of the materials area, a bulging expandable folder clutched in her arms.

"Yes, Miss Silva, right here." Miriam picked up a neat stack of rustling onionskin sheets and extended them.

"Don't give them to me, Miriam—put them in your outbox."

Miriam took the chiding without comment as Silva turned her attention to me.

"Don't bother the receptionist when she's working, Ted."

"Was just thanking her, s'all."

"For what?"

"Ran into her on K Street after work yesterday. She gave me directions on what bus I should take ta get home."

"You seem to have trouble with directions, Ted," Silva said, glancing conspicuously at the table where I'd left the map.

"I'm all done studying, Miss Silva. Gimme a quiz, I'll pass with flying colors."

So she did, rattling off a string of addresses. I promptly identified the best routes. She thought she had me on the last one, rebuking me for saying I'd take Alabama Avenue Southeast instead of Bruce Place to get to Suitland Parkway. I wasn't surprised that she didn't apologize when I pointed out that Bruce Place dead-ended in a park.

"Put the map away then and get Philip's keys—your first deliveries are ready."

"Yes, ma'am."

"And knock on Mister Himmel's door—he wants to see you before you go."

I nodded, stubbed out my cigarette, and shot Miriam a parting smile. Could I set up a date for us that night? I wondered. How soon could I start questioning Miriam about who came and went from H & H on a regular basis? Finding a way to get her to talk about Logan Skerrill would be tricky—I couldn't ask her directly. I set these questions aside to focus on Himmel. What did he want?

I knocked, entered at the *come in*. Himmel was standing, looking out his window, though there wasn't much to see, just the brick wall of the building across the alley. Gray smoke wafted from a cigar in his left hand.

"Please, be seated," he said to the window.

I sat and lit up.

After a long pause, Himmel turned to face me, but he didn't return to his desk. "I'm told it's important for bosses to have the office with the best view," he said.

"I wouldn't know nuttin' 'bout dat, Mister Himmel."

"No, I suppose you wouldn't. As it happens, this is the only office here with a view." He glanced at the window, as if I was supposed to compliment it.

A blind alley, yeah, I get it. Risky for a clandestine communist—and a foreign national—to be dropping metaphors like that. I hoped it meant Ted Barston had passed muster.

"Philip and I read more about your father last night, Ted."

"Dat's good."

"Shame what happened to him."

"Yeah, and den some."

"Pardon?"

"Just a saying, s'all. More dan a shame, I guess you'd say." I hoped I wasn't overdoing it—Ted Barston didn't seem like the kind of guy who grieved.

"Yes, well, I think you will make a good addition to our staff, Ted." Himmel let that statement linger, like the smoke from his cigar, watching me closely.

I added to the smoke and said, "M'sure glad ta hear dat, Mister Himmel. Like I was telling Miss Silva a little bit ago, nobody's gonna be disappointed in me."

"That's good to hear, Ted."

"And I'm all set ta make my first deliveries."

"Yes, Philip and I just discussed your use of his automobile."

"Dat's not gonna be a problem, is it?"

He exhaled. To judge by the smoke, Himmel liked fine cigars. I turned my head subtly to glimpse the band—sure enough, a Montecristo.

"No, it won't be."

"Okay, den. I better get ta it, hey?"

He nodded. I stood and reached to carefully stub my Old Gold out in a glass ashtray reefed with cigar ash.

"One last thing, Ted."

"Yeah, Mister Himmel?"

"On some of your deliveries, the client will give you a package to bring back here."

"Okay, no problem. You want I should give dose packages to Miss Silva or Mister Greene?"

"Neither of them, Ted—I want you to bring the packages to me." He gave me a long, steady look.

"Sure thing."

"I don't want you to say anything to Nadine or Philip about these packages. Do you understand, Ted?"

"You bet, Mister Himmel."

"Good."

And with that I left, tingling with excitement—and alarm.

CHAPTER 14

COULD BARELY FOCUS ON MAKING MY FIRST DELIVERY, I WAS SO BUSY thinking about what had just happened. It seemed too good to be true. Ted Barston waltzes into H & H, bluffs his way into a job, and the next day he's tapped to be a courier. Would I have time to take the packages to the Navy Building before giving them to Himmel? We had labs, we could open packages and reseal them without leaving a trace—at the Funhouse, they'd given us a demonstration. I could set everything up with Terrance, who could make sure everything was waiting. The lab boys would snap pictures, fix the packages back up, and I'd be on my way.

Then it hit me, while I was driving north on Thirteenth to deliver a box of clippings to a one-man law firm: Was Himmel setting me up? No package to pick up, just a trap to walk into. The delivery would look legitimate, but I'd be waylaid before I got to the door, shot on the street, or, more likely, in an alley—the manifest would tell me to come to a rear entrance. As I lay bleeding to death on the cobblestones, just like Logan Skerrill, the shooter would turn out my pockets and run off with my delivery to make it look like a robbery. Which is exactly how the Metropolitan Police would work it, if they spent any time on the case at all. How could you solve a random robbery gone wrong, the killer not knowing that this particular deliveryman had nothing of value to take? But Paslett and the O.N.I. would come down on H & H like Thor's hammer—wouldn't Himmel, Silva, and Greene realize they'd be in the crosshairs if I was killed? Unless they planned to be in the wind as soon as my body hit the pavement.

I pulled over to calm myself, setting the parking brake of Greene's rusty '31 Ford. I needed to talk to Terrance, needed to set up a meeting. He could help me figure out my next step. He also could get me Barston's discharge papers to show Silva the next morning.

I dropped a nickel in a druggist's telephone booth and dialed the number I'd memorized. It didn't ring at the Naval Building—if I was being followed, my tail could stroll in after I left and ask the operator for the last number dialed. That's why Embassy 3518 rang at the Irving Street Apartment Hotel. The owner was a carefully screened civilian, one of dozens paid modest retainers by the O.N.I. When the telephone rang, he would say, "Irving Hotel," nothing more. If I heard anything different, I'd hang up immediately. The telephone rang twice, then a gruff voice:
"Irving Hotel."
I said, "One of your residents, Hal Evans, told me you have a vacancy."
"I'm sorry, that room's been filled."
I hung up and checked my watch: 10:17. At that moment, Terrance was receiving a similarly coded telephone call. Within thirty minutes, he would be at the pre-arranged meeting point we were using while I was undercover. If he was out of the Navy Building, Paslett would take his place. I had just enough time to make my delivery to the lawyer, get to the rendezvous, then finish my other drop-offs.

MERLE PREAK, ATTORNEY AT LAW, WASN'T A HIRED GUN, JUST A HARRIED little man in a vest and rolled-up sleeves who scraped out his living handling divorces. Now I understood why he hired H & H to clip announcements from the classifieds, the kind that read *To whom it may concern: From the tenth day of April, 1945, I am no longer responsible for any debts other than those contracted by myself, signed.* . . . Unfaithful husbands took out ads like that to protect themselves from vengeful wives who might run up the limit on a credit account at Hecht's or Woodies. Unable to afford a secretary, Preak used H & H to sniff out traces of domestic strife and warring spouses so he could call and offer his services. He barely acknowledged me, motioning me into his cramped office. Took the box, dropped it on a wooden chair along the wall, and scribbled his name on the manifest, not bothering to respond to my parting *Have a nice day, sir.*

Paslett had come with Terrance to the meeting point, a billiards parlor on Ninth and F. According to the O.N.I. file, Barston had liked to play nine-ball, so it wouldn't look suspicious if he killed an idle hour shooting stick. The commander and Terrance had both changed into civvies, my partner wearing faded dungarees, a black T-shirt, and a tan zip-up jacket. A bull of a man, Terrance naturally looked like a Teamster or a mechanic—he fit in perfectly. Paslett didn't. Probably thought his creased gray trousers and white shirt with red pinstripes made him look like a shipping clerk, but his posture and bearing were all wrong; life as an officer had made it impossible for him to slouch, sprawl, or scratch himself like a real clerk. Watching Terrance take a shot, the commander held his cue ramrod-straight, like a swagger stick. I could make a game or two of nine-ball with Terrance look natural, the cocky Barston loafing on his first day of work, but billiards with a second man who looked so out of place was a dead giveaway.

Terrance shot me a look as I approached their table. *What could I do?* The parlor was long and expansive. Ceiling fans hung from beams joining the walls, swirling cigar and cigarette smoke into wispy clouds. The bar was in the rear, half of its stools occupied even at this early hour, lone men sipping shots and beer backs. A radio murmured the news, two hustlers practicing bank shots eyed us over. Ignoring them, I took a cue stick from the wall rack and nodded my greeting to Terrance and Paslett.

"How's it hanging, Barston?" Terrance said as he bent over the table to shoot. They were playing nine-ball.

"Awright."

Paslett asked, "Found a job yet?" Trying to sound nonchalant.

I hid my wince. Even in character, he sounded like a superior officer.

"Yeah, sorta." I lit an Old Gold and inhaled greedily. "Deliveries, part-time."

"That doesn't sound too bad." Terrance missed his shot. Intentionally, it looked like, to put Paslett at the table.

"Dunno. Gotta show 'em my discharge certificate tomorrow. Dey might not like what it says."

My partner ticked his chin, indicating he understood what I needed. "You're just making deliveries, whatta they care about where you been?"

"Dis real ball-buster runs da office, she's already got it in for me."

"But somebody must like you there, huh?" asked Paslett, who had made one shot and missed the next.

"Yeah, da owner, he and me hit it off real good. He remembered my pop."

"What kinda deliveries you gotta make?"

"Dese small packages, nuttin' heavy."

"Sounds easy," Paslett said.

"Yeah, 'cept sometimes, m'supposed to also make exchanges."

Terrance nodded absently, methodically chalking his cue. "You supposed to inspect the returns, before you accept 'em?" Translation: Will you be able to bring the packages to us?

"Dey didn't tell me." *Maybe, maybe not.*

"Well, you'll get the hang of it." This from Paslett, his way of saying, *Figure it out, Voigt!*

"Yeah, I guess so. Just hope da first customer don't blame me for him not liking da goods." *What if I'm being set up?*

"Shoot the messenger, huh?" Terrance remarked as he sent the cue ball hurtling across the felt at the nine ball. Too hard, boxed the pocket.

"Happens, don't it?"

Paslett said, "You do a good job, I'm sure you'll have nothing to worry about." *If you don't make any mistakes, you'll be fine.*

"Gee, thanks." Which charitably translated as *Not helpful*, but more accurately said—

"Aw, fuck, Ted, you worry too much," Terrance piped up. "Oughta let me do your worrying for you." His way of saying he'd watch my back, that he'd tail me the rest of the day and stay close, ready to jump in if I was being set up.

I nodded, trying not to let my relief show. "Yeah, dat's a good idea."

Paslett missed a shot at the nine ball, Terrance didn't. I leaned my cue against the table and racked balls one through nine in the wooden triangle as the commander took a seat and lit a cigarette. I sank the five ball on the break but missed the one ball on my follow-up.

"What're you using to make deliveries?" Paslett asked.

"Dis real rustbucket, belongs ta one'a da managers."

"Owner musta really taken a shine to you, let you borrow the staff's vehicle like that."

Terrance, out of the commander's view, rolled his eyes. I pretended to concentrate on my shot at the three ball, my partner having made two shots. I wanted to finish this game and skedaddle—if I didn't finish my deliveries pronto, Silva and Himmel would get suspicious.

After I sank the three and four balls and was lining up a ricochet to bank the nine ball in, Terrance said, "So are you the only delivery guy?" *Can you tell us anything more about the staff before you have to leave?*

I couldn't think of a safe way to tell them what Griffin Crieve had told me about Himmel, Silva, and Greene being Russian spies, so I decided to keep it simple.

"Well, besides dat ball-buster I told you about—Silva, Nadine Silva's her name—dare's dis fella Greene, Philip Greene, I guess he's an account representative or sometin' like dat. A real fussbudget, telling me not ta smoke, asking do I know my way around da city, on my case. But da receptionist, dis gal Miriam, she's nice. I got a feeling she and me are gonna get on real good." *I'm working her as a source to see what I can find out about Logan Skerrill and the clipping service.*

"Yeah? A hot tamale, this Miriam?" Terrance asked with an impish grin.

"More like a burrito, but yeah, hot, real hot."

We all laughed, then I took my shot and banked the nine ball straight in.

"Nice shot," Terrance said. *You're doing a real good job so far, partner.*

Paslett nodded, then asked, "How about this Silva gal? She a looker?" *Should we check her out?*

"Oh, yeah, a sweet piece'a tail, tall brunette with sharp looks, but she likes ta play hard ta get." *Absolutely, but she won't be easy to shadow.*

I checked my watch and racked my cue. "Well, I gotta run, boys. Don't wanna run late on my first day."

"See you around, Ted," my partner said. *Don't worry, I'll be watching you the rest of the day.*

"We oughta do this again," Paslett said. *We'll need to meet, soon.*

"I dunno, I'm awful busy for a while." *Don't push it, let me set the pace.*

"Well, whenever you can make it."

I hid my smile. Not having to *sir* a C.O., getting him to agree with me—a lieutenant j.g. could get used to that, real fast.

FINISHING MY ROUTE THAT AFTERNOON, I FELT PRETTY GOOD. TERRANCE was watching my back and he'd have Barston's discharge certificate at our pre-arranged dead drop by that evening. He was pleased with my work, so was Paslett. Sure, he was prodding me, but he'd eased off when I'd reminded him how much I'd accomplished so far. I'd become Barston, I'd gotten a job at H & H, I'd bagged Miriam as a source. If that wasn't enough, it looked like I'd soon be working as Himmel's personal courier. If I could just figure out a way to divert those packages to the O.N.I. labs. . . .

If, if. I should have known better than to weave my laurels yet. *Ifs are Sirens, steer clear.* So an officer had told us at the Funhouse. We had heard so many bromides like that during our training, they had stopped registering. As I soon had reason to regret.

CHAPTER 15

I DIDN'T SPOT TERRANCE AS I DELIVERED THE REMAINING PACKAGES, but I never doubted he was close by. None of the remaining clients had packages for me, and I couldn't help but think I'd lost my nerve by asking my partner to shadow me. Himmel probably wanted to make sure I was reliable before he trusted me to bring him something.

I pushed that worry aside as I sped around Northwest D.C., double-parking or pulling in front of fire hydrants (what did I care if Philip Greene racked up tickets?). I needed to plot my next moves. Miriam needed to be more than an easy lay if she was going to be a good source, I realized. What she had wanted, what she'd told me to do to her the night she took me home—well, it had been pretty obvious I wasn't her first quick roll in the hay. But the way she'd clung to me after she fell asleep, her arms wrapped tight around me, hinted that she wanted more than a man—or men—to haul her ashes. She wanted a steady, a sweetheart, a joe who'd treat her right. I must be that guy, I decided, the one who treats her right, who brings her flowers and whispers sweet nothings into her ear.

It wouldn't be easy—Ted Barston wasn't the courting kind—but I saw how I could play it. Ted would tell Miriam about his troubled boyhood, about a pop who neglected his son because he was so busy organizing strikes and leading the union. Ted would tell her about youthful scrapes with the law, about how his pop thought he could beat his boy straight. Miriam's folks had taken in foster kids, it was a story she could understand. Ted would confess his dope habit, tell her all about how it had landed him in the brig. Then he'd drop hints he wanted to pull his life together. He couldn't talk about settling down, but the lovey-dovey act should open Miriam up like a tin of sardines.

But how to get her to talk about what went on at H & H? How to find out how often Logan Skerrill had visited the office? My gut told me Miriam was no Red, she was just a receptionist. Himmel, Silva, and Greene were the core of the cell, and other members who came to the office must pose as clients or potential clients. So the trick was to get Miriam to talk about things she'd seen that looked ordinary, but weren't. My angle in was Silva. She rode Miriam hard, she didn't like me. If I could coax Miriam to join me in carping about Silva when we weren't at work, I could get Miriam to tell stories about H & H. Hopefully, Logan Skerrill would come up, I might learn who had a reason to kill him.

As I parked the Ford, I decided to ask Miriam out to eat that night, after work. Then I'd pick up my discharge certificate at the dead drop. *Time enough to squeeze in a date with Liv, too?* I wondered. I could leave a message at her rooming house, inviting her to meet me at the Little Palace that evening. After the dead drop, I could drop by my flat, change clothes, and swing by the diner. We couldn't spend the night together— I had to wake up on my cot at the Jefferson Club as Ted Barston—but even a few hours with Liv, as myself, as Ellis Voigt, sounded awful good after my day so far.

Greene made a show of checking his watch when I came in. "How'd it go, Barston?"

"Dandy. Only got lost eight times."

He gaped, started to sputter.

"Aw, I'm kiddin' you," I said, clapping him on the shoulder. "What I'm s'posed ta do with dis?" I fluttered the manifest with the recipients' signatures.

"I'll take that!" He snatched the sheet from my hand and ostentatiously walked over to the front counter. "Please file this, Miriam."

"Yes, Mister Greene."

Standing behind Greene, I rolled my eyes at Miriam, who kept a straight face. But Silva saw me and strode over.

"Ted, fill out your time sheet, then you're done for the day. We'll see you at nine sharp tomorrow."

"Yes, ma'am!"

She shot me a dirty look but said nothing. She headed toward her office, Greene on her heels, calling, "Nadine, Nadine, I wanted to ask you about . . ."

I said, "Miss Miriam, could I have my time sheet, please?"

"Of course, Mister Barston."

She pulled my card from the box on the counter. I marked the time— 3:45—and signed my initials and handed it back.

"Did you have a good first day, Mister Barston?"

"I did, Miss Miriam. Gonna celebrate, too."

"Are you?"

"With a special friend, I hope."

"Oh?" She arched an eyebrow. "You hope?"

"Well, I gotta ask her ta join me, don't I?"

"You better call her soon, to make sure she doesn't already have plans."

"Yeah, be a real shame if she couldn't join me at Ferrara's, on Twelfth Street, at six, huh?" I smiled.

"It would be." A smile back.

And with that I left, thinking that Miriam might be a sharper tack than she looked.

I TOOK A ROUNDABOUT WAY BACK TO THE JEFFERSON CLUB, MAKING unpredictable stops on corners and in front of shop windows, to check to see if I was being followed. When I was certain I was in the clear, I popped into a People's Drugstore to call Liv's rooming house. She was still at work, which was good, because I needed to leave a cryptic message, just in case I was wrong about not being shadowed.

"Yeah, I wanna leave a message for Liv," I said to the girl who answered the telephone.

"What is it?" A racking cough followed her terse question. Probably a G-girl too sick to work, couldn't get any rest because the telephone rang all day with calls for her housemates.

"Tell her Buck Mulligan will be at the Martello tower tonight at eight-thirty if she's free."

"Who? Where?!" Another painful-sounding cough.

When she was done clearing her throat, I slowly repeated my message and hung up before she could ask me where the Martello tower was.

The permanent odor of the Jefferson Club reminded me I needed a hot bath and a shave. I fetched the razor and a change of clothes from my rucksack and headed to the Turkish Bath House on Eighth. For a quarter, you could take a long, hot steam; for a nickel, the washroom attendant gave you a handful of mentholated shaving cream. Reclining on the smooth stone bench, I closed my eyes and let the wet heat soak into my pores. Two men next to me were having a hushed conversation about tract housing and the current price for an acre of land in Annandale. Their murmurs and the warmth made me drowsy. I dozed, if only briefly. After toweling off, I shaved and dressed, ran a comb through my wet hair. I found myself whistling as I left the bath house. No dreams of Delphine last night, I realized. Maybe being Barston for a while was good for me.

FERRARA'S, WHERE I WAS MEETING MIRIAM, WAS AN ITALIAN RESTAURANT crammed into a narrow storefront. No sign, just a chalkboard. Dirt-streaked windows, festooned with drooping nets of yellowing garlic heads, probably deterred many would-be diners, but I'd heard the prices were cheap, the servings plentiful—just the sort of place Barston would take a date.

Didn't take much to nudge Miriam into talking about H & H. As soon as our first glass of Chianti was poured, she was off to the races, marveling at how Himmel lived in a suite at the Wardman Park Hotel, complaining about what a "louse" Greene was and how he thought he was "so important," even though Silva ordered him around "like a nigger."

" . . . every goddamned chance he gets, he takes it out on me," she finished. "'Miriam, that's not the way *we* file invoices,' 'Miriam, surely you know better than to use capital letters in an address.'"

"Yeah, he's a real pud," I said. "How come he ain't in uniform?"

She smirked and said, "Says he's flat-footed."

Our food came. I'd wanted the *osso bucco*, but Barston struck me as a spaghetti and meatball kind of guy, so that's what I'd ordered for both of us, with garlic bread.

"Well, if dat bitch Silva starts ordering me around like dat, I'm outta dare," I said.

"Wish I could quit," Miriam said glumly, looking at me with expectation.

My cue to ask her why she didn't quit. Then she'd tell me all about her big dream, the one she was saving her money for. Every G-girl and steno I'd dated in D.C. had one, a plan that was going to lift them out of their dreary routines of filing and taking dictation. My guess, Miriam was going to beauty school as soon as she had the dough, then was going to open her own salon.

"How come you let her push you around?" I asked instead.

"Who, Nadine? Well, see, I need to work a little—"

"You gotta stand up ta bullies like her," I interrupted, my mouth full of meatball. "Like I was saying yesterday, you gotta push right back when dey start shoving."

She nodded politely, but I could tell I was making her uncomfortable. Miriam had spunk, but not enough to stand up to Silva. I'd seen that moments after walking into H & H, when Silva had tongue-lashed her in front of me and the staff. So I changed the topic—and struck gold.

"How come she's such a bitch, Silva?"

"She's always been mean. But ever since her boyfriend bit the dust, she's been on a tear."

"Was he overseas, her fella?" Hiding my excitement.

"No, he lived right here. Guess how he died?" Miriam's eyes grew wide.

I shrugged, as if I didn't give a damn, and shoveled noodles into my mouth.

"He got murdered, can you believe it?" she said excitedly.

"No kiddin'? How'd dat happen?"

"He got shot with a gun, that's what happened." Miriam giggled at her lame joke, so did I.

"For real, yer not yanking my chain?" I asked.

"Honest injun. And it just happened like a few days ago."

"Was he bent, this guy?"

"Nobody knows. See, the thing is, Ted, we're not even s'posed to know he got kilt!"

"How come?" Still packing the spaghetti away, like it was my last meal.

"I don't know. He used to come in to see Nadine at the office, but then all'a sudden, he stopped, like two, three weeks ago."

"So how do you know he bought it?"

Miriam wiped her mouth primly, looking like the cat who's just got the mouse, and laid her napkin down. Her plate was still half-full. *Would Ted finish her food?* I decided he would.

"You done with dat?" I asked.

"Oh yeah, go ahead, Teddy. So anyways, Norman—he's one of the clippers, he's the one who always wears braces instead'a belts, older guy—he goes to see Philip after everyone's left. The door's closed so he knocks, and Philip, he yanks the door open and tells Norman, 'whatta you want, can't it wait till tomorrow?' and Norman can see right in, and guess who's in there, all red-eyed from crying?"

"Silva."

"Right! Boy, I didn't think she had a teardrop in her body. Anyways, she drops this newspaper she's holding and comes rushing out and Philip goes chasing after her—see, I happen to *know* that Philip's got a huge crush on Nadine, so he wants to comfort her and all that—and Norman's just standing there, see, he can't help himself, he wants to know what it's all about, so he peeks at the paper Nadine dropped on Philip's desk and it's folded to this article about a murder near the Navy Yard." She smiled triumphantly at me as I mopped up the sauce on her plate with the last piece of garlic bread.

"So how'd dis Norman know it was Silva's fella? Coulda been anyone."

"There was a photo of the guy who got kilt. Norman recognized him."

"What's his name, Silva's squeeze?"

"Lincoln Skerrill," Miriam announced.

I didn't correct her. I stacked her now-empty plate on top of mine, pushed both to the side, and lit up.

"Well, dat's sometin', all right," I commented.

"Yeah, but you know what the real kicker is?"

I shook my head.

"She didn't even go to his funeral, can you imagine! She must not'a loved him one bit. Just showed up to work like it was any other day."

Because if she had shown up, Terrance would have taken down a detailed description of her as well as of any other out-of-place mourners. My partner had attended Skerrill's military service, held while I was cramming to become Ted Barston, to take note of who came. That Silva knew to stay away meant that Griffin Crieve was right about her, Greene, and Himmel. She could mourn all she wanted, as long as she did it privately—the cell must be protected, at all costs. I found it awful hard to believe that Skerrill had been dating Silva without knowing that she was a Red, and that she and her cronies were up to no good. I had to check the urge to prod Miriam to tell me more, so that I didn't look suspicious. But getting her to gossip from now on would be easy-breezy, as long as I kept her happy.

With that in mind, I asked her why she couldn't quit her job just yet, and she launched into an exuberant recitation of her big plan. Sure enough, beauty school, her own salon. All so real to her, a story she'd obviously told countless times to whomever would listen, that all I had to do was nod and say *sure* or *great* now and then. Maybe that's why a nice girl like Miriam had bee-lined to a bum like Barston. She hadn't noticed he never really listened, that he was awful good at plastering a fake smile on his nodding head as he was actually thinking about himself. Her last guy had probably told her to shut her trap every time she tried to talk about beauty school—now here was Teddy Boy, enrapt as he listened. I thought about Liv and her desire to go to the South Pacific after the war. Liv and Miriam couldn't be more different, as far apart as Ted Barston and Ellis Voigt were, yet both girls had the same glow in their eyes when they talked about their dreams, about their futures.

Barston and I sure didn't get excited when we considered our futures. Maybe we had more in common than either of us thought. At least Barston was a man without a past. He had a history, sure, facts I'd memorized as if preparing for a high school exam. But he didn't have a past, that ebb and flow of memory that laps over our thoughts every day. And my past was distracting me from listening to Miriam. First a memory of Liv, now one of Delphine: her telling me her big dream, so many years ago when we were kids. Nodding as Miriam went on, I was stuck on the thought that if I'd never met Delphine, I wouldn't be sitting across from Miriam at that moment. Didn't make sense, but who ever said the past does?

CHAPTER 16

I PAID THE BILL AND TALKED MY WAY OUT OF SEEING MIRIAM HOME. *Gotta see a pal from my Navy days, kiddo.* Yeah, all right, she answered, starting to pout, till I whispered in her ear. Then she brightened and didn't even seem to care that I left her standing on the corner as I crossed the street. I turned once to wave, then hustled down Massachusetts, toward Mount Vernon Square. I had to get to the library before it closed to pick up Ted Barston's discharge certificate.

Terrance didn't much care for our dead-drop site. *I hate libraries,* he'd said during our lunch at Margie's. *How can you hate some place you've never been?* I'd shot back. *Funny,* he'd growled through a plume of cigarette smoke, but he'd agreed to the set-up. On an earlier visit to the library, I'd determined that Dr. William Sherlock's *Practical Discourse Concerning Death* had only been checked out once. In October 1921. Not a title likely to find another borrower, especially after I surreptitiously ripped the catalog card from its drawer and gave it to Terrance, so he could find the title. Sure enough,

Barston's dishonorable discharge was folded into the book, along with an unsigned note from my partner: *I should read this book sometime—looks like a real gas!* I chuckled, ripped the note into tiny pieces, pocketed the certificate.

Outside the library, I hopped on a bus to get to my flat, so I could change clothes before meeting Liv at the Little Palace. Breaking cover was pretty reckless, strictly *verboten*, and some kind of dumb, for sure. But as long as no one from H & H wandered into the diner—and what were the chances of that?—Ted Barston and the investigation were safe. Just an hour or two with Liv, I told myself, then I'd become Barston again and return to the Jefferson Club.

As a precaution against being tailed, I switched buses, doubling back on Fourteenth Street for a few blocks, and took a roundabout way to my flat. So far, I'd seen no signs of a shadow since starting my job at H & H, but I had to be sure. Franklin D. was right at the door when I came in, mewling to beat the band. I hadn't been able to feed him since I'd gone to see Griffin Crieve two days earlier, but there were still mice in the walls and, in a pinch, he could use the flap in the back door to go scrounge in the alley. Maybe he was just lonely.

"Why don't you get yourself a girlfriend?" I asked him. "She's welcome to live here with you."

He looked at me as if he expected me to start making cat-sense any second. When I didn't, he gave me a stern squawk and bumped my calf.

"Awright, awright, I hear you."

I went into the kitchen, opened up two cans of Spam, and heaped the hash into his well-licked dish. Topped off his water bowl. Maybe Kleist, my landlord, could feed him for a while. But I didn't want Kleist to know I was away. If someone came around asking about Lieutenant j.g. Ellis Voigt, U.S.N., the less Kleist knew, the better. I lit a cigarette, wondered, *Could Liv stay here?* Flicked that idea away with the first ash. Talk about reckless! I'd have to lie to Liv about why I was away, I'd compromise the investigation, Kleist would evict me for having a subletter.

I hurriedly changed into Ellis Voigt's clothes—creased brown trousers, La Playa two-tone sport shirt, and Russetan wingtips—and left by the back door while Franklin D. was still bent over his dish. Checked the Timex:

ten to nine. I was twenty minutes late, but then, had Liv ever been on time? Hell, I didn't even know if she'd show.

But there she was, sitting in a booth. I shot Gerald a tropical sunrise of a smile, he grunted an acknowledgment.

"Buck Mulligan? For real?" Liv greeted me. Looking exquisite in a gun-blue belted dress with half-sleeves and sharp collar points.

"Figured it out, didn't you?"

"Not exactly how I pictured a Martello tower," she said, gesturing at the brightly lit diner.

"Well, D.C.'s no Dublin, either, is it?"

"It sure isn't. Thought you'd never read *Ulysses*."

"Whatever gave you that idea?"

"Well, when I told you I'd finally gotten the book from the library, you mighta said 'I've read that.' Wouldn't most people?"

"Am I most people, Liv?" Trying out my tropical sunrise smile on her.

She laughed, flicking a lock of hair away from her brow, and for a moment I felt happier than I had in weeks. Months, even.

"Besides, I didn't want to give away the ending," I said, taking her hand and squeezing it.

"Don't start now—I just started the last chapter."

"So, Liv."

"El?"

"How will you be?"

"Ever-wonderful."

"That a word?"

"Is now."

"Hungry?"

"No. You?"

"Could do dessert."

"Share?"

"A'course." I caught the attention of Gerald, who was hovering nearby, rearranging shakers.

"Yes, you want?" he asked, still bent over a table.

"Banana cream pie."

"Two?"

"Just one."

"Coffee?"

"Yeah, please."

He nodded briskly and strode away.

Liv asked, "What're you reading these days, Professor Mulligan?"

"Pulp."

"*True Detective?*"

"Close, very close."

"What's your favorite story?"

"This one about a boy who grows up on the waterfront, runs away to join the Navy."

"Like you, huh?"

"Only in Chicago, we called it the harbor, not the waterfront."

Our pie and coffee came. I slid into the booth next to Liv, so we could share our dessert side-by-side, like two love-struck teens. Warmth of her leg, rustle of her dress, the way she tipped cream into her coffee and stirred once, the dainty press of her fork into the soft meringue—I could watch Liv do nothing special all day long and still feel like a million bucks. Just like with Delphine, in Chicago, all those years ago.

"You're due for a visit to the library," Liv said.

"If only I could find the time."

"You have time for me, right?"

"A'course."

"So make a date with me."

"Didn't I just?"

Rolled her eyes. "Another one. And I'll take you to the library. For *that* date."

"And find me something better to read?"

She nodded excitedly, like a child who's just been asked if she likes the circus. "Game?"

More than you could ever know, I thought. But as long as I was using the library as a dead drop, I couldn't set foot in it as Ellis Voigt.

"How about Lowdermilk's instead?" I said, referring to the downtown bookshop.

"S'long as I get to pick your book, sure."

"Natch. So tell me about *Ulysses*."

She set down her fork and told me about her struggle to get through the chapter set in the hospital. About how she read it over and over, hoping it would make sense. About how she finally went to the library in search of assistance.

"Went through two dictionaries, El—neither were any help!" she exclaimed.

My stomach tightened, my heart beat faster. What the hell had I been thinking, telling Terrance to use the library as our dead drop. Liv was there all the time—for Christ's sake, I'd *met* her there. If I ran into her while posing as Ted Barston. . . . What other bone-headed mistakes was I making? I glanced away from Liv, still happily telling her story, and surveyed the diner, looking at other patrons, my panic growing. The elderly man bent over a bowl of soup at the counter—had he come in after me? The middle-aged couple eating casserole at a nearby table—were they watching us? If I couldn't pull off being Ted Barston, if I blew this case—

"Liv, I'm sorry, I gotta go." I hurriedly kissed her on the cheek and lurched out of the booth, tossing some bills to Gerald on my way out. I didn't dare look back at Liv. Hustled home, frantically changed into Barston's clothes. Straight out the back door, ignoring Franklin D.'s unhappy meowing, taking alleys and backways to get out of the neighborhood. I didn't think Liv would come to my flat after the way I'd left, but I had to avoid seeing her, had to get to the Jefferson Club, pronto. As long as no one had followed me, as long as I didn't make another mistake, the investigation was safe. I could only hope Liv would give me a chance to explain why I'd run out. Now I regretted kissing her as I fled. An empty gesture, obscene even, worse than a Judas kiss.

Couldn't worry about all that now, had to focus on being Ted Barston. *I'm not Voigt, I'm Barston*, I thought. *Liv's not my girl, Miriam is.* What was she doing tonight, I wondered. Too late to call on her, of course, but thinking about a date with Miriam that *might have been* helped me forget about the debacle with Liv. I could have taken Miriam to the movies after our Italian dinner. Sure, Barston was supposed to be broke, but Miriam wouldn't ask questions, wouldn't even wonder where he got the money to take her out—and I had plenty of money to fund a few decent dates for

Barston and Miriam. Could have asked about which beauty school she wanted to attend, or about her folks, or the dress she had on layaway at Woodie's—hell, anything at all so long as it had to do with her life. She was one of those girls, you ran across them all the time—clerks, stenos, waitresses—who were expected to listen, not talk, who were expected to follow instructions, not ask questions. Ask them how they were doing and they'd say, "Just dandy, sir," no matter how miserable or lonely or confused they felt. Miriam yearned for attention, wanted to fall in love. So what if her dream was a cliché, one shared with countless other unimaginative girls her age? It was hers, she had the same right to be as happy as Liv. Lieutenant Ellis Voigt needed her as a source, he was using her; but that didn't mean Ellis Voigt, who was, for all his flaws, still a decent man, couldn't ensure that the character he was playing treated her right. As it was, Barston was going to beat a hasty departure from Miriam's life the instant the investigation ended—the least he could do in the meantime was give her some happiness while he was around.

Thinking about Miriam, and mulling ways Barston could be nice to her, calmed me down. My pulse had stopped racing by the time I got to Ninth Street. *Just need a full night's sleep*, I told myself, and that sounded like a simple, good idea. Until I saw Terrance sitting in our Chrysler, parked two blocks away from the Jefferson Club.

CHAPTER 17

IG'S UP, I THOUGHT AS I WALKED TOWARD THE BEAT-UP CAR— Terrance had seen me with Liv. Instead of anger, relief. I wasn't cut out for undercover work, was I? My successes so far—passing myself off as Barston, getting a job at H & H, cultivating Miriam as a source—were flukes. If I was a natural, like Logan Skerrill, I never would have made a date with Liv. Never would have used the library as a dead drop. Terrance had no choice but to report me to Commander Paslett, who'd dress me down, berate me, abuse me, humiliate me. I'd be demoted and exiled, probably to a rust-bucket tanker in the Pacific. I squared my shoulders, took a deep breath, and drew the Old Gold I was smoking down to my fingertips. I was washed up, but I was determined to follow tradecraft one last time.

Walked past the car, only glancing at the man in the driver's seat, as any passerby would. Continued down Ninth Street and turned west on E Street, stride casual but steady, the walk of a man headed home, while checking for signs of a tail. Dropped a cigarette so I could look behind me, used the reflections of shop windows to check angles. As I passed the statue of Casimir Pulaski, just before reaching Pennsylvania Avenue, Terrance slowly drove by. I dipped my chin, to let him know I hadn't been followed, and he pulled to the curb. I quickly got in on the passenger side, he drove away, neither of us spoke. On E Street I'd promised myself that I wouldn't confess first, that I'd let my partner make the first move.

"We got a serious problem," Terrance finally said, his voice taut.

"I know," I answered firmly.

"You do?" Surprised.

"Well, you wouldn't be here if there wasn't."

"Ain't that the truth." He smacked the dashboard lighter down and fished a cigarette out of his jacket pocket. "Where the hell you been, anyways? I been sitting up on that fleabag hotel for more than an hour."

So he hadn't seen me with Liv! All my doubts vanished, the self-recriminations disappeared.

I said, "I was on a date with Miriam, she's the receptionist at H & H. Got something juicy, too."

"Yeah, like what?"

"Tell me our problem first."

The lighter popped, Terrance reached. He pressed the glowing end to his smoke and inhaled. I took the lighter from him and fired up an Old Gold.

"Goddamned Bureau, that's our problem." As in the Federal Bureau of Investigation.

"They know about Barston—they know about me?!"

"Not yet. But it's still the mother of all snafus, let me tell you."

And tell me he did, after parking in the lot of the George Washington University Hospital, a short drive up Pennsylvania. (Good place to talk unnoticed—who pays attention to other cars when they're rushing to see a sick relative?) After our meeting at the billiards parlor, Paslett had assigned a young civilian employee, a woman named Frances Traub, to tail Nadine Silva. I knew her slightly. She was about twenty-two, as fresh-faced as they come, round cheeks, curly brown hair.

"I was against *that* idea," Terrance said, shaking his head.

"How come?"

He glared at me. "Besides that she's a broad? And that she's never done undercover work?"

"B-Three ran her on an op last year and she did fine."

"Did I mention she's a broad?"

"All right, all right, what happened?"

"Paslett gave Traub the description you gave us of Silva, then let her off the leash. Sent her out, just like that."

"So Silva made her? I tried to tell you she'd be tough to tail—"

"I know, I know, we went over all a'that, Traub said she got it. But it wasn't Silva who made her."

"Who, for chrissake?"

Traub, it turned out, had done nothing wrong. She had set up across the street from H & H and waited for Silva to leave, which she did around six-thirty, while I was at dinner with Miriam. Traub had followed her up Fifteenth Street, to a druggist's, where Silva bought chocolate and the latest issue of *Collier's*, then to Scott Circle. Here, Silva sat on a bench, read her magazine, ate her candy bar. Might have been a drop (leave the magazine, folded, on the bench, or drop the brown paper drugstore bag in a trashcan) or a meeting (contact sits down, asks for a light), but no, Silva took everything with her when she got up and walked to the nearest bus stop on Massachusetts Avenue. Traub boarded and took a seat several rows behind Silva. When Silva disembarked at Union Station, Traub stayed on for another stop, just like she'd been trained, keeping an eye out the bus's rear window.

After Traub hopped off, a man in a suit stepped out of a parked sedan. Said he was lost, asked her for directions. Traub told him that she was late for an appointment, couldn't help him. That's when he leaned in close to whisper that she was under arrest and better not make a scene.

"Lemme guess," I interrupted. "Guy in the suit had a partner, and they both got a boss named John Edgar."

"Gee, how'd you guess?"

"So the Bureau's on to H & H. Now we know they're Reds for sure." Which I already knew, but since my visit to that loon Griffin Crieve hadn't been authorized, I kept that detail to myself.

"Yeah, and thanks to your little Miss Traub, now the Bureau knows we're on to H & H, too!"

"It's not her fault, Terrance—how was she supposed to know the F.B.I. was following Silva the same time she was?"

"She shoulda seen 'em," he grumbled.

I let that ride. "What'd they do with her, the Bureau boys?"

"Hell, they thought she was a Red, too! Took her in, worked her over but good. Yelled at her about the Espionage Act, told her she'd fry in the chair if she didn't tell the truth about why she was tailing Silva."

"But why would one Red tail another?"

"They weren't trying to make sense, just looking to scare the daylights out of her. Finally, after two hours'a her telling 'em she's just a lowly clerk for O.N.I., she's got no idea what they're talking about, they thought to call Paslett and check her story out. Dumb bastards."

The Bureau knowing we were looking at H & H was a serious problem. No doubt, a memorandum of the Bureau's interrogation was on its way to J. Edgar Hoover's swish sidekick Tolson, who lived with the director. Those two would stay up well past their bedtime, plotting a way to short-circuit our investigation. But I had a much more pressing concern.

"You said the Bureau doesn't know about me—yet. Tell me about that 'yet.'"

"So these two clowns—Slater and Reid are their names, sound like a coupla shysters, don't they?—anyway, they call Paslett and he tells 'em to bring Traub to him. Commander calls me, we're waiting in his office. Those two stroll in like the King of Prussia—"

"Jesus, Terrance, skip the play-by-play!"

"Okay, okay, hold your horses. So they read us the riot act. Whatta we think we're doing, sending a pup like Traub after a known communist, they've been watching Nadine Silva and H & H, how dare we bull our way into their case. Know what the commander says?"

"Who's Nadine Silva?"

Terrance gaped at me. "How the hell d'you know that?"

"Just a guess. But when it comes to slow-waltzing the Bureau, no one's better than the old man."

"Got that right. Well, I just about fell outta my chair. Shoulda seen Slater and Reid—that question took the crease right offa their trousers."

"And Traub, she hadn't given anything up while they were questioning her?"

"Nope. All she told 'em was, she was on a training exercise, she was supposed to follow a stranger she picked out on a sidewalk. Paslett backed her up. He musta given her that story to use in case anything went wrong." He added, grudgingly, "I guess for a broad she did okay."

"This Slater and Reid, they didn't believe Paslett, did they?"

"Hell, no. But what could they say? They got nothing to prove otherwise. And once they realized they'd just told the head of B-Seven, O.N.I., that they're investigating H & H as a communist cell, they clammed up tight and skedaddled."

That was good to hear. Maybe the memorandum headed Hoover's way wasn't such a problem. Slater and Reid would slant their report to cover their blunder of tipping off the O.N.I. But one way or another, Hoover would learn about our investigation.

"So they don't know anything about me? Yet."

"Right. But you know they're gonna turn us upside down to find out what we're doing."

"They got your name, that means they're gonna identify me as your partner, and it'll take 'em all of fifty-nine seconds to see I've disappeared—"

"Don't worry, Paslett's two steps ahead. Soon as those two clowns left and he dismissed Traub, we cooked up a doozy of a scheme."

"Do tell."

"All right, you're gonna love this. We pulled your jacket and yanked everything out for the last two months. Paslett's got his pets in Seven-R typing up back-dated field reports, orders, transit documents, everything to show you're in Iceland, at the N.O.B. at Hvalf—hell, I can't pronounce the rest of it."

"Iceland!"

"Yeah, haven't you always wanted to go?" He pushed the dash lighter in again.

"What the hell am I s'pposed to be doing in Iceland?"

"Who cares? Point is, Bureau can't check to see if you're actually there."

"So when they see me at H & H, they'll know me as Ted Barston. They dig into my background, I'll still be Barston—as long as Seven-R did their job right."

"Right."

"They're gonna go to my flat and talk to my landlord—he's gonna tell—"

"We're on it, don't worry. Bright and early, before the Bureau can figure out who Ellis Voigt is, me and Paslett are gonna swing by and have a little chat with your landlord—what's his name?"

"Kleist."

"Kleist. He's a Kraut, right?"

I nodded.

"By the time Paslett gets through with him, he's not gonna dare breathe a word to the Bureau except to sing the song we give him about how you're in Iceland."

"Think it'll work?" I asked, still doubtful.

"Abso-fucking-lutely, no doubt in my mind." Terrance tossed his butt out the window. "Hey, what'd you get outta that receptionist you're banging? You said something juicy, right?"

"Aw, it's nothing," I answered. "Just a rumor about Silva's boyfriends—I gotta check it out before I report anything."

CHAPTER 18

DIDN'T TELL TERRANCE THAT LOGAN SKERRILL HAD DATED NADINE
Silva not because I didn't trust my partner, but because I didn't want him
to tell Paslett, not yet. I knew the commander, I knew he'd want to beat
the Bureau at their own game by nabbing the cell at H & H first. He'd
start bulldogging me, pushing me, damn the risks, to bring in evidence of
espionage and how Skerrill had fit in.

Which raised an awfully important question: What, exactly, was Himmel's cell up to? The F.B.I.'s monitoring of Silva confirmed the ranting of
the malodorous Griffin Crieve that Himmel, a.k.a. Pavel Nevelskoi, was
a Russian spy, aided by Greene and Silva. Crieve had disparaged Himmel,
calling him an "ink-stained vulture" who had accomplished nothing. Yet
Crieve had also told me he was surprised the Bureau hadn't as yet swept
up the Russian and his two lapdogs.

Why not? If the Bureau knew Nevelskoi was using an alias, agents could
arrest him on trumped-up immigration charges and hold him indefinitely

while they grilled him, pressing him to give up his co-conspirators and tell all. The Russian embassy would protest, but not too hard, because if Nevelskoi did crack, he'd have to be disowned. That toad Hoover loved getting headlines like *Red Spy Ring Nabbed!* So why hadn't the Bureau made its move yet?

John Edgar must want to catch Himmel red-handed, I realized—to grab hard evidence of what Himmel's ring was passing to the Russians. The Bureau didn't know the details, but it knew Himmel's cell was into something big and that time was running out to nail them. Agents were watching Silva, probably Greene and Himmel, too—zilch again. Now the Bureau knew O.N.I. had joined the fox hunt, and John Edgar would do everything he could—and I'd not as yet seen any limits on his everything—to throw us off the scent. But that was Paslett's problem, not mine. *I* was in the cell, and the Bureau didn't know that. If the commander and my partner's plan worked, if they were able to "send" me to Iceland, then I could bore deeper into the cell, undetected.

At the Funhouse, we were trained to think about unknowns second—always start with what is known. *Known facts, known facts*, an officer had yelled at us, and we'd repeated the phrase in unison, like novitiates learning a sacrament. What you know will point you to what you need to know, he'd finished. To date, these were my known facts. One, Himmel's cell was a spy ring. Two, Logan Skerrill had dated one of Himmel's spies, Nadine Silva. Three, the Bureau knew about the spy ring, but it didn't know what the espionage was. Four, Skerrill had been assigned to the Bermuda Special, the hush-hush trip made by one of our destroyers last fall. The possible connections between these four facts pointed me toward what I needed to know. *If* I learned what the Bermuda Special had done, and what Skerrill's part had been; *if* I discovered how much Skerrill knew about Silva and what he'd told her, then I'd likely know why he'd been killed. And once I knew the *why*, I could figure out the *who*. I'd strung a lot of *if*s from the tails of my known facts, but at least I now knew what I must do, as Ted Barston, in order to render all those *if*s into facts. Starting with Nadine Silva, the Red Queen of K Street.

I WOKE UP ON MY COT AT THE JEFFERSON CLUB FROM A FITFUL SLEEP, fraught with unsettling dreams, vividly remembered. Delphine watching me mutely from a tavern's dim corner, F.B.I. agents hovering around me, Terrance laughing and drinking as I sat alone in a distant booth, Franklin D. pacing the table, mewling at me. I washed up in the stinking bathroom at the end of the hall, wondering why I was bothering, and walked to the Automat on F Street to get breakfast. Scrounging a few nickels from my pocket, I bought a Danish, an apple, and coffee. The place was packed, but I found a spot at a table with three construction workers wolfing down ham sandwiches and cherry pie. The chair's last occupant had left behind that morning's *Times-Herald*, so I caught up with all the news I'd missed the last few days. Easy to forget there was a war still on, Ted Barston took so much of my attention. The Seventh Army had taken Munich, the Navy was planning fresh operations close to the Jap home islands. Hirohito was still going ahead with a public appearance at a shrine for the war dead, or so the Japs were reporting. *Plenty more to add to that shrine*, I thought.

Philip Greene shot over as soon as I entered H & H, interrupting my *Hiya, Miss Miriam!*

"Barston, we need you to get going pronto this morning," he huffed, thrusting the clipboard with the delivery manifest into my hands.

"Awright, awright, keep your pants on." I winked at Miriam, who suppressed a giggle.

Need to do something special for her, I thought as I followed Greene to the storeroom. Buy her some cosmetics, to show I remembered her beautyschool dream? Not Barston's style, though. He was more likely to filch flowers from a cemetery. One way or another, I needed to keep Miriam talking about Silva and Skerrill.

Greene pointed to a precipitously leaning stack of boxes. "Here's today's delivery," he announced.

"All a'dat?"

"Yes, and everything needs to reach our clients by one, so get going. Make sure you distribute the weight evenly in the back seat and trunk, I just had the rear springs repaired last fall."

"Maybe you oughta help me load up den, hey?"

"Oh no, I'm much too busy this morning. Besides, loading *is* the deliveryman's job."

It sure is, I thought as I roughly tossed the heavy boxes into the back of Greene's car, noting with satisfaction the creaks and pops of the rear springs. Before I got going, I put my discharge certificate in Himmel's inbox—if Silva wanted to see it, she could ask him.

The manifest spelled out the expected time of the deliveries, which were scattered all over town. To stay on schedule, I had to hustle. Went to a law office way up Connecticut Avenue, then to a hole-in-the-wall office in Southeast called the Anacostia Recording Company. Delivered two boxes to a Georgetown University sociology professor who kept me five minutes to complain about how the draft had taken his best graduate students.

How to get at Silva? I wondered as I yanked a parking ticket (second of the day) from underneath Greene's windscreen wiper and tossed the citation into a curbside trash can. Any attempt to ask about her personal life would set off klaxons—she'd make me as a mole. I could only pump so much out of Miriam before that well went dry. Anyway, Silva didn't like or trust Miriam, so I doubted she had ever confided in her about dating Skerrill. Had Silva kept a trinket of the relationship, had she failed to erase all traces of the late, not-so-great Logan Skerrill? Only one way to find out, I decided—I needed to toss Silva's flat.

But the last delivery distracted me from planning my break-in. *Joseph Charles* was the recipient listed on the manifest, and Silva herself had written his name on the envelope; I recognized her stately cursive. An obvious pseudonym (two first names, very sloppy), but the address was even more suspicious. *2111 Florida Avenue NW* turned out to be a Quaker church, or Friends Meeting House, as a modest sign in the tiny yard announced. With its gabled roof and flagstone walls, the meeting house looked more like a wealthy family's residence than a place of worship—perhaps it once was. I walked in, feeling uncertain and conspicuous. Was I supposed to find the sexton and ask for Joseph Charles? Wait for someone to acknowledge me? The nave was airy and bright, sunlight streaming through paned windows. In an unusual arrangement, two sections of pews faced one another, separated by a wide aisle. I vaguely remembered that Quakers didn't have preachers, that congregations sat in silence until an inner light or spirit moved them to speak. My inner light was flashing red—I might as well have come in with a bull's-eye pinned to my shirt. The vast room was empty, every step I took creaked on the ancient wooden floorboards. In the rear, a staircase led to a mezzanine and tiered balconies with more pews, an ideal vantage from which to observe someone undetected. Was this the setup I'd feared on my first day as Ted Barston, deliveryman? I told myself that Himmel wouldn't dare arrange a hit in a church—imagine the headlines!—but who knew, maybe the Reds had gotten to the Quakers, too.

I slipped into a pew beneath the mezzanine, so at least I couldn't be seen from it, and stood stock-still. If I couldn't move without making noise, then no one else present could, either. I scanned the balcony like a hawk, looking for a hidden figure. Nothing. The nave remained quiet, but I couldn't stay in the shadows much longer without looking suspicious. Heart pounding, I stepped into the aisle and called out, "Hey, I got a delivery for Joseph Charles. Anybody here?"

No response. Could I just leave the envelope? I wondered. But every recipient had to sign the manifest. If I returned without Joseph Charles's signature, Silva might fire me. Maybe *she* was setting me up, trying to get rid of me for botching a delivery. That didn't seem right—too complicated. Just as I was about to call out again, a windowless door in the rear of the nave opened and a middle-aged man in a rumpled charcoal gray business suit strode out.

"Yes, yes, that's for me, sorry to keep you waiting." He tried a disarming smile, but it was ninety-eight percent nervous, a cat's whisker away from twitching. He had soft features: round cheeks, indistinct chin, fleshy eyelids. His thinning brown hair was combed back from a broad forehead.

"Pastor Charles?" I asked.

"Oh no, I'm not the pastor here, I just—well, I help out the Friends now and then."

Feigning boredom, I handed over the envelope and held out the clipboard, pointing at the signature line. He scribbled illegibly.

"Have a nice—"

"Oh wait, I have something for you," he interrupted, reaching into the inside pocket of his suit coat. I thought I'd checked my flinch, but fright must have shown in my face, for his own eyes widened for an instant before he looked away. *He's just as afraid!* I thought as he handed me an unmarked, sealed envelope. "That's for Mister Himmel," he said.

"I'll make sure he gets it, sir. Have a nice day."

"Yes, thank you, thanks very much. And, uh—you have a nice day, too!" With that, he turned and practically scurried to the door he'd come out of.

I left by the front and got into Greene's Ford. Whoever Joseph Charles was, he wasn't a friend of the Friends, otherwise he wouldn't have said *I'm not the pastor here.* Yet he knew enough about the meeting house to know it would be empty at this time, just before one o'clock. That's why the delivery times were spelled out on my manifest. But if Himmel had given the instructions, why had Charles been so nervous?

I nosed the Ford around the corner and watched Charles get into a late-thirties Plymouth parked behind the meeting house. He swung out onto S Street, going east. I let him get two blocks ahead, then fell in behind. Tailing him was a big risk, but I wanted to find out who Joseph Charles really was, and I wanted to take a peek at the envelope he'd given me. I needed to do both within the hour, because if I wasn't back before two, Silva wouldn't believe my lie that I'd taken a lunch break after the last delivery.

CHAPTER 19

CHARLES WAS EASY TO FOLLOW. HE HEADED NORTH ON CONNECTICUT Avenue and drove just under the speed limit, passing only a slow-moving truck, letting the traffic flow around him. I stayed several car-lengths behind, also leaving plenty of space between my car and other vehicles, so that I could make a sudden turn if needed. But I got lucky. A half block north of Tilden, Charles turned left into the National Bureau of Standards campus. I drove by and parked in the half-circle driveway of a towering apartment hotel for a few minutes, resisting the urge to open the envelope on the passenger seat. *First Charles, then the goods*, I told myself. I quick-dragged an Old Gold, tucked the envelope under the passenger seat, then pulled into the southbound lanes of Connecticut and made the same turn Charles had.

The campus, more than a hundred acres in size, was as crowded and cluttered as the patch of tempos on the Mall. Some of the buildings were several decades old, constructed of brick, with tall, airy windows; but the majority of the structures were made of wood and were clearly meant to be temporary, lacking basements and decorative features. Several laboratories seemed to be converted airplane hangars. Terrance and I had once come to the campus as part of an investigation of a crooked Navy Yard machinist who was substituting inferior lenses in binoculars so he could sell the real McCoy on the black market. Even though we were wearing uniforms, Terrance and I had been required to present our O.N.I. identification cards to an armed civilian guard. The National Bureau of Standards sounded like a snooze of a government agency, but its responsibilities included calibrating the ideal gram weight for gunpowder, determining the tensile strength of parachutes, and perfecting Kenotron rectifier tubes for radios. It wasn't possible to count the number of military secrets locked away on this campus, there were so many. That's why there were guards, that's why Ted Barston wasn't getting past the gate. But I didn't need access—I just needed a name.

I braked to a stop next to the sentry box and rolled down my window. The guard started to address me but I cut him off.

"I gotta talk ta Joseph Charles—he works here."

"Who?" His eyes narrowed in suspicion.

"Fella in a Plymouth, he's wearing a suit, he probably got here a little while ago? I made a delivery ta him but dare's been some kinda screw-up, so I—"

He leaned over the sill. "Look, pal, you've made some kinda mistake."

"S'my stupid boss who's made da mistake. Look here"—I thrust the clipboard at him—"you see dat signature? Joseph Charles, it says. He was my last delivery, but my boss is saying I didn't make it, dat I forged dat signature. So I gotta have dis Charles call my goddamned boss ta tell him he got da package."

"How did you know this Charles was coming here?"

The guard was sharper than I'd expected. But in for a dime, in for a dollar.

"He told me! Said he was late for work here and it was my fault, even d'ough I got ta his place right when I was supposed ta."

"Well, you're gonna have to take it up with your boss," he said firmly, watching me closely, waiting for me to ask to see his clipboard. If I did that, he'd call for more guards so I could be detained and questioned—ruses at the gate were old, old spy tricks.

"Look, can't you just check ta see if anyone named Joseph Charles has come in here today?" Before he could say no, I added plaintively, "Look, chief, I can't lose dis job—I got Four-F'd 'cause I got dis heart murmur—goddamned doctors won't even clear me ta work in a factory or nuttin'. At least if you check, I can tell my boss I tried ta find da guy."

"Awright, lemme look."

As he turned to take his clipboard from a hook in the wall, I tilted the rearview mirror to catch the sill of the sentry box. Just as I'd hoped, he set the clipboard down as he scanned the names. I followed his gaze down to the last entry, marked 1:11 P.M.

He looked up. "Nope, no Joseph Charles."

I thanked him, cursed my imaginary boss one more time, and backed the Ford up. The guard had told the truth: no one named Joseph Charles had entered the National Bureau of Standards campus at 1:11. But Dr. Taylor Nagel had.

WITH NAGEL'S NAME, TERRANCE COULD NOW RUN A FULL BACKGROUND check. He was damned good at mining the files, directories, and records that bless each of us with official existence. Educational accomplishments, legal transgressions; licenses to drive, marry, and open a business; births and baptisms; debts, divorces, foreclosures: Dr. Taylor Nagel might be a spy, but he was a citizen, too, and the paper traces of a life lived so far had to be substantial.

I drove south on Connecticut and pulled into the National Zoo's entrance to examine the envelope Nagel had given me. The driveway was expansive and lined by shade trees; as long as I stayed in the car, looking like a joe picking up his wife and kid, no one would bother me. The envelope was white, standard-sized, and free of all markings other than Charles's hastily scribbled signature across the flap. I'd have no trouble buying an envelope exactly like it at a stationery store or druggist's, no trouble forging the signature. Which meant it didn't matter how I opened the envelope.

I tore off the flap and tapped out a sheet of pale blue graph paper folded in three. With the chatter of monkeys and the gleeful shouts of kids carrying from the primates' enclosure, I stared at a perfectly ordinary picture that made no sense: in crisp, straight blue-pen lines, an outline of two one-room buildings with flat roofs and thick walls. Like a mirror image, the structures were side-by-side and exactly alike, except for the interiors. The first building contained a large square marked *radio*; the second, a rectangle labeled *transmitter*. Neither structure had windows, save for two small portals set into the facing exterior walls. A thick pencil circle around the portals was labeled *sheathing*. The only other marking was above the radio: *10/1m*, it read, with three wavy lines floating above.

I was no wireless expert, but I knew that radio transmissions didn't require protective structures and sheathed portals. The "radio" and "transmitter" were substitutes, cut-outs for the actual equipment depicted. I had no idea what that gear was, but I bet the recipient did—this drawing surely wasn't the first one Dr. Nagel had passed to H & H.

The picture was simple enough for a child to copy. Or Ted Barston, hurriedly sketching with a stubby pencil on the torn envelope. The drawing was to scale—a tiny but legible formula in the lower righthand corner read *1:15*—but did I have time to make my lines the same length as the original's? I checked my watch: it had stopped at 12:54, just about the time I'd arrived at the Quaker meeting house. Cursing the entire company of Timex, from its president and board down to its charwoman, I estimated how much time had elapsed since my encounter with Nagel. At least thirty minutes, which left me a half-hour at the most to render my copy of the drawing, buy a replacement envelope, and return to H & H. So much for a facsimile; an approximation would have to do. I drew quickly, silently appreciating the basic lessons in draftsmanship we'd received at the Funhouse. At this, too, Logan Skerrill had excelled, demonstrating an aptitude for a naturally straight line. He had been able to draw, to act, to charm; to get ahead and impress his superiors. *And look where it got him*, I reminded myself.

I carefully folded my copy and slipped it into my pocket. Firing up the Ford, I got back on Connecticut and drove south. There was a People's Drug Store on Dupont Circle, I could buy an envelope there. No spots, so I double-parked, not bothering to click the flashers on. Inside, I found the stationery I needed lickety-split, but—just my luck—only one clerk was on duty, and the line was long. I hustled back to the druggist's counter.

"Ring me up, pal, huh, I'm in a hurry."

He didn't look up from the pills he was sorting. "No can do—see the sign?"

Prescriptions Only—No Exceptions! read a small placard taped to the sliding glass window.

"C'mon, all's I'm buying is one lousy envelope."

No answer, just a long shake of his head. Now I'd lost my spot at the check-out. If I'd been thinking, I could have slipped the envelope into my shirt and strolled out before I even got in line the first time. No choice but to wait now, glancing with dread at the wall clock. *1:51.* Tick, tick. . . .

When I finally got to the cash register, I waved the envelope at the clerk, slapped down a nickel, and rushed out without waiting for my two cents change.

"S'ppose you think you're more important than the rest of us, huh, Mac?" The question came from a joe in a gray flannel suit, pinned tie, and homburg. He was standing in front of the Ford, his arms crossed.

"What?"

He turned his glare toward Greene's car, as if it had just said a dirty word to him. "Can't be bothered to find your own parking spot, so you block the rest of us. Because of course we don't mind waiting for you, do we?" He capped his sarcasm with a wave of his hand at the gleaming Packard I'd parked in, obviously his car.

I almost lost it, could feel the anger ripple through my innards and tighten my arm muscles. Just as the flash bulb of the police photographer's camera had brilliantly lit, for a split-second, the alley where Logan Skerrill had been killed, I saw, in finely etched detail, the next minute. I'd approach Mr. Peeved Citizen, offer a sheepish grin, start to apologize—and then sucker-punch him, right in the gut, leave him breathless and unable to stand. I'd catch him by the elbow and walk him to the curb, let him down gently, telling any curious passersby that he'd tripped and almost got hit by a car. But I couldn't afford a scene, couldn't risk a good Samaritan running over to help, couldn't take a chance on this joe getting his voice back and yelling for a cop.

"Get da hell outta my way," I growled, pushing past him and yanking open the driver's door, which I hadn't locked.

"Wha—Hey! You can't talk to—"

I slammed the door shut on his sentence. For a moment he appeared ready to plant himself in front of the car, but then he had the much better idea of stepping back to avoid being run over. I squealed the tires getting back into traffic, cutting off a car and earning myself a long, angry honk. Maybe that driver would get out so he and my new friend could carp about the general deterioration of polite society.

If there were bats out of hell overhead, I beat them speeding back to H & H, pulling into the alley at—I hoped—a little past two. I refolded the drawing of the two structures and sealed it in the envelope I'd just bought. After studying the signature on the original envelope, I quickly scrawled *Joseph Charles* across the flap. A handwriting expert could tell the difference, but I was betting that neither Himmel nor Silva had such training, that they wouldn't even look closely at the signature. Even if they did, I was confident my copy would pass muster. At the Funhouse, we'd been trained in the basics of forgery. How to study initial strokes, measure ascenders, gauge pen pressure, avoid hesitation marks. I slammed the car door shut and went in by the rear door.

Himmel scrutinized the envelope, which I brought him straight away. He held it by the corner with his thumb and forefinger, peering at it through his reading glasses, then turned it over and studied the signature on the flap for a long, agonizing moment. *Did I leave a damp mark when I licked the glue?* I suddenly wondered with dread. Himmel set the envelope down, smoothed it flat with his fingers, and looked at me impassively. I checked the urge to ask if anything was wrong—I was just Ted Barston, a dishonorably discharged shipfitter second class who did what he was told and didn't give a damn what his boss was up to.

"This is all Mister Charles gave you?" he asked.

"Yessir."

"Nothing else?"

"If he had, it'd be right dare in front'a you, boss."

He nodded slowly. "Ted, do you know the story of Pandora?"

"Never heard'a him," I promptly answered. Barston, of course, wouldn't know the legend of the young girl who had opened a box she should have left closed.

"Good. You should keep it that way."

"Sure thing, boss," I said breezily, lighting up as I left his office. Why hadn't I checked the flap before I came in! I reminded myself that I didn't know if Himmel had noticed anything wrong with the envelope. I did know I had looked it over before I got out of the car—surely I would have noticed a trace of saliva, a tiny gray stain, along the flap. With all my training, I couldn't have made that kind of blunder, right? But I couldn't picture the envelope as it had appeared during my last look. *Your memory must be a camera*, we'd been told over and over at the Funhouse. *Take picture after picture*. I'd been so worried about being on time, I'd forgotten this elementary rule.

No choice but to forge ahead. Himmel, himself well-trained in spycraft, might just have been trying to unsettle me, dropping hints that an innocent man wouldn't think twice about but that a plant like me would fret over. And moles who are always looking over their shoulder don't see what's in front of them. But I had to stop worrying about the envelope and concentrate on my next tasks: deliver my copy of Nagel's drawing to Terrance and Commander Paslett and toss Silva's flat while she was still at the office. Miriam had mentioned that Silva never left before five o'clock. I had just enough time to set up my meeting with Terrance and Paslett, find out where Silva lived, and break in. I could only hope she didn't have a roommate, a dog, or nosy neighbors.

CHAPTER 20

ON MY WAY OUT OF H & H, I GAVE MIRIAM A WINK AND A FOLDED NOTE. *Hey, kiddo, wanna go dancing?* (the note read). *Meet me at the Rainbow at 8.* I needed to keep her happy, keep her thinking she was my gal, and see how much more I could squeeze out of her about Silva and Skerrill. From a telephone booth in a diner, I called the Irving Street Apartment Hotel, using a coded message to schedule a meeting in two hours with Commander Paslett and Terrance at the billiards parlor. I needed to know why Skerrill had been posted to the Bermuda Special. If Paslett had any reservations about giving Terrance and me the goods on that mission, he'd fast forget them once I handed over my copy of Nagel's schematic.

The odor of grilled onions and frying hamburger meat reminded me that I hadn't eaten for hours. I bought two burgers to go, smoking a cigarette while I waited for the counterman to wrap up my order. I caught my reflection in the mirror behind the coffee urn. Greasy hair, stubble, circles under my eyes. *You look like hell, Barston*, I thought.

DAVID KRUGLER

I greedily ate the sandwiches as I finished the walk to the Jefferson Club, using the brown paper bag as a napkin. A grand old dame in a worsted skirt suit and a hat with a feather boa wrinkled her nose in disgust as she passed by. Whatever else happened that day, I'd done a bang-up job of offending proper society.

The Jefferson Club lobby was empty save for a wizened old-timer wrapped in a blanket, murmuring to himself. Most of the residents were either "working"—cadging, panhandling, going through trash cans—or already spending their wages at the nickel beer gutbuckets that had settled on Ninth Street like flies on dogshit. I unlocked my cubicle and retrieved the burglary kit from my rucksack. I'd only packed a few picks, a tension rod, and a shim, but if I couldn't get into Silva's flat with just those tools, I deserved to be sent back to the Funhouse.

SILVA WAS IN THE DIRECTORY. HER FLAT WAS ON H STREET, NE, JUST east of the rail tracks leading into Union Street. I took a bus, disembarking a few blocks away so I could get the lay of the land. H Street was a wide stretch of clothing, shoe, and jewelry shops rubbing shoulders with druggists and diners. Silva lived on the third floor of a brick building typical of the neighborhood: on the first floor, a mom-and-pop store, in this case, a hat shop, with inset show windows; and above, two floors of apartments, their narrow windows overlooking the street. I walked by, briefly glancing at the racks festooned with hats. The afternoon sun inked shadows on brick walls. I doubled back through the alley. The rear lot of Silva's building contained a ramshackle garage and a garden that must have been abandoned the previous fall. Matted parsley and sage plants, their leaves shriveled and black, looked like discarded mopheads. I swiftly mounted the exterior wooden stairs. If anyone asked, I'd been sent from H & H by Silva to fetch a file she'd forgotten. But if the second floor tenants were home, they didn't come to their rear window to see who was coming up the steps.

I knocked loudly. If a dog barked, I'd leave; if a roommate answered, I'd pretend to be a panhandler. No response, so I turned to the spring lock, which had a run-of-the-mill five-pin tumbler. I inserted the tension rod and a small pick, nudging the triangle-sized pickhead to rake the pins while leaning close. At the Funhouse we'd been trained to stand upright while we

152

worked a lock, so that a casual observer would think we were just having trouble with the key. The lock yielded in less than a minute. I slipped in and shut the door, checking to see if I'd broken a thread or freed a slip of paper tucked between the door and frame. Nothing.

I shut the door behind me, looked around. Living room with the usual furnishings and a few framed photographs on the plaster walls. Silence except for the tick of a clock on a side table and my breathing. Two windows overlooked the street, a sickly fern on the sill. To my left was the kitchen, a galley. I started in the lone bedroom, which directly adjoined the living room—no hallway. The bed, a double, was unmade, the rumpled sheets and quilt bunched up on the left side, smooth on the right. So she'd slept alone. The night stand was cluttered with hair pins, an alarm clock, and a cork coaster atop a precarious stack of books on Renaissance art. No ashtray. In the drawers I found a manicure kit, lipsticks, condoms, a pad of paper, dull pencils. I bent to look beneath the bed; nothing but dustballs. I went through the dresser drawers, checking the neat stacks of sweaters, sorting through a frilly mass of panties and brassieres. On the wall were two framed diplomas, a B.A. and M.A. in art history from Columbia University, and a photograph of Silva standing in front of a sun-dappled fountain with three other young women. The closet was a mess: stacks of books that had fallen over, boxes of notebooks filled with notes, a card file with a timeline of Italian art, empty suitcases, a pile of winter coats that resembled a hibernating bear, and hanging clothing. The bathroom was tiled in postage-stamp-sized ceramic pieces that looked recently scrubbed. Nothing unusual in the medicine cabinet: cough syrup, aspirin, toothpaste and brush.

I moved into the living room. Two tall bookcases jammed with works on art, world history, and political theory. A long, low couch with matching chair. Coffee table bedecked with a gargantuan ceramic ashtray and six matching coasters. In the front closet, a card table, four folding chairs, and several empty hangers. On the wall, framed black-and-white photographs of a European-looking city—my guess, Rome. A magazine rack next to the couch held old issues of *Look*, *Time*, and a directory for federal offices in Washington.

The kitchen was well kept. No dishes in the sink, stovetop wiped clean. The icebox held some cold cuts, sliced cheese, and a jar of mayonnaise.

And eight bottles of beer. The freezer was empty save for two trays of ice cubes. I checked the cabinets: a box of pasta noodles, a can of tuna, a tin of oatmeal. I pawed through the oats, to see if Silva had hidden anything there, but she was smarter than that.

I went back into the living room and sat down on the sofa. The table clock read 3:13. Still lots of time, but I didn't want to push my luck. I hadn't expected to find much during my cursory walk-through, just wanted to get a feel for how Silva lived. What she ate, read, wore; how she relaxed and what was important to her. So far, I knew she was not a wartime newcomer to the capital because she lived alone in a decent-sized apartment. She had money, or came from money—Ivy League degrees in art history don't come cheap—but she didn't display any photographs of her family. Her bedside reading told me Silva was still interested in art. The boxes in the closet told me she had once worked as a teacher or a college lecturer. Had she planned on becoming a professor? Managing a clipping service was a big step down, but not if Silva believed she was serving a greater cause than educating young minds about Raphael and chiaroscuro. So when had she turned Red? Did she come from a progressive background, were her folks well-heeled do-gooders who believed in *noblesse oblige* and all of that? Had she seen fascists force-feeding castor oil to communists while living in Italy?

Reminded myself the *why* didn't matter. What had been Silva's relationship with Logan Skerrill? There were a few signs Silva wasn't as attentive as she should have been in concealing her secret life. The beer in the icebox, the oversized ashtray on the coffee table, and the folding chairs in the front closet hinted at late-night gatherings. Not with H & H's stables of spies, of course—that would be a yawning breach of security. More likely, Silva was a roper, a recruiter, the over-educated sophisticate who searched for Red-leaning civil servants in positions of interest to the party.

I knew I shouldn't make too much of it, but why did she keep a directory of federal offices next to her magazines? To look up the people she met at parties? It was illegal for federal employees to belong to the Communist Party, but, like a parent's admonishment to never open *that* drawer, the ban had only increased the party's allure. Left-leaning bureaucrats with an itch for excitement were ripe fruit for the likes of Silva and Himmel. Sitting on the sofa, I could easily envision the set-ups. Invite the targets over for a casual evening of drinks and conversation, let the topics drift to politics, let the guests reveal what they *honestly* think about Roosevelt and the New Deal. Subtly plant the notion *there's got to be a better way, yes . . . ?* Invite them back, take a book from the shelf. Press it into their hands, implore them to read it for discussion *next time.* Meanwhile find out everything possible about the mark: Is he valuable, can he be turned, what can he pilfer or copy from the files in his office?

What else had she neglected to hide? I remembered what Miriam had told me, that this ice queen and ball-buster had shed tears at the news of Skerrill's untimely death, even seeking comfort from the toad Greene. The photograph of Silva as a student in front of the fountain—had she kept up with her college girlfriends? If she missed art enough to still study it, to keep her notes, maybe she still corresponded with her fellow art lovers.

I checked the urge to light up—leaving the trace aroma of Old Gold in Silva's flat would be pretty stupid—and got back to work. Now the real search was under way. I returned to the bedroom closet. When it comes to the sentimental, most people are predictable; they like to hoard mementos, keepsakes, and special objects in one place. A cedar-lined hope chest, the back of a dresser drawer, an orange crate on a closet shelf. What was dear to Silva—the notes, outlines, and papers of her budding career as an art historian—was in that closet; maybe a trinket or letter from Skerrill had been cached there, too.

But no. I riffled book pages, shook notebooks by their spines, studied every folder tab. I scrutinized the souvenirs Silva kept in a shoebox (ticket stubs from art museums, dinner menus, and concert programs). Every object related to Silva's time abroad and her study of art. I squandered precious minutes on this useless exhumation before I realized my mistake: like all people who lead double lives, Silva had learned to separate her worlds, to conceal her divergent identities. If she ever opened a line between them, she first took every precaution possible. She wouldn't keep anything she'd gotten from Logan Skerrill, because she knew no matter how well she hid it, someone like me would turn it up. Besides, Skerrill was too smart to leave a written record of what he'd been doing for H & H. As much as I hated to admit it, he'd done an awful slick job of tricking Terrance and me into believing he was a homo during our search of his boarding house.

If there was anything to find, Silva had left it. And it would be right out in the open. No cryptography, nothing complex, just an ordinary veneer to pry off. Of course, that's what made this type of deception so effective—if you didn't know which object held the secret, you couldn't crack it. Was it the grocery list, the notice from a bookshop that the title she had ordered had arrived? My search was methodical and slow—too slow, in fact. By four o'clock, I'd only gotten through the kitchen and half of the living room. I needed to leave, pronto—hell, I should have left fifteen minutes earlier. What if Silva got a headache and left work? What if she was getting her hair set at four-thirty and wanted to come home first? Reluctantly, I put down the stack of bills I'd been reading and left the flat. No one saw me going down the stairs, and I walked three blocks down the alley before returning to H Street.

For all my trouble, I'd only turned up a letter posted to Silva three weeks ago from one Brenda Lawler, of 148 E. 61st Street, New York. Most of the letter was chatty, several long paragraphs about Lawler's husband and son, a party she was hosting, some rationing tips she'd picked up. I got the impression that Silva and Lawler had been classmates—was Brenda one of the girls in the photograph by the fountain?—but I couldn't be sure. Only one passage seemed noteworthy, so I memorized it:

> . . . well, Nads, sorry to go on for pages about myself and all these trivial little happenings without commenting on your problem. Here's my two cents: dump him! You're far too daz- zling and beautiful and smart (dare I say "a catch"? tho I know how you loathe that word because it smacks of that most bour- geois of institutions, marriage!) to tolerate a philandering dog, whatever his tricks. (Didn't we forswear sailors ages ago? No matter.) Anyway, send him packing, Nads, and find yourself a better man. Call anytime if you want a heart-to-heart, we'll reverse the charges.
>
> All my love . . .

The sailor must be Logan Skerrill, he'd been cheating on Silva; she'd caught him, she'd confided in a dear friend. But like the clues hinting that Skerrill had been a fairy, something felt off. I had no trouble believing Skerrill had two-timed Silva. At the Funhouse, Skerrill had bragged about his conquests, which wasn't unusual, we all did, but he had topped the rest of us by detailing the showdowns he set up with the gals who thought they were his steadies. He'd leave out a mash note from another broad, or show up for a date wafting another woman's perfume. From the smug way he had told these stories, you could tell that's what stoked his coals, revealing his betrayal and getting these poor girls to beg him to be true. Manipulators like him have no trouble finding weak girls.

But Silva wasn't such a woman, and that's what felt wrong about the letter. If I had to guess at what had fired the sparks between "Nads" and Skerrill, I'd go with the mutual attraction they felt as two cold-hearted operators who believed in the same cause. If Silva thought or knew Skerrill had been unfaithful, it seemed more plausible that she'd up the ante, that she'd play her own game, not send a weepy confession to a girlfriend.

So what did the letter mean for real? Did it mask something related to H & H's espionage, or was it simply just what it appeared to be, a personal letter from an old friend?

CHAPTER 21

THE THING ABOUT TOSSING A STRANGER'S FLAT: GETS YOU WONDERING if it's ever happened to you. Or, in this case, Ted Barston. If Himmel, Silva, and Greene suspected Barston wasn't on the level, could they find out where he was flopping? The Jefferson Club didn't keep a register, and I was pretty sure no one had ever tailed me there, but so what? The Reds knew good tradecraft, they could easily send someone around to the Ninth Street fleabags with a description of me as Barston, maybe even a photograph secretly snapped when I was coming or going from H & H. But did it matter? They could turn the rucksack inside out, nothing in it would trace back to Ellis Voigt.

Hell, a toss of my basement flat on Caroline Street wouldn't turn up much of anything, either. The arrangement I had with the landlord Kleist, the favor he owed my pop—I hadn't known how many months that was good for when I arrived in D.C., so I hadn't moved in much, just my clothes and a few books. Even now, when I knew I had the place for at least the war's duration, I still lived light. I didn't keep letters from my folks and brother, ripped them up as soon as they were read. I had some framed family photographs, had toted them with me wherever this war had sent me, but they were now in my box at Riggs Bank. Told myself it was to keep them safe, but looking at them day-to-day had unsettled me. Wasn't sure why. Got along with my folks, my brother, too. Maybe I felt guilty shredding their letters beneath their smiling faces in the black-and-white photographs. But if someone ever tossed my flat, I didn't want them reading my private correspondence or looking at the pictures on the wall, as I'd just done to Nadine Silva.

When I arrived at the billiards parlor, Paslett and Terrance were playing eight-ball, two bottles of Schlitz on the rail by the table, smoke untwining from my partner's cigarette as he missed a shot at the five ball. I nodded as I walked to the bar, returned with a cue and my own beer.

"Hiya, Ted, how's tricks?" Paslett asked. He'd improved his wardrobe: dungarees, corduroy shirt, sleeves rolled up. (I wondered how Terrance had broached *that* subject.)

I shrugged and said, "Ain't been bit by a dog yet."

"Still making deliveries, huh?"

"Had worse jobs."

Terrance said, "Nobody misses you, that's for sure." With a crooked grin. His way of telling me that he and Paslett had set up the Iceland cover story to keep the F.B.I. from finding out who Ted Barston really was.

"Gee, thanks." I slipped the envelope out of my pocket and handed it to Paslett.

"He sent it in care'a dis Joseph Charles, two-one-one-one Florida Avenue. Dat's da last place I was staying." Translation: the package for Himmel had come from a man using a pseudonym at that address.

"Careless of him," Paslett remarked.

I nodded—not a bad set-up, that. "You know how dose eggheads are. Get a doctorate, dey lose all common sense. Anyways, after da letter got returned, Nagel remembered I got a new address."

Terrance returned the nod. *Dr. Nagel, got it.*

"What's he up to?" This from Paslett.

"Busy all da time, he says. Hardly ever leaves his office. Dey just made him headmaster at Holy Cross Academy."

The commander hid his confusion, but my partner nodded. He remembered that a private school, Holy Cross, was located east of the National Bureau of Standards campus.

Terrance asked, "He got any work for you?" *Will you pick up any more packages from Nagel?*

"Who knows, I'm awful busy dese days." *Doubt it, and I'm still working the receptionist, still trying to find out what Skerrill did for H & H.*

"Well, nice of him to drop a line," Paslett said as he chalked his cue and took a bead on the twelve ball. He missed.

"You two ever gonna finish dis game, hey?" I said with a grin.

"Keep your pants on," Terrance growled, taking a long drag on his cigarette. He stubbed it, picked up his cue, and ran the table, putting a soft kiss on the eight ball to drop it in the side pocket. "Rack 'em, hot-shot."

I set the balls and took a long drink of beer as Terrance broke. The envelope was gone. I hoped Paslett had been subtle when he pocketed it. My partner sank the four and the seven on the break and was considering his options when I asked, "How was our buddy's trip ta da Caribbean?"

Paslett clenched his jaw. Obviously, he didn't want to talk about the Bermuda Special. Because he couldn't figure out how to cloak his answers or because he wasn't ready to tell us what he knew? Another bad sign: Terrance kept his gaze on the table, methodically chalking his cue. Blue powder sifted from the cube, the commander's pause continued. *C'mon, c'mon. . . .*

"He never got there," Paslett blurted out.

"No? Thought dat was a sure thing."

"Uh-uh. Where he got sent, he said it was just like being underground."

Underground—Skerrill had been part of a secret mission. But Terrance and I already knew that. So what else was Paslett trying to tell us?

"But the air turned out to be just fine," the commander added.

Underground . . . worried about the air . . . a canary in a coal mine? Then it clicked: the Canary Islands. The destroyer had gone to the Canary Islands, in the Atlantic. Terrance still looked confused. I whistled, soft and low, warbling—he got it.

"Seems like an awful long trip to make these days," my partner said.

"Well, he needed to bring a new friend home." Translation: somebody important who couldn't find his own way to the States.

I thought quickly. The Canary Islands were Spanish territory. Franco was neutral, but he leaned Nazi. A German trying to escape Hitler could, with the right papers, get to Spain, get to the islands. But how did he make contact with the Allies? And who the hell was he? Sending a destroyer across U-Boat-infested seas to fetch one man was a hell of a risk. Was he a scientist, a Wehrmacht general, a Nazi official? Whoever he was, it smelled like an O.S.S. operation.

"Dis new guy, he must got friends in high society," I said.

Paslett nodded vigorously. Around the Navy Building, *Oh, So Social* was our jeering nickname for the Office of Strategic Services because so many of its officers were East Coast, high-society elites.

"Yeah, plenty'a other suitors, too," the commander said. Meaning, O.S.S. wanted to keep him; so did Army and Navy intelligence.

That's why the War Department had taken charge of the mission, I realized, and why we'd horned in by sending officers from O.N.I.'s Special Activities Branch, Skerrill included. So who'd claimed the prize? Maybe the Bureau had jumped into the fray, too. One of Washington's oldest rumors was that John Edgar had copies of lesbo letters in Eleanor's hand, leverage he could have used to force F.D.R. to let the Bureau take over. Now that Roosevelt was dead, the letters were no good, but the Bermuda Special had gone and returned six months ago.

Terrance and I were on the same wavelength.

"Who's the lucky bridegroom?" he asked.

Paslett said, "Damned if it didn't end up being my old football buddy."

That threw both of us, though we feigned knowing nods. Paslett was Annapolis, sure, but he'd never been on the gridiron. Was he trying to tell us—

"Boy, you can't win any bets with him, can you?" Terrance blurted out.

"Nope, but hope springs eternal," Paslett replied.

Now I got it. Every autumn, Paslett and his friend General Leslie Groves wagered fifty bucks on the Army-Navy game. Groves was big-time, that rare breed who could soldier and politick, a Pentagon dandy who still had the respect of the men who served under him. That's why we'd been surprised by the news he'd been sent to Los Alamos, New Mexico, early in the war. *What, we're worried about Pancho Villa riding again?*, I'd cracked to Paslett at the time, but he didn't know any more than the rest of us. Since then, we'd picked up bits and scraps. Item: Scientists—physicists, mostly—were, like iron filings drawn to a magnet, clumping together in Chicago, Manhattan, and Los Alamos. Item: Army had built a secret city and plant in the Great Smoky Mountains National Park in eastern Tennessee. Item: The Senate committee investigating waste and fraud in war contracts had stumbled onto missing millions but Secretary of War Henry Stimson had told its former chairman, Harry S. Truman, to back off. That mix of secrecy, moolah, and scientists could only mean one thing—some kind of weapons project.

Terrance had won our game, but I didn't bother to rack the balls. We fell silent, sipping our beers and smoking. O.N.I. had placed Logan Skerrill and the other Special Activities officers on the Bermuda Special to find out all they could about the "new friend" being picked up in the Canary Islands and why he was being sent to New Mexico. If Skerrill had succeeded in learning all of that, then we had to assume the Soviets now knew, too. Terrance sighed and stubbed a cigarette. He gave me a baleful look as Paslett stood, watching me intensely. Different expressions, same thought. *You gotta get more on Skerrill.* The diagram I'd copied was part of the puzzle— hopefully Navy scientists could figure out what it meant—but that wasn't enough. And I didn't need either of them to figure out a way to tell me.

"Well, so long, see you next time," I said, and left.

I HAD TIME TO KILL BEFORE MY DATE WITH MIRIAM. I WASN'T ONE TO show up for dates with liquor on my breath, but I figured Barston had no such qualms. I parked myself at a corner tap, all pine paneling and lazy ceiling fans, and chased flat beer with rye shots. The Rainbow, where I was meeting Miriam, was a low-rent dance hall in Southwest D.C., not far from the waterfront. It was popular with enlisted men who chafed at the rules of U.S.O. and Women's Battalion socials, where the chaperones bussed in G-girls for two hours of punch and chit-chat and always did a head-count as the girls filed back onto the bus. The Rainbow attracted khaki-wacky teenage girls and lonely wives whose husbands were overseas. If you still couldn't score, the local cops let prossies trawl K Street, a block away. The Rainbow used to be popular with Negroes until several dozen sailors and marines charged in one night, swinging clubs and bats while provost guards loafed outside, chatting and smoking. The cops were nowhere to be seen. The Negroes didn't go quietly, but when they started to give as good as they were getting, the provost guards jumped in with their billies—some even led with their rifle butts. From that night on, the Rainbow was lily-white.

I found Miriam at the bar, fending off a pimply adolescent private who was squeezing close so he could drape a skinny arm around her shoulder.

"Go fish, Mac, she's taken," I growled.

His eyes flashed. I shifted my stance, getting ready to knee him if he wanted to play rough. He sneered, I clenched my fist, but he thought better of brawling and moved on.

"Hey, kiddo, what's cookin'?" I dipped to give Miriam a kiss.

"Ooh, tastes like somebody's been celebrating already."

I scowled and said, "Da hell dat's s'posed ta mean?"

"Nothing, Teddy, I just—do you want another drink?"

"Nah, I don't wanna drink—did we come here ta dance or what?"

"Sure, honey, let's go dance."

She slid off the stool, I took her roughly by the hand. I hadn't noticed that Miriam had barely touched her drink, something tall with vodka or gin, but it was too late to change my mind. Barston was no Prince Charming, but I was laying it on a little thick. The confab with Paslett and my partner had aggravated me. I'd scored big with Nagel's drawing, but Skerrill still hovered out of my reach, taunting me, like a skeleton that drops in front of you at a Halloween haunted house and then jerks out of sight. I was deep inside the Himmel cell, I'd identified a National Bureau of Standards bigwig who was passing secrets to the Reds; yet I felt like I was stumbling around, groping in the dark. It was my own fault, I realized. I'd assumed that Miriam would be packed to the gills with rumors, gossip, and secrets about H & H and all who'd passed through its doors. And she had given me everything she knew about Silva and Skerrill's relationship, but I could hardly expect a communist cell as watertight as Himmel's to let anything related to espionage leak to the staff. That same flawed thinking had guided my toss of Silva's flat. What had I expected to find, a goddamned diary with dated entries detailing the who, what, and why of the Bermuda Special?

DAVID KRUGLER

My predicament wasn't entirely my fault. Paslett nurtured his own mis-
guided assumptions about my undercover work. He believed just because I'd
gotten the delivery job, I'd completely fooled Silva, Greene, and Himmel.
Not by a long shot. Greene bought my act, but the other two still watched
me like peregrine falcons. How many more packages could I divert before I
was caught? Being a lieutenant j.g. U.S.N. was no protection—the uniform
sure hadn't saved Skerrill. As for Skerrill, Paslett didn't realize that my
placement inside the cell only enabled me to observe what was happening
now, not what *had* happened. Whatever Skerrill had told Silva and Himmel
about the Bermuda Special was long done and gone, whisked on to Himmel's Soviet handlers, no traces left behind. Spy cells weren't government
agencies, they didn't leave paper trails, a fact Paslett, who had never done
undercover work, didn't get. But I couldn't make excuses, I couldn't ask
Terrance to argue on my behalf. All that mattered were results, and I had to
get them. *Just gotta be ready to roll with the punches*, I told myself as I forced
a smile at Miriam on the dance floor.

A prophetic resolution, as it turned out.

CHAPTER 22

THE BAND AT THE RAINBOW WAS LOUD AND MEDIOCRE, A MOTLEY pile-up of hacks who couldn't make the grade at class joints. They mangled last year's hits and wrung out tired standards. The trumpet player kept looking at his instrument with mild surprise after each number, as if he still couldn't believe he'd managed to get it out of hock for that night's gig. Not that the patrons cared. No one came to the Rainbow for the music, he came for the noise, the scene, the booze, the girls. I tried to shut out memories of my visit to the Lotus with Liv, of what we'd talked about in between trips to the dance floor, but the more Miriam prattled, the more pressing the memories became.

"What's wrong, Teddy?" Miriam whined in my ear as we slow-danced to a lackluster cover of "Like Someone in Love."

"Nuttin', kiddo."

"You're not mad at me, are you, Teddy?"

I mumbled something, lost in a recollection of Liv, her teasing question that night at the Lotus. *So you don't think there's anything literary about pulp fiction?*

"D'you want to get a drink?" Miriam asked.

"Nah, let's stay out for anudder number." *Did I say that?*

"Okay, sure, baby." *You implied it.*

"Havin' a good time, toots?" *Enlighten me, my favorite femme fatale.*

"A'course, Teddy, thanks for taking me out." *So you're hit by a car, El, you lose your memory. But who you've just lost, the man of the last three years—what if that's not who you really are? What if you've been living a lie, and now you gotta find out why you had to become someone else, and who you were before that?*

"Sure, toots, anytime." *I'd spring for the movie, Liv, but literature? C'mon. . . .*

"Teddy . . ." *Forget the plot, El, and think about your moral dilemma. There's a moral dilemma in that plot?*

"Teddy . . ." *To part the black curtain hiding your past, you have to sacrifice everyone you love. You learn your secrets, but now you're alone, solitary—are you finally, truly yourself? Tell me that's not the stuff of literature.*

"What, whatta you want?"

Miriam squirmed in my arms. "You're holding me too tight, Teddy, it hurts!"

I hadn't realized how hard I was gripping her hand and waist.

"Sorry, toots. Just can't get enough'a you, hey?" *The stuff dreams are made of, maybe, but literature? I don't think so.* And the thought of Liv's delicious laugh that moment at the Lotus took me right back to the cry of her climax in my bed that night, a memory so sharp I felt a flutter in my stomach.

"I wanna drink, Teddy."

"Sure, toots, whatever you want." I let go of Miriam, she followed me to the crowded bar.

Get ahold of yourself! I thought. Needed a bit of amnesia myself, to shake Liv loose from my mind. But until a car came along and hit me, I had to make do with rye and beer chasers.

MIRIAM MATCHED ME DRINK FOR DRINK; WE NEVER MADE IT BACK TO the dance floor. I made a few half-hearted attempts to get her to talk about Silva and Skerrill, but she wanted to talk about beauty school, so I gave up. Fed her questions, kept her going. *What's da best beauty school in D.C. . . . yeah, uh-huh . . . Whatta dey teach youse gals. . . . yeah, uh-huh . . .* I didn't know how much longer she'd be of use, but best to keep her on a string for as long as I was Ted Barston. When I couldn't think of anything else to ask about beauty school, I spun a woeful tale of Barston's rough boyhood and frequent run-ins with the law. Miriam clucked and cooed like a mother hen, tenderly squeezing my forearm when I told her about my dope habit and how it had landed me in the brig. "Oh, Teddy, that's just awful," she kept saying. Around midnight, I wrapped my arm around her and took her home. She didn't mind my grip now—hell, we both needed it to stay on our feet.

Don't bed her, I told myself. But thoughts of a roll in the hay were awful tempting. Miriam was lusty, a real baller. Who would an A-1 lay hurt? Barston wouldn't think twice, didn't I have to keep in character? Wasn't like I was being unfaithful to Liv, right? Being Barston brought certain obligations, forced me to do things that Ellis Voigt would never do. Besides, I wasn't Liv's only boyfriend, she must have had other lovers, though that didn't make her a roundheel. The way she lived her life, it just didn't follow the habits of other girls, like going steady or angling for the altar. If Liv had a good time with a date, if he was interesting—a poet, a painter, an actor—she probably went to bed with him. Didn't make her sex-crazed, it was just another way to connect. At least, that's how it felt with Liv and me.

But I knew, even through the alcohol haze, that thinking about Liv's love life was an easy dodge. Miriam was falling in love with Barston, a man who actually didn't exist. Even if he did, the Barston in her eyes was a much touched-up photograph. Where others saw crudeness, she saw toughness; what others called bluster, she embraced as charm. Could the same be said about the Liv of Voigt's star-struck gaze? Was the girl of my dreams, with her barefoot late-night strolls and her South Pacific dream, for real just a quirky dilettante? Maybe Miriam and I, Ellis Voigt, had more in common than I'd realized. We'd both made the mistake of falling in love with our wishes, not real people. The difference, of course, was that I knew Miriam's love would soon shatter, while I still had the opportunity to change so I could keep Liv. That's why I was hesitating, as Barston, to take Miriam to bed. But a conscience was a luxury neither Barston nor Voigt could currently afford.

"S'all going to hell anyway!"

"Whassat?" Miriam slurred.

Jesus—I hadn't realized I'd thought aloud. I spun Miriam into my arms, gave her a big, sloppy kiss to cover the mistake.

"Hey, the party's still going!" she exclaimed as we swayed our way down her block.

"What's dat?"

"My brother Kenny, he's throwing a party."

And so he was. A man with a hat over his face was sound asleep on the porch, a couple was necking beside him. The front door was open, the parlor crowded. Cigarette smoke drifted like fog over a dozen conversations. Miriam and I pressed our way into the dining room. Overfull ashtrays and empty bottles littered a table that had been pushed against the wall. A drunken man carrying a case of beer swayed into the room. "Reinforcements have arrived!" he shouted. We took two beers, I popped the bottle tops with a church key lying on the table. I didn't need any more alcohol, but the cold beer went down quickly—despite the cool evening and several open windows, the house was sweltering.

"C'mon, I want you to meet Kenny," Miriam said.

"Who?"

"Kenny, my brother, silly—'member?"

"Oh yeah, good ol' Kenny, sure."

She took me by the hand and tugged me through the house, stopping friends to ask after Kenny. Several shrugs, a headshake, then a sober-looking joe with slicked-back hair and a crooked nose eyed us over before leaning close to say something in Miriam's ear. I caught "business" and "later"—no matter, Miriam didn't listen.

"He's upstairs," she told me, making for the stairs. I lurched along, like an oversized rag doll attached to a little girl's hand. Neither of us turned around when the man shouted, "Hey, what did I just say?"

We found Kenny in a large, brightly lit room, a study or office of sorts: battered wooden desk, scattered chairs, end tables, a sofa. The door was shut, but Miriam flung the door open after knocking and calling out, "Hey, Kenny, it's me!"

Four heads turned to stare. All men, quiet, sober, as tense as cats on a crossed path. Watching us, not moving but coiled. I wasn't so drunk that

I missed one of the four slip his hand inside his jacket and shift his weight slightly.

"Hey, Mirs, you just getting here?" the man behind the desk asked. Smiling, but an edge to his voice. Mid-twenties, brown-blond hair grazing his collar. Acne scars dappled his cheeks, but that only added to his rakish looks: sharp jawline, bright blue eyes, an aquiline nose.

"We were out to the Rainbow," Miriam announced.

"Who's we?" Looking at me, no smile.

"Ted Barston," I said firmly, stepping forward to shake his hand. "You must be Kenny."

He didn't stand, didn't extend his hand. "Why don't you wait downstairs for me, huh, Mirs?" Looking right past me.

"Well, okay, whatever you say, Kenny, I just wanted you to meet Teddy here, you know, the fella I been telling you—"

"Sure, Mirs, we'll have a nice long chat, but not now." These last four words fell like stones on the floor. "Wade'll go with you."

A nod from Kenny brought one of the other men to his feet. He was skinny and ugly, with a patchwork face: weak chin but a broad nose, beady eyes but bulbous eyelids. He wanted to look like a gangster, but, like his face, his clothes clashed. Jacket didn't match his pants, tie was off. The points of his unbuttoned collar splayed out, which made him look even thinner. But he moved quickly, and I didn't like the way he looked at me as he put his arm around Miriam's waist to lead her out. *Whatcha gonna do about it, pal?* his expression challenged me. I didn't give a fig who pawed Miriam, but I didn't need trouble, not now, when I was so plastered. Wade looked familiar, but I didn't place him until we were downstairs—he was the guy who'd been sitting by himself in a chair the night I bedded Miriam.

"Go get us some beers, Mirs," Wade said, laughing at his lame rhyme.

"Don't call me 'Mirs'—you're not my brother," she shot back.

"Then go get us some beers, *Miriam.*"

I felt like I was on a playground. Miriam stomped off, Wade eyed me over.

"What's your name, Mac?"

"You heard me upstairs," I said evenly.

"Don't matter. Mirs goes through so many guys, we don't bother with their names."

I ignored that crack and lit up. The situation was easy to read. Wade had once made a pass at Miriam, she'd spurned him, he couldn't push it because she was Kenny's foster sister. So he stroked his manhood by sniping at her dates. I vaguely wondered what kind of "business" Kenny was conducting upstairs. Didn't matter—what he was up to had nothing to do with my investigation. *One more beer, outta here*, I thought. At the Rainbow, I'd imagined what another roll in the hay with Miriam might be like, and the booze had only whetted my desire. But I had to be up bright and early. If only I'd listened to myself instead of getting cute.

Instead of beers, Miriam came back with a fifth of rye and three glasses. She poured generous belts, we toasted uneasily.

"What's Kenny doing upstairs?" Miriam challenged Wade.

"Bizness. Which is none'a your bizness."

"He told me he was done dealing."

"Dealing what?" I asked without thinking, though the answer was obvious. This neighborhood was a choice spot to score dope, chockfull of two-bit hustlers and dealers like Kenny who worked on consignment for a local crime boss.

Before she could answer, Wade said menacingly, "You better shut your trap, sister."

I took a step toward him. "You better watch your mouth, *brother*." I didn't want a fight, but Ted Barston wasn't the kind of guy who'd let his gal get pushed around by a punk.

"Yeah, what if I don't?" he smirked. "What're you gonna do about it?"

I didn't answer, just stared him down. He didn't back off. Little guy with a big mouth—I had to expect him to fight dirty. Sensing the tension, people around us had stopped talking.

"Why don't you go back upstairs, Wade," Miriam interrupted our staring contest.

"Cuz Kenny told me to watch you two till he's done talking bizness, *Mirs*."

"Leave Ted alone," she shot back.

Goddammit, I thought. No man wants his gal to stick up for him, ever.

"Man, you're some kinda cream puff, aren't you?" Wade taunted.

Just walk away. Barston would've already decked Wade by now, but Voigt couldn't afford a distraction, he had a lot to do. Then Wade noticed the track marks I'd simulated on my forearms.

"Well, whattya know, Miriam's on her high horse about what her brother does, but it looks like her loverboy's itching for a hypo him—"

I lowered my shoulder and charged him, using my weight and height to plow him right through a clot of stunned partygoers, driving him against the wall as I gripped his right wrist. Women squealed, beer bottles fell, a man's hand flailed at my arm. Wrenching Wade's arm around his back, I pinned him and began pounding his face against the wall. His forehead thudded, the cartilage in his nose crackled, blood smeared the plaster; a tooth bounced off my shoe. I remember screaming obscenities, I remember one, three, and then more hands finally gaining purchase on my shoulders and pulling me off Wade, who toppled unconscious to the floor.

"Hold him, hold him," someone shouted, but no one tried hard to stop me when I wrenched free and made for the door. A woman stared in horror and scuttled away, as if fleeing a snarling dog. I heard a thunder of steps on the stairs—Kenny's boys, coming to see what the commotion was. I raced out the door and went straight to the back yard, where I crouched behind an overgrown shrub. They'd expect me to flee down the street, which gave me a chance to go down the alley and zigzag my way out of the neighborhood. I checked the urge to run, moving slowly, quietly, climbing fences and jumping gates until I got to Virginia Avenue, where I waved down a hack. My hands were still shaky when I collapsed on my cot at the Jefferson Club.

CHAPTER 23

HAD ONLY THREE HOURS TO SLEEP, BUT I WOKE UP ALERT, TENSE, wired. I'd tried to ignore that punk Wade, but when he noticed my faked hypo marks, I'd no choice but to give him a beating. Kenny and his crew were drug dealers, they knew what dope fiends looked like for real—I couldn't take a chance on one of them questioning my cover. But I should've just decked Wade with a one-two punch to his weak chin. I'd lost it but good, never been so enraged in my life, and calling it Barston's animal instinct didn't excuse my loss of control. Couldn't afford fury, not while I was undercover, might make an even bigger mistake. Also couldn't shake the image of the blood smear Wade's pulped face had left on the wall, or the gut-twisting sound his broken nose had made as I continued to pound his head. No doubt about it, he was in the hospital. Kenny wouldn't call the cops, but Miriam would tell him where I worked. Wade was just a minion, he was expendable, but I'd given Kenny a big Bronx cheer by taking apart one of his boys in his home—he'd want revenge. An awful lot of people had witnessed the scene, word would spread on the street, Kenny *had* to come after me.

I hoped Kenny wouldn't blame Miriam for what had happened. Sure hoped she wouldn't let on that she'd fallen for Barston. She could just tell Kenny that she'd just met Barston, they'd only been on a few dates—maybe that'd save her. Kenny was her foster brother, but she'd talked about him like a blood relation, and a real brother wouldn't let Wade's friends avenge his beating by roughing up Miriam. I hoped. I'd done her dirty by thrashing Wade, but in a way I was relieved. Last night's booze had besotted my thinking. I didn't need Miriam anymore, didn't have to string her along any longer. As a source, she'd given me all she could about Skerrill and Silva's relationship. For sure, I owed her an easy let-down when Barston broke up with her. Maybe I'd take her out to a fancy dinner, to the Pall Mall Room at the Raleigh or Harvey's on Connecticut. I could get some cash from my lock box at Riggs, tell Miriam to get all dolled up, even spring for her to get her hair set and buy some new makeup.

But Miriam had to wait until everything shook out at H & H. Had to focus on the investigation, had to think through my throbbing headache, the pain in my right hand. Despite the hangover, a realization: trying to follow Skerrill's cold, cold tracks was useless. Silva, Greene, and Himmel were too smart to leave traces of his subversion. What I must do instead, I saw, was collect the remaining pieces of Himmel's puzzle. I didn't know how they fitted together, but I sensed that the Bermuda Special, the diagram I'd copied from Nagel, and the secret millions pouring into secret Army labs in New Mexico and Tennessee were all part of that puzzle. With Skerrill dead, Himmel was hustling to finish his mission. I was the Johnny on the spot, the only man who could find out if the Reds were about to put everything together. I still needed to figure out who had wanted Skerrill dead, but the puzzle, the big prize, had to come first. Once I had it, Paslett would let me break cover, let me quit H & H. I would molt Barston's scabrous skin and become Lieutenant j.g. Ellis Voigt, U.S.N., once again.

These realizations cheered me, but I still felt and looked like hell. Bloodshot eyes and dark circles, the persistent headache. I needed to ice my hand, sore from gripping Wade's head so tightly, but there was no time—I had to get to H & H.

SILVA GLARED AT ME WHEN I ENTERED. SHE WAS BEHIND THE counter, no sign of Miriam.

"You look like something the cat dragged in. What will our clients think, seeing our delivery boy in such a sorry state?"

That I need a drink? Best to keep that thought to myself. I consoled myself by imagining her reaction if she knew I'd been through her underwear drawer the day before.

"Greene got da manifest ready?"

"He'll be up in a minute. Your appearance wouldn't have anything to do with Miriam calling in sick today, would it?"

"Miriam's sick? Dat's too bad. I oughta pick up some chicken soup for her after my deliveries."

"That's not an answer to my question."

"No, I don't know why Miriam's sick. Maybe we got da same bug, me and Miriam."

The glare got colder. "Nice try, Barston. Don't think I haven't noticed the little winks and nods you two exchange. If I find out she called out because she was with you last night, you can rest assured this will be your last day of employment here."

"How many ways you want me ta say it already—I don't know why Miriam's sick. Why don't you ask her and quit hasslin' me?"

She didn't back down, not a bit. "You were supposed to bring in your Navy discharge, Ted, where is it?"

"Ask Mister Himmel—I gave it ta him."

Greene scurried up, interrupting the standoff. "Everything all right, Nadine?" he asked.

She didn't even look at him or reply, just kept staring me down. For an instant, I wondered if she'd noticed something amiss at her flat and suspected me. *No way, no way,* I told myself. You're Ted Barston, you're steamed because your boss is a ball-buster, play it out. So I didn't break my gaze, either.

Greene didn't like being an ignored spectator. "Nadine, what's going on here? Is Barston giving you—"

"Nothing's going on, Philip: Ted and I were just discussing his need to be more presentable."

He eyed me over, wrinkling his brow in disgust and stealing a look at Silva to see if she'd noticed. She hadn't.

What a toadie, I thought.

"Dat my list for da day?" I reached for the clipboard in Greene's hand, but he pulled it away.

"Yes, yes, this is your manifest, but I need to tell you the following before you . . ."

He droned on. Mrs. McClellan had complained about improperly mounted clippings, there was a note of apology in her package, etc., etc. Silva turned on her heels and strode to Himmel's office, no doubt to see the discharge certificate and then to insist I be fired. I was certain Himmel wouldn't say yes. There had to be more packages he was waiting on, the diagram from Nagel couldn't be the last one.

"Are you listening, Barston?" Greene squawked.

"Yeah, sure, be nice ta Mrs. McClellan and tell her about da note." I took the clipboard and held out my hand for his car key. He dropped it grudgingly.

"Remember what I told you about the springs!" he called out as I left.

I pretended not to hear him.

MY HEADACHE HAD ONLY GROWN WORSE, SO I STOPPED OFF AT A TAVERN a block from my first stop and downed a shot of rye. That helped. I bought some Listerine to kill the whiskey smell. The morning went fast, one delivery after another. I shut out all thoughts of the investigation and what I needed to do. I was in a groove as Barston, chatting with clients, buttering up the elderly Mrs. McClellan by complimenting her on the fruit basket she was passing off as a hat.

I made such good time, I treated myself to eggs, hash, potatoes, and a Schlitz or two at a greasy spoon on Seventeenth and Columbia.

"Beer with breakfast, I like it," the counterman said.

"Dis is lunch, hey," I shot back.

On my way to the final delivery, to one Randall Kovacevic, I went into Western Union and sent a telegram to Liv at her rooming house—one of the other girls was sure to be home to sign for it. REPORT OLD FRIEND MISBEHAVED STOP (it read) APOLOGY DUE ALSO DANCING DINNER AND

MORE STOP PREPARED TO DELIVER LOTUS TONIGHT EIGHT STOP YOUR SUP-
PLICANT L STOP

Meeting Liv when I was supposed to be in Iceland was even more stupid and reckless than my last date, the one I'd fled like a kid with a curfew, but I had a plan. I'd say that I'd wanted to tell her, on the night we met at the Little Palace, that I was being sent to Iceland, but I hadn't been able to break the news. Weak tea, sure, and a lie, but all that mattered was not losing Liv. If she believed I was going to Iceland, then hopefully we could pick up when I "got back." If she hadn't already left for the South Pacific. No way that could happen until we put the Japs down for good, I reminded myself, and the way they were fighting, that was months off.

Randall Kovacevic's address was a residence, a third-floor flat in an apartment hotel on A Street, SE. My manifest listed the flat number, 3F, but out of instinct I checked the mailboxes. The label on 3F's box was a typed slip of paper with Kovacevic's name—it had been taped on. I carefully peeled back the tape. Underneath was a handlettered card: *R. Kudlower.*

"Sloppy, very sloppy," I muttered. Whoever had trained this Kudlower and Nagel, the scientist from the National Bureau of Standards, had botched his job but good. I wondered if it had been Greene. Maybe Himmel hadn't had the time to train his spies properly. More likely, he didn't care what happened to them after he got what he wanted. Another reminder that time was running out on me.

I went up the stairs and down a dimly lit, creaky corridor with a worn runner. I knocked and got a *Who's there?*

"H & H Clipping Service, got a package for Randall Kova, Kovacev—"

"Okay, okay, come in," the door swinging open.

Another rookie mistake. If Kudlower didn't want his neighbors to over-hear his pseudonym, he should've opened his door immediately. Hell, he shouldn't have been couriering out of his flat to start with—at least Nagel had taken the precaution of meeting in a place he had no connection to.

I held up a fat envelope. I'd checked the contents in the car: nothing but clippings from the papers' Federal Diary section, which reported Congres-sional committee hearings, assignments, and actions. Awful boring stuff, a cover, I assumed, for the real reason I was there.

Kudlower grabbed the envelope. He looked to be my age, mid-twenties, with an Irish complexion, freckles and fair skin. Husky build, but he was going soft, a paunch tugging at his sweater. His flat was small and common. Murphy bed (down, unmade), kitchenette, bathroom with just a toilet and sink. For furnishings, a table with fold-down flaps, a few chairs, a divan. I noticed, stacked on one chair, a dozen or so thick volumes bound in black leatherette covers, the kind with a sleeve to put a title card in. I could only read the card attached to the top volume: *Department of the Interior Appropriation Bill for 1945, Hearings before the Subcommittee of the Committee on Appropriations.* Maybe the clippings weren't a cover, maybe Kudlower actually used them in his job.

"Sign here, please, Mister Kova—how da you say yer name?"

"Kova-cev-ick," he said, scribbling a signature.

Wrong again. In high school, I'd known a kid named Petrovic—Serb names ending in a *c* were pronounced as *ch*.

"Hold on, I got something for you," Kudlower said. He went into the kitchenette and returned with a letter-sized envelope. "Will you take this back with you?"

"Sure, you bet."

Now Kudlower couldn't get me out of his flat fast enough, crowding me to the door. I examined the envelope as I thudded down the stairs. Just like the one Nagel had given me, it was plain white, no markings, sealed with a lick. I'd have no trouble replacing it. I checked my watch, which had started working again after I'd banged it twice: a quarter past one. Plenty of time to see what R. Kudlower was passing on to Himmel and make a copy.

Only I never got the chance. Two men fell in stride with me as I rounded the corner of Seventh and A, headed to the car. They'd been standing outside a Peoples Drug Store, smoking, looking at boxes of cigars in the display window. But I knew that trick, too—I could see their reflection as easily as they could see mine. The one on my left wore a gray suit, wrinkle-free white shirt, and a blue tie with a pebble pattern. You could have used the crease in his trousers as a letter opener, and the polished toes of his black wingtips shone like the North Star. He looked about forty, slight build, average height, with a jutting jaw and a slightly bent nose. The man on his right was short and stocky, not as neatly dressed. His blue jacket was unbuttoned, his gold and red tie carelessly knotted. He had a stub of a nose, small ears, and dark eyes with heavy lids. I had dealt with enough F.B.I. agents to know the look, to know how they approached a mark on the street. I should have been ready for this, I realized. If the Bureau was watching Silva, for sure it was also watching the people suspected of spying for Himmel. As the two men caught up with me, I slipped Kudlower's envelope under my manifest, hoping they hadn't noticed it when I passed them.

"Hey pal, mind if we talk to you?" the sloppy one asked.

"Buzz off," I answered.

They didn't like that. Mr. Neat double-timed and planted himself in front of me, forcing me to halt.

"Outta my way, Mac," I growled.

"You can't spare a minute?" The sloppy one again, this time touching my forearm.

"Get yer filthy hands off me! Leave me alone!" As I wanted, my angry cries stopped passersby.

"Cut it out," Mr. Neat said, quietly but firmly. "You're going with us, and it's up to you, pal, you wanna go easy or hard."

"For what?" I shot back. "I ain't done nuttin', I'm just working here. Leave me alone!"

"Say, what's the trouble here?" asked a concerned citizen, a Rotarian-looking fellow in a suit and eyeglasses.

Now Neat and Sloppy had no choice but to badge him and the other onlookers. They stepped back, and a whistle from Sloppy brought a sleek black Plymouth sedan to the curb. Neat opened the rear passenger door and hustled around to the other side as Sloppy pinched me right below my elbow, grabbed my clipboard, and pushed me into the car. A man will do exactly what you want if you know how to hit the nerve, as Sloppy did—I'd learned that same grip at the Funhouse. He made sure my head banged the car's ceiling as I went in. I'd expected that cheap shot, for gumming up their roust, but I hadn't expected the knock to bring my hangover back. And I had a feeling I'd be going without a drink for a while.

CHAPTER 24

I KICKED UP QUITE A FUSS IN THE PLYMOUTH, SQUAWKING ABOUT MY rights and how I was going to lose my job, working myself into a Barston-worthy tantrum. The two agents and the driver, another standard issue G-man, pretended not to hear me, until finally Mr. Neat couldn't take it anymore.

"Stop the car, Loula," he ordered the driver, who dutifully pulled to the curb. (With a name like that, I understood why he got stuck driving.)

"You wanna get out, go ahead, get out," Neat addressed me. "But the second you leave this vehicle, we're gonna arrest you under Section Six-eighty-three of the Espionage Act. Then you can have all the lawyers you want. If you shut up and stay in the car, you're not under arrest. We'll have our little talk, then you'll be free to go."

"For real?" I asked, though I wanted to laugh in his face. Only the Bureau could come up with a gimmick like that: you're free to go, but if you leave, then we'll arrest you, so you better do what we want.

He nodded sternly. I canned it. We drove to the Bureau's headquarters in the Department of Justice building, an impressive structure. Fluted columns held up friezes and sculpted panels, the decorative aluminum window trim shone bright. The Stars and Stripes fluttered above the Constitution Avenue entrance, but Loula took us to the loading dock. The Bureau didn't have jail cells in the building—anyway, I wasn't under arrest, right?—but it did have some awful nice interrogation rooms in the basement, or so I'd heard from Commander Paslett. Opaque glass, hidden mics, and Hollywood-quality film cameras, specially designed chairs to make a sitter uncomfortable.

Loula stayed in the car as the two agents got out and led me into the building. Clerks and janitors stepped to the side as Neat and Sloppy walked me down a long corridor. John Edgar's vaunted files—tens of thousands of index cards on suspect Americans and aliens—were rumored to be kept somewhere here, but I wasn't getting a tour. Neat unlocked a windowless door and motioned for me to sit in a chair with its back to the door. An old, old interrogator's trick, that. To my right and left were observation windows; directly in front of me was a gray metallic screen. I couldn't catch any reflection from it, but I was certain that anyone on the other side could see the entire room.

My chaperones sat down side-by-side across from me. The table between us was burnished metal brightly lit by humming overhead fluorescents.

"I'm Agent Slater, my partner's Agent Reid," Mr. Neat announced. "The quicker you answer our questions, the sooner you're outta here." Slater and Reid, the same two agents who had picked up Traub and confronted Paslett and Terrance at the Navy Building.

"Why da hell are you hassling me?"

Reid wagged a finger at me. "He said *answer*, not *ask*."

I shot him my best defiant Barston look but didn't smart-aleck him. Already my legs were starting to hurt—the two front legs of my chair were slightly shorter than the rear legs.

"Okay, your full name and place and date of birth," Slater began.

I told them, grateful for the hours I'd spent in my flat, drilling the facts of Ted Barston's brief, unhappy life into my head. The Bureau doesn't do the good cop, bad cop routine—Hoover thinks it's amateurish. His agents grind down their prey with relentless questions about their lives, habits, and everyday comings and goings. This approach lulls you into a false sense of security. Who can't answer questions about where he grew up and what his pop did for a living, easy-breezy, right? But after a while, you get restless, anxious, frazzled. All the probing causes you to doubt your own memory. You worry that if you forget something, make a mistake, they'll accuse you of lying. Once the G-men have you on edge (and aching to take a leak), they spring the questions they really want answers for. And if you hesitate, if you hem, haw, and er, then it's bad cop, bad cop all the rest of the way. Hell, by the end it's going to be bad cop, bad cop no matter what.

I wasn't worried about passing the "This Is Your Life, Ted Barston" test, and I was confident that the Bureau, even with its enviable resources, hadn't learned anything more about Ted Barston than Paslett's researchers. As long as I kept my facts straight and flashed Barston's temper, I'd be okay. Easy, breezy. . . .

". . . your father was pretty important in the I.L.A.," Reid was saying.

"Yeah, so?"

"The I.L.A. was and is a communist-affiliated union, led by known agents of the Soviet Union, responsible for a wave of disruptive dock strikes in the New Jersey ports throughout the nineteen-thirties."

"Thanks for the history lesson, can I go now?" But you can't bait Hoover's boys, they shrug off insults like a duck sheds water.

"Why'd you seek employment at H & H?" This from Slater.

"Cause I needed a job, whattya think?"

"Why that particular establishment? You have no work history with clipping services or the newspaper trade. Why not a machinist or shop position?"

Now I was in a bind. Why would a guy like Barston ask for work at a clipping service? It looked fishy, but I sure as hell didn't want to tell them about Griffin Crieve.

"Maybe Mister Himmel's a friend'a mine," I decided to say, defiantly.

"Had you been in contact with Himmel after your release from the brig?" Slater, still.

"No."

"How'd you know he needed a delivery man?" Now Reid.

"I didn't."

"You just went to see him out of the blue?"

"Hell, yeah! Goddamned Navy left me flat broke, what else was I s'posed ta do?"

"Find a job in Charleston," Slater interjected.

"Or go back to New Jersey," Reid suggested.

"I hate Charleston, nobody I know's left in Joisey."

"Why D.C.?" Slater asked.

"Didn't have da fare ta get ta New York, figgered I could find work here da same as anywhere else."

"Did you know Himmel ran a clipping service before you picked Washington?"

"Nope."

The two agents exchanged looks. I was taking a big risk, but I had to get them off the subject of why Barston had ended up in Washington—that was the weakest link in my chain.

"How exactly do you know Himmel?" Reid pressed. "Start by telling us about the first time you met, where it was and when, who introduced—"

"I never met da man before I walked into his business, okay?"

"You said he's a friend."

"I said *maybe*. Anyways, you know I was kidding, da way I said it."

"All right, then why'd you go to Himmel?" Slater leaned over the table.

"A friend told me ta look him up."

"Name, occupation, and address of the friend."

"Uh uh," I said. "Go ahead and arrest me, 'cause I ain't giving you dat name."

If they did arrest me, I was in a heap of trouble. Because they really would use the Espionage Act, and an obscure provision of the law allowed suspects to be detained for forty-eight hours before arraignment, to allow the government to ensure that "state secrets" would stay secret after a suspect appeared in court. But I was gambling that Slater and Reid didn't want to take that step. They didn't want a case against Ted Barston, they wanted to stop the espionage; and if they arrested me, then the envelope I'd picked up from Kudlower (posing as Kovacevic) would become evidence and would have to be shown to a defense attorney.

My hunch was right—sort of.

"All right, let's set that question aside and talk about this envelope," Reid said smoothly. Like a magician's card, it had appeared out of nowhere—he must have had my clipboard on his lap.

"What about it? Last guy I made a delivery ta, he gave me dat."

"What's in it?"

I shrugged. "Hell if I know—I don't open da packages."

Slater asked, "Doesn't it strike you as strange that H & H's clients are giving you envelopes after you make deliveries?"

"Mister Himmel told me some of 'em might, so I should just bring da envelope or package or whatever ta him."

Reid perked up. "Have you picked up a lotta packages for Himmel?"

"What, you think I count 'em? C'mon, pal."

"That's 'Agent Reid,' not 'pal,' Barston, and you'd better answer the question," Slater said.

"I did! Goddammit, I'm just da delivery boy, I take whatever's listed on da manifest ta da addresses dey give me, and if dey give me sometin' for Himmel, I take it back ta da office for him, end'a story."

"And you've never opened one of these envelopes?"

"Nope."

"Maybe you should open this one," Reid said quietly. He slid the envelope toward me.

"Want us to get you a letter opener?" Slater cracked.

Bastards, I thought. They didn't have a warrant, the chances of convincing a federal judge they had probable cause for picking me up were fifty-fifty. If they opened the envelope, it might not be allowed as evidence in a trial to nail Himmel et al. for espionage. But if I opened the envelope voluntarily—and Slater and Reid would swear under oath that I had, backed up by an edited cut of the film they were shooting of the interrogation—a federal prosecutor would have all that he needed. I wouldn't be charged, of course, not after my real identity was revealed, but I had to do whatever I could to preserve my cover.

"Fuck you both," I snarled, crumpling the envelope into a ball and throwing it at Slater's head.

"Goddammit!" Reid shouted, smoothing the envelope out as if it were a ten-thousand-dollar bill.

Slater jumped out of his chair and raced over to the metal screen on the wall. He rapped twice, no doubt a signal to stop the filming and the recording.

"Gimme back dat clipboard and da envelope," I ordered Reid. I jumped up, kicked my chair over. "You keep telling me I ain't under arrest, so I'm leaving, understand? I'm going back ta work and if you wanna know what's in dat envelope, you come ask Himmel, because—"

Slater punched me in the left kidney. I knew the blow was coming—he'd come around the table as I was yelling at his partner—so I'd shifted my posture slightly to take the hit on my lower back. But there wasn't much I could do to soften the rest of the workover. Reid pinned me in a half-Nelson while Slater, grinning like a kid who's trapped an alley cat he wants to torture, let me have it: blow to the solar plexus, leaving me gasping; one-two punch to the kidneys; knee to the groin. Reid released me, I fell to the floor, instinctively drawing my knees up and covering my head with my arms.

"Looks like boyo's got experience taking a licking," Reid commented.

"Curled up just like a tater bug," Slater said, chuckling.

But they were done. They'd left no visible marks, and after a while I'd be able to walk on my own. I'd be pissing blood for a week, but who'd believe a guy like Ted Barston if he claimed two F.B.I. agents had given him a beating?

They grabbed me by the shoulders and hauled me to my feet.

"Pick up your chair," Slater commanded.

I did, shakily—if Reid hadn't been holding onto my bicep, I might have toppled over.

"Sit down." Slater again.

They returned to their seats and glared at me.

"We know about you and Himmel and your pals Silva and Greene," Reid said matter-of-factly. "Pretty clever of you commies to set up a clipping service to move the packages. We've been watching all of you for a while now. So you can drop the dumb lunkhead act, Barston. Your dad was a Red, so are you. One way or another, we're gonna get the name of this friend who sent you to H & H."

Was that true, had the Bureau put H & H under full surveillance? Silva, yes—she was being watched. But if the Bureau knew with certainty that

H & H was a front, John Edgar would have placed two-man teams on every employee, including me. Bureau boys would have watched me make deliveries, meet twice with Commander Paslett and Terrance, and (Jesus H. Christ!) send a telegram to Liv an hour ago. But the fact I was now being interrogated by Slater and Reid proved I hadn't been tailed for long, because the Bureau would have identified Paslett and Terrance as O.N.I. officers after the first meeting at the billiards parlor. Hoover would have raised hell with the director, who probably would have ordered Paslett to bring me in. So Slater and Reid were fishing. They *suspected* H & H was a front, but they didn't know how all the parts and players fit together. They were on to Silva, but they didn't know who Himmel really was, I realized, which is why they were pressing me about him. They knew this Kudlower character was hinky—that's why they'd been watching him—but they didn't know the details. By squeezing me, they hoped to connect the dots. If I wanted to get out of there with my cover intact, the "dumb lunkhead" act was my best play.

Reid slid the crinkled but intact envelope over the table. "Open it."

"If I do, then can I go?"

"Of course," Slater said too quickly.

"For real?"

"He said yes, didn't he?" Reid snapped.

"All right, den." I opened the envelope, and we all three stared at what slid out.

CHAPTER 25

A STAMPED POSTCARD AND A HANDWRITTEN NOTE. *DEAR H & H* (THE note read), *the enclosed was inadvertently included in my last delivery. I am returning it to you for its proper disposition, R. Kovacevic.* The postcard was also in cursive, but in a different hand. The picture showed Los Alamos, New Mexico, at sunset, orange, umber, and cinnamon hues coloring a desert vista of mountains and scrubby trees. On the back, the following:

> Hello B! What a grand time we're having out here in the country at the Five-Five dude ranch. Everything we need is right here, we don't have to go anywhere. Enormous meals, horse rides through the canyons, bonfires at night—$$$$ well-spent, every penny. And the people we're meeting, you wouldn't believe it. People from the island, mountains, and plains. We're rubbing shoulders with dancers, violinists, actors,

even a few gymnasts. Would love to stay the whole year, but we have to come home. Wish you were here (giggles)! All our love, L & A.

Slater and Reid scrutinized the note and postcard for a long moment before handing them over. I took my time reading, pretending to be a slow reader so that I could memorize every word. The postmark, dated April 18, 1945, looked real, but postal markings are awful easy to forge.

"What does that card mean?" Slater demanded.

"How da hell should I know?"

"It's obviously some kind of coding."

I shrugged and set the card and note down; Reid snatched them up.

"I wouldn't know nuttin' 'bout dat, I'm just da delivery guy."

Slater glared at me, but if he knew anything about how commie cells worked, then he knew I was telling the truth: the courier must never know anything about the contents of his packages.

"What does Himmel do with the envelopes you bring back?" Reid asked.

"He makes paper airplanes, whattya think?"

"What d'you know about Himmel?" he asked, ignoring my wisecrack.

"He's an okay joe, for a boss. Can I go now? You said if I—"

"Where's he from?"

"Guthrie, Fresno—I got no idea."

"He's no Okie," Reid shot back.

"Yer da F.B. of I., why don'tya take a look at his birth certificate?"

"Good idea, I like that—maybe we oughta make you an honorary agent," Slater said sarcastically.

"Where's he from?" Reid asked, still unperturbed. He was the bright penny in this duo, trying to lead me.

"Freedonia."

"Funny. You oughta tour the Catskills this summer. But you know what's even funnier, Barston?"

"Why don'tya tell me?" Faking a yawn.

"How you just showed up outta the blue. Brig, bus, bingo—suddenly you're on the doorstep of H & H like a newborn abandoned by his mother. And Himmel takes you right in, a dishonorably discharged shipfitter, a dope fiend, a sad sack with no friends. Except the one friend you don't want to tell us about, the one you said told you to go to Himmel."

Chill right down the spine. Slater's knowing nod unnerved me further. *Are they on to me?* Too late to change my act now—I'd already put everything I had on Red. If I didn't give them something, they'd keep digging, keep clawing the tree like bloodhounds until the bark scraped away. My cover wasn't that thick, it couldn't withstand a full-tilt Bureau siege. Maybe I had no choice but to tell them about my visit to Griffin Crieve. After all, that loon had bought my story—why wouldn't Slater and Reid?

"Griffin Crieve," I said, and left it at that.

They exchanged looks. Then Reid laughed. "Still the funny guy, huh? But we're not joking anymore, Barston. You give us the name—"

"Crieve, comma, Griffin. Got a big ol' house off Logan Circle. Lotsa pretty stained glass, can't miss it."

"How d'you know Griffin Crieve?" Slater asked.

"I met him when I was a kid. Came ta da docks ta rally da boys. Like you said, my pop was big in the I.L.A. Crieve liked him."

"But that had to be, what, eight, ten years ago? Why would you go—"

I stood up. "I'm done, got it? Goddammit, I already told you if you wanted more, you'd better arrest me. Instead, I get beat up, you make me open dat envelope, and you say I can go after all'a dat. So fuck you both, I'm leavin'!"

It took all my strength to keep my hands from trembling. I'd rattled them, sure, but I couldn't know how they'd react. Work me over again? Take the plunge and arrest me? Try to sweet-talk me into staying?

"All right, Barston, you can go," Reid said, finally.

"For now," Slater added.

THEY BOTH ESCORTED ME OUT, NEITHER SAYING A WORD UNTIL WE reached Tenth Street.

"Count on seeing us real soon, Barston," Reid said.

"Go ta hell," I answered gleefully. A family of tourists was passing by, an American Oil Company map of Washington clutched in the father's hand, so I wasn't worried about a parting shot from my new friends. The family gaped, mother shooed them along. Slater and Reid would give me my comeuppance with interest next time we saw one another, but this must be the last time I was alone with these two, I realized. I didn't know how I'd do it, but I had to avoid run-ins with the Bureau. For sure, Slater and Reid were going to order a twenty-four hour shadow on me. What they didn't know about Himmel's spy ring, they thought I knew—or could lead them to what they needed to know. A fulltime tail was a rough turn, it would tax all my skills learned at the Funhouse, it meant I'd be hard-pressed to set up another meeting with Terrance and Paslett. Keeping my date with Liv that night was out of the question. Or was it?

But seeing Liv, that was small fry. I still had a hell of a lot to learn about Himmel's espionage, and I was no closer to identifying who could have murdered Logan Skerrill than when I set foot in H & H—that had to change, and change quick. I was caught up in intrigue and events I didn't as yet fully understand, but this much was crystal clear: I was fast running out of time to finish the job I'd been sent to do as Ted Barston.

BY THE TIME I GOT BACK TO GREENE'S CAR, IT HAD COLLECTED TWO more citations. I promptly filed them in the nearest trash can and drove pell-mell to K Street. I parked in the alley so I could come in through the rear and go straight to Himmel's office without having to deal with Silva or Greene.

Himmel was bent over a stack of papers, twirling a pencil. I must have looked a mess, my clothes rumpled and my hair wild from Slater and Reid's beating, but he was only interested in my hands. Empty, my palms flat against my dungarees.

"No envelope for me, Ted?" He set the pencil down.

I sat down without waiting for an invitation and lit up. It hurt like hell to inhale—the G-men had bruised my ribs but good—but sweet Mary, that Old Gold tasted wonderful. "Coupla boys from da F.B.I. picked me up when I was leaving da last address."

"The F.B.I.? Why would they arrest you?"

"Dey didn't arrest me, Mister Himmel. Dey just wanted ta talk ta me. And see what was in da envelope Randall Kovacevic gave me."

He reached for his box of Montecristos and took a cigar. He rolled it gently in his hands, tapping the tip against the desk. "I see you gave it to them. The envelope."

"Didn't have much choice."

He found his clipper, snipped the cigar, and brushed the pinched end into the ashtray. "But you were never under arrest, hmmm?"

I took a long, satisfying drag on my cigarette, exhaling the plume toward the overhead fan, which caught and twirled my smoke. I was reminded of the cotton candy machine at a carnival, the way the blades turn and spin, the pink sugar going round and round. "Dey said if I didn't talk ta 'em, dey'd arrest me."

"I don't understand how they could take the envelope if you weren't under arrest." He frowned.

The hell you don't! A Soviet agent, perplexed by an intelligence agency playing cat-and-mouse with a mark? But Himmel had to play his part, so did I. "All's I can tell you, Mister Himmel, is dat dey said if I didn't cooperate, dey'd arrest me. Dey promised if I opened it for 'em, I could go."

"That strikes me as, hmmm, what is the word I want here?"

"Un-American."

"Yes. Un-American, perfect. I will be sure to let our attorney know of this outrage. Did you get the names of these F.B.I. men?"

"Slater and Reid." I spelled the names for him; he made a show of scribbling them down on his pad.

"So, Ted." He set the pencil down and struck a match to light his cigar. A plume of gray smoke obscured his face for a moment.

"Yeah, Mister Himmel?"

"What was in the envelope the agents forced you to open?"

In the car, I'd decided I wouldn't tell Himmel that I'd memorized the note and postcard. That was the action of Lieutenant Ellis Voigt, U.S.N. But Ted Barston, for all his bluster and don't-give-a-damn posturing, was grateful to Himmel for the job, was eager to please. So I had to give him something. "Well, dey didn't lemme see it all dat long, you know, what was in da—"

"Just tell me what you saw, Ted."

"Sure, Mister Himmel. All right, so da first thing dat slid out was a note from dis Kovacevic fella, and it said sometin' about how da other thing had been given ta him by mistake in his last delivery, so he was sending it back so we—H & H, he meant—could give it ta whoever it belonged ta."

Puffing on his cigar, he motioned for me to continue.

"Okay, all right, so da second thing, it was just a postcard, from some place in New Mexico, Los, Los Alma"—I stumbled over the name, to see if he'd correct me, but his expression remained impassive, so I continued. "Anyways, it was just a postcard from dis place in New Mexico from dese people who just signed dare name 'L' and 'A' to someone called 'B.'"

"What did the postcard say?"

"What postcards always say. We're having fun, wish we could stay longer, wish you were here—dat kinda stuff."

"Did L and A say where they were staying?"

"Think it was called da Five-Five Dude Ranch."

His eyes flickered. *Should I give him more, to find out what he's most interested in?* I could let Terrance know all about Himmel's reaction when I sent my partner a message.

"Dey must like dis ranch an awful lot, Mister Himmel, because dey said it was worth all da money dey was spending."

"Did L and A say how much the ranch cost?"

"Uh, no, I don't think so."

"What, exactly, did the postcard say about money, Ted? Do you remember?"

"Well, lemme think, da way dey put it was, okay, it was 'money well-spent, every penny.' And dey used dollar signs instead'a da word 'money.'"

"How many dollar signs, Ted?"

"Hell, I don't remember. Three? Maybe four."

He glanced at the pencil, then turned his gaze back to me, exhaling cigar smoke. *He wants to write that down*, I thought. Why did he need to know how many dollar signs had been used?

"... Ted!"

"Sorry, Mister Himmel, what did you say?"

"What else did the postcard say?"

I decided to withhold the mention of dancers, violinists, actors, and gymnasts. Sloppy spycraft, to refer to such unusual occupations, a red flag that Paslett and Terrance should be able to decipher without too much work. The ranch must refer to the hush-hush military installation in New

Mexico that Paslett had mentioned at the billiards parlor, so the dancers, et cetera, must identify *who* was at the base. Himmel would want that detail awful bad, but I had to give him something else instead: "Well, da only other thing I remember is, dey said dey wanted ta stay longer, like I told you, but dat dey had to come home."

Himmel nodded and rolled ash off his cigar. I was already on my third Old Gold of the conversation.

"And there's nothing else you can tell me about that postcard, Ted?" His voice quiet, too quiet.

"No, Mister Himmel. Sorry 'bout dat." I checked the urge to say something about a bad memory. *Don't overdo it.*

"That's too bad, Ted."

He knew I was holding back, but I was determined to stay the course. The dumb lunkhead act, Reid had called it. I wondered if Nevelskoi ever tired of playing Himmel. For sure, I was bone-tired of being Barston.

"What should I tell Greene about da manifest?" I asked. "Da F.B.I. agents, dey kept it."

"You will have to tell him you lost it."

"He's gonna wanna fire me. Silva, she's gonna—"

"Let me handle those two, Ted."

"Okay, Mister Himmel. So you want me back here tomorrow morning?"

"Yes. But I need you to do something important in the meantime."

"Sure, anything."

"Keep an eye out to see if you have any new friends between now and tomorrow." Translation: you'd better watch for the Bureau's shadow.

"Gotcha." And with that, I left.

I TOLD GREENE I'D BEEN MUGGED—CONVENIENTLY, THAT EXCUSED my appearance—and I'd forgotten to retrieve the clipboard after I picked myself up off the sidewalk. He was more worried about his car than anything else, but Silva, of course, overheard everything and bolted over to grill me about the mugging. How many guys jumped me, where had it happened, had I called the police, on and on. I cut her off by saying I'd told Himmel everything and was going home for the day. I needed a drink fierce, to kill the aches and throbs from my beating.

Three shots of rye and beer backs in a Seventh Street gutbucket steadied my nerves and cleared my head. As I drank, I puzzled over the name of the ranch and Himmel's intense interest in the number of dollar signs on the postcard. Five-Five . . . what was the number five taken to the fifth power? I dug a grubby pencil stub from my pocket and worked out the figure: 3,125. Say the dollar signs represented zeros. That yielded a total of 31,250,000. As for the sender, Kudlower, posing as Kovacevic, lived near Capitol Hill. He had stacks of Interior Department appropriations reports in his flat. Jesus, how could I have not seen it right away! Kudlower was the cell's money man, he was tracing how much money was being spent on the military installation in New Mexico. And, with the reference to dancers, violinists, actors, and gymnasts, he must be trying to tell Himmel *what* the project was.

CHAPTER 26

LEFT A TWO-BIT TIP AND HUSTLED OUT ONTO SEVENTH STREET, blinking in the bright afternoon sun. I probably shouldn't have had that third shot and beer, but I was still able to pick out my shadow from the Bureau. He was across the street, milling around a newsstand. Blue suit and gray fedora, brim tilted against the sun. Looked young, real young, collar not quite tight, tie askew, like he was wearing his pop's shirt. He held a magazine, was leafing through it, but obviously not reading, his eyes darting to assay my side of Seventh Street. The news-jockey, perched on a stool inside his shack, glared at the agent with open hostility. When the agent saw me, he immediately dropped his gaze back to the magazine.

Observations pushed through the rye. Boy G-man was green, making rookie mistakes like loafing around a newsstand, pawing a magazine. When the news-jockey told him to buy it or beat it, Boy G-man badged him—hence the eyefuck. Boy G-man didn't know what to do next, now that I'd emerged from the bar. Waiting for me to head out, telling himself to give me a block like he'd been trained, then fall in. Question: If Ted Barston was important enough to glue a shadow on, why hadn't the Bureau sent out an experienced man? Answer: Slater and Reid were short-handed, every man they could spare was already busy trying to crack H & H. They hadn't expected to see me make a delivery to Kudlower, but it was their lucky break. *Because now they knew how Himmel sent the collection basket around to his spy ring.* By tomorrow, perhaps even tonight, Slater and Reid would have a seasoned two-man team watching me, and I'd be hard-pressed to shake them. Drawing Boy G-man as my shadow that afternoon was my lucky break, because I wanted to confirm my hunch about Kudlower and the pseudo-postcard from Los Alamos, New Mexico, before I contacted Terrance and Paslett. To do that, I had to cut my new friend loose.

My destination was Capitol Hill, but I needed to get cleaned up—shave, haircut, change of clothes—before I set foot in the vaunted halls of Congress. I headed south on Seventh, my gait a bit too stiff, like a drunk trying to walk sober. I stopped in front of a burleycue theater and gaped at the cheesecake posters, using the glass case's reflection to spot my tail. He was directly across the street, crouching to tie an already properly laced wingtip. *Tsk, tsk—didn't they teach you anything at the Academy?* My plan was to kite him along Seventh Street, to the amusement arcade between H and G Streets. The barrel vaulted arcade had a wide mall lined with shooting galleries, bean bag tosses, pinball machines, and countless kiosks hawking junk for tourists. Noise, crowds, flashing lights, kids underfoot—I could lose Boy G-man by ducking down one of the myriad side aisles and out an unmarked exit. But then a tout sidled up and asked if I wanted a bite of the real thing—suddenly I had a much better plan.

"How much, hey?" I asked.

"Ten bucks, plus the room." He was a skinny guy, with a long nose and an oversized jaw like a horse's, baring teeth begging for a trip to the dentist.

"Okay, but dare's a joe across da street, looks like vice? He gonna be a problem?"

Horseface picked out Boy G-man immediately and grinned maliciously. "Nah, he ain't gonna be a problem—this is the last he's gonna see'a us. C'mon."

He deftly turned into a narrow passage running alongside the theater's exterior wall. I followed. He pushed open a gate, veered left, and knocked in code on the theater's steel-plated service door: two long, two short, a drum of his fingers. The door lurched open, we ducked in, the door closed. I never saw the doorman—it was dark, and Horseface didn't pause, leading me up a metal staircase and down a dimly lit, narrow corridor. He opened a door to another hallway. Just before we entered, I heard a banging on the theater door. We could just hear Boy G-man's shout: "Hey, open up in there!"

Horseface cackled. "C'mon, almost there."

This corridor led into the adjoining building, which on Seventh Street had the edifice of a rooming house. Maybe the first two floors were rooms for let, but the third floor was all prossies, guarded by a rock-solid slab of man who cried ex-boxer. Pouchy eyes, cauliflower ears, fists hanging from his wrists like wrecking balls.

"Tell Tiny whattya want, pay him, enjoy," and with that Horseface pounded down the staircase we'd just come up, his work done.

Tiny, natch—that kind of irony passed for humor in the underworld.

"Any requests?" Tiny grunted, taking me in with a practiced, bored eyeover.

"Nope, just a clean girl and a nice quickie."

"A boy to make his mother proud," Tiny deadpanned, holding out his massive palm. "Fifteen bucks, knock on door four."

"Must be awful nice rooms," I said, peeling bills off my fast-dwindling roll.

"Class acts deserve classy digs," Tiny said with a straight face.

Behind Door 4, I found a brunette who looked about nineteen, the teenage chubbiness still in her cheeks. She wore a black shift with lacy hems that clung to sturdy thighs and plump breasts. She was reclined on a sagging mattress in a steel bedframe, knees bent, head resting on her palm, reading a magazine. She looked up without interest.

"Hey lover, where you been?" she cracked.

"Comedians, all'a you," I replied.

"I'm Jean."

"John. But you already knew dat, hey?"

"Leave the jokes to the pros, honey—easier on all'a us that way." She straightened up and tossed the magazine to a nightstand with a cracked top. I'd expected *True Romances*—wrong: *Time*. She had a pleasant face stuccoed with lipstick, mascara, and rouge. Eyebrows plucked into perfect arcs and manicured nails were the House's way of telling tricks that the girls were clean. She reached for a bottle of lotion, tapped a dollop out, and worked it into her palms. The sound was unsettling, like the suction of mud on your boots.

Tell her my kink was I wanted to hear stories? Act nervous, make excuses, wait for her to say *S'allright, happens to all good boys?* All sorts of angles I could take to avoid banging this prossy, but I couldn't afford attention, couldn't risk a scene. If I acted strangely, Jean might signal for the heave-ho, and Boy G-man was likely still sniffing Seventh Street, desperate to pick up my scent. I needed to give him time enough to realize he'd screwed up and had to call for help, then make my exit. And the easiest way to gain time enough was to—

"Gotta undress yourself, lover—this ain't a full-service station," Jean said, her eyes narrowing. I caught her glance at the hotel bell on the nightstand. One *ding*, and we'd get a no-knock visit from Tiny.

"Then just the usual," I answered, unbuckling my belt. *Dis is Barston's treat*, I told myself. I hadn't paid for it since I met Liv, wasn't about to start now; but Teddy, he had a lot of lays to make up for his time in the brig, didn't he? I clung to that question as Jean pulled up the hem of her shift with a practiced turn of her wrists.

BOY G-MAN HAD VANISHED WHEN I TOOK MY LEAVE. I FLAGGED A HACK and had him take me north to Massachusetts and on to Dupont Circle. By the time reinforcements arrived from the Bureau and started their grid search, I'd be long gone. I told the driver to drop me off at the intersection with New Hampshire, then I cut across the plaza inside the circle. Kids ran about, playing tag and tussling as their mothers laughed, talked, smoked. Buses disgorged scores of office workers who fanned out across the plaza to finish the trudge home. There was a little barbershop tucked away on Hopkins, a half-block more alley than street, where I could get cleaned up before heading to the Hill. I'd never been there, nobody would recognize me.

A shave never felt so good. I closed my eyes and let the tension ease from my shoulders as the barber ratcheted the chair back. The steaming hot towel leached out the rest of the rye, the mentholated shaving cream cleared my sinuses. As the razor scraped a careful, slow path across my cheeks and jaw, I imagined all my troubles swirling away with the stubble-flecked cream. Paslett's persistence, my dreams of Delphine, Himmel's watchful gaze, Greene's pestering, Silva's scolding, Miriam's cloying, Slater's sadistic grin—all of it gone, down the drain forever. Let my thoughts drift, and drift up, a daydream as high as the sky, starting with a headline. *Naval Lieutenant Cracks Red Spy Ring Wide Open.* . . . Sure, I could be the source, the leak, could think of a way to get it to Drew Pearson or another columnist without leaving fingerprints. That kind of story breaks, I'm ruined for future undercover work. Leverage that, right, wheedle Paslett into fixing a decommission. Sprung from the Navy, a free man, I can go to the South Pacific with Liv! We can layover in Chicago—hell, we'd have to change trains there anyway—and visit my family. Stay a few days, maybe a week. Even make it a surprise, not let them know I was coming and with a guest to boot. The jubilation on Mom's face when I came through the front door would be the best present I ever gave her—we hadn't seen each other, I hadn't seen Pop or Eddie either, in two years. Mom and Pop would love Liv. And strolling once-familiar streets and the old neighborhood with her, maybe, just maybe, I'd finally shake myself free of the dreams of Delphine, shake off the chains that—

"Just a trim?" the barber asked my reflection in the mirror, his scissors upheld.

"No, buzz it down," I told him. My haircut was reg, but I'd always left enough up top to comb a part. I wasn't sure why, but now I wanted it short, right down to the scalp. I didn't think Barston would mind.

I tipped the barber fifty cents and walked to Connecticut, headed south until I found a second-hand clothing store. My clothes were rumpled and soiled—I couldn't go to the Hill looking like a bum. I bought gray-checked trousers and a white dress shirt; the owner let me change in the back. A block from the Mayflower Hotel, a Negro shoe shine spiffed up my brogans. Then I flagged a hack and was on my way to the Senate Office Building to see a gal named Teresa Herndon.

SHE WAS ONE OF THE FIRST PEOPLE I'D MET IN D.C., AT A DANCE sponsored by the Women's Battalion No. 1. Teresa had come from California to work in the office of Senator Hiram Johnson. May 1942: the Japs had just taken Corregidor and thousands of GIs, and for all the crepe, punch, and music, the social felt like a wake. Couples danced listlessly, clutching each other as if they might collapse, like those marathon dancers from the Roaring Twenties. I'd milled in a corner, rolling an empty punch glass in my hands, thinking an awful lot about the half-bottle of whiskey back in my flat.

"Instead of a band, they oughta just have a fat man with a fiddle," a short brunette said at my side. Tight curls falling to her shoulders, enviable tan, resonant voice.

"Nero," I said.

"Rome's burning, isn't it?"

"Tonight, feels like it."

She thrust her hand out for a hearty shake. "Teresa."

"Ellis."

"Had enough fun yet?"

"You mean it's already started?" I did my best to look mortified. She bought it, for a half-second, then grinned.

We ditched the dance, wandering streets lined with rowhouses until we ended up on the Taft Bridge, looking down at the silver shimmer of Rock Creek. Found a diner on Calvert Street and drank too many cups of coffee, talking easily and freely, somehow avoiding The War. Around two-thirty we both yawned at the same time and broke into laughter. I walked her to her boarding house; we parted without a kiss. Had ourselves a three-week romance, something between a fling and going steady, two new arrivals helping each other settle into the boomtown. Teresa's sense of humor eased the stress of my training at the Funhouse, she loved to go out dancing, she ate like a lumberjack and didn't put on a pound. Yet we ran out of things to talk about, responsibilities piled up on her at the Capitol, the Funhouse kept my hours irregular. When she asked if I wanted to play tennis—she was a girl's state champion runner-up—I knew we were through. No bitterness in the split, call it a drifting away. Think we both sensed The War was leading us down two different paths, hers ending with a husband, house, babies, mine ending just about anywhere but at a hearthstone.

I found Teresa in the front office of Johnson's suite.

"Ellis?" With uncertainty, from behind an ornately carved desk.

The haircut, right—and I was out of uniform. Also, getting beat up by two G-men and taking a tumble with a prossy had probably put a different color on my cheeks.

"Hey, Teresa." Startled by my own voice. The longer I talked like Ted Barston, the more natural his accent became.

"What brings you by?" She wore a crisp white blouse with shiny black buttons and wide cuffs. She'd cut her hair and set the curls to lie tight against her forehead.

"Time for a cup'a joe, maybe a slice of pie?"

She looked down at a stack of carbons. "Hate to be rude, Ellis, but we're awful busy today."

"It's business, won't take long. Scout's honor." I waggled my fore and middle fingers.

"You were never a Boy Scout."

"Yeah, but the Navy's made me clean and reverent."

"Okay, Ellis." Smiling just like that night. "Gimme a minute."

She went into a rear office, returned wearing a wide-brimmed hat and clutching a glossy black purse. We left by the Constitution Avenue doors and went to a diner a half-block away. Teresa shot me a curious look as I steered us past several empty booths up front. No way I was sitting by a window. I made sure I was facing the door. A heavyset waitress ambled over, we ordered coffee and the shortcake.

"O.N.I. got something'a interest coming through Senator Johnson's committee?" Teresa asked, looking relieved when I shook my head.

"What can you tell me about the Senate committee investigating war contracts—the one Truman used to chair?" Call it instinct, call it a hunch—hell, call it a stab in the dark, but the thick books with the black covers in Kudlower's flat weren't run-of-the-mill government publications. The Government Printing Office used cheap beige cardstock to bind reports like the one Kudlower had on the Interior Department's appropriations. I'd seen those black covers once before, when a lawyer from that Senate committee I'd just asked Teresa about had visited the Navy Building.

"What d'you want to know?" She sounded guarded.

"Got this fraud case, might connect to something the committee's investigating." Casual, noncommittal.

"A friend'a mine works in the office of the new chairman, so I've heard a few things. "

"Who's the new chairman?"

"James Mead, of New York."

The cake and coffee came, we stirred sugar into our cups, took a few bites of the cake.

"What kinda staff's this Mead got for his investigations?" I asked.

"Awful small. Wanna say four lawyers and two investigators, something like that." Giving me a quizzical look.

"It's the investigators we might have to call. Know anything about them?"

"One used to be in the F.B.I.; Flanagan, think his name is."

Surprise, surprise.

"And the other guy?" I asked.

"A staffer who used to work for Senator La Follette, of Wisconsin."

"Know his name, too?"

"Kurlander—no, Kudlower, that's it. I've only met him once."

Ditto the surprise. She snuck a look at her watch.

"Just one other thing, Teresa—I was wondering, can you tell me how the committee comes around on an investigation?"

"Oh, that's easy—people come to them. Whistleblowers, unhappy employees, competitors who lost the bid. They probably spend most'a their time going through mailbags and taking calls."

"At some point, Flanagan and this other guy have to go in the field."

"Right. And the lawyers usually go with. Bust in waving subpoenas, followed by movers with boxes to cart out all the records—quite dramatic." She finished her cake, pushed the plate aside.

Time to fish. "But with the war winding down, the committee must not be too busy."

She leaned over the tabletop. "This is a 'Can't remember who' conversation, right?"

"A'course. Matter of fact, if anyone asks, you never saw me."

She nodded absently, as if I was joking. I didn't tell her I was supposed to be in Iceland.

"Right before Roosevelt picked up Truman as his running mate," she told me, "there was lotsa talk on the Hill that Truman had stumbled on something huge."

"Yeah?"

"Missing money—and lots of it."

"How much?"

"Millions, fifty, sixty, maybe more."

"Where'd the trail lead?"

"That's the thing—no one could follow the money all the way. Came through the appropriations bills and hearings, but then just disappeared. Like down a black hole."

"Fifty million dollars and no one can find it?"

"S'what I hear. But you know how the rumor mill works. Probably it was five million that just got some compound interest as the story passed around."

"Mead must not be the bulldog Truman was, to give up looking."

Teresa shook her head.

"So what happened?" I asked.

"Okay, more rumor. The committee sent one of their investigators to New Mexico to dig around—it was their one solid lead."

"He find anything?"

"I don't know. But I haven't heard anything more, and you know if they found the money it'd be front-page news." She glanced at her watch again.

I took the cue. Dropped a dollar bill on the table and walked her back.

"Thanks, Teresa," I said at the Senate Office Building entrance.

"Yeah, sure."

We smiled at one another awkwardly. I pulled open the massive door for her.

Just before she passed through the vestibule, I asked, "Do you know which investigator they sent to New Mexico—the F.B.I. agent, or this Kudlower fella?"

She thought for a moment.

"Kudlower."

CHAPTER 27

I F I WAS LUCKY, I HAD ALL NIGHT BEFORE THE BUREAU'S BLOODHOUNDS picked up my trail, so long as I stayed away from the Jefferson Club, H & H, and Miriam. Beyond that, Slater and Reid hadn't the foggiest about Ted Barston's pals and haunts. The more they looked, the less they'd find—because until Paslett brought him to life, Barston didn't exist in Washington, D.C. For sure, the agents would get suspicious after a while, they'd smell a plant, a hothouse creation. *Black orchids*, one of my Funhouse trainers had called concocted identities like the one I was using. They didn't grow in the wild, you could only produce them in a laboratory. Once the Bureau boys figured out Barston was a cover, it wouldn't take them long to trace ol' Teddy Boy back to Paslett—they already knew O.N.I. was poking around.

Terrance, Liv. I needed to make the most of my free hours to brief my partner and do everything I could to salvage what I had with Liv. If she showed at the Lotus. After the way I'd left her in the lurch at the Little

Palace, I couldn't much blame her if she'd ripped up my telegram. Awful hard to believe I'd sent it just that morning. Ted and I, we'd been through a lot in the last few hours.

I boarded a streetcar headed north, giving Union Station a wide berth. If the Bureau thought Barston was going to take a powder, they'd have men watching the entrances. I had no particular place in mind, just wanted to get out of downtown. At Rhode Island Avenue I hopped off and entered the nearest Peoples Drug Store, went straight to the telephone booths, dropped a nickel for Embassy 3518, and waited to hear "Irving Hotel."

I said, "I'm looking for John Gostling."

"He ain't here. Leave your number."

"Dupont four-one-one-eight."

He hung up, I lit up, cracking the door to let the smoke out. I'd just crushed the butt when the telephone rang. I pushed the door shut and picked up.

I asked, "Should I take the number forty-eight bus from Hoboken?"

"No, you want the number fifty-three from Jersey City," Terrance answered.

Only the two of us knew this question and answer—we'd come up with them before I went under.

"Can you talk?" I asked.

"Are you at the bus station now?" *No.*

"We got problems, we gotta meet pronto."

"Well, that's good, I guess." *Okay, where?*

"Meet me at McMillan Park, the benches in front of the reservoir in an hour. Don't tell Paslett, leave him behind."

"Okay, I'll meet you at the station." *See you there—alone.*

I hung up and lit another cigarette, exhaling with relief as I left the drugstore. The smell of fried onions and sizzling hamburger wafted from the diner next to the drug store. I was as hungry as a junkyard dog, but I didn't have time to eat.

TWO MEN SITTING ON A PARK BENCH WOULD DRAW ATTENTION, SO WE got in the car—the beat-up Chrysler we always got stuck with—and went for a ride, Terrance driving. He pointed us southwest on Rhode Island.

"Nice haircut," my partner said, pushing the dashboard lighter in.

"Thanks. Was Barston's idea."

"What's our problem?"

"The Bureau. Two'a their boys hauled me in for a chit-chat this afternoon."

He looked over sharply. "They were following you?"

"No—they were watching the guy I was making a delivery to, followed me out."

Terrance didn't say anything. The lighter popped, he pressed the glowing coil to his cigarette. I lit up, too. No easy way for him to ask *Did your cover hold?*, so he was waiting for me to tell him, in whatever way I decided.

"This delivery," I went on, "guy's name is Kudlower but he's going by Kovacevic. Strictly amateur. Used his own flat, taped the alias to his mail slot. Had an envelope for me to take back to my boss, Himmel."

"Aw, shit."

"Don't worry, I memorized the note inside—you can write it down to take back to Paslett."

"But now the Bureau's got a piece of our evidence."

"S'alright, they got no idea what they got. But now they know how H & H is collecting, and the only reason I can be here is because they put a pup on my tail after they cut me loose and I shook him easy. By the time they find me next, pros'll be on the beat."

A nod, an exhale of smoke. This was our last meeting while I was under, we had to make it count. I took a long drag of my cigarette.

Terrance asked, "So what angles are they working, the Bureau?"

"All right. They've been on to H & H for a while, we know that—hell, if the old man hadn't gotten ahold of the Bureau's report on clipping services, we never would'a found 'em. But if John Edgar thought Himmel was using his delivery man as a courier, I would'a been followed from day one."

"Instead they were watching Silva."

"But not Nagel, that scientist I got the first envelope from. So they must not know about him."

"So why Silva? And how'd they find this Kudlower?"

"Silva, I don't know yet. Kudlower, I know how. After I shook my tail, I went to see a friend a'mine on the Hill."

"Jesus H. Christ, Ellis, you're s'posed to be in Iceland!"

"Don't worry, she's not gonna tell anyone she saw me."

"A woman who won't talk? You gotta be—"

"I asked her about the Senate committee that investigates war fraud," I cut in, "the one Truman used to chair. This Kudlower, he's got a mile-high stack'a appropriation hearing reports and who knows what else in his flat, but they're not G.P.O.-issue, he's got 'em in these fancy black leatherette covers. Remember seeing those?"

He nodded. We'd both been interviewed by that lawyer from the committee during his visit to the Navy Building.

"So what I found out is, Kudlower's one of the committee's two field investigators. And the other guy, name of Flanagan, guess who he used to work for?"

"Sonofabitch—the Bureau."

"Bingo. I don't know if this Flanagan got put on the committee's staff because they already suspected Kudlower or he just got suspicious the more he worked with him, but however it happened, the Bureau's on to Kudlower. And Kudlower's dirty—he's telling the Reds how much money is being spent at that base in New Mexico."

Terrance whistled lowly. "How much?"

"Over thirty mil, if I figured right. Pull over, I'll give you what I got."

Terrance steered to the curb. We were on Sixteenth, alongside Meridian Hill Park. Its steep rock walls loomed over the sidewalk, the street lamps pooled dim yellow light on the uneven slabs. No one around—it was a long, steep trek for several blocks here, no shops or diners, nothing. My partner flicked on the dome light and pulled out his notebook.

"Okay, first thing in the envelope was a brief note." I recited the message verbatim, Terrance copied every word.

"Any unusual markings?" he asked.

"Nope. Second thing was a postcard." I described it, going slowly, closing my eyes, picturing the postcard in my mind, just as I'd been taught at the Funhouse. *Your memory's better than you think*, the training officer had drilled into us. Terrance scribbled furiously, peppering me with questions after I finished. The denomination of the stamp, its image, the cancellation marking—was it straight or off-center? A good question, that—the P.O.

rarely rolled a neat postmark across a piece of mail. Thanks to Terrance, I remembered the cancellation was straight.

"Dollars to donuts, it's a forgery," he commented.

"Oh yeah. Okay, so here's what it said." Again, I recited the postcard's text, noting the punctuation and describing the handwriting style, how the writer looped his l's and crossed his t's. My partner hit me with more questions. Any hesitation marks, did the card look handled or new?

"Anything else you can remember?" he finished.

I closed my eyes one more time, turned the card over and over in my mind—nothing new. I shook my head and lit a much-needed cigarette. I resisted checking my watch. *It takes as long as it takes*, I told myself. If this briefing went past eight, I just had to hope Liv was patient. If she showed.

"All right," Terrance said, starting the car and easing back into traffic. "Tell me how you came up with thirty mil outta this."

I told him how the name of the ranch, the Five-Five, had struck me as odd, and how Himmel had wanted to know how many dollar signs the writer had used.

"If you use those dollar signs as zeros after five to the fifth power," I continued, "you get thirty-one million, two hundred and fifty thousand dollars."

"Yeah, maybe." Dubious.

"You don't think so?"

"Hell, I don't know, Ellis—these kinda ciphers ain't exactly our cup'a tea."

True enough.

"M'sure Paslett's got some pencil-and-slide-rule boys he can put on it."

"Sure, sure. So when you told Himmel about the card, how much detail did you give him?"

"Christ, Terrance, as little as I could! But I had to give him something, so it didn't look like I was holding back." Terrance had only worked a cover a couple of times, and years ago at that—he'd forgotten about all the challenges, about how you were constantly balancing the investigation against your false front.

"Okay, okay, don't get hot, m'just asking is all."

Last thing I needed was a go-around with my partner, so I asked, "What'd you and the commander dig up on that egghead scientist?"

Terrance nodded, taking a long draw on his cigarette before briefing me. Taylor Nagel was forty-six, born in Chillicothe, Ohio. A.E.F. during the Great War, Ohio State University afterward, 1924 B.S., electrical engineering. First job, Precision Instruments of Newark, New Jersey. Came to D.C. in 1930 to the National Bureau of Standards. An expert on the measurement of radium, co-wrote the 1931 X-ray safety code. Now hush-hush work on radiological measurement and standards. Wife Claire, three kids, house in Friendship Heights, in Northwest D.C.

"Has he been to New Mexico?" I asked.

"Not that we could tell."

"What about that special passenger the Bermuda Special brought back?"

"Paslett did a little more digging, called in some favors. This has gotta stay way under your hat, Ellis, this is—"

"Terrance, c'mon!"

"Yeah, sorry—being around the old man all the time, it's got me spooked, you know? Every time he talks to me, he swears me to secrecy, like I just got outta training."

"So whatta we know?"

He exhaled audibly. "Our friend is Gerhard Trechten, some German physicist. Nazi party member, college professor, internationally known, all'a that. According to O.S.S., Trechten was last spotted working outta an underground lab or factory the Krauts got in the Harz Mountains."

"What's so special about this Trechten?" I didn't ask how Paslett got an O.S.S. report—I didn't want to know.

"Ever hear of 'uranium'?"

I shook my head.

"Me neither. But when Paslett found out this Trechten's some sorta specialist in uranium, I tell you, Ellis, he looked like a ghost: the blood just drained right outta his face."

"Is it a weapon, uranium, why is—"

"I got no idea, Ellis—I don't know uranium from Uranus. All I can tell you is that Paslett is shitting bricks thinking about how Skerrill was aboard the Bermuda Special with this Trechten."

"Did he go to New Mexico for sure, this Trechten?"

Terrance nodded grimly. "Yeah, we confirmed that. But what he's doing, what's going on down there, beats me. And if Paslett knows anything more, he ain't saying."

I thought for a moment. Say Skerrill got the dope on Trechten, maybe even talked to him aboard the ship. He tells all to Himmel, who rousts his spies, orders them to give him everything they got on what's happening down in New Mexico. So Nagel delivers, Kudlower delivers—Skerrill continues to give what he can until he gets killed. Who else did Himmel have on the string, who else was going to make a delivery to him? And would I be the one to courier it?

"You'll check out this Kudlower next?" I asked.

He nodded. "What're you gonna do?"

"I think Himmel's still got some deliveries to collect, so I gotta make sure I'm the one who collects."

"What're you gonna do about the Bureau?"

"I'll have to shake 'em. Himmel, he knows I got a tail now, he told me to step light—I take that as a sign he's counting on me to figure it out."

"Seems to trust you an awful lot."

Something off in his tone? And why that phrase? *An awful lot.* I shook off the suspicion. Staying under like this, longer than I'd ever done cover work before, was giving me the jitters.

"Yeah, this Barston cover's working great," I said.

"So what about Skerrill—got any leads on who killed him?"

"Maybe." I told him about my toss of Silva's flat, about the letter I'd found hinting at two-timing. And I finally told him what Miriam had told me the night I took her to the Italian restaurant: Silva and Skerrill had been lovers.

"So the jealous hubbie of Skerrill's other gal knocks him off? I don't know. . . ." His voice trailed off.

"If Skerrill picked the wrong broad and she's got a hubbie with a temper, it's a possibility. I bet if we ask Durkin"—the city detective sergeant we'd taken the case from—"he'd tell us half the homicides in D.C. come outta marriages gone bad."

"Do you know who Skerrill had on the side?" Still doubtful.

"No," I admitted. "But the gal I'm banging, H & H's receptionist, she's a gossip. Called in sick today, but I'll pump her tomorrow."

"I guess Himmel's got no reason to bump off Skerrill, not with what he was giving him."

"Right! That's what's been nagging me ever since I went under—why would any'a the Reds wanna kill Skerrill? He was their goddamned golden goose."

"Well, here's hoping that roundheel knows something." Translation: you don't have a lot of time to wrap this up, partner, not with the Bureau breathing down your neck.

"She hasn't let me down yet."

Terrance saw me glance at my watch. Ten after eight.

"Where you want me to drop you off?" he asked. We were on Connecticut now, headed north.

"Right here's good."

"What're you gonna do the rest of the night?"

"First thing, eat a horse—I'm starving. Then I'm gonna get some rack time. Haven't had a decent night's sleep in I don't know how long."

He nodded absently, watching traffic in the passenger's side mirror, pulled to the curb. "Need anything?"

"Yeah, money—d'you bring any?"

"Yeah." He reached into his inside jacket pocket and handed over a rubber-banded roll.

"How much?"

"Two yards." A crooked grin. "Don't spend it all in one place."

"Why not? S'my last night without a chaperone."

A brief laugh. Then a straight-on look at me. "Watch your back, partner."

"Always." I got out, shut the door, leaned in through the open window. "I get any more deliveries, I'll call the Irving Park line, tell you what I can. Same if I come up with who did Skerrill."

"Yep." And with that, he merged and continued north on Connecticut.

As soon as the Chrysler's taillights were out of sight, I stuck out my arm and flagged a hack. I handed a fiver over the bench before I'd even shut the door.

"Lotus Club, pronto."

"You got it, pal."

CHAPTER 28

THE HACK PULLED UP HARD IN FRONT OF THE LOTUS—THE RIDE HAD only taken five minutes. Quarter after eight, either Liv was here or she wasn't. I paid the cover, hustled past the fountain with the fake flower, surveyed the ballroom. Liv wasn't one to sit at a bar with a drink, she'd charm her way into a tucked-away spot and an extra candle and open a book and lose herself in the world of those pages, oblivious to the sharks eying her, circling close to ask—

"Got time for a supplicant?" I asked, trying to hide my excitement at finding her. Sitting in a clamshell booth by herself, a ginger ale and book her only company.

"I don't know, what's he supplicating?" Looking over the top of *Ulysses*.

"Not the usual."

"What's the usual?"

"Forgiveness."

"Instead?"

"The future."

"Because . . . ?"

"Because 'how will you be' is more important than how you've been. Or, in this supplicant's case, what he did." *How will you be?* Liv's quirky greeting. Being Ted Barston was giving me a new appreciation for it.

She set the book down. First time *Ulysses* had crossed the Lotus's threshold, for sure. "Some people might say that's, I don't know—"

"A cop-out?"

Tick of her head.

"But we're not some people, are we, Liv?"

A long laugh.

I relaxed a little, eased into the booth. "I had a reason for what happened, you know, that night, but it's no excuse—"

"El, you don't have to explain," Liv interrupted gently. "The future, right?"

I nodded, relieved. Forgetting the past—hell, forgetting just the day up to that moment sounded like an awful good idea. In the last twenty-four hours, I'd gotten drunk twice, beaten a man within an inch of his life, abandoned a girl who thought I was her guy, got roughed up by the F.B.I., and screwed a whore. But then, I hadn't done any of those deeds—Ted Barston had.

A girl in a brocaded tunic glided up, I ordered a Tom Collins, another ginger. I lit up, grinning like an idiot schoolboy at Liv.

Who asked, "What happened to your hair?" Smiling back.

"Lost a bet."

"Makes you look different."

"Better?"

"No."

"It'll grow back."

"So, El."

"Liv."

"How will you be?"

"Happy. Warm. Content."

"Yeah? How?"

"Not how, where."

"So where's happiness, warmth, and contentment?"

"Far from here," I said.

"Far from here's not a where."

"Way west, how's that?"

"How way west?"

"Depends."

"On?"

"How far you want to go, Liv."

Our drinks came. She took a sip, her gaze on me. Always so expressive, her eyes, now inscrutable. "Not 'go,' El," she finally said.

"No?"

"Plunge."

"It's a deep ocean, the Pacific," I said. Voice even, steady, my eyes fixed on hers.

"You sure, El?"

"Haven't dived to the bottom, if that's what you're asking."

Faintest of smiles, sip of her soda. "It's not a dive, either, El. A plunge."

"Plunge, got it."

She watched me closely for a moment. Then parted her lips to speak. *Do you?* I thought she was about to ask. Instead:

"Dance?" she asked.

"Sure." I forced a smile and took a long drink of my Tom Collins. Had I pushed too hard, too soon? But hadn't she asked me to come visit when she told me about her plan to move to the South Pacific after the war? And she'd told me I needed to get out of the Navy. What else could that be but an invitation to go with her?

I pushed these questions out of my mind as we took the floor. Liv had come, she was happy to see me, we were having a good time. *Just enjoy the moment*, I told myself. A prisoner of Barston, I shouldn't even be out as Ellis Voigt—Paslett would keel-haul me if he found out—so I had to remind myself how fortunate I was just to have an evening with Liv.

Dexter Pierce and the boys were hot, ripping through "Hindustan," "Hell's Bells," and a Woody Herman number. We'd broken a sweat by the time they slowed it down for "I'll Be Around," sung slow by a slender chanteuse in an ecru sheath of a dress decorated with glinting sequins.

Couldn't have weighed more than ninety-eight pounds soaking wet, but did she have pipes, a voice like scotch on half-melted ice. Liv wore a dark blue knee-length skirt and a black V-neck blouse with banded half-sleeves. No stockings, legs bare—wasn't anything to like about rationing except the ban on nylon. We laced our hands together and I wrapped my left arm around her waist, slow-stepping like two kids at dance class. Too bad my stomach chose that moment to rumble, testily reminding me I hadn't eaten since lunch.

"Can I buy this gal dinner?" I murmured in Liv's ear, her face pressed to my chest.

"Mm-hmm."

The two hundred dollars Terrance had given me was burning a hole in my pocket. It was supposed to tide Ted Barston over for the rest of the investigation, but a vision of a T-bone on a platter surrounded by mounds of mashed potatoes told me otherwise. Plenty of restaurants close by. Olmsted's on G, Alfonso's on L; the Casino Royal was a stone's throw away.

The song ended, we gently parted, still holding hands. I led Liv back to our booth to collect her scarf and library book. The band started up, a foot-tapping, jazzy number I didn't recognize, then the musicians abruptly stopped, the clarinetist cutting off a high note. From the bar, whooping and whistling. *A fight*, I thought. *Good thing we're leaving.* But I was way off.

Our cocktail server rushed over, her face flushed. "Did you hear?" she asked.

Another burst of shouts from the bar drowned out my "Hear what?"

"The Krauts surrendered!" she yelled over the noise. "The war's over in Europe!"

Liv squealed with delight and squeezed my hand tighter.

"Jesus Christ, for real?" I asked.

The server bobbed her head excitedly. "Now all we gotta do is finish off the Japs!" She darted away to spread the news.

A hush fell over the ballroom as a bartender shot through the swinging service doors, a Motorola portable clutched above his head like a trophy. The news was on, but we were too far away to hear. No matter—whatever the broadcast said launched a raucous round of cheering and whistling.

Dexter Pierce lifted his baton, the boys jumped into a Latin number. A conga line formed on the floor, people rushing from the bar and booths to join it.

"I can't believe it," I said to Liv.

"I knew we were close, but still," she said, awe in her voice. "Know what this means?" She pulled herself close, breath hot in my ear, hand gripping my bicep. My mouth went dry.

"What?"

"Soon as we beat the Japs, I can go to the Pacific."

I can go to the Pacific. Not *we*, not *you and I.* Dammit, I had pushed too hard. Or was Liv just testing me? Maybe I was reading too much into her words, maybe she was just waiting to hear me say, *Yes, I'm ready to take the plunge.*

"About that, Liv—"

But she didn't hear the rest of what I said. More cheering from the dance floor as two of the Lotus's girls wheeled in a cart laden with champagne bottles in ice buckets, followed by girls carrying trays of glass saucers. The conga line effortlessly bypassed them.

"Champagne! El, can we have some?" Liv spun around, her smile like a sunset, orange and rose-tinged and fleeting, her black curls bouncing against her forehead, a faint sheen visible in the "V" of her blouse, bracelet dangling from her wrist, fingers laced with mine as the crowd cheered the first bottle's pop, a cascade of bubbles dousing bystanders, Dexter Pierce and his boys now raising the roof with a bebop take on "Stars and Stripes Forever," the trumpeter blowing so hard it looked like he was about to flutter off the stage—if I ever forget everything and everyone I've ever seen and known, Jesus, let me keep that scene, that moment, that heat, that ache for the taste of the champagne we never got on the night of May 8, 1945.

Because just as I was about to shout "yes, yes, yes" to Liv, I spotted Boy G-man across the ballroom, hat in hand, looking around frantically, trying to push his way through an impenetrable crowd blocking the dance floor like the Great Wall of China.

CHAPTER 29

T HE TELEGRAM! I SHOULD'VE KNOWN THAT SLATER AND REID WOULD relentlessly track my steps—that's why they'd kept the H & H manifest. After letting me go, they had visited all the clients I made deliveries to and had questioned them, searching for another spy. At every stop, they had surveyed the block, looking for places a courier for a Red spy ring might visit. Diners, druggists, taverns—and Western Union. Of course a photograph had been taken of me from behind the one-way glass while I was being interrogated; a technician had probably developed and printed it before Slater and Reid had worked me over. *Sir . . . ma'am, have you seen this man today? You have? What did he do. . . .*

The idiot sent a telegram to his girlfriend while he was undercover, that's what he did. How could I be so stupid, so reckless? Now Slater and Reid had Liv's name and knew where she lived—for sure they'd gone to her rooming house. Where one of her gabby housemates immediately told them Liv was off to the Lotus Club to meet her beau. Had I ever sent her a letter, had she written my name down in her address book, had they searched her room yet, were they waiting on a warrant? But I had no time to think about the other mistakes I might have made, because if I didn't get Liv and myself out of the Lotus pronto, my goose was cooked but good.

"Liv, Liv, I've got to—I've got a better idea," I shouted, tugging her hand. She looked up, perplexed.

I pasted on a smile and said, "Live free, right?"

Thank God—she finished the mantra for me: "And the rest will follow."

"So follow me." I checked the urge to look in Boy G-man's direction or at the bar, where Slater and Reid were likely scanning the patrons' faces. No way Boy G-man was sent solo, not after losing me earlier. My only hope was that Slater and Reid hadn't put a man on the club's rear exit, that they'd expected to surprise us inside the club. Maybe later—say, in a half-century—I'd marvel at my good fortune. War ends, celebration throws off my shadows.

Liv's hand clutched, I took us to the back of the club, steering us around neckers, the tail of the conga line, and men and women queued up at the telephone booths, jabbering away as they waited their turn to call loved ones. I popped open the service doors with my free hand and hustled us through. Except for a teenager in a stained apron, the dishwasher I guessed, the area was deserted.

"Go get some champagne, kid," I shouted.

He didn't need any more encouragement. Stripped off his apron, shot out the swinging doors. I looked around hurriedly, hoping I'd guessed right. The girls had wheeled out the champagne from here, the bottles must have been stored in a cellar or locker, would the girls have thought to lock it? They hadn't—the windowless door on a narrow room racked with wine and spirit bottles was wide open. I let go of Liv's hand, darted into the dark room, grabbed a dusty wine bottle. I pulled out my roll and peeled off a ten-spot, dropped it where the bottle had lain.

What gives? Liv's expression asked.

"Forget the Lotus and its conga, we're gonna celebrate in the street." I tried to turn my panic into enthusiasm. "We're gonna toast our way down Fourteenth to the Mall, straight to the top of the Washington Monument if we want!"

"Oh, there's gotta be so many people outside by now!"

"Damn straight, let's spill on out." I pointed to the exit.

We ran out, Liv first. I grabbed a wine key off a counter and pushed the door firmly shut. When Slater, Reid, and Boy G-man finally worked their way to the back, they'd find nothing but a dirty dishwasher's apron to ask if a young couple had come this way.

I led us down the alley. I thought we might need to keep to it for a few blocks, in case the Bureau had spotters outside the Lotus, but as soon as I saw the crowd on Fourteenth Street, I knew we were free. Street and sidewalks packed, joyous Washingtonians chattering, hugging, kissing, clapping each other on the shoulders. We weren't the only ones who'd thought to bring booze—whiskey, beer, and bubbly were being passed from one hand to another. All traffic halted, no one caring, a chorus of horns adding to the cheering, passengers and drivers getting out to join the party. A streetcar, beached like a shipwreck, was empty save for its operator, who leaned out his window, talking happily with the crowd.

"What'd you buy us to drink?" Liv asked with an impish smile.

I wiped dust from the label and read haltingly. "Vosne-Romanée, Les Chaumes, Nineteen twenty-eight."

"That a good year?"

"Let's find out." I pulled the cork, with difficulty—it started to crumble as it came out, but eventually I worked it out and tossed it high over the crowd.

"You forgot glasses," Liv said, teasing.

"Where are my manners?" I took a draught and passed the bottle to a giggling Liv. I'd worried I'd grabbed a dud, the wine was so old, but it was awful good, the best wine I'd ever had, with hints of fruits and a spice I couldn't quite identify—

"D'you taste nutmeg, El?" Liv asked, handing the bottle back.

"That's it!"

We flowed with the crowd, south on Fourteenth, to F Street. Garfinckel and Co. had turned on all their lights, even though the department store was closed. Through the revolving door we glimpsed the cleaning crew leaning on their mops, grinning, waving. A stockboy was dancing with a store dummy in one of the display windows, spinning her around until her arm fell off, much to the crowd's delight.

"Let's go to the White House, see if Truman comes out!" Liv shouted.

"You got it!"

Still holding hands so we didn't get separated, we moved down F Street, sharing the bottle with one another, passing it to anyone who looked in need of a drink. By the time we reached the Treasury Department grounds, just east of the White House, the wine was gone. Snippets of excited chatter floated past, like leaves stirred by an autumn breeze. *Six weeks tops for the Japs, you wait and . . . No way Hitler's dead—betcha anything the Russkies got 'im, they're just . . . Yeah, but do I want him to come home that soon* (burst of laughter) *. . . Y'all gotta be kidding, it's the federal guv'ment, they're a'gonna keep . . .* We headed for the rear lawn of the White House—if Truman was going to make an appearance, it would be on the balcony of the residential quarters. As if to match the gesture of Garfinckel and Co., the spotlights on the grounds had been turned on, bathing the White House in brilliant light. "We want Harry, we want Harry," we chanted with the crowd, but the new president didn't step out.

"Ready for that dinner I promised?" I shouted to Liv.

"Who's gonna be serving tonight?"

"I know a place."

That place being the Willard Hotel, just two blocks away. Its twelve or so stories loomed over Fourteenth Street, the Stars and Stripes snapping from a flagpole atop a turret. Mansard roof layered like a wedding cake, the lobby a tribute to Versailles or the Winter Palace.

"Here?" Liv asked, incredulous.

"S'our lucky day, Liv, I came into a windfall."

"You sure?"

"Yeah, I counted it twice."

"Funny guy. You know what I mean." Looking at me searchingly. Didn't I know I couldn't impress her with a fat roll and a fancy dinner?

"S'what I want, Liv."

So we strode in past the marble columns and underneath the glittering chandeliers to the stately restaurant, where I greased a dour maître d' ten bucks to convince him that I *had* a jacket, but an over-exuberant passerby had sprayed it with champagne just before we arrived, and he didn't want me to ruin their fine upholstery by wearing it in the dining room, did he?

More silver on our table than in my mother's wedding set, menus bound in Moroccan leather, a head waiter trailing acolytes: assistant waiter, wine steward, bus boy, crumb collector, candle lighter. An orchid unfurling from a crystal vase, napkins rolled in gold rings.

"I've never been in a place like this, have you?" Liv whispered. Except for an elderly couple bent over soup tureens, not talking as they ate, the restaurant was deserted.

"Nope. S'why we should have the Maine lobster, don't you think?"

"For real?"

"I've never had lobster, have you?"

Shook her head. And order the lobster we did. The pleasure, the joy, the delight that animated Liv's face as she took her first bite, golden and shiny with drawn butter—that alone was worth the cost of our entrees, and the bisque, and the Waldorf salad, and the Chateau Montrechet the wine steward recommended. Were we using the right fork, did we keep our napkins folded properly? Neither of us cared, happily lost in a conversation about books and plays and music. No talk of work, or friends, or even of the war. By the time we'd finished our coffee, and our discussion of a play Liv had volunteered to be a stagehand for, it was well past ten, the elderly couple was long gone, and the head waiter was gliding around the edges of the dining room, like a cutter on maneuvers, glancing at us constantly. I signaled him over, paid the bill, took Liv by the arm. We strolled into the lobby. V-E celebrants still flowed down the streets, but the crowds had thinned. The war in the Pacific was still being fought, tomorrow was another workday, like any other.

"El?"

"Liv."

"Take me home."

"We are home."

Her head came off my shoulder, eyes wide. "What, no—El, you can't, we can't . . . the dinner, that lobster, that was—"

"Liv, please listen to me." Looking her straight in the eye now. "I've been on this assignment, it's a mess, it's a snafu, it's consuming me. I've given up everything, even my flat, and I don't know when or how it's gonna end. But I do know this—I'm free tonight, I'm free till the morning, and when I knew I'd have this night, all I could think about was how I wanted to spend it with you. I didn't know the war was gonna end, but it did, and that's gotta be some kinda sign, that I'm with you, so please, stay here with me." I meant every word, down to my marrow, and for once wasn't every word I'd uttered true?

"Okay, El," she whispered.

I went over to the front desk and told the clerk I wanted a room.

"No luggage, sir?" With a raised eyebrow.

A fiver lowered it. One night in the Willard cost more than I made in a month, but it wasn't my dough, was it? I counted out the bills, he whisked them off the polished counter, unhooked a key from an ornately carved mahogany rack. The bellhop took us up, not knowing what to do with his gloved hands without bags to carry. I still tipped him fifty cents.

We wandered through the suite, as awestruck as two kids ogling Woodie's Christmas window displays. Liv oohed the velvet divan and walk-in closet with sliding pocket doors, I aahed the veneered bar with a glass martini pitcher and silver ice bucket. Oil paintings of landscapes on the wall, fabric wallpaper, Persian rugs. Polished desk with blotter, embossed stationery, Mont Blanc pen set. Chandelier with adjustable lighting, Art Deco sconces on the wall. Leather-bound room service menu, two Bakelite telephones. Liv plumped down on the divan and kicked off her pumps, I checked out the bathroom. Marble walls and a vanity mirror with lights, like in a diva's dressing room. Two sinks, upholstered chairs, soft thick towels stacked high on a padded footstool.

"Liv, c'mere and look at this tub—there's room for four people in it, easy, and there's a radio built into the wall."

No answer.

I turned around, starting, "Liv, you gotta—"

Didn't finish. She was standing in the doorway, striking a pose. Hands on her hips, elbows out, left leg straight, right leg slightly bent, toes forward. Chin turned slightly, to offer her face in profile, black curls brushing slender shoulders. Naked except for powder-blue lace panties and a matching brassiere. The chandelier bathed her in soft light, brought a golden hue to her smooth legs. A silver chain necklace nestled between her breasts, pale rose nipples visible through gauzy lace.

She said, "The closet looked pretty bare, so I thought I oughta hang up my clothes."

"Good idea," I said. But my clothes didn't make it to the closet.

AFTERWARD, WE DREW A BATH, LOUNGING IN PLUSH ROBES WE'D found in the bathroom closet, watching the bubbles mound, the steam rise. Liv stood first and let the robe drop to the tiles, her alabaster skin still damp from our lovemaking. She lowered herself into the water, arms outstretched and back erect, until the bubbles covered her breasts. I followed her in. A bath had never felt so good. Just like the shave I'd had earlier, the water, almost too hot to bear, leached away the dirt, the filth, that being Ted Barston left on me.

For a long, exquisite moment, neither of us spoke. Mute, sated, happy, we had no need of words. Being in that bath was like being free of the past and the future, adrift in an independent present that if you're lucky—no, careful—might never run out.

"S'nice, isn't it, El," Liv murmured eventually. Head on my chest, knees poking through the suds, hand resting on the tub's coping.

"Yes." All the words the English language has, and that was the only one that fit, right then. *Yes.* I started to drift off, a stir of water from Liv's toes brought me back.

I said, "Liv, about what we talked about at the club, about you going to the Pacific."

"Oh, El, let's not—"

"No, it's all right, I'm not going to say what you think."

No reply.

"What you said," I continued cautiously, "about taking the plunge—I get it, I really do."

"Are you sure, El?" She slid up and effortlessly turned, crossing her legs as she faced me. Her hair lay wet against her neck, rivulets traced her collarbone and chest.

"Yes," I answered, and left it at that. *Yes, I get that you're not going to plan your move, you're not going to pick a date and book a ticket, or even pick a place.*

One day, you're going to take the plunge, head west to San Francisco or Los Angeles, maybe Hawai'i—wherever will get you where you want to be. And if I'm going to go with you, I have to plunge, too.

"All right, El." She reached for my hands, squeezed them.

"But Liv, there's something I gotta tell you now. It's not about the Pacific, something else." I thought about how much I'd risked to even be here with her. And I thought about the morning at my flat, when I'd told her about Delphine. How much could one more revelation hurt me? The wrong way to think about it, I realized. *Could that revelation help me?* Exposure a huge risk, strictly verboten—"layaway suicide," a Funhouse trainer had called it, trusting an outsider. The first payment, the first "tell no one," comes hard and slow, you'll resist, but then when nothing bad happens right away, the second, third, fourth payments come fast and easy. "If you can't keep your mouth shut, get out of intelligence work before someone shuts it for you," our trainer had said ominously. We'd all nodded obediently, but none of us—not me, not Logan Skerrill, not one of the other handpicked recruits—had believed we'd ever have trouble keeping mum. We were the best of the best, right, eager to be spies in our nation's service, itching for skulduggery, braced for adventure. Maybe that's why my lips had loosened, my discipline had slackened—I wanted out. I wanted to live free, like Liv had been telling me since the night we met. *Just tell her, take the plunge, see how it all—*

"This something else, could you call it a secret?" Liv asked quietly.

"Yes."

She turned her hands, so that both our wrists faced up. "What color is blood, El?"

"Red."

"Uh-uh. Blue." She dipped her chin at the veins visible under our wet skin.

"Only till you bleed."

"But if you never get cut, your blood stays blue."

"Awful hard, going through life never getting cut."

"Oh, I know—believe me, I know. But keeping our secrets blue, that's something we can all do, if we really want."

CHAPTER 30

S O I DIDN'T TELL LIV MY SECRET, I KEPT IT BLUE, JUST LIKE SHE'D said. Sounded silly, her advice, a folk saying that smart people would make fun of. But I already knew enough smart folks—Liv was the only wise one I knew.

At seven the next morning, I left her sleeping peacefully in the Willard's king-size bed, her hair mussed gently on a plump pillow. I hadn't told her the F.B.I. would soon question her about one Ted Barston. If I warned her, Slater and Reid would see it in her face the instant she answered the door, no matter how much she tried to act like she had no idea why they were there. As for her reaction when they showed her a photograph of me as Ted Barston, I just had to trust that Liv would immediately make the connection between the secret she thought I'd wanted to tell her and the reason the F.B.I. wanted to talk to her. She was quick-witted and unimpressed by authority—she wouldn't flinch when she saw my picture. Or so I hoped. If she did crack, if she blurted out *But that's El!*, I might, just might, still have enough time to finish my work before Slater and Reid traced what Liv told them back to me. But only if I got busy early, and a little luck came my way.

I walked to a diner and filled up on coffee, eggs, bacon, and hash browns as I read all about the Germans' surrender. I was lucky to get a paper, copies were selling so fast—early birds were slapping nickels down on the newsstand counter like rubes at a ring toss. A sea of ink had been spilled for the four-inch headline: *Krauts Call It Quits; Japs Fight On.* The copy itself was predictable, packed with quotes from high hats and brass, the usual suspects from Congress, the man on the street. Easy to miss on page six was a two-column story about the Japs' 32nd Army's counteroffensive on Okinawa. It had failed, Buckner's Tenth Army was preparing to punch back, heavy casualties expected. The V-E celebration was going to end unhappily in a lot of marines' and GIs' homes when the Western Union boy came knocking.

I didn't spend much time wondering how the German surrender would affect the hush-hush weapons program in New Mexico. General Groves wouldn't let up, not one second. If anything, he'd put the eggheads on double-time. Whatever was being built in the desert, the Pentagon wanted it ready before the Japs called it quits. To test it, justify the cost, let the world know what Uncle Sam had—however you cut it, we weren't spending millions of dollars for something to go on the shelf. Which meant the Russians had to be getting antsy, too, pushing Himmel to wrap up his operation.

Paid my tab, left a big tip. Only twenty-two dollars remained of the two hundred Terrance had given me, but that didn't worry me. If all went well, I wasn't going to be Ted Barston much longer. I considered coming into H & H through the alley but after losing me twice, the Bureau would have men watching every approach. *What the hell,* I thought. The day he'd arrived, Barston had strutted in like a rooster, he might as well go in like one on his last day.

About a block from H & H, I saw Miriam on the northwest corner of Fourteenth and I, sitting on a bench, slump-shouldered, her head bent. A hat concealed her face, her purse was slung over her shoulder. Silva must have canned her. No way I could talk to Miriam without the boys from the Bureau seeing me, but that was okay. Franklin Square, a park, was directly across the street, we could talk there unheard.

"Hey, kiddo, whattya doing out here?" I called out.

"Oh Ted, oh, I'm so glad you're here, everything that's happening, I—" A bout of blubbering prevented her from finishing. She was a wreck, a god-awful mess. Mascara running, face puffy, eyes red. I'd expected that—but not the bruises. One below her left eye, another on her right forearm. It looked like someone had wrenched her arm, leaving a purple-blue grip on her pale, soft skin. *Goddamned Kenny*, I thought. He couldn't find me to avenge what I'd done to his boy Wade, so he'd taken it out on his foster sister instead.

"Hey, what happened?" Laying on concern.

"Nadine fired me!"

"Just now?" Trying to sound surprised.

"Soon as I walked in the door! Teddy, I tried to come in yesterday, but I couldn't, I just couldn't, so I called in sick—and I was, I really was, and I was so worried about you and—"

A bus pulled to the curb, drowning her out. A gaggle of late-arriving office workers dashed out the door, rushing past us to get to their desks by nine.

"C'mon, kiddo, let's go across ta da park and siddown, hey?" I reached for a hand, helped her to her feet.

"Teddy, I'm so happy you saw me!" she exclaimed as we crossed Four-teenth. "I was about to get on that bus, and I didn't think I'd ever see you again."

"Hey, you been on my mind all morning." I steered us toward a bench beneath an elm, where I could see anyone approaching. "Now, what's dis 'bout Silva giving you da heave-ho?"

"Teddy, she found out I told you about her boyfriend."

"What?" Trying to sound confused, not alarmed.

"'Member how I told you about her boyfriend, the one who got shot near the Navy Yard?"

"Yeah, I guess so."

"And she didn't even go to his funeral, 'member that?"

"Yeah, yeah, but what's dat gotta do with her canning you?"

"She says I'm a gossip, Teddy! That I tell stories and cause problems. But I don't do that, do I? You're the only one I told that story to."

Silva hadn't fired her for being a gabber, but I couldn't tell her the real reason. Silva was on to me, her suspicions had grown, somehow she'd figured out I was pumping Miriam for information. Instead:

"Aw, kiddo, she didn't can you because you like ta talk—dat's bull, and she knows it. Naw, she's just jealous, s'all, 'cause you got friends, you got a steady, you got a plan, yer going ta beauty school. What's she got? Nuttin'!"

"Thank you, Teddy. I just knew there had to be some other reason. See, everybody knows Norman's the gossip—he's the one who told me about Silva's boyfriend getting killed, 'member how I told you it was Norman who told me?"

"Sure I do," I said, holding back a sigh of relief that Miriam hadn't as yet wondered why Silva would accuse her of gossip if I was the only person at H & H Miriam had talked to. She wasn't the brightest penny, Miriam—and what did it make me for exploiting her sweet dumb trust of Barston as much as I could?

"And he's the one who told everybody about how her boyfriend was having an affair, not me."

"He said what?" Trying not to sound interested.

"He eavesdropped on her talking to Mister Himmel one day, Teddy, and then went around and told everybody in the office—everybody!—that her boyfriend was cheating on her and she'd gone in to tell Mister Himmel all about it."

"Yeah, he's da one with da motormouth, not you, kiddo." And how lucky for me that Norman liked to pry, liked to gossip, liked to cause disruptions.

"Why would Nadine tell her boss her boyfriend was two-timing her?"

Because, kiddo, the late, great Logan Skerrill wasn't cheating on Silva—he was cheating on the Reds, on Himmel's spy ring. Now I saw it, everything clicked. Skerrill, star of the Funhouse and O.N.I.'s Special Ops, hadn't been content just to give all to the Reds while serving as a naval intelligence officer—the sonofabitch had the balls to go to the Bureau and sell himself as a mole. He was crazy enough to try it, Hoover was arrogant enough to buy it. Ol' John Edgar saw a chance to roll up a Red spy ring and cripple a rival agency by running Skerrill as a double agent. But Silva found out, she got guidance in a coded letter, the one I read when I tossed her flat, before going to Himmel. Who'd taken control of the "affair" by icing Skerrill. And Himmel was too careful, too good to do the job with his own hands—he would have looked for a patsy, a fall guy, a dope he'd tricked into killing Skerrill.

"I dunno, who cares?" I mumbled to Miriam.

I glanced around. Like stray cats sniffing fish scraps in an ashcan, the Bureau's boys had crept closer. Number one, on the bench down the path, no hat, blue overalls, posing as a factory worker still on a V-E bender, tilting a bottle in a paper bag to his lips. Number two, a guy in a blue suit pretending to read the newspaper at another bench. For sure number three was behind us, probably some joe tossing bread crumbs to pigeons. Slater and Reid had pulled out all the stops.

"Listen, kiddo, I gotta get in dare"—I jerked a thumb toward K Street— "before Silva cans me, too. But I'll see you tonight, I promise."

She looked up with alarm. "Don't come to the house, Teddy—"

"Did Kenny do dis, 'cause'a what I did ta his boy?"

"Teddy, Wade's in the hospital, he's gonna be there at least a week, they say, and—"

"Who knocked you around, kiddo?"

She looked down. "It was Kenny, but he was real mad, Teddy, on account'a what you did, and he thought I knew where you lived and that I was lying when I told him I didn't know. But I wouldn'ta told him even if I did know, Teddy, you gotta believe me, because Kenny, I've never seen him so mad, they're looking for you, him and his boys, they might even try to get you at H & H—"

"Lemme worry 'bout Kenny, okay, kiddo? You got some place else you can stay?"

"No, I'll be all right there, don't worry—Kenny's real sorry, he apologized—"

"Hey, how about's you and me meet up at da bar across from dat Italian restaurant we went to, remember, on Twelfth Street? Tonight, eight o'clock?"

"Oh, that'd be wonderful." She looked up, smiling, a joyous expression on her battered face. "You'll be there, Teddy?"

"You bet, kiddo. You just sit tight and wait, okay, in case I'm a little late?"

And with that, I gave her a quick peck on the lips and hightailed it to H & H. Tried not to think about my previous intention to let her down easy, to take her out for a big night and coax her into believing that Barston didn't want to leave her, but that he had to go. Stupid of me to believe that the investigation would yield such an opportunity. No, not stupid—selfish. "Props," we'd learned to call them at the Funhouse, the people you cajoled, manipulated, and conned while working undercover. Poor Miriam, she didn't even rate as a mark, like Himmel or Silva—she was just a prop. I'd told myself that I'd expiate my deception by treating her right at the end. But had I ever truly meant to do that, or had I just salved my conscience by resolving to be decent, just once? Barston had seduced Miriam, pumped her for information, then abandoned her. Worse—he'd wrecked her relationship with her brother. No matter that he was a dope dealer, violent and volatile, and not even her blood sibling. Kenny was the only brother she had, and what Barston had done at the party, his assault of that punk Wade, was unjustified. If he'd just walked away from Wade, ignored the taunts, no one would have examined the feigned hypo marks, no one would have questioned them. The pressures of being Barston had increased to the bursting point, but Miriam, not Barston, had paid the price.

As long as I was being honest with myself, then I needed to stop referring to Barston as if he were really another person, his actions beyond my responsibility and concern. I, Ellis Voigt, had assaulted Wade, my actions, my choices, had led to Miriam being beat up by her foster brother. And now I had lied again to her, promising to meet her that night just so I could get away from her and see my investigation to its end. How long would Miriam wait at the bar, telling herself through drink after drink that her Teddy was going to show? Who—what—had I become?

CHAPTER 31

I WASN'T EVEN OVER THE THRESHOLD WHEN SILVA GOT IN MY FACE, A finger held high to forestall any protest.

"You're late, Barston—I'm docking you the entire morning's pay. If you're late again—"

"You'll can me? Just like you did Miriam, huh?"

Her smile gave me chills. "Oh, did you run into our ex-receptionist just now, Barston, is that why you're late? Offer her some solace, a shoulder to cry on? Least you could do after what you put her through."

I should've known Silva would wring everything she could out of Miriam before canning her. So now Silva knew all about our night at the Rainbow and what I'd done to her brother's punk at the party.

"I didn't leave dose marks on her."

"But you deserted her, didn't you, Barston? Thrashed that kid and left her to face the music for you."

Nothing I could say to that—Silva, damn her, was right. Like a coward, I'd let Miriam take the fall. Did Silva know I'd run to protect my cover? She suspected I wasn't who I claimed to be, but how much did she know?

I said, curling my lip in contempt, "Why don't you just can me now, hey? Your pal Philip can make da deliveries today."

Her eyes narrowed almost to slits, she said nothing.

"Dat's what I thought, toots."

One crack too many. Greene, who'd been hovering nearby, pretending to go through some invoices, shot over and drilled a finger into my chest.

"You watch your mouth, Barston." His breathing was fast and shallow, his other hand clenching into a fist.

I checked the instinct to seize his finger and whirl him around to pin his arm. Instead: "Or else?"

"Or else I take you out back and teach you some manners."

"Ooh, some ettey-kette lessons, I like dat. How much you charge per hour?"

He grabbed my shirt by the buttons, using both hands. I pressed my hands into a V and shot them upward between his arms, breaking his grip. That put him off-balance, but he recovered quickly, moving into a boxer's crouch: knees bent, fists held out on either side of his chin, eyes darting, watching my hands. Anybody can ape what they pick up from the movies or a three-card bout, but watching my hands, not my eyes—that showed Greene had actually spent some time in the ring. Picked on as a kid, he'd probably gone to a gym to learn a thing or two. I adopted a fighter's posture, too, circling in the opposite direction.

"Oh, for God's sake, you two," Silva said with exasperation, but it was Himmel's booming voice that halted our scrapping.

"Enough! Philip, get back to work. Barston, in here."

I straightened up, dropped my arms, smirked. Greene was slower to ease off. "Lemme guess, you wanna say 'dis isn't over,' don't you?" I said breezily.

Whatever he mumbled, I didn't catch. Silva started to say something to him, he cut her off, gesturing wildly. Himmel had already gone back in his office. I strode past the desks of clippers, ignoring their stares and whispers. Flashing on what Miriam had told me the night I took her to dinner at the Italian restaurant. *Silva orders Greene around . . . Greene thinks he's so important . . . he's got a huge crush on her . . . when she found her boy-friend had been killed, Greene went to comfort her.* That last detail didn't jibe. Silva and Skerrill lovers, sure; Silva heartbroken at his death, not so much. Had Miriam's source, the clipper Norman, lied about seeing Silva crying in order to add drama to his story? But maybe it wasn't Silva I needed to be thinking about. Considering the way Greene had just come after me, maybe I needed to be thinking about him.

"Sit down, Ted," Himmel said in a neutral voice.

I sat and lit up. Himmel was playing with one of his cigars, studying the clipped end, cradling his lighter.

"Any friends follow you to work this morning?"

"Three in Franklin Square. Probably anudder one in da alley."

"Oh, I'm sure of that. A long tail, no?"

"Lost 'em twice yesterday." Hoping he wouldn't ask for the details.

"Good for you, Ted. Because you must do it one more time."

He slid a scrap of paper across his desk, I picked it up. *1831 Columbia Road 3B*, it read. I handed the scrap back, he set it on fire and dropped it into the ashtray.

"They cannot see you go in or come out, understand?"

"A'course."

"And obviously they cannot pick you up prior to your return."

I nodded dutifully.

"Good. Philip has already loaded the car, the manifest's on the front seat."

I stubbed my cigarette and stood. "Mister Himmel, can I ask you a question?"

"Yes."

"Seems to me, I'm not gonna be much good as yer delivery man if I got the Bureau on me all'a da time."

"No, probably not." Not saying more, waiting to see how I'd respond.

"So maybe I oughta get anudder job after today."

Now Himmel lit his cigar, taking his sweet time, puffing methodically, rolling the cigar to get an even burn. "I will say this, Ted. If you finish today's delivery without trouble, we will discuss your future. Not here, of course, you shouldn't come back here again."

"Where d'you want me to meet you?"

"Library of Congress reading room. I'll be there all afternoon, I have some research to do."

"Okay, Mister Himmel." I didn't ask what I should do with Greene's car. Exhaling gray smoke, he said, "Good luck."

I DIDN'T SEE ANY OF THE BUREAU'S BOYS WHEN I CAME OUT INTO THE alley and got into Greene's car. Probably the spotter was high up in a neighboring building, using binoculars to watch the door. I wondered if Slater or Reid had risked jimmying Greene's car to take a look at the manifest, decided they hadn't. They'd trust in their ability to stay on me like white on rice. I'd gotten lucky twice, they were determined not to let it happen again. To shake them a third time, I needed a lot more than luck.

I fired up Greene's jalopy and nosed out onto Fifteenth Street, turned north. The car was riding low, its backseat piled high with boxes of clippings. I picked up the first tail just shy of Massachusetts Avenue. A peasoup-green Model A Ford, blackout covers still attached to its bug-eye headlamps, a driver and passenger, hats pulled low. They might as well have stenciled "F.B.I." on the door panels, they were so obvious, but I couldn't make the second car. Bureau procedure was, the first car shadows, the second stays ahead, typically driving parallel streets a few blocks away, using radio dispatch to stay in contact. That way, the backup car could fall in if the mark managed to shake the tail. I needed both cars behind me, which was going to take a bit of fancy driving.

I swung a left on Massachusetts, which pointed me northwest. I drove just under the speed limit, staying in one lane, nice and easy. The Ford stayed three to four cars behind, its driver confident enough to allow vehicles to block his sight line for two, three blocks running. At Dupont Circle I switched on the left turn signal and slowed up, as if I was waiting to get into the inside lane. A gleaming Studebaker honked, I ignored him. The Ford had tightened up, to keep in view—as I wanted, he'd already moved into the inside lane. I waited until a delivery van was almost flush with me, then I swung a hard right on Nineteenth and hit the gas. The car I'd cut off—an Olds or Buick, I didn't have time to take a close look—stomped on his brakes, then his horn, rolling down his window to scream obscenities at me. Which I deserved—I'd shaved that move awful close, you probably couldn't even have slipped a sheet of paper between our bumpers. Now my tail had no choice but to take the circle around and double back. So was the backup car following us from the north, say on P or Q, or was he taking a southerly route, M or N?

Either way, he picked me up at Nineteenth and Florida, just before Nineteenth takes a westerly bend. A mid-thirties Pontiac sedan, gray with black trim, also a driver and passenger. Lot of juice under that hood, which is why it was the preferred getaway car of many a bank robber. Considering how stingy Hoover was, the car probably had been a getaway car. I slowed back down, then swung a last-moment left on Wyoming. Just as I'd hoped, the Ford was back in the hunt, catching up with us when I turned right on Connecticut. They knew I'd made them, they didn't care, and they were about to find out I didn't care either.

I floored the accelerator when I reached the Taft Bridge, then tried to shove the brake pedal right down through to the pavement. The tires screeched, the rear end swung out, bringing me to a stop at a right angle to the sides of the bridge. I put the car in neutral and engaged the parking brake. The Chevy's front end jutted into the first lane of oncoming traffic, southbound drivers honked angrily as they swerved out of the way. The Ford and the Pontiac pulled to the curb about five car lengths back, but none of the G-men got out. Northbound traffic was already backing up.

"You idiot, move your car!" the first passing driver yelled at me.

I got out, leaving the door open, and leapt on top of the trunk. "You wanna see what we're giving to the Russians?" I shouted at my shadows. "Well, come and get it!"

I jumped down, yanked open the rear passenger door, and pulled out three boxes of clippings. Bentbacked, I ran as fast as I could to the railing. The G-men tumbled out of their cars when they realized what I was doing and raced toward me.

Too late—I heaved the boxes over the railing, a burst of paper whipping past my face as the lids blew off, the folders and envelopes opened, and a week's worth of newspaper clippings and associated documents scattered down to the Rock Creek and Potomac Parkway.

"Christ almighty!" one G-man shouted.

"Grab him!" his partner yelled.

The fastest of the four was a lithe young guy who didn't let his wing-tips and suit jacket slow him down. I had a head start, but he closed the distance fast—I was sure glad I'd left the driver's door open and the engine running. I slammed the door, almost trimming off his fingertips. I released the parking brake, shifted into first, and popped the clutch as he fumbled to draw his weapon. The sight of a man with a gun caused a southbound driver to swerve into the guardrail. The car behind plowed right in, the agent had to jump out of the way. A pileup, what a great idea. I clipped a northbound car, forcing him into the other guardrail; the car behind had to come to a complete stop. The remaining G-men raced back to their cars, but I had five, maybe eight minutes before they cleared a path and came after me, another ten before they spotted me—if they were lucky. And that was all the time I needed.

ON THE OTHER SIDE OF THE BRIDGE I TURNED EAST ON CALVERT, WHICH took me to Columbia Road. I pulled into the alley behind the building at 1831. They'd check the streets first, my G-men friends, before they got to the alleys, so that bought me a little more time. I entered through the rear, went up the stairwell. The door to 3B was chipped and peeling, the runner in the corridor dirty and patchy. Grimy walls, dim light. A toilet flushed at the end of the corridor, a fat man came out of the bathroom buckling his belt, his undershirt untucked. He barely glanced at me before ducking into his room, the door snicking shut. A deadbolt shot home.

I knocked, waited. Knocked harder, called out I had a delivery.

"Hold on," a male voice grumbled loudly.

A long moment, then 3B's deadbolt clicked and the door opened a crack, the useless safety chain dangling in front of the man's face.

"What?" he challenged me.

"Delivery. H & H Clipping Service."

He undid the chain. I came in, shutting the door behind me. He was wearing only gabardine trousers and a white T-shirt. No socks, no belt, no dress shirt. He looked about thirty. Dark eyes, long nose, clipped mustache. His black hair looked like he'd run his fingers through the part just before letting me in. The flat was small, just a parlor and a bedroom, its door closed. In an alcove with a dingy curtain, a sink and towel rack. No kitchenette, no closet. He didn't sit down, instead picking up his cigarettes from an endtable speckled with glass rings.

"You don't have anything," he said, finally noticing my empty hands.

"Musta forget it in da car," I said evenly.

He shrugged, lit up, took a long drag, said, "Hang on," in a tired way. He was as uninterested in play-acting as I was. He opened the bedroom door and went over to a dresser in the corner. A peroxide blonde was lounging on the end of the bed, wearing only an ill-fitting peach slip, a cigarette in her hand. He mumbled something to her, she didn't respond. She turned her head to study me, her expression blank. The eyeover was fleeting. She was wearing an awful lot of makeup for a woman still in bed at ten in the morning. Bright lipstick, curled lashes, rouged cheeks.

He came back with an envelope, pushing the bedroom door shut behind him.

"My gal," he said as he handed me the envelope. "We're taking the day off, you know—still feeling last night's celebration." He mustered up a weak smile.

"Sure," I said. She was strictly trade, a pro all the way, but what did I care? He knew he might have to spend the day waiting for the courier, might as well treat himself to some entertainment. I turned to leave, adding over my shoulder, "Oughta tell you, I'm real popular, got lotsa friends dis morning. Dey might come a'knockin'."

"Okay, thanks," he said unenthusiastically, checking his watch.

Cheap bastard, I thought, pounding down the rear stairs, the envelope folded and tucked in my rear pocket. But if he ended up being questioned by the Bureau because he stuck around to get his money's worth out of the prossy, that was Himmel's problem, not mine.

CHAPTER 32

THE SMART MOVE: DITCH GREENE'S CAR, COPY THE CONTENTS OF the envelope, deliver it to Himmel at the Library of Congress. Then, break cover, come up for air as Lieutenant Ellis Voigt at the Navy Building. Forget the Iceland story, try not to think about how Paslett would blow his stack when I strolled in. Because once I gave him this last delivery and told him that Skerrill hadn't just been a Red spy—he'd also been a mole for the Bureau—the commander would calm down lickety-split. What I'd given Terrance and the commander so far was enough to roll up the cell, to arrest Silva, Greene, and Himmel on espionage charges. Throw each into solitary, start sweating them, get each to turn on the others. John Edgar would go nuts, he'd storm up and down the Potomac like Napoleon, blustering and yelling about how this was *his* operation, who the hell did O.N.I. think they were screwing with; but once Paslett let it leak that Hoover had run a turncoat naval intelligence officer as his own mole without telling anyone, the brass would cold-shoulder that toad but good. Sure, we had our tussles, O.N.I., O.S.S., and all the rest, but when it came to stiffing the Bureau, we closed ranks tight.

What I did instead: drove to the Jefferson Club to retrieve the rucksack from my cage. I hoped the lock had held, that none of my lovely neighbors had jimmied the hasp. I'd been absent a long time, other residents would've noticed. Keeping Greene's car on the streets was a pretty big risk—the Bureau would be dragging D.C. with every net they had and putting an A.P.B. out with the local cops. But a half-hour, maybe forty-five minutes, was all the time I needed with the car, then I could abandon it.

I pulled up in front of the Jefferson and, for once, fed the meter—I couldn't afford a parking ticket right now. Dashed in, took the smelly stairwell two steps at a time. Sigh of relief, my cage still locked. Let myself in, knelt and groped for the rucksack under the foot of the cot. Swept up dustballs and grit. "Fuck, fuck, fuck," I muttered, panting from my run. Then I remembered: I'd last left the bag under the head of the cot, to keep it away from the door. I slid forward and pulled the rucksack out on the first grab.

Bounded right back down the stairs, leaving the lock and key in the hasp, a gift to whomever found it first. Any joe who lived at the Jefferson Club couldn't have too many locks. Tossed the rucksack on the front seat, flipped down the driver's sun visor. Good citizen Greene had dutifully clipped his vehicle registration to the back side. He'd listed 1224 Euclid Street, 2R, as his residence. Could be fake, or a dead drop, or a pinko pal who collected mail for Greene and passed it on. Only one way to find out. I shot up to Massachusetts, then headed north on Thirteenth, hoping the A.P.B. hadn't caught the ears of a bored patrolman loafing in his prowl car at Logan Circle. Got to the house without trouble and parked in the alley.

Greene bunked in an ordinary D.C. rowhouse, three stories, narrow, brick, enclosed rear staircase tacked on. I shouldered the rucksack and took Greene's keys with me—dumb bastard had given me his ring, so I had his house key. If any neighbors asked, I was still Ted Barston, H & H's delivery man, sent by Greene to fetch an important work file he'd forgotten. But I didn't see anyone as I hustled up the brick path from the alley. The unfinished wooden steps clattered as I went up to the second floor. Greene kept his landing neat, just a doormat and a stack of old newspapers.

Flash of panic as I unlocked the door: Did Slater and Reid know where Greene lived? What if they had a man in the alley, watching the house? Figure the Bureau wouldn't think I'd come here, that I had no reason to? The longer I was in the wind, the more places they might look. Slater was crafty, methodical—he might just think Ted Barston *would* hide out here because he'd assume the Bureau would never think to make a house call. To be safe, I had to be quick.

So, stepping into the tiny kitchen, locking the door behind me, surveying the scene, the counter with bread box, butter dish, bowl of fruit . . . *I'm you, Philip Greene, I'm a loyal foot soldier in the Red Crusade, I do what Himmel and Silva tell me. Got a crush on Nadine, hate it that she lets that smug prick Skerrill haul her ashes. A real golden boy, Skerrill, I've never liked him, hate how easy everything comes to him. I've got talents, I'm a true believer, how come they don't ask me to do more? Then Silva comes to me, red-eyed, upset, terrible news that shocks and thrills me: Skerrill betrayed us to the Bureau! Tears streaking her face, letting me hold her close, whispering, "Will you help us, Philip? We must protect what we're doing. . . ." "Yes, anything," I tell her, right away, no hesitation, exhilarated—finally, my chance!*

More thoughts as Greene . . . *So how would I have done it, what mistakes did I make? Getting Skerrill to meet, not hard. Location, that alley in Southeast—harder sell. Why there? he'd have asked. Tell him a fellow traveler lives there, a friend of the cause, something like that. Tell him, meet me in the back, we'll go in together. Have Himmel back me up—yes, yes, important meeting, want you both to go—to clinch it. I've cased that alley but otherwise never been there. The gun's easy—Himmel gets it for me, promises it's untraceable. I practice using it behind an abandoned farmhouse in upper Montgomery County. Don't have to be an ace—I'm gonna shoot Skerrill at close range—but that piece has gotta fit like a glove. I get there early, of course I don't drive, I take the Pennsylvania Avenue streetcar and walk the rest of the way. So far, so good. Skerrill strolls down the alley ten minutes late, but dammit if he doesn't sense something's off, honed instincts telling him that meeting in an alley to go into a house isn't quite right.*

Then my second mistake: instead of plugging him right away, without saying a word, I confront him. Just had to tell him we'd found him out, didn't I, had to let him know why he was being killed, as if he wouldn't have known as soon as I pulled the thirty-eight. He doesn't waste a second, jumps me before I finish my condemnation, before I can get the gun out of my waistband. We struggle, we throw punches—thank God I took those boxing lessons as a kid. Damn glad I brought the roll of pennies, too, clenched in my left fist. Those two wallops daze him long enough for me to get the thirty-eight out. I don't even remember how many shots, even though I remember how he grunts, how he gasps, the red marks from my knuckles on his cheek and the ragged scratch from my ring as he falls.

How much noise? A street brawl, shots fired, gotta go, can't stick around to see if he's dead, gotta trust in the weapon, the shots, the close range. Run west, out of the alley, slow to a brisk walk to get back to Pennsylvania Avenue. No one sees me, I'm sure. If any of the residents peeked out during our argument, what did they see? Two white men fighting, one gets shot, the shooter runs away. A colored block, that stretch of M, poor people, soon to be forced to move because the Navy Yard bought out their landlords. How much are they going to cooperate when they find out the dead man was a naval officer?

And Greene had figured right—Terrance and I had gotten nothing from our canvass of the alley and its residents.

"But were you smart enough to get rid of the gun, Philip?" I murmured as I looked around his living room, lined with bookcases and potted ferns. I checked my watch: 11:18. I was up hard against my self-imposed deadline to search Greene's flat, five minutes left. I could push it to ten minutes, but no more, not even close to the time needed for a thorough search. Anyway, how likely was it that I would find the gun? But Greene, having killed a man, might have grown anxious. What if Himmel received orders to take care of the trigger man? The Russians were like that, paranoid, ruthless—years of loyal service did you no good if someone in power gave an order. How many officers on the General Staff had Stalin killed just because he got a little suspicious? Greene might—he just might—have kept the gun, believing it offered him protection.

I unshouldered the rucksack, dug out cotton gloves, the kind photograph retouchers use, pulled them on, ran a finger along a shelf. Clean, no dust. Nothing out of order here, even the *Collier's* and *Harper's* magazines aligned perfectly on the coffee table. Funny, place as neat as Skerrill's rooming house. Seemed a century ago that Terrance and I had searched that room and interviewed the landlady. What did this tell me, that everything's just so, exactly where he wanted, where he could find something immediately. . . .

That if I kept the gun against Himmel's strict instructions to toss it, I'd hide it in plain sight, where I could get to it easily, but I wouldn't stash it someplace obvious. The thirty-eight's not in a plastic bag taped to the toilet tank, it's not in the breadbox, it's not behind the books, it's not under my mattress. What I'm worried about: If they decide to eliminate me, they'll try to make it look like a robbery, like I came home and surprised a burglar and got shot in the struggle. They'll send someone I'll let in, someone Himmel would vouchsafe, someone who'd put me at ease, then—bang-bang. So long, Philip Greene, thanks for taking care of our traitor Logan Skerrill. So I want my gun where I can reach it without tipping off my would-be assassin. What I'm gonna do when I let him in, I'm gonna walk toward the kitchen, like I'm about to ask if I can make some coffee, which leads me right past this coatrack, right past this old suit jacket hanging behind the raincoat, and when I turn to ask about the coffee, I reach right into the side pocket and—

Bang, bang. I cradled a thirty-eight in my gloved hands, the same type of weapon used to shoot Logan Skerrill, held it up to the sunlight streaming in through Greene's front window. No sign of prints, but maybe Greene had rubbed it clean, just in case the cops tossed his place? A wiped gun wasn't my problem, I decided—one for the prosecutor.

Definitely my problem: the illegal search. If the gun matched the shells that Durkin, the city detective, had retrieved from the alley, then pinning the killing on Greene was easy-breezy—but only if the gun was admissible. Which it sure the hell wasn't now, not even with a judge who hated Reds. Put the thirty-eight back, call Terrance and tell him to call Durkin to get a warrant? No good, either; I'd have to give a sworn statement. Spinning a yarn wasn't hard—I could say Greene had bragged about being an enforcer for Himmel, about being an A-1 gunslinger—but I couldn't break cover, not yet, not until I made a copy of the envelope in my back pocket and kept my meeting with Himmel at the Library of Congress. Even if I found a way to make the statement, it took time to get a warrant. What if Greene got rid of the gun while we were waiting? Paslett might not care, he was only concerned about the espionage. Identifying Skerrill's killer wouldn't be as important to him, not after he found out Skerrill had betrayed the O.N.I. Good riddance, right?

But nailing Greene for Skerrill's murder was important to me. Which is why I dropped the thirty-eight in my rucksack and hightailed it out of the flat.

CHAPTER 33

I STASHED THE THIRTY-EIGHT UNDER THE PASSENGER SEAT OF GREENE'S car, making sure it was within reach of a driver with arms shorter than mine. As in, the arms of the car's owner. At Logan Circle I took Vermont Avenue south to I Street. Pulled up in front of Iceland's Chancery, stopped right under a NO PARKING sign that threatened immediate towing of violators' vehicles. We had an important base in Iceland—hell, wasn't I supposed to be there that very moment?—so keeping Iceland's diplomats happy was important. If the Chancery called the city to complain about a dented Chevy in its *No Parking* zone, that Chevy wasn't staying long. And once the city looked up how many parking violations that particular vehicle had lately racked up, the owner wasn't getting his car back anytime soon.

I hadn't even finished dashing across I Street toward the La Fayette Hotel when a guard came running out of the sentry box, waving his arms and shouting. I pretended not to hear him, rounded Sixteenth Street. When

I was out of sight, I entered the hotel and went straight to the lobby, which offered a fine view of the Chancery. The guard, I was pleased to see, had returned to his box and had a telephone receiver in his hand. I fired up an Old Gold, reached for the *Evening Star* on the coffee table in front of me. I was halfway through my second cigarette and the front page section when the city tow truck rolled up. The Chancery guard watched with his arms folded, a satisfied look on his Icelandic face as the driver started chaining the Chevy's bumper. I finished my smoke, folded the newspaper, and headed to the bank of telephone booths on the far wall.

"Daley," my partner answered gruffly.

"It's Voigt, can you talk?"

"Jesus, what're you doing, calling direct?"

"Listen up, partner, s'all breaking open. Himmel had me make the last pick-up this morning, it's in my back pocket, m'supposed to give it to him now. Not at H & H, he wants me to come to the Library of Congress."

"Fuck, they're about to split."

"Bingo."

"Can you get the package to us first?"

"No, we got something else we gotta do and quick."

"What?"

"Pick up Durkin and go straight to H & H—I need him to arrest Philip Greene, and I need you there when it happens. Remember Greene, he's the office manager?"

"Yeah, yeah—what's the charge?"

"He did Skerrill."

"For real? Why?"

"Remember that little problem I got with our friends from the Bureau?"

"Yeah."

"Guess how John Edgar's boys found out about H & H."

"You're shitting me."

"Nope, Skerrill was working for the Bureau. I don't know why, yet—maybe he got worried, thought he was about to be discovered, so he offered himself as a mole to the Bureau to dig himself out, or maybe the Bureau got to him first and flipped him."

"Nice'a the Bureau to tell us," Terrance said bitterly.

"Don't worry, they're gonna get what they deserve."

"How d'you know Greene got the job to take care of Skerrill?"

"I got proof. Have Durkin send a man to the city impoundment lot to search a Chevy with tag number one-six-three dash four-nine-five. That's Greene's car, he keeps a thirty-eight under the seat. Durkin needs to get that weapon tested pronto." I listened to the sound of rapid scribbling.

"S'not proof till the gun matches the slug from the alley."

"Durkin got a matchable bullet, remember? Get the gun and the bullet to their ballistics—"

"Shouldn't we wait to pick Greene up till they test the gun?"

"We don't have time. Besides, I want the test results to come in while we're questioning Greene—I wanna shove that report right under his nose."

"What if the bullet doesn't match?"

"Then tell Durkin to tell his boys to write up a fake one. What we gotta do is, we gotta sweat Greene, get him to confess."

Long pause. "I better check with the commander, he's gonna wanna—"

"No, no—listen, Terrance, don't tell Paslett. We'll tell him we had to move too fast, there was no time—and there isn't, there really isn't."

"Shouldn't we arrest all of them at once? I mean, if we take Greene outta there, they're gonna run."

I checked my watch: 12:07.

"Not if you move now—Greene always takes his lunch break at Cheryl's Luncheonette, it's on the west side'a Twelfth, a tick or two north of K." I described Greene: short, solid build, comb-over, tortoise shell glasses, mustache. "Grab him there, they won't know what happened over at H & H."

"You sure he'll be there?"

"Yeah, yeah, I've been working with these people a while, I know their habits. Get Durkin, arrest Greene, and bring him to the Fifth Precinct. And make sure the city boys get the gun outta Greene's car. Don't let him call a lawyer or anybody. I'll meet you at the Fifth."

"Okay." Still dubious.

"Terrance, if we get Greene to confess to killing Skerrill, we can force him to roll on the rest'a the Reds. With what I've brought in from being Himmel's courier, we'll know how much they know about New Mexico and how far it's gone."

"All right, gotcha. Hey, what about the Bureau, aren't they still tailing you?"

"Nope, they're too busy picking up litter in the Rock Creek Parkway."

"Huh?"

"I'll tell you after we grill Greene."

"Okay."

I hung up. With the telephone booth door still shut, I took the envelope out of my pocket. Another plain white business envelope, no markings. I could probably ask the hotel desk clerk for a replacement, wouldn't even have to stop at a druggist's or stationer's on my way to meet Himmel. Flash: What if the deliveries I'd handled, including this one, had some kind of invisible marking, a watermark that only showed up under blue light? Then Himmel would know I'd opened them. I lit a cigarette to calm my racing pulse, my churning stomach. *Okay, okay, okay, if Himmel suspected Ted Barston of compromising his operation, he'd have done something right away, right?* Fire me, call the police and accuse me of stealing—or arrange the hit I'd worried about during my first day, when I'd had Terrance follow me to make sure I'd be all right. But just because it hadn't happened the first time didn't mean it couldn't still happen. As in, this afternoon. *What if, what if, what if . . .* a man could *what if* himself into panic and paralysis. And I sure as hell couldn't afford that at that moment.

I ripped open the envelope. Inside, nothing but a white slip of paper. *Yes,* it read. Nothing but that single word. *Yes. Yes!?* For that slip of paper, I'd led four F.B.I. agents on a wild goose chase, I'd thrown a week's worth of newspaper clippings into Rock Creek, I'd caused a traffic jam and pile-up on the Taft Bridge—all for one lousy word? Was Himmel playing some kind of joke?

He expected me to get caught! He didn't expect me to shake the Bureau's tail, I realized; I was just the decoy. By keeping the G-men busy, I freed up Himmel to receive, unnoticed, the package he was actually waiting to receive. Or was I running scared, hearing the bay of hounds that weren't really on my trail? Jesus, I was frazzled, my nerves raw and heart pounding, struggling to think straight. I deep-dragged my smoke till I calmed down a bit. Whatever Himmel's motive, I was going to follow through with his instruction to meet him.

I pulled open the booth door and went to the front desk. Sure enough, the clerk gave me a plain envelope when I asked nicely. I sealed up the slip of paper, had the doorman hail me a hack. I couldn't wait to see Himmel's face when I found him at the Library of Congress.

WHEN I FIRST GOT TO WASHINGTON, I USED TO SPEND A LOT OF TIME in the reading room of the Library of Congress. Mahogany desks encircle the circulation counter, cream-red marble columns support a dome, gold leaf adorns every corner and lintel, as profligate as ivy. Two-story alcoves with cast-iron shelves and narrow spiral staircases are lined with books. On clear summer afternoons, bright light pierces the dome's leaded glass, illuminating certain desks—surprised readers look up, blinking, when the sun catches their spot. Sometimes I didn't even read, just sat thinking about nothing in particular, content to listen to the quiet sounds of a library at work. Occasional coughs, rustle of turning pages, scratch and whisk of energetic note-taking, rickety ticking of a book cart's caster, thud of a call slip being date-stamped. Perhaps I needed a contemplative refuge from the O.N.I., from the pace and press of wartime life, hard to say now. Whatever the reason, my last sojourn to the library had occurred more than a year ago.

If Himmel was surprised to see me, he didn't show it. He was sitting near a column in the outer circle of desks. Didn't greet me, just motioned toward one of the alcoves and set down the book he was reading, *The Cathedrals of the Rhine and North Germany.* He ascended the staircase, I followed. We entered the stacks, walked single file between two long shelves to the rear wall, turned right, kept going. The stacks created a maze of books, easy to get lost in despite the straight rows. Alongside the section of books on the Ancient Near East, Himmel halted. We hadn't seen or heard anyone else—you could spend hours in the stacks without encountering another human being.

"So?" he asked.

I wordlessly handed him the envelope.

"Difficult?"

I shrugged.

"You have done a good job, Ted."

"Thanks."

He studied me in a clinical, detached way, the way a doctor might if you told him you had a medical problem.

"Dat it?" I asked.

"Yes."

Funny. But I kept my expression impassive, too. "What's gonna happen ta H & H, Mister Himmel?"

"Now that you have brought the Federal Bureau of Investigation into my affairs, you mean?"

Had to let that slide, couldn't get angry—had to stay Ted Barston, eager to keep the job, playing the part to the end.

"Well, if I did anything ta make dat happen, I'm sure sorry, Mister Himmel."

"I know, Ted. Still, I must let you go. Your efforts to finish this last task for me are appreciated, but Miss Silva informs me that you didn't complete any other deliveries today."

"No, sir, couldn't get ta 'em."

"My gratitude will be apparent when you pick up your pay envelope from Miss Silva."

"Okay." *That's it, that's all?* But that was Ellis Voigt's question, not Ted Barston's. "Guess I better let you find da way out," I said.

Himmel didn't answer, just walked back down the row of books. I followed silently. We exited the stacks and clomped down the alcove's staircase. Himmel returned to his desk, picked up his book, and resumed reading, looking just like a professor doing research. I kept on walking and didn't look back.

Maybe there was more to the message I'd just delivered than I first thought. *Yes, our meeting is on.* Or, *Yes, you should proceed.* But who was Himmel meeting (possibly), what should he proceed with (possibly)? Himmel appeared to think we'd never see each other again. I wasn't so sure. But until I knew more about what that *Yes* meant, I couldn't say how, or where, or why we would meet.

CHAPTER 34

FLAGGED A HACK RIGHT OUTSIDE THE LIBRARY—NO SHORTAGE OF CABS on the Hill—and gave him the address of the Fifth Precinct. *What if*s gnawed at me the whole ride. What if Terrance had ignored me, had gone to Paslett for instructions? What if he and Durkin hadn't found Greene? What if Durkin couldn't find the ballistics expert, what if they couldn't whip up a report—real or bogus—on such short notice?

I paid the driver with the last of my O.N.I. cash and hustled into the police station, a red brick building with stone lintels set above tall windows. In the waiting area a sullen-looking couple sat on the wooden bench near the entrance. Cigarette smoke drifted up toward the clattering ceiling fan; the piebald floorboards creaked as two patrolmen walked out. At the reception desk, a man clutching a parking ticket was arguing with the sergeant. I waited impatiently, furiously dragging on an Old Gold. I wasn't in uniform, didn't have my O.N.I. identification card, couldn't cut in. Finally John Q. Citizen stomped off, ticket still in hand.

"Detective Sergeant Durkin's expecting me; so's the naval officer with him."

The sergeant, a thin man with slicked-back brown hair, eyed me over. "They're busy."

"Like I said, they're expecting me."

"All right." Still not believing me. He stepped to the rear counter, picked up a telephone, dialed an in-house number and murmured something. Waited, said yes, hung up. Came back and pointed to the corridor to my right. "Second door on the left."

Terrance answered my knock. I stepped aside as my partner came out—I didn't want Greene to see me yet.

"You got him?" I asked.

"Yeah, you could say that."

"What happened?"

"Didn't go easy, s'all." Massaging the knuckles of his right hand.

"Lemme guess—says he's as innocent as the pure driven snow."

"A'course. If he says one more time we got no proof . . ." Expectant look.

"Get the gun?"

"Durkin says they did. I haven't seen it."

"Where is it now?"

"At the police lab. Durkin's pretty put out, says it usually takes a week to get a ballistics report, outta the blue we want it in a hour for a case we took from 'em, boo-hoo, boo-hoo."

"We'll get him some flowers when this is over. Are they gonna put something in front of us pronto?"

Terrance checked his watch. "S'pposed to be here by two at the latest." I turned my wrist: 1:27.

"Perfect. All right, what we're gonna do is, I'm gonna push Greene hard on Skerrill, soften him up for when the ballistics report gets here."

"Ellis, he's stubborn like a mule—keeps shouting for a lawyer, not just any shyster, someone he says he's got on retainer. S'making Durkin awful nervous—and me, too, I gotta say." Translation: we couldn't delay Greene's call much longer. And it wouldn't take an attorney long to get a message to Silva and Himmel.

"I got that covered, we're gonna get everything we need outta Greene right now."

"We better, 'cause Paslett's gonna wonder where the hell I am pretty soon and what's going on."

"Don't sweat it, we're gonna nail Greene for doing Skerrill and then we're gonna roll up the Reds at H & H before the Bureau can make their move. The old man's not gonna care we didn't brief him first, trust me."

Terrance studied me closely. His expression uncomfortably reminded me of Himmel's long look at the library. "Okay, your show, let's go," he finally said, opening the door.

The interrogation room was small and windowless. Glazed ocher tiles on the lower half of the walls, yellowing plaster with hairline cracks to the ceiling. A sturdy wooden table scarred with scratches and cigarette burns. Durkin was seated facing the door, Greene had his back to it. Terrance and I came around and sat on either side of Durkin.

Greene's eyes slitted in anger when he recognized me. "You! I shoulda known! How much are they paying you, you goddamned worthless—"

"Zip it, Greene," I cut in, using my normal voice. "M'not Ted Barston, I'm a naval intelligence officer. We've been on to you and your Red pals at H & H for a while now."

That shut him up. He glanced nervously at Terrance, who was in uniform, then Durkin.

"Don't look at them, look at me," I barked. "We know all about that traitor Logan Skerrill. Only before we had enough to bring him and the rest'a you in, he got himself killed. What a coincidence, huh?"

"I didn't kill him and you know it." Voice steady, surprise gone. He was quick, had to credit him that.

"Yes, you did. Let's start with the reason why. Your boy Skerrill got too cute. Went to the F.B.I. and cut a deal with John Edgar, told him he was a Red, he'd betrayed the Navy, but maybe he could make things right by doing a turn as a mole for the Bureau. Some big brass balls, huh? But he knew Hoover'd bite. What does the Bureau care if Navy's in the dark? Way Hoover sees it, he and his boys oughta be the only ones chasing Reds. And what Skerrill promised to bring in, that'd be plenty to cover asses high and low once Navy found out what was going on. But we play rough, too. Enter Ted Barston."

I paused to light a cigarette, see if Greene piped up with another denial. But he was smart, kept still, waiting to see how much more I'd spool out.

Concentrating, memorizing everything I was saying. Expecting he'd be relating it all to Himmel soon. I didn't dare look at Terrance—laying all our cards on the table before the first bet had to be making him pretty edgy. Durkin already had a cigarette going, was staring at the ceiling, bored. Looked like he was counting cracks.

"So guess what I learned while being your gofer, Greene?" I asked.

No response.

"Your boss Himmel's running a whole ring of spies. Uses the clipping service to hide the pick-ups. Set up a profitable business, use your real deliveryman to courier the goods. Only your latest deliveryman made copies'a everything he brought in."

That got me a nice eyefuck, but he still kept quiet.

"What with that, and all the arrests we're gonna make, our commander's awful pleased, especially since the Bureau still has no idea we beat 'em at their own game. But here's the icing for our cake: we got the guy who killed our resident Benedict Arnold."

"The hell you do," Greene said flatly.

"Himmel found out Skerrill was walking both sides of the street," I went on, "so he arranged to bury his mole for good. All he needed was a loyal foot soldier to carry out his orders." I pointed at him.

"Uh-uh, not me, you're not gonna frame me."

"Nobody's framing you, Greene. You're our man, and don't believe for a second that Silva and Himmel are gonna lie for you. To get out from under the charges we're gonna lay on 'em, they'll roll on you pronto."

"What about my alibi for that night?" he asked. Watching me closely.

Fuck! Fuckety, fuck, fuck! How could I have forgotten to check on his whereabouts!? I was so certain the gun proved he was the shooter, so taken with my imagining of Silva seducing him into the murder, that I'd forgotten to check his alibi. And if he could produce eyewitnesses—trustworthy ones, not fellow commies—who saw him far away from that alley that night, my case went belly-up. What if the ballistics expert couldn't match the slug to the thirty-eight? Wouldn't take much of a lawyer to make hash of our—no, *my*—evidence. At the arraignment alone, Greene's lawyer could raise these doubts and get a low bail, easy-breezy. Once he walked on a bond, Greene was certain never to return for his day in court.

"Did you check?" Greene pressed. "Seems to me, if the Office of No Intelligence or whatever it is you call yourselves these days wanted to prove—"

"Shut up," I snapped, leaning forward to stare him down. "What night was Skerrill killed?"

"Shouldn't you know that?" Smirking.

"Don't wisecrack me. What night was he killed?"

"I don't know, why would I? I had nothing to do with him or his murder, you can't—"

"If you can't tell us what night he was killed, how do you know you have an alibi?"

That tripped him up, but only briefly, his eyes darting, still fixed on my glaring face. "I don't need to have an alibi—I didn't do anything! I can prove where I was *any* night'a the week. Tell me the date, I'll tell you where I was."

"We already know where you were, Greene—we checked. Nobody knows where you were, nobody you know claims to have seen you that night."

"You're lying."

"We checked, Greene, believe it."

"So what? You got any eyewitnesses put me at the scene? What's your evidence? Know what I think? This is all a ruse, some two-bit trick to get me to admit to what you're claiming, that H & H is some sorta spy ring. Which is crazy, just flat-out crazy talk."

I grinned at Terrance. "Doesn't even need a lawyer, does he? He can defend himself."

"Yeah, oughta save his nickel to call his mother, huh?" my partner cracked.

Durkin grinned as Greene stormed and sputtered about how we'd better let him call his counsel or else. He was still going when the door opened and a patrolman entered and handed a slim gray folder to Durkin. He glanced at it, slid it over to me. I looked at him, he ticked his chin—the bullet and weapon matched.

"Guess what this is, Greene?"

He was back to giving us the silent, sullen act.

"A ballistics report. We just matched a slug taken from the murder scene to your gun."

The color drained from his face. "What? I don't own a gun, that can't—lemme see that!" He lunged forward, but I pushed the folder to Terrance, who laid his meaty fists atop it.

"The thirty-eight we found under the seat of your car today? You don't own that?"

His eyes widened behind his glasses, he shook his head furiously. "No, no, no—that isn't mine, I've never owned a gun—you! You planted it! You've been driving my car every day, hours at a time, you put it there!"

"Greene, how could I have possession of the gun that killed Skerrill? We've been investigating his murder since it happened. Simple, how that works. First we look for motive. We find out you, Himmel, Silva, and Skerrill are working for the Russians. We find out Skerrill was a mole for John Edgar. Bingo—you, Himmel, and Silva now got an awful big reason to want our fair-haired lieutenant dead. So now we look for opportunity. We check on where Himmel was that night without him knowing it. He clears. We check out Silva, too. Guess what, Greene—she clears. Only you don't, nobody we talk to can say where you—"

"Now I know you're lying," he cut in. "If you had checked me out for real, my friends woulda told me, no way they talk to stripes without telling me."

I stared him down. "You sure about that, Greene? Absolutely, positively? Willing to bet your life on it? 'Cause that's what's at stake, a trip to the gas chamber, this was premeditated murder, first degree all the way."

"That bullshit doesn't scare me."

"No bullshit, Greene. This"—I tapped the ballistics report—"proves it. We got motive, we got opportunity—with the gun, we got the way you did it. Shot Skerrill at close range and left him to bleed to death like a rat—"

"Your gun'll never be admitted. You say you found it in my car? Where's the search warrant? I never saw it, I'm the car's owner, nobody served me. Your search was illegal, so your gun—which you planted, don't think I won't be able to prove that—will get tossed out."

Durkin had stopped staring at the ceiling, was now watching Greene intently. Thinking, maybe this commie's right, maybe there's no case here.

I didn't dare glance at Terrance—we had a helluva lot more at stake here than Durkin, and I'd asked my partner to trust me.

"Know where your car is now, smart guy?"

"Doesn't matter, your search was illegal." Shrugging.

"City impoundment lot, that's where it is," I continued. "Turns out Ted Barston racked up quite a few parking tickets while he was making deliveries and you forgot to pay them. So your car got towed."

He started sputtering. I cut him off.

"So the thirty-eight you killed Skerrill with and stashed under your front seat was discovered while your vehicle was in the custody of the Government of the District of Columbia. See, until you pay those tickets, Greene, the car doesn't belong to you. It's being held as security for the debts *you* owe the city. Right, Detective Sergeant Durkin?"

"You bet," he answered immediately.

Now I looked at Terrance. He was suppressing a grin, good.

"You think you got it all figured out, don't you?" Greene addressed me, his temper in check. "This frame, you think it's solid on all sides. Nice'a you to tell me your angles, that's gonna be a big help to my attorney. You think 'cause you're all in uniform, you got badges and authority and your *laws*, you can do whatever the hell you want. I'm done talking to you fascists, hear me? I've told you to let me call my attorney, and you damn well better, right now."

Was he hoping I was bluffing? Or didn't he care? He had bigger balls than I thought if he was willing to clam up, go to jail, and take his chances at trial. Which were pretty good, though I wasn't about to admit that to anyone, not even Terrance. Because if Greene could produce a solid alibi, if we couldn't wring out a witness or two from the Negroes who lived in the alley, the ballistics and my story about motive probably weren't enough to convict him. But that was a problem for another day. Right now, I had to keep him from calling his lawyer. We couldn't stall him any longer—I had to convince him to decide *not* to make the call.

"Okay, Greene, you wanna call your shyster, we'll let you. But there's one more thing you oughta know before you do."

"That tired old trick?" He snorted derisively. "I already know everything I need to, all I need—"

"If you really wanna make the call, we'll just drop the murder charge and you can walk outta this room a free man."

"What?!" he exclaimed.

Terrance grunted in surprise, or dismay; Durkin shot me a look.

"You heard me. If you want a lawyer so bad, we'll release you. But you should know there's two agents from the F.B.I. waiting in the corridor. They wanna talk to you in a bad way and they're not worried about your lawyer one bit. Turns out, Section Seven-ninety of the Espionage Act allows federal authorities to hold a suspect for forty-eight hours without arraignment or counsel during wartime if said authorities convince a judge that this time is needed to protect the state's interests with regard to the espionage."

I leaned forward until my face was just inches away. His breath stank of coffee and onions, his cheeks were flushed. Stared right back.

He asked, "If you're butting heads with the Bureau, why would you let them have me?"

"Because we've got the ringleaders, we've got Himmel and Silva in custody. You're small fry, Greene, but don't think the Bureau's not gonna wring you dry. And because you killed Skerrill on federal property, they can still hang a murder rap on you."

"So what d'you want from me?"

"We want you to think long and hard about your choices here. You wanna take your chances with the Bureau, or you wanna take your chances against our case? We'll give you the rest'a the day and night to make up your mind, but you gotta do it alone—no lawyer."

He bit his lower lip, furrowed his brow. Putting on an act. No way he'd walk out, believing G-men were hovering outside. He knew the Bureau was on to H & H, knew everything I'd said about Skerrill being a mole for the Bureau was true. In a lucky break for me, the mistakes I'd made—not checking out Greene's alibi, moving the gun from his flat to his car—had helped me convince Greene not to call his lawyer. He'd seen through my bluster about the search of his car, and he was sure he could beat our charge at trial. The Bureau wouldn't be so easy.

"Okay," he finally said. "I'll hold off calling my lawyer till I decide what to do."

"All right," I answered calmly. "My partner and I'll get rid of the G-men, then we'll take you to a holding cell."

We scraped our chairs back, left the room. Terrance's grin told me he thought I'd planned everything out, that my blunders had actually been feints. I saw no reason to set him straight. Like Liv said, keep your secrets blue.

CHAPTER 35

S O WHERE ARE THE BUREAU BOYS FOR REAL?" TERRANCE ASKED ME in the corridor, still grinning.

"Like I told you on the phone, picking up trash in Rock Creek."

I enjoyed his *What gives?* expression for a moment, then told him how Ted Barston had thrown several boxes of newspaper clippings off the Taft Bridge after proclaiming them to be stolen documents. Terrance's guffaws turned more than a few heads: patrolmen, a female dispatcher walking by; even the desk sergeant poked his head in the hall to see what was so funny.

"They're gonna figure out you rooked 'em."

"Not till after they get their shoes muddy."

He clapped me on the shoulder. "Wish I coulda seen Hoover's fat face when he got that call."

"Yeah, me, too. But I had to shake 'em, had to get that final package."

He shook his head. *Not here.* I nodded as he went back into the interrogation room to give Durkin the "all clear" signal, so he could take Greene to a cell. Then we left the precinct house and I followed my partner to our car, parked on the street.

A pleasant May day, clouds rolling across a powder blue sky, light breeze teasing the budding leaves on the trees lining the sidewalk. We left the windows rolled down, lit up.

"So?" Terrance asked.

"'Yes.'"

"Yes what?"

"*Yes.* That's all the message said, the word 'yes.'"

"You gotta be shitting me."

"Nope."

"What'd he say when you gave it to him, Himmel?"

"Nothing. Said I did a good job, then gave me grief for bringing the Bureau down on the clipping service and fired me."

"Think he's on to you?"

"If he was, would he'a let me fetch this last envelope?"

"What if it's a decoy?"

"Could be." I told him how I thought Himmel hadn't expected me to shake the Bureau's tail, that he'd expected me to get picked up.

He listened, brooding, dragging hard on his cigarette. "Something's not right, Ellis. This Himmel, he seems awful relaxed for a Red about to lose his spies. Why wasn't he in the wind the second you told him the Bureau had picked you up?"

"Because he needed this last delivery."

"For a message that just says 'Yes'? Doesn't add up."

My partner was right but now wasn't the time to fix our math. "Let's forget about Himmel for a second," I said. "What d'you and the old man have on the other messages I brought in? The schematic from the X-ray expert and the postcard about New Mexico?"

He exhaled smoke. "Paslett's due to get reports back on 'em any minute. Otherwise, we know about the same as when we talked last time. What we got down there, in New Mexico—very hush-hush, very secret, m'sure it's a weapons project, but what exactly, I don't know, Paslett doesn't either. My guess, it's our version a'the V-2."

As in the V-2 rocket, the unmanned, guided bombs the Germans had lobbed at Britain in their dying days. The Nazis were now one-day down, but you could bet your last dollar we were still scrambling—as were the Russians—to build our own rockets. Except:

"How do X-rays fit in? Or this uranium you mentioned before?"

"How the hell would I know, I'm no goddamned Einstein."

"Awright, forget the weapon, here's what I think Himmel's up to. He's calm, he's not worried because he's already got almost everything he needs to give to the Russians. God only knows how much he passed on before I showed up, but figure what I delivered was the last of it. So he's done, he's out—he's never going back to K Street again."

"Doesn't care about Greene or that Silva broad."

"Right—let 'em take the rap, what does he care? Everybody's expendable to the Reds."

"Okay, okay, that's why Himmel ordered Greene to kill Skerrill—he wanted us to investigate and arrest the shooter." He snapped his fingers. "Bingo! Just like that, Himmel's taken care'a his mole and found a patsy."

"Right! See, another thing is—I didn't tell you this on the phone—is I think Himmel told Silva to get lovey-dovey with Greene to get him to do Skerrill. Greene's got the hots bad for Silva, wouldn'ta been hard for her to sweet-talk him into it."

"Which means we can arrest Silva as an accessory. There's another problem taken care of for Himmel."

"S'long as Greene decides to face the murder rap. Which I bet he will—he thinks he can beat it at trial. Hell, he's still trying to be a loyal Red, right—that's why he won't take his chances with the Bureau. Wants to protect the spy ring at all costs. What the dumb bastard doesn't realize is, he *is* gonna protect Himmel—but it's gonna put him and Silva in prison to do it."

"Yeah, yeah, this makes a lot more sense." An urgent look. "Where is Himmel—he still at the library? Jesus, we gotta pick him up before he runs."

"For what? We got nothing to hold him on. We got nothing to prove he passed anything to the Russians. We need to know how he meets with—"

"We can arrest him for Skerrill's murder, same as Greene."

"With Greene we got the gun—Himmel, we got nothing."

"Awright, let's pick him up for receiving stolen documents. That X-ray drawing you brought in from the National Bureau of Standards—that's a crime, taking classified plans, more than enough to hold him."

"Except he didn't receive a stolen blueprint, just a drawing anyone could've made. No markings on that sheet, nothing to prove it came from a government agency. Himmel's lawyer would have him out in no time."

"For chrissake, Ellis, you wanna help me figure this out then!" Face red, frustrated.

I couldn't blame him, either. But now it was time to suss out Himmel, to make his actions add up. I was ready to lay it out, fingers crossed tight, hoping that two plus two finally produced four. "Okay, partner, take it easy. Remember I said Himmel's got almost *everything*?"

"Yeah?"

"Means he's not gonna run today. He's got one more pick-up to make, and he's gonna do that in person. That message just says 'Yes'? That's to tell him the meeting's on, but I don't even think Himmel needed to get it, because he was counting on the Bureau taking me in and not letting me go. On the off-chance I made it, he gets confirmation but there's nothing in the envelope to incriminate him."

"So who's he meeting?"

"I don't know. But I'm gonna try to find out right now. You go back in and get Durkin, get over to H & H and arrest Nadine Silva. If she's not there, try her flat." I gave him the address.

"What're we supposed to do with her?"

"Nothing. Stick her in a cell, don't let her call a lawyer. When we can't put her off anymore, we'll grill her, see if we can get her to turn on Greene. Then we'll do the same to Greene. One of 'em cracks, then we can build a case against Himmel."

"How we gonna know what you find out about Himmel?"

"Don't worry, I'll call Paslett soon as I know something, tell him where you can find him."

"I don't know, Ellis, we might be a little off the reservation here—"

"Trust me, partner, okay? I haven't let you down yet, have I?"

HE DID TRUST ME, NOT HAPPILY, SHAKING HIS HEAD AS I GOT OUT. NO offer of a ride, or money—I was on my own. I hailed a hack, had him take me to the Riggs Bank across from the Treasury Building. Left the meter running as I went in to make a withdrawal. O.N.I. had paid for my splurge with Liv at the Willard, least I could do was cover my remaining expenses. I paid the driver and started walking. Eventually, I'd catch a bus, but I had time to spend, I needed to think. *Tried* to think, jumbled observations didn't count. Almost twenty-six years old, eight years in the Navy. Didn't want a promotion, didn't want to stay in uniform. All these years, striving to prove my worth and talents, begging for undercover work before the war ended, like a second-stringer during the fourth quarter. *Put me in, coach.* Careful what you wish for, right? Now that I'd been undercover, now that I'd seen firsthand what you had to do to succeed—just ask Miriam—I'd lost my stomach. Or nerve. Both, probably. If Barston and I could pull it off, if we could bring down Himmel's spy ring, could I leverage that score into a decommission? But then what? Hadn't seen Mom, Pop, and Eddie in two years. Take the train back to Chicago, stay in my old room? Christ, that was no life for a grown man.

But neither was the one I had. Lived alone, two suitcases would pack me up. Had a cat, sort of. More flings than girlfriends. Couldn't quit hoping for more with Liv, couldn't evict Delphine from my dreams. Be funny if it wasn't pathetic: seven to one, women outnumbered men in D.C., and I wanted two women I couldn't have for very different reasons. What if I couldn't get out of the Navy before the Japs called it quits? Liv wasn't going to wait, not her style. *Live free, rest will follow.* If I really wanted to go with her, then I needed to leave the same day she did, damn the consequences. Plunge means *plunge.* Maybe Liv didn't want me to go? Maybe just muster out at the Navy's pace, get married, go to school. Normalcy. Even though I sensed, deep down, that would just be a different type of undercover assignment. Thought of the Austrian novel I'd never finished reading the year before. *Der Mann ohne Eigenschaften.* The man without qualities. Ladies and gentlemen, Ellis Voigt, a.k.a. Theodore Barston, a.k.a. whoever he cannot commit to be, today, tomorrow, forever.

At Longfellow's statue, a decision: being namby-pamby was for the namby-pamby. Hopped on a northbound Connecticut Avenue bus, let the view distract me. Fountain at Dupont, bustling shops, churches, McClellan's statue, lions at the foot of the Taft Bridge. No trace of my crime, the accident long-cleared, the boys from the Bureau gone. Couldn't see if they were still afoot in the Parkway, retrieving clippings, but I hoped Boy G-man, at least, was still down there, snagging his trousers on brambles.

I disembarked at Calvert and walked the long block to the Wardman Park Hotel, atop a well-manicured hillock, looking over D.C. like a Sphinx. Best view in the city, I'd been told, if you were fortunate enough to have an upper-floor suite, didn't matter which side—the building's Greek cross-shape gave all top-dwellers a fair share of the vista. Rates to match, too. I wondered where Himmel's rooms were, recalling Miriam's question when she'd told me, on our second date, that Himmel lived in the hotel: How'd he afford it? Communism being what it was, you'd think his Russian overseers would expect a proletariat address, or, if he must keep up appearances, something petit-bourgeois. The Hotel 2400, say, or a flat in a T Street rowhouse.

House dicks are expert at picking out loiterers. On top of that, the Lebanese and Irish embassies were, for the duration of the war, located inside the Wardman, and both legations had guards roaming the halls. I could get a drink in the lobby bar, sure, nurse it, order another, but what were the chances Himmel would pass through? Residents had their own entrances, their own elevators. I didn't want to stick out, didn't want anyone to remember my face—I sure as hell couldn't call Himmel to see if he was in. But a very desperate Philip Greene could.

I strode across the lobby to the telephone booths and shut myself into one. Thought: *Greene eats his words, he's got a low voice, now he's panicked, he's going to rush to say everything at once.* Had to practice, had to fool Himmel, couldn't let him guess Ted Barston was playing a game with him. I cleared my throat and said, "Mister Himmel, it's Philip Greene"—stop. Voice pitched too high, sounded strained, fake. Also, why would Greene use his last name? He was the only Philip in the office. "Mister Himmel, hello, it's Philip, from the office"—stop. Pitch better, but I was speaking too slowly, still sounded too formal. *Greene's scared, he's desperate, gotta sell that.* "Mister Himmel, it's Philip, listen, I'm in a jam, the cops arrested me"—stop. Better, much better, the phrasing rang true, the voice was closer. I ran that line four or five times, feeling Greene's urgency, hearing his voice in my head.

As a precaution, I partially unscrewed the telephone's speaker—this way, it would rattle when I jiggled the handpiece, making it sound like a bad connection. Then I dropped a nickel to call the switchboard, so it registered as an outside call.

"Wardman Hotel, how may I help you?" a pleasant female voice asked.

"Henry Himmel, please."

"Guest or resident, sir?"

"Resident."

"Just a moment, sir."

A click as she patched me through, three rings, pick-up.

"Yes?"

"Mister Himmel, it's Philip, listen, I'm in a jam, the cops arrested me"—I tilted my head back, mumbling as I shook the instrument for a moment— "need your help."

"You have the wrong number," hanging up.

No matter, he was home; if I'd guessed right, not for long. But how to follow him without being spotted? Had to assume Himmel knew the same tricks, the same tradecraft as I did. He'd be looking for tails when he left the Wardman. If I could see him, he could see me. But if I could find out where he was headed . . . ?

I left the booth, bought a *U.S. News & World Report* at the gift shop, and took a seat in the lobby facing the residents' elevators, close enough to hear the doors open. With my penknife, I carefully cut a slit into the center of the magazine's fold. By tugging the covers apart, I could see through, but an observer would have to look close to notice the peephole. And who lingers on a man reading a magazine in a hotel lobby?

Read an article predicting the Germans would hold out till the end of May. Some news, some report. In the Washington column, a blurb about the closing of the Thomas Jefferson Memorial for renovations. Was halfway through a tearjerker on war widows when Himmel exited, a leather satchel in hand. I closed the peephole, kept the magazine close to my face, now turning my gaze to the wall mirror. Himmel exited and said something to the doorman, who promptly whistled for the next hack in line. Looking like a man in a hurry, Himmel got in the rear, no tip for the doorman. I'd eyed that doorman over when I came in—study everyone, everything, the Funhouse had taught me. Pegged him as a swish, not sure why, hadn't heard him speak, hadn't caught a lisp. Maybe that little stutter-step when he hopped to, the way he'd checked his reflection to see that his bowtie was straight? No choice but to trust my instinct now. I folded a ten dollar bill into a tight triangle, dropped the magazine, and hustled out.

"Oh, no, he's gone," I exclaimed. Trying not to lay it on too thick.

The other doorman grinned maliciously, my guy shot him a disapproving look. "Can I help you, sir?"

I turned and gave him an imploring look. A knowing look. The doorman's eyes flickered as he studied me. *Sell it!* I commanded myself.

"All right, he's angry—well, so am I!"

"Who, sir?"

"Henry, that's who. Did a distinguished-looking gentleman carrying a leather satchel just get into a cab?"

The other doorman was shaking his head in disgust. He edged away, in no mood to overhear a swish sob story.

"A guest did just leave, sir. With a satchel."

"Oh, I knew it." I lowered my voice, leaned close, smiled conspiratorially. "What's your name?"

"Jonathan, sir." Dropping his eyes toward his polished brass nameplate.

"Oh, of course, how silly of me not to notice!"

"Perfectly all right, sir."

Lowering my voice, I said, "Jonathan, thank you for telling me that Henry left and that he went to the . . ." I held out my hand to shake, palming the bill.

"The Automat on F Street? Is that where you'd like to go, sir?"

"Yes, it is!"

He whistled for a hack, I tipped him a quarter to keep up the show. At swank joints like the Wardman, the staff were under strict orders not to reveal where guests went, but I'd guessed right about Jonathan, had found a way to get his sympathy. Fellows who have to hide who they are ought to look out for one another, right?

CHAPTER 36

T HE AUTOMAT, TOUGH BREAK. LOUD, BRIGHT, OPEN FLOOR—TABLES only, no booths, no dark corners. No waitstaff—that was the whole point. Twenty-four hours a day, as long as you had a pocketful of nickels, you could get something to eat from the gleaming glass and chrome cabinets lining the walls: salads, sandwiches, casseroles, soups, pie. Drop a nickel, turn the knob, lift the door. Take your dish, close the door, watch a replacement roll up. Find a table, wolf down your dinner, swill your coffee, and watch others—enlisted men, laborers, G-girls, clerks—do the same. Himmel would be on high alert, for sure, facing the door, back to a wall, using the countless glass doors and cases to observe reflections. He'd be there ahead of me, no time to set up even if there was a place to roost. No time for a disguise, wouldn't fool Himmel anyway. So what to do?

I told my hack we needed to make a stop before the Automat, anything he could do to gain time would fatten his wallet. Anything turned out to be: running two red lights, cutting off a delivery van, and a nifty detour down Florida Avenue to Twenty-third Street instead of staying on Connecticut.

"Lights are timed, see," he growled over the seat, slowing down to the speed limit—we hit nothing but green at every intersection the rest of the way.

"Keep the meter on," I told him as I rushed into the Navy Building, using a side entrance on the Mall. I hadn't been back since I went under as Ted Barston, I needed to keep my head low and stay unnoticed if I could. Fortunately, the office I needed was on the ground floor.

"Well, look what the cat dragged in," a gaunt old man in work clothes and a shop apron greeted me. Shock of bristly gray hair like a Fuller Brush, piercing eyes, liver-spotted face. Long arms and a skinny frame made him look gangly but he was as dexterous as a surgeon.

"Good to see you, too, Filbert."

"Heard you were in—"

"Iceland?"

"Yeah, there."

"I'm back and I wanna buy you dinner at the Automat."

"Gee, a two-bit meal, aren't I glad I got outta bed this morning?" He turned his attention back to the guts of the radio or telephone or whatever the hell was spread out on the table before him. Professor Gadget, we called him, O.N.I.'s expert on all things electrical.

"And give you a chance to field test that miniature transmitter you were telling me about a while ago."

Looking up, he said flatly, "It's not ready." But I could see the interest in his eyes.

"Filbert, do this for me, and I'll convince Commander Paslett to marry his youngest daughter off to you."

"The fat one? No thanks. I'll take a bottle of single malt Scotch from Islay instead."

"Deal," I said, though I had no idea what he was talking about.

"S'pose we gotta go right now."

"How'd you know?"

"Because the day one'a you bastards tells me there's no hurry is the day I retire."

I forced a grin and tried not to look anxious as he took down a wooden crate from a shelf packed with tubes, wires, casings, and circuit boards. He set down the box, took off the top, and began inspecting the contents. Turned dials, flipped toggles, snapped a battery into a socket. *C'mon, c'mon* I wanted to say but I held my tongue. Finally he put the top back on the box and started to untie his apron.

"You can do that in the car, Filbert—we gotta go."

"Aw, for chrissake," he grumbled, but he picked up the box and I hustled him to the waiting cab.

Soon as we were under way, he was like a kid on Christmas, showing off his loot. "So what we got here, what I did is, I took a Stancor Twenty-P with a C.P. transmitter, but I built the modulator myself—no way ten watts gives you the range you need, and I opened up the frequency range, using Meissner one-tube regenerative receivers, so we can go anywhere from one to seventy megacycles. . . ."

I nodded, repeating *uh-huh, uh-huh* like it all made sense, waiting for him to take a breath. "Filbert, if you're sitting at a table next to someone, will I be able to hear what they're saying?"

"Have you been listening to a word of what I've been telling you? The microphone's got a range of twenty feet and with the amplifiers I got here on the board, you're gonna . . ."

This time I concentrated and what I thought I heard was: Filbert had custom-built a one-way, wireless radiotelephone. The receiver (me) could hear everything the microphone picked up by listening on an adapted field telephone with a headset. He had designed the microphone to look like a pen—the sender let it jut from a shirt pocket.

"Now, if this works the way it oughta, the next step is, what I'm gonna do is, I'm gonna wire it to a Dictaphone disc, so we can—"

"Filbert, how're you gonna hide the microphone wire that connects to the board? Our mark, he's awful suspicious, somebody sits down near him with that gizmo, he's gonna know—"

"Think you're the only one who's ever done field work, hot-shot? All I gotta do is run the wire through my sleeve before I go in. I put the box on the chair next to me and plug into the jack while I'm doing that. This mark, if he looks over, all he's gonna see is a poor old man stopping off for his dinner after an errand." He held up his rig. I hadn't noticed at the Navy Building, but Filbert had installed his contraption inside an old wooden box with *Bekin Hardware* painted on the side, the letters faded.

"That looks pretty good," I said.

He shrugged. "Only box I had that was the right size."

The cabbie pulled to the curb a block away from the Automat, as I'd instructed him. I passed him fifteen bucks on the six-fifty fare and ignored Filbert's bug-eyed reaction.

"Well, look at Mister Moneybags, tipping hacks like there's no tomorrow while the old man only gets—"

"Two bottles, okay, Filbert? I'll get you two bottles of that bourbon you want—"

"Scotch! There's a big difference."

"Okay, okay, let's go!"

I flung open the door and led Filbert to the alley behind the Automat. "Lemme do the talking, okay?"

"Yes, your highness."

Ignoring that crack, I pounded on the metal door marked DELIVERIES. A chunky teenager in a spotless uniform of white pants, shirt, and garrison cap opened the door and looked us over.

"No salesmen," he began.

"Step aside, sonny," I cut him off, "we're here on an important military matter." I stepped forward, he backed in, we came inside. "Show him your card, Filbert," I said.

The kid gawked at the out-held O.N.I. identification card as I told him what we were going to do: my partner was setting up a top-secret telephone in the service area, and the kid had to make sure no one bothered us.

"Can you handle that?" I finished.

"Yessir!" he exclaimed, chopping off a not-half-bad salute.

"Good. Where's the best spot, Filbert?"

The old man was all business now, surveying the kitchen like a cat burglar looking for the silver. "Here," he ordered, pointing to a long aluminum table cluttered with baking utensils. "Get all this crap outta my way," he barked at the kid, who jumped to. Filbert assembled the radiotelephone, flicked a switch, grunted approvingly when it began to hum. Walking to the rear wall, the circuit board under his arm, he lifted the pencil microphone to his lips and chin-ticked for me to lift the headset. As soon as I had it on, Filbert whispered, "Got any sisters, Voigt, 'cause that boy looks awful horny and you owe him."

I grinned and gave him a thumbs-up.

"What'd he say?" the kid asked me eagerly.

"He said you'll make a fine sailor."

"For real?"

"Sure thing, kid, now go keep guard for us."

He scrambled away as I described Himmel to Filbert. He nodded briskly and exited into the alley, carrying the wooden box. The pen microphone was in his shirt pocket, its wire running down his sleeve, out of sight. Just as he'd said, all he had to do was set the box on a chair, connect the jack, and keep his left arm at his side.

I sidled up to the service doors and peeked through the portal window. Sure enough, Himmel was sitting at a corner table, facing the door. Across from him was a slender, young, intense-looking man. Dark eyes under thick, arched brows, black hair parted to the side, Brylcreem glistening. High cheekbones, narrow chin, thin wrists jutting from crisp white cuffs fastened with silver links. Navy blue sweater, yellow tie, herringbone jacket. They were already talking—nothing I could do but wait for Professor Gadget to get settled and wired.

He didn't dawdle, Filbert, but he still had to buy a slice of pie to keep his cover. Wisely, he left an empty table between himself and Himmel, who eyed him over quickly, then turned his attention back to his contact. Filbert looked like a harmless old man with an ordinary box. I hurried back to the baking counter, giving the excited kid a thumbs-up. I fitted the headset on and got out pencil and notebook. A loud crackle as Filbert connected the cord to the circuit board's jack, a brief humming, then—

... *don't care, don't give a damn* (Himmel's contact, his voice surprisingly deep).

All right. Himmel calm, waiting.

What you call improvising, I call security.

Yes, I see. Another meaningless agreement. When your man breaks the rules, you let him explain, let him talk as long as he wants—only way to find out if you've been compromised.

This blind devotion to couriers, I just don't understand it.

The old ways, they have their uses.

But this is the oldest way of all, isn't it? A tête-à-tête?

Yes.

Don't worry, I wasn't followed, not once since I left the desert.

That's good.

But enough chit-chat, right?

No reply from Himmel. A shrug, perhaps upturned palms?

How's your memory?

Excellent.

Because what I'm about to say, you must commit to memory.

All right.

Don't you want to know why?

No. Proceed.

Long pause, sounds of the Automat filling the silence: clatter of plates, murmur of conversation, burst of laughter from a distant table. I wished I could see what was happening. Was Himmel staring down his contact, trying to end a very risky meeting with someone who'd traveled such a long way to say something in person to the handler he was never supposed to meet? Then:

Fine, I'm only going to say it once: to diffuse the Uranium two-thirty-five, use uranium hexafluoride and a metal filter with submicroscopic perforations. Do not use a mass spectrometer. Got that?

Yes. How do you know this?

What, a Ph.D. in physics from Yale at twenty-two isn't sufficient bond?

What a blunder! Boasting, giving away his biography—I scribbled happily.

How do you know this? Himmel unfazed, staying in control.

Look, even a brief summary would take all night and you wouldn't understand a word anyway. So how's this: our visitor from afar was indispensable in helping my team reach these conclusions and conduct the necessary tests with rousing success. And in a coupla months, maybe less, the whole world's gonna find out what a big, big bang of a success we've pulled off.

Very good.

Now, as long as you remember exactly what I just told you, your physicists will know what to do with this.

A whisk, a scrape, something sliding. Had to be an envelope, its metal clasp dragging across the laminated tabletop. No response from Himmel.

Now you can tell me something. I've learned my contact on that trip met with an untimely demise.

Yes, he did. Himmel's voice flat.

An accident?

He was murdered.

By whom?

The local police are still investigating.

And they'll get their man, right. (Sarcastic laugh.) *Now memorize this: this is my last delivery, my last contact.* Scrape of chair, echo of steps; Automat sounds again, and Filbert's shallow breathing. Then a loud crackle as Filbert disconnected. I peeled off the headset, dropped it to the counter, stared at my shorthand notes, the jumbled pieces fitting together. . . .

Boy Genius from New Mexico gives Himmel instructions on Uranium 235 . . . not the first reference to uranium—Terrance says Paslett blanched when he heard it earlier. Terrance on the hush-hush base in New Mexico: *my guess, it's our version a'the V-2.* Millions of dollars rushed through Congress, no public record, no hearings, funneling straight into New Mexico. Boy Genius to Himmel: *my contact on that trip met with an untimely demise.* Boy Genius running scared, blustering past the fright, asking casually about his contact but then saying: I'm done, got it? Not wanting the same fate as his contact, a.k.a. Logan Skerrill, both men aboard the Bermuda Special, fetching that runaway German scientist. Worth the trouble, worth the time—said German *indispensable.* Two months, maybe less: bang, bang, predicts Boy Genius. Can't be V-2s, he's too proud of what he's done, has to be something new, original, out-of-the-blue. With uranium. Can you make a bomb from uranium? No idea, a question for the physicists, for Paslett—all I know is: down in New Mexico, they've built some kind of bomb, a real doozy. Japs are still fighting. Bang, bang, Tokyo?

Can't know, not my job. This is: thanks to Boy Genius, the Reds have the last piece of the puzzle to build their own bomb. And thanks to Skerrill, the F.B.I. knows the Reds know a lot about that bomb. But my pals Slater and Reid, they don't know about the last, vital step needed to finish the bomb. Only Himmel and I do.

The alley door burst open, a breathless Filbert rushed in, clutching his wooden box.

"I was too far away, didn't hear anything—did you get it?" Practically quivering with excitement.

"Your rig worked great, Filbert—I got it all."

CHAPTER 37

GAVE FILBERT CAB FARE, TOLD HIM TO TELL NO ONE WHERE HE'D BEEN, and swore the kid to secrecy. Then I exited through the alley, walking around to F Street to wait for Himmel. Sound tradecraft: let your contact go first, give him time. Himmel would stay at the table, maybe refill his coffee. Figure he had men waiting outside. Boy Genius had told Himmel, *Don't worry, I wasn't followed.* Himmel'd figure he was wrong, just hadn't seen his shadows all the way from New Mexico. The Reds were awful careful, awful suspicious, wouldn't let a source like him roam free, not after he sent word he was leaving the reservation to make his delivery in person. Final one, too, according to him. *This is my last delivery, my last contact.* Maybe, maybe not. Parting ways with the Reds wasn't so easy. Better avoid Washington's alleys, Boy Genius.

I smoked a Lucky Strike, glad to be done with Barston's Old Golds. Wishing I had time for a drink or three. Dusky sky, day giving way, city cast in twilight's unreliable light, distances hard to gauge, lights blinking on in buildings, curtains being drawn. At ten to eight, Himmel came out of the Automat and stepped to the curb, looking for a hack. One pulled to the curb, he opened the rear door. I sprinted forward and jumped in behind the driver right after Himmel shut his door.

"Hopin' you got a moment ta talk, Mister Himmel," I said.

"We already had our talk, Ted."

"I know, but sometin's come up I wanna tell you about."

"All right." Calm, unfazed—just like at the Automat.

"Jefferson Memorial," I told the driver.

He nodded at me in his mirror and headed west to Fourteenth. I didn't tell Himmel why we were going there, he knew. Public space, wide open—neutral ground, good for us both. Did he know the memorial had just been closed for renovations? I figured no, city happenings not his concern. Short ride, long silence, neither of us talking, hack quiet, too. Almost fully dark when he dropped us off. Funny how that happens, last light goes so quickly on spring nights.

I paid the driver, we got out. I motioned toward the memorial, relieved to see a temporary wooden fence encircling the marble base. Even better: the gravel path beneath the cherry trees, the route Liv and I had taken during our closed-eye stroll, was blocked off, so passersby couldn't come around to the west side.

"It's closed," Himmel said.

"S'alright, Thomas Jefferson doesn't need to hear any of this." In my normal voice.

He gave a faint smile, looking around to make sure we were alone. "You shouldn't have been able to find me."

"Shouldn't have been able to overhear your conversation, either."

He shook his head, not believing me, reaching into his jacket for a cigar.

"'To diffuse the Uranium two-thirty-five, use uranium hexafluoride and a metal filter with submicroscopic perforations, do not use a mass spectrometer,'" I said softly but clearly.

His head snapped up, right hand still holding the unlit cigar to his lips. Had to give him credit, he recovered quickly. Didn't sputter, didn't demand to know how. Just—"You are resourceful, aren't you, Lieutenant Voigt?"

"Could say the same about you, Pavel Nevelskoi."

He smiled, took his time lighting the cigar.

I lit up, too, trying to kill the shake that wanted to overtake my hands.

He said, "It will not do you any good, that name. No more than the names Lenin, or Stalin, or Trotsky." Legends, aliases, pseudonyms—the Russians were masters. Not that it mattered who Pavel Nevelskoi was for real.

"Gotta say, you played along perfectly," I said. "I just about pissed my pants when I saw you at H & H."

"You hid your surprise well, lieutenant."

"Wasn't so easy, fooling Silva all that time."

"No, she is quite observant."

"How did you know the Navy would send me in with a cover?"

"That's not important now. What is, is that the result has worked to the benefit of both of us."

"How's that?"

But he didn't answer, instead asked, "How did you trace Skerrill to H & H?"

"Our internal security detail observed him entering the office. We're prohibited from using clipping services, so my partner and I followed up." I didn't tell him that Paslett, working off the partial report obtained from the F.B.I., had suspected the clipping service was a front.

"Very thorough. How lucky for us, that your superior selected you to go—what is the phrase you Americans use, under cover?"

I said, "Yeah, it was his idea for me to get a job with you."

"Yes. Your approach was quite unusual, but, I think, suited the situation."

"How come you didn't already have a deliveryman?"

"We did—Philip made all the deliveries. After you came in, I told him and Nadine that I had asked the party to find someone else we could use and that you had been sent. Philip believed me, but Nadine, she wasn't so easily persuaded."

"Like you said, she's awful observant. But she went along, always the loyal Red."

He shrugged, puffed on his cigar. We'd walked to the south side of the memorial, its dome and colonnade dark.

"Musta been hard to set up her lover," I said. "But she knew it had to be done after she got the letter meant to sound like a note from an old friend, telling her to dump Skerrill pronto. That was the order for the hit, wasn't it?"

Again, no reply. He was still wondering how much I knew, letting me tell it. I had nothing to lose by opening up, but I couldn't let him get suspicious, had to keep him thinking I had something important to tell him.

"So you told her you'd take care of it. But she didn't know what that would feel like, did she, till the news broke." I laughed. "No way to avoid reading about it, is there, at a clipping service? And when she realized it had happened for real, she got emotional, even shed a few tears for Logan Skerrill, her lover boy and fellow Red."

"Are you trying to coax me into telling you why we had Skerrill killed?" Smiling contemptuously.

"Don't be shy, I know he was working for the Bureau."

"If this is true, this is a very good reason to kill him, yes?"

"If you say so."

He laughed cynically. "Now who is being shy? You took pleasure in what you did."

"No."

"I don't believe you." Drawing on his cigar, squinting at me through the plume of smoke. "Skerrill was your rival, he was better than you, he was the darling of the Office of Naval Intelligence. You, Voigt, struggled to complete your training and you failed in your first field assignment, couldn't even fool those *ersatz* fascists."

"How did you find out Skerrill had gone to the Bureau?" I asked calmly, ignoring the taunts.

He shrugged. Translation: you're not meant to know, you're just the hired hand used to take care of a problem.

"He always was too clever for his own good, wasn't he?" I pressed. "Always wanting more excitement, more risk."

"His motive for helping the Bureau doesn't matter anymore, does it?"

"Nothing matters to Logan Skerrill anymore."

A harsh laugh. "Is that why we are here, Voigt? Do you need reassurance, do you want me to say you are safe, as long as you keep quiet?"

"No, I'm here to tell you the police have arrested Philip Greene for Skerrill's murder."

"I already know, he called me—"

"That was me. Pretending to be him."

"To see if I answered." Understanding immediately that was how I'd followed him.

I nodded.

Himmel said, "How clever of you. But it's true, Greene has been arrested?"

"Yes. I framed him for the killing of Skerrill." Remembering how I'd imagined myself as Greene after I broke into his apartment, imagining him killing Skerrill, pretending that he'd hidden the gun in the jacket hanging on his coat rack. I'd had the gun with me the whole time, of course—it had been in the rucksack at the Jefferson Club. But I couldn't imagine myself out of this spot. "I planted the gun in his car, then let it get towed," I continued. "Once it was in the city impoundment lot, we could search it without a warrant. Of course the gun matches the bullet taken from the body."

"What if he has an alibi for that night?"

"Probably he does—that's why he's eager to go to trial."

"What do you mean?"

"When he yelped for a lawyer, I threatened to hand him over to the Bureau to face espionage charges. He thinks our case is weak—hell, he knows he's innocent. Why wouldn't he go into D.C. Superior Court instead'a facing up to the Bureau for crimes he knows he's guilty of?"

"I see. I suppose I should thank you."

"For?"

"Protecting the cell. That must not be easy, you must still feel some allegiance to the Navy."

"I'm protecting myself more than anything, aren't I?"

Laughing, he said, "Yes, but as I said earlier, the results are serving both of us nicely."

I let that ride and said, "I convinced my partner that Silva put Greene up to the murder, so she was also arrested today. They're gonna put the same squeeze on her—'take an accessory to murder charge or we'll turn you over to the Bureau.' I thought you'd want to know all this. They'll see through the scam soon enough, Greene and Silva, but not until you've had time to roll up your operation."

"Very helpful, Voigt. Maybe too helpful."

"Come again?"

"What is it you want for doing this? Please don't tell me you did this because you consider yourself to be, how did you put it, a 'loyal Red'?"

"I'm not asking for anything," I answered in a steady voice.

We'd reached the fencing enclosing stacks of stone and brick for the memorial's renovation. If anyone was looking across the Tidal Basin, the cherry trees along the bank obscured our figures. No lights, no shadows. I checked the urge to look around—I'd already done that, a minute ago, when Himmel wasn't watching my face. We were alone.

"I don't believe you," he said firmly. "Is it that you want to say what my contact told me at the restaurant? That you are also finished, you want nothing more to do with us?"

"I'm not that naïve, Mister Nevelskoi. Once in, you never leave, right?"

He laughed softly. "You make it sound like a life sentence, lieutenant. Don't you know—"

I leapt forward, catlike, squeezing the trigger of the thirty-two I'd slipped from my waistband as I pressed the barrel with its homemade silencer just beneath his heart. I just caught his cry, thrusting the handkerchief I'd wadded up with my left hand into his open mouth. Took him to the ground, tossing the gun so he couldn't grab it. He struggled underneath me, kicking, flailing, biting. I turned my head, dug my toes into the ground, clutched fistfuls of grass, seeking purchase, weight. Had to smother him, had to keep him quiet, wait for him to bleed out, had to trust in that single shot. I pushed the gag in harder, took a vicious bite on the pad of my thumb, gritted my teeth against the pain. He managed to knee me, I shifted my weight. His right hand worked free, pounded my back. Then—

He went limp. I didn't dare move, fearing he was playing possum. Tried to control my rushed breathing, so I could listen for his breath, but I was panting like a dog. I lay on top of Himmel, my shirt soaked with sweat, my left hand throbbing and slick with blood from the bite. Finally I thought to reach around for the hand lying on my back, fumbled to find his wrist, awkwardly pressed two fingers against the still-warm, damp skin. No pulse.

I rolled off but didn't stand. Had to stay low to the ground in case the muffled sounds of our struggle had cocked a faraway ear, had caused someone across the Tidal Basin to stop and ask, "What's that?" On my hands and knees, I searched for the thirty-two, found it five feet from Himmel's body. A year ago I'd found that weapon during the search of a suspect's billet, had taken it without telling anyone. The serial number was filed off, the suspect drew a ten-year sentence for black marketeering and theft of government property. Figured someday I might need an untraceable weapon. So I'd outfitted the thirty-two with the type of silencer they'd taught us to make at the Funhouse, wrapped it in an oiled rag, and put it in my safety deposit box at the Riggs Bank, along with the forged passport and 854 dollars in cash that I now also carried.

I crept over to the body and searched Himmel's pockets until I found a sealed envelope. Ripped it open, pulled out a complicated schematic that made no sense. No matter, had to be the item Boy Genius had passed to Himmel at the Automat. I pocketed it—thankfully, there was no bloodstain on the envelope, just on my shirt. A small caliber wound, upward into the heart, the bleeding had been mostly internal. I hadn't wanted a mess, didn't want to leave a trace of what I'd done. Guess I'd learned a lesson or two from killing Logan Skerrill.

CHAPTER 38

WHAT HAPPENED WAS, I FELL IN LOVE WITH DELPHINE. SIXTEEN years old, both of us, just starting our junior year at Chicago's Lakeview High in the fall of 1935. Delphine: raven-haired, slender, black eyes, dusky skin, five feet tall maybe, second generation Sicilian. Intensely quiet, like she had plenty to say but no one to say it to, only a girlfriend or two. Not like the other pretty girls, who roamed the halls in chattering packs, parting the between-bells crowd like fire engines—no, Delphine drifted alone from class to lunchroom to yard with a flickering smile. I first noticed it in English class. After mentally tracing the curve of her calf into the folds of her pleated skirt, after noting her tiny waist and the swell of her hips, her breasts, the brightness in her almond-shaped eyes—all that beauty rushing into my impressionable sixteen-year-old head, but it was her smile that stuck and took over my thoughts. Was she, like me, thinking about how stupid our classmates were? How dull and washed-out our teachers were? What observations, what daydreams, teased out that smile? And why didn't I have the goddamned nerve to drift alongside her in the corridor and ask her? Then:

"Do you think he's weak, like he says?" Asking me, casting her gaze at Mr. Jurgensen, our English teacher, as class ended one October morning.

"Who?" Practically struck dumb.

"Macbeth." Watching me closely, no smile now. Wondering, *Is he just like the others?*

"No," I answered firmly.

"Then what is he?"

"In love."

"Convince me."

So I did, walking her to lunch, jabbering about the play and how dense Jurgensen was, about how he didn't get that Macbeth wasn't as weak as he seemed, that maybe he wasn't being manipulated, maybe he was plotting, scheming, letting murder into his mind because he was in love with Lady Macbeth.

"Funny how that happens," Delphine said.

"What?"

"That the woman takes the blame."

I'd never heard anything like that before, as my face must have shown.

"Don't believe me, huh? Ask Ophelia." And with that she stood, picked up her tray, and walked away without a look back. Knowing I was watching, knowing I'd caught her smile, knowing I'd stay up all night re-reading Hamlet, knowing I'd sidle up in the corridor the next morning, bleary-eyed but jazzed, ready with my response.

Every lunch after that day, together. My friends teased me mercilessly; I barely heard them, stopped even seeing them, their faces dull white blobs, one indistinguishable from the other. Maybe that's what's best about first love, never to be repeated: everyone around you blurs and falls out of focus, like a Greek chorus, off-stage. Only me and Delphine, bright and vibrant, the sun shining only for us. Disdaining the Rainbow Rink and Riverview Park—roller skates, Shoot-the-Chutes, the Tunnel of Love, they all seemed like two-bit entertainment for kids, yesterday's news for two sophisticates like us. We went to the Preston-Bradley Theater to see plays staged by the Federal Theater Project; we hung out at a coffee shop where Delphine had befriended a group of regulars, writers for the W.P.A. who collected life stories from Uptown residents. We listened intently as they regaled each other with that day's "catch," a game they played, telling tales about the folks they'd interviewed—you had to guess which stories were true, which ones false. They were only a few years older than us, college students forced out of school by the Depression and cub reporters cut by struggling papers, but they were emissaries from another world that appeared, through our teenage eyes, to be carefree, independent, smart.

Delphine and I went to countless movies together, all that fall and into 1936. One Saturday, in the balcony of the Uptown, the first matinee, no one else around, we'd slipped under the "Closed" sign dangling from a velvet rope and snuck up the stairs. Entranced by "The Petrified Forest," watching Gabrielle clutch Alan as he dies.

"When a woman puts her hands on a man's back like that in a movie, it means they're lovers," Delphine whispered.

"Gabrielle and Alan never slept together," I whispered back.

"They never got the chance, did they?" Her breath hot in my ear, my hand on her thigh. Both of us knowing the next film didn't start for forty-five minutes, both of us knowing the ushers wouldn't come up, not if we were quiet. Mostly quiet.

We knew we'd be together after we graduated, never had to talk about it, didn't have to make a plan. Delphine was determined to go to college, she wanted to be a professor—not a teacher, a professor—and spend her life teaching students the right way to read Shakespeare, Dos Passos, Thoreau. No money for me to go to school, I hoped I could get on with the W.P.A. and join the coffee shop crew, then come home every night to Delphine. No tuition money for her, either, but at home she needled her pop, Rosario, dropping lines like "After I get my first degree" or "I should give Northwestern another look." He'd shake his fist at her. "You're'a not'a gonna go to no college!" She'd give it right back, the two of them yelling. Took me a couple of visits to realize they were play-acting, her pop laying on the thick Italian accent to tease me, Delphine delighting in my discomfort. In truth, Rosario had flawless English—he'd arrived in the States as a young boy—and was studious, well-read. But not bookish, like his daughter, who read for the joy of it. Rosario was an organizer for the

Congress of Industrial Organizations, hellbent on putting a union card in the hand of every laborer he could buttonhole outside a factory gate or shop entrance. He read so he could persuade, recruit, build the industrial army. I should have caught on when I scanned the titles of his impressive library. Kropotkin, *Memoirs of a Revolutionist*. Lenin, *Key Speeches*. Marx, *Theories of Surplus Value*. In Italian, books by Pareto, Gramsci.

Rosario liked me, let Delphine bring me home to dinner. He was a natural-born teacher. Where others argued, he asked. *But what is a fair wage, Ellis?* Letting me ramble, listening intently, then saying, *There's a book I think you might like to read*. Going to his library, pulling the title off the shelf, pressing it into my hands. Not, *you must read*, nor, *I want you to read*. Unlike so many believers, whatever their religion, Rosario understood that a change of consciousness could not be imposed, it had to be invited in by the willing. But I do not believe, and never have, that he intended to bring me into the fold, that he wanted me to join the party. At least not before May 30, 1937.

That spring, Rosario served on the leadership committee of the Steel Workers Organizing Committee. The Wagner Act had legalized collective bargaining, the steel owners didn't care. When Republic Steel shut out its workers, the C.I.O. vowed to fight. A picket was scheduled for May 30, Memorial Day; Delphine and I plastered the north side with handbills. Delphine's mom warned Rosario not to take us, arguing with him. She was not well-read, her people had come from Sicily as contract laborers, but sometimes a peasant's wisdom is keener than the intellectual's book-learning.

What a sight! Outside the mill, hundreds of workers amassed, spread out in a field, moving toward Republic's main gate. Day bright and sunny, warm. Rosario darted back and forth, beckoning to stragglers, urging them to get in line. Delphine and I handed out signs, until they were all gone. *Republic Steel vs. The People*. The strikers chanted, "Who builds America?," answering, "We do, we do!"

What we saw as a rally, Republic saw as a siege. In front of the gate, more than one hundred Chicago police stood in a solid line, billy clubs and sidearms already in hand, a fleet of paddy wagons parked close by. Delphine and I looked around for Rosario, who was thirty yards or so in front of us, arguing with a police captain. "We've got a legal right to peace-fully picket," Rosario shouted, the officer just shaking his head. The chant changed: "Let us through, let us through!" The police shifted, pressing closer—when a striker shook his fist, a patrolman clubbed his forearm and pushed him to the ground.

"They can't force us out, there's too many of us," Delphine shouted to me.

The first shots barely registered, a burst of pops, puffs of smoke, cries of alarm. We were buffeted by workers running away from the police charge. I grabbed Delphine's hand and turned to run, too, but she yanked me forward.

"C'mon, let's get Pop before he gets shot." She saw my doubt, saw my fear. "Mom'll kill me if I don't bring him home," she cracked.

I forced a smile and said, "When you put it like that."

We pushed forward, but the retreat was pell-mell, everyone running, a stampede. I wanted to lead—I was a foot taller than Delphine, I could see over most heads—but she stayed in front of me, pulling at my hand. We got clipped on the shoulders, we had to zig and zag, but somehow we managed to stay on our feet. A bug-eyed barrel of a man charged at us, I yanked us out of his way just before he knocked us down. Then we were clear, away from others, and in the rush to catch my breath, I didn't notice a body lying close, not until Delphine spoke.

"My God, what have they—"

I never heard the shot, only saw her head turn suddenly, her chin slumping—she looked like she'd dropped something. Until she collapsed.

THE DOCTOR ROSARIO MANAGED TO FIND TOLD US IT DIDN'T MATTER that twenty minutes had elapsed before he could see to her. She'd died quickly, he said, probably didn't feel anything. The doctor lied—I watched Delphine die. She sputtered, unable to speak; her breathing rasped, wheezed, rattled; she shook my hand away when I tried to hold it; her eyes fluttered. Did she hear me screaming for help, did she see the tears streaking my face, did she hear me promise everything would be all right?

Not that it mattered. Because Delphine couldn't hear me when I told Rosario I wanted revenge, that I wanted to help the party destroy the men who arranged for steel workers and a teenage girl to be mown down like rabbits, shot in the back, left to die in dirt. Sure, I hated the cops, but Rosario had taught me they were just stooges, dupes, the hired guns of the men who really mattered, the men who rigged the system to make themselves filthy rich. The men *I* would make pay, one day.

After the funeral, after the union's memorial service for the fallen—Delphine and nine men dead—Rosario gave me a street address, had me memorize it. *Don't write anything down, you understand?* I responded, *Yessir,* as if I were a buck private. Three days before my high school graduation, I went to the address, nighttime, knocked. Steel door, plain brick one-story building on an industrial block, no lights. I repeated what Rosario had told me to the man who answered my knock. He let me in, led me wordlessly to a shop floor. No introductions, no preamble—for the next two hours, I sat on a wooden chair under a dim bulb and answered every question imaginable about my upbringing, my family, my education. Three men, sitting just outside the light, faces not visible, just disembodied voices and a hovering cloud of cigarette smoke. *If we want to see you again, we'll let you know,* they said. When Rosario didn't contact me for a week, I was sure I'd failed the test—and I didn't dare call him. Then, as I sat despondently at the coffee shop early one afternoon, waiting for the W.P.A. crew to come in, a scrap of paper fluttered to the table. I looked up, saw only the back of a man leaving. A different address scribbled down, no time given. Figured I was supposed to arrive at the same hour as my first visit. Two different men gave me a battery of written tests. They barely spoke, handing me sheets of paper. *Start . . . Stop . . . Start . . . Stop.* After three hours, *You can go now.* No word about contacting me.

I sweated it out two weeks, June almost gone, my folks on my case to get a job, before the next message found me. Yet another address, different men again. They told me I'd passed, was I ready to go on? *Yes, yes, yes,* I babbled, expecting they'd now give me my membership card and have me sign a roster—dumb kid! Anyone wants to join the Communist Party of the United States of America, all he has to do is ask, pay his dues, sign his name. But the party sure as hell doesn't want to record the names of its recruits for industrial and government espionage, doesn't want any trace of their presence. Just like Rosario had said. *Don't write anything down, understand?* So:

"We want you to join the Navy, Ellis."

"What if the Navy won't take me?"

"Then you're of no use to us."

I enlisted the next morning.

I THOUGHT ROSARIO WOULD BE PROUD, BUT HE WAS A WRECK, HIS clothing disheveled, stubble on his face, the flat a mess, Delphine's mom nowhere to be seen. The windows were down and the curtains were drawn, air stale, Rosario unwashed—the stench of grief. Leaving, I knew I could never see him again. To keep my party cover, I needed to stay away from known communists, suspected communists, parlor pinks, fellow travelers—anyone who skewed Red. But that wasn't the only reason. When Rosario finally looked up as I told him what I was doing, I realized he wasn't listening to a word I was saying. His red-rimmed eyes gave away his thoughts: *Why didn't the bullet hit him?* No matter what I did for the party, I could never bring Delphine back to him. Whatever I was about to do, I had to do for myself, by myself. *And for Delphine,* I resolved as I shut the door on her broken father. I was a month shy of my eighteenth birthday, and I believed I was invincible, indispensable, and destined to be a hero. How different our lives would be if, at eighteen, we could know that we are not, and never will be, any of these things.

CHAPTER 39

I DRAGGED HIMMEL'S BODY TOWARD THE CONSTRUCTION FENCING AND covered it with a tarp I pulled from a stack of lumber. Buttoned up my jacket to hide the bloodstain. Lit a cigarette and walked east on the footpath, trying to keep a leisurely pace. A man out for a stroll, taking the night air. Crossed Route 1, passed under the Southern Railroad tracks, walked into the Tourist Camp in East Potomac Park. Not too many tents this time of year, but I wasn't the only one enjoying the evening.

"Howdy!" a stocky man called out.

"Evening!" I responded heartily. Duck a stranger's greeting, he's sure to remember you.

He was walking a terrier that got awful excited about my pants as I passed, straining at his leash, growling.

"Bruiser! Behave now." Over his shoulder, "Sorry about that."

"Not a problem." Good thing dogs can't talk; what tales they'd tell.

The Tourist Camp abutted the Potomac, and I'd always noticed a skiff or small boat pulled up on the gravelly shore whenever I drove over the river. I walked up to a rowboat anchored with a cement-filled coffee can.

"Mind if I take her out for a little row?" I called out to an elderly couple sitting in lawn chairs.

"Go right ahead!" the man said cheerfully. "Lovely evening, isn't it?"

"You bet!"

"You just get in?" his wife asked.

"Yep, just pitched my tent in the back row."

"Hope you're not too close to the tracks," the man said, motioning; "those trains run day and night."

"Oh, don't you worry, I'm a heavy sleeper," I answered with a big grin, spooling the rope round my arm and lifting the anchor into the bow. Pushed off, hopped in, mounted the oars, dipped.

Lovely evening, indeed. Lights twinkling in the Pentagon across the Potomac, waves wriggling like eels, breeze teasing the cherry blossoms. I rowed hard, relishing the strain in my shoulders, the rough feel of the oars in my hands. The exertion eased the sting of my memories and the pain in my hand from Himmel's bite.

The Reds mostly left me alone my first year in the Navy. Wanted to see how I'd do, wanted to see if I could parlay my training as an Aviation Ordnanceman at the Great Lakes Training Station into an ensign's commission. That took studying and plenty of boot-licking, but I got the commission and went to Officer Candidate School. Easy to forget my secret, except I'd been told to read the Lost and Found section of a local paper every day. *Lost: young beagle, tan and white spots, answers to Cato, last seen in Hull Park, call Admiral 9356, reward* was my summons, my signal to come to a windowless warehouse. I was too dense to get the joke, to see that I was a dog on a leash, cocking an ear at his master's voice. (Delphine would have seen the metaphor right away.) I thought they were briefings, that what I was telling my handlers about Navy procedures and training was valuable intelligence, but their questions only meant to make me feel important. They were checking up on me, making sure I was advancing toward the true prize: an assignment in the O.N.I., which came not long after Pearl.

Just as a different group of handlers in another city was tracking a bright penny named Logan Skerrill. Funny how we never caught on to one another at the Funhouse. Had to give the Reds credit, they made me feel like I was the only one. Watertight security, every cell sealed off like the compartments of a submarine. By the time I wised up, finally grasped what Rosario had known all along—nothing we did could ever bring Delphine back—it was too late to get out. The Reds had recorded every "briefing," they had photographed me passing copies of documents from Paslett's files to my courier in Washington, an American whom I only knew as Michael. It was Michael who warned me, who immediately saw through my request to lie low for a while.

"We don't get to decide that, John—they do." He ticked his head over his shoulder, the sort of gesture only someone standing next to you will notice.

Himmel might have laughed when I said, "Once in, you never leave," but only because he knew it was true. If I'd tried to break free when I first wanted to, the Reds would have sacrificed me and Michael, staging it so that our separate deaths looked like accidents. No one would ever know we'd been spies or that we'd even known one another.

I steered the rowboat alongside the retaining wall by the Jefferson Memorial and tossed the anchor onto the grass. No one around, but I had to hurry. The construction might not deter a passerby, a dogwalker might happen along. Hopped the fence, heaved two large stones over; they thumped into the soft ground. Cut a length of rope from a tarp stretched over sacks of mortar mix and put it and the stones into the boat. Now the hardest part: dragging Himmel's body to the boat, getting it in. If I rolled the corpse over the gunwales, the thud would carry loud and clear across the Tidal Basin. There was a naval barracks in West Potomac Park, a guard might investigate, flashlight in hand. But how else to do it? I peeled the tarp off, set it and the rope in the boat's bow. Thought: he's not dead, he's drunk, too soused to stand. How would someone manage that? Scrambled over to the body, crouched, and reached behind me. Grabbed the arms and wrapped them tight around my shoulders, trying not to shudder. Carefully, taking deep breaths, I stood slowly, grunting with the effort—Jesus, he was heavy. Crab-walked to the water's edge, rolled him to the grass, then pulled him to a sitting position, legs draped over the retaining wall, shoes dangling over the dark water. The body listed but didn't fall. I slipped into the boat, moved the port oar out of the way, and tucked the tarp between the boat and wall, to muffle the impact I couldn't avoid. Staying seated to keep the boat stable, I reached for a foot, placed it over the gunwale, reached for the other foot. Leaning forward, I grabbed a fistful of shirt, ignored my pounding heart. No way to know if my plan would work unless—

I sprang to my feet, yanking the body toward me with all my strength. The boat dipped, the portside slammed into the retaining wall, the tarp thankfully absorbing most of the noise. Bear-hugging the body, I fell back, my rump just catching the center thwart. Waves spread, the oars rattled, I was panting into a dead man's face; but I'd gotten Himmel aboard.

Let go of the body, lowered it. Dragged the anchor aboard and pushed off, mounting the port oar as I drifted. Dipped, pulled hard, pointed the bow toward the river. Once I was on the Potomac, I could wrap the body and stones in the tarp, lash it tight. The current would carry me to the Long Bridge, where I could briefly tie up. Then, so long, Henry Himmel, a.k.a. Pavel Nevelskoi, a.k.a. unknown.

HIMMEL HAD CONTACTED ME THREE WEEKS EARLIER, THOUGH OF course I didn't know who he was then. A classified had summoned me. *Lost: silver pocket watch, inside cover engraved* K.B.L. *to* F.R.W., *on April 20 near Judiciary Square, reward.* I'd been promoted from beagle to watch. We met in a diner on F Street. What I'd been told was, the morning after I saw the ad, I should be in a booth along the west wall, order a Denver omelet, and set a folded *Times-Herald* next to my plate. The city's conservative daily, funny.

"We have a favor to ask," Himmel said as soon as he sat down. He studied me, taking my measure.

I took a bite of omelet, waited. He probably knew more about me than my parents now did. Where I lived, what I did off-duty, how many spoonfuls of sugar I stirred into my coffee every morning.

"A friend is moving, I can't be there to see him off," he said. "Could you go in my place?"

"Permanent move?"

"Yes."

"When?"

"Wednesday night." Watching me closely now.

Couldn't answer quickly, couldn't hesitate long. "You'll introduce us beforehand?" I decided to ask.

"Of course. At the usual place."

My last bite of omelet went down like a stone, I took a long drink of water to keep from choking. "I'll be there."

"Good." And with that, he left.

Protocol was, give the contact plenty of time. Finish your food, read the paper, drink another cup of coffee—you're just a joe getting a late breakfast, better look like it, don't act like a commie agent who's just been ordered to kill someone.

I wiped my mouth, dropped the wadded paper napkin on my plate, and walked at a leisurely pace to the men's room. Went into the stall, puked up the omelet, the hash browns, the coffee. No one else in there, I was able to wash up and pull myself together. But I didn't sleep a wink that night.

"The usual place" meant the dead drop Michael and I used. Locker 4-A, Union Station, we both had keys. The next morning, I retrieved a canvas bag with a single sheet of paper and a thirty-eight wrapped in a cloth. On the sheet, a description of the man I was supposed to kill, the site, the time, nothing more. Himmel had referred to the mark as a friend, codeword for a fellow Red, but nothing in the description flagged him as Logan Skerrill. *White, 26 years of age, five feet, eleven inches tall, 155 pounds, brown hair and eyes, will answer to William.*

"William?"

The man turned, shoes whisking on the alley's cobblestones. He wore tan slacks, white shirt, no tie, hands thrust into the pockets of his windbreaker. I was gauging his height and weight, just noticing that his hair was curly, a little long in the bangs. *Shoot now!* But his face looked familiar, I'd seen him before, I slipped the weapon back—

"Jesus Christ, is that you, Voigt?" He strode forward, coming closer; I checked the urge to run. How the hell did the mark know my name, what was—

"Skerrill!"

We faced each other, only a few feet apart, no one else around, the alley dwellings dark. He had taken his hands out of his pockets and tensed his arms.

"Oh, this is rich, this is too much to believe—they recruited you? Good ol' earnest Ellis Voigt, working class schmuck from Chicago, barely making it through the Funhouse"—*pull the gun, do it now!*—"you're the one I'm s'posed to meet?"

I'd squandered my second chance—he came up with the answer to his own question, instantly understanding why I was there. Logan Skerrill, Boy Wonder, always one step ahead of everyone else. He sprang forward, turning his shoulder, using his forearm to knock me off balance, trying to drop me. No punches, just as we'd both been trained: *get your opponent to the ground, break an arm, smash his hands.* I twisted my torso, his forearm glanced off my chest, but he reached for my right wrist as he planted his left leg behind me, now trying to flip me on my back. I broke free, reached into the left pocket of my jacket and gripped the roll of pennies I'd brought along, just in case, swung a roundhouse from my waist right up to his jaw. The blow staggered him, put him back on his heels—he'd been expecting me to counter with a move we'd been taught. But I wasn't going to beat Skerrill using our training—he was better than me. In the streets, in the alleys, anything goes, and fighting dirty was the only way I'd win.

The rest of our fight happened just as the coroner had guessed, except that the punch to Skerrill's abdomen was my second one and I missed the solar plexus. He didn't double over, instead started backing away, looking around for a weapon—a board, a rock, anything. I closed in, feinted a left jab as I delivered a straight punch to his nose, the pennies clutched in my right fist. Crack of bone, blood sprayed. Right roundhouse, again to the nose. Unnecessary, but I wanted to inflict pain. Two jabs, left-right, cut his cheek—I'd forgotten to take off the ring Delphine had given me—and then the left hook to the chin. My hands ached, I dropped the pennies into my pocket, reached for the thirty-eight. Skerrill was still on his feet, still looking for a weapon. Saw a broken cobblestone, somehow managed to pick it up without falling over. I aimed for his chest, missed wide, my hands shaky, the bullet hitting his left thigh. He grunted and fell to his knees as

I strode forward, firing two more shots, one below the rib cage, the other to his heart. Bang, bang—just like the coroner had said.

I dropped the gun into my pocket and ran—lights were coming on, someone had come out on his porch. I darted into a dark passageway between two alley dwellings, hopped a fence, raced across M Street, zigging and zagging my way out of the neighborhood. Somewhere in my flight, I wrenched the ring off and dropped it down a drain. Silver and amethyst, with a firebird spreading its wings over the band. Wasn't expensive, sentimental value only, thank God I'd never worn it on duty—I'd only slipped it on that night for luck. Probably could have kept it, hidden it. Didn't even think about the thirty-eight till I got home. Keeping the weapon was reckless, risky, stupid—but it saved my skin. Just ask Philip Greene.

WHY HAD HIMMEL PICKED THE ALLEY NEAR THE NAVY YARD? AS I finished tying the rope around his tarp-wrapped body, I wondered: Did he use that alley because he knew it belonged to the Navy, because he wanted O.N.I.—he wanted *me*—to get the investigation? I would find out in the morning—but only if I finished the task at hand.

Approaching the Long Bridge, I steered toward a pier, quickly tied a tautline hitch to the wooden buffer. I pulled the body aft, checked my knots, slid his legs over the sternsheets. Lifted his torso, pushed him into the water, released. For a heartstopping moment, the shrouded body drifted, rolling slightly, not sinking—I flashed on it floating right up on the Tourist Camp shore, people gawking and buzzing as I rowed up. But the dead don't bleed—they don't swim, either. A release of air bubbles as the stones won the battle of gravity, the tarp disappeared. Would the body stay down, buried in the muck of the Potomac's bottom? Probably not, it would dislodge eventually, wash up miles downriver, cause a stir. But that would take months, and decomposition would prevent an identification. They'd try to match the teeth to the dental records of missing persons, but the Russians sure as hell weren't going to file a report when they realized Himmel had disappeared.

I tossed the gun into the black water, untied the boat, rowed back to the camp. What I'd just done didn't release me from the grip of the Reds, it didn't make me safe. The N.K.V.D. had special sections, counterintelligence units that forayed across the States like a pack of wolves: never seen, seldom heard, littering hardscrabble landscapes with the carcasses of their victims. They'd trace every one of Himmel's last steps to find out what had happened to him. Not out of loyalty, or justice, or even retribution—the Reds would want to know if they'd been compromised. I had no doubt the N.K.V.D. would find me. Killing Himmel didn't protect me, it just bought me enough time to figure out what I'd do when the Russians came for me.

CHAPTER 40

M Y BASEMENT FLAT WASN'T MUCH OF A HOME, BUT THAT NIGHT it felt like a castle. Peeled off my clothes, stuffed them in a bag to dump the next morning. Hid the cash I'd taken from my bank box and the envelope with the schematic. No sign of Franklin D., I'd been gone too long, he'd given up on me. Returned to the alley, roamed to another block—wherever he'd gone, I hoped he could survive on the streets again if no one took him in. Just before I fell asleep, I remembered my broken promise to Miriam to meet her that night and wondered what she'd done when I never showed. Let a guy on the make bed her? Returned to her abusive foster brother Kenny? Another stray I'd taken in and abandoned, Miriam.

I thought putting my uniform on in the morning might feel strange, like I was dressing for a masquerade party, but it didn't. The uniform fit nicely, it was clean and pressed, I knew exactly who I was supposed to be when I wore it. No time for breakfast, only a Danish from a bakery on U Street.

I got off the bus a few blocks from the Navy Building and thrust the bag with my bloody shirt and jacket into a trash can behind a haberdashery.

Terrance had fallen asleep at his desk, his head resting on his forearms. He stirred, looked up blearily, wincing at the cricks in his neck and back. Didn't speak a word, just lit a cigarette and inhaled, glaring at me. He'd been there all night, looked like hell.

I sat down, lit up, and said, "Reason I didn't call in is—"

"Save it, you got a bigger problem brewing right now."

Not *we, you*. Bad sign. "Like what?" I asked, trying for unconcerned.

He picked up a sheet of paper, studied it, still blinking the sleep from his eyes. "D'you know a Lavinia Burling?"

"No."

"Guess she goes by the name 'Liv,' whatever the hell that means, works as a typist at the Office of War Information—"

"Liv? Liv! How do you know about her?"

"So you do know her?"

"She's a gal I date now and then." Trying to reel back my surprise.

"Uh-huh. But you don't know her full name? Even though she's your gal?"

"She's not my girl, Terrance—just a broad I bang every now and then." Trying not to wince at my words.

"Uh-huh." Still not believing me.

"Why're you asking about her?"

"Because your buddies from the Bureau are in the commander's office asking about her, and I'm supposed to—"

I sprang from my chair and raced to the door, didn't hear what Terrance shouted after me. Probably that I was supposed to sit tight till I was summoned. But doing what I was told wasn't going to help me, not now.

Paslett's door was closed; I could hear raised voices. Checked the urge to barge in, knocked like a dutiful junior officer.

"I said no disturbances, goddammit!" Paslett thundered.

"Lieutenant Voigt, sir. Requesting permission to enter."

Long pause, then, "All right."

Seated in front of the commander's desk, Agents Slater and Reid, cigarettes in hand, both men turning to look at me. Ignored them, staying at attention till Paslett nodded. Caught Reid's smirk as I dropped the salute. As if he and his partner didn't yessir John Edgar and stand ramrod straight every time they entered his sanctum.

Paslett glowered at me, didn't speak.

I said, "Lieutenant Daley tried to stop me, sir, but I didn't listen."

"There's a surprise," Reid chortled.

"What happened to your accent, Barston?" Slater asked sarcastically.

Paslett turned the glare on them. "You two wanna make jokes, you can slink back to the Justice Building now."

That wiped the smiles right off their faces. No defense of me, that whipcrack, just Paslett reminding them whose office they were sitting in.

"Agents Slater and Reid were just telling me about a girlfriend of yours, Voigt." The commander picked up a copy of the document Terrance had. "Lavinia Burling, a typist—seems you were out with her two nights ago. Excuse me—*Ted Barston* was out with this gal."

"Not Ted Barston, sir, me. Liv—Lavinia—only knows me as myself."

"And why were you out with her when you were undercover?"

"I broke cover, sir. To go on a date." Sugarcoating that fuck-up wouldn't help, I had to play it straight.

"Do you always telegram your girls to ask 'em out? When you're supposed to be undercover?"

"No, sir." Standing stock-still, taking it.

"In addition to fouling up your investigation, commander, Voigt cost us a lotta time and effort," Reid said. "Four men on the street just to find out where he'd been, which is how we got the telegram. On top of that, he caused a traffic accident on the Taft Bridge so he could throw boxes of clippings onto the parkway—it took us several hours to collect all those papers!"

"Then we had to track down the girl," Slater chimed in. "If it hadn't been for V-E, we'd a'had ahold of her then and there, but they ran out the back of a club and got lost in the crowds."

"Save your excuses for Hoover," Paslett growled, "and finish what you came to say."

"All right, commander. When this gal finally told us who Voigt was, we had to scramble to check her out—what you have there"—Reid motioned at the document—"is just the preliminaries. So far, this Burling looks clean, but we can only know for sure after we carry out a thorough investigation."

When this gal finally told us who Voigt was. Liv had held out as long as she could, but I should've known she didn't stand a chance against the Bureau. Slater and Reid had bullied her, told her she'd be fired from her government job, threatened her with prosecution under the Espionage Act, all the while demanding she give them my name. *Just his name, that's all, then we'll leave you alone.* And when she couldn't take it anymore: *Ellis.* She didn't know my last name, didn't matter—they would've forced her to say she knew I was in the Navy. A naval officer working undercover, first name Ellis; it hadn't taxed the Bureau's resources to identify me.

Slater and Reid were trying to bury me *and* cover up the operation they'd run with Skerrill. Couldn't blame them, couldn't get angry—you play with scorpions, you risk getting stung. As they were about to find out.

"Sir, have they told you about their little game with Skerrill?"

"Game?"

"Now hold on"—"Goddammit," Slater and Reid sputtered, but I cut them off.

"Skerrill was a Red, just like you figured, sir. He confessed all to the Bureau, which decided to run him as a mole to penetrate the spy ring at the clipping service." I smiled at the two agents. The office was awful small, but their eyefuck was a thousand yards long. "Did he come to you, or did you just get lucky and stumble across him?"

"Is this true?" Paslett asked them, an ice-cutter edge to his voice.

"With all due respect, commander, you're not authorized for briefings on that ongoing investigation," Reid said.

"Lieutenant Skerrill's dead, Agent Reid," Paslett bore down. "Did the Bureau hire a soothsayer to talk to his ghost? Is that what I'm not *authorized* to hear?"

Dumb play, trying to pull rank on a naval commander in the Navy Building, but the two had no choice—Hoover would skin them alive if they admitted they'd had Skerrill on a string.

Slater said, "Commander, we'd be happy to informally deliver a message to the director about your interest—"

"Don't hide behind Hoover's skirts—you came to me! Tell me I got an officer who's off the rails, urgent, urgent, must meet right away, and now you wanna clam up?"

"We're here about Voigt!" Reid exclaimed. "He's the officer who's fouled everything up! We're here as a courtesy. Commander, we could arrest him this moment but instead we've come to ask you what you're—"

"Sir, these two may not be authorized to talk about Skerrill—what about me?" I cut in.

"Proceed, lieutenant." He held up a hand at Slater and Reid's protests. "Like I said, you two can slink back to Justice any time you want."

They stayed put, they needed to hear what I said. Just as I'd hoped, Paslett wanted them to hear it, too. Skerrill turning Red, that was a stain on O.N.I., an embarrassment we wanted to keep quiet; but the Bureau running him as a mole without authorization was a secret Hoover wanted to keep. Paslett wanted *him* to know how much we knew. Quid pro quo, you keep mum, we will, too.

"Skerrill was walking both sides of the street, sir. I don't know when, or why, but he must've come to the Bureau—"

"You don't know that!" Slater shouted. "You can't prove we didn't pick him up."

"I also can't prove you both got two-inch pricks, unless you wanna stand and drop your trousers."

Before they could fire back, Paslett said, "No more interruptions, understand? Otherwise, I debrief Lieutenant Voigt by myself."

Slater lit another cigarette, furious; Reid slumped in his chair, scowling.

"You're right, I can't prove he came to you," I continued. "But odds are, he did. If you had something on him, you woulda swept him up and leaned hard. Knowing Skerrill—and I did, we went through training together—he woulda bluffed you, knowing you couldn't hold an officer without informing Navy. So he comes to you, gives you something fat and juicy so you know he's a real Red, then he hooks you but good by promising to bring you more if you don't charge him or tell us we've been compromised."

Paslett asked, "Why would Skerrill expose himself, Voigt, if no one was on to him?"

300

"That was his way, sir. He loved being in control, loved manipulating everyone. Look at his jacket, look at how he got started with that Mexican operation, changing it on the spot to put himself at the center. It worked, suddenly he's Boy Wonder—for us and the Reds. You'd think that'd be enough excitement, but it was like a drug with him, sir, he needed more. What's more dangerous than being a double agent? Being a triple agent."

"So what'd he bring the Bureau that was so fat and juicy?"

"I don't know, sir," I said slowly, drawing out *I* and *know*. Paslett caught my cue. The Bermuda Special, the German scientist, the New Mexico project—that's what Skerrill had brought them.

"What about the spy ring at the clipping service?"

"Whatever he gave the Bureau, he gave them, too." Which meant every O.N.I. operation Skerrill had a finger in had been compromised, an intelligence agency's worst nightmare. Had to give him credit, Paslett hid his dismay well, didn't wince, didn't sigh. Thank God he didn't know the whole truth.

"How'd the Reds find out he'd gone to the Bureau?"

"They followed him, sir." Just a guess, but Himmel wasn't around to contradict me, was he?

Reid studied me closely. The Bureau would've been extra careful when meeting with Skerrill, they would've had shadows on him to make sure he wasn't being followed. Reid didn't believe me—didn't matter. Thanks to Paslett, he and Slater were gagged until I finished my account.

"Himmel moved fast, sir. He's the head of the clipping service—we dig deep enough, we're gonna find out he was born in Russia, sir, I'm sure of it. He's the Soviets' conduit, he gets everything to the embassy."

Paslett was nodding along, tapping his finger on the desk, jazzed. I hadn't forgotten what he'd said the night he assigned the case to me and Terrance: coded cable traffic from the Soviet embassy had shot up recently. Hell, maybe what I'd just said was true—coded cables *did* transmit the espionage to Moscow.

"So what Himmel did is," I went on, "he tricked Philip Greene, one of the clipping service managers, to shoot Skerrill. Greene's got a crush on the other manager, Nadine Silva—but she was Skerrill's gal. Himmel told her to get lovey-dovey with Greene, to tell him that Skerrill had betrayed them all, that he had to be taken care of. Greene's a loyal commie, plus he's jealous of Skerrill—he didn't need to be asked twice to be the trigger man. Once I found the gun, well . . ." I shrugged—the rest didn't need to be said.

"He denies shooting Skerrill, you know." Slater could no longer contain himself.

"Yes, I know," I replied matter-of-factly, "I interrogated him."

"Nifty trick you pulled on him," Reid said, "but it's not gonna work."

Paslett said, "What Agent Reid is trying to tell you, Voigt, is that the Bureau has removed Greene and Silva from the custody of the Metropolitan Police and is currently holding them on federal charges."

As in, espionage. Fine by me, no way Himmel told Greene or Silva who I was—what if he had needed me to take care of one of them? The local police wouldn't protest, Skerrill's death wasn't on their books, we'd taken it from them. Didn't matter if Slater and Reid believed Greene was innocent, they were going to use the evidence I planted to leverage Greene on the espionage charges. As long as Paslett believed Greene had killed Skerrill, no one would investigate further.

"All right, that's enough," Paslett said. "Agents Slater and Reid, we're done, you can go now."

No protest, but after they stood, Slater said, "Commander, if I were you, I wouldn't count on Voigt telling you everything you need to know." Translation: once we finish grilling Greene and Silva, we'll know inside out how much Skerrill compromised O.N.I., and we'll keep that to ourselves unless you start playing nice.

But Paslett was in no mood to swap olive branches. "Don't tell me how to do my job, you two-bit government gumshoe. The Bureau shoulda gone to Forrestal"—James Forrestal, the secretary of the Navy—"as soon as Skerrill came in off the street. You tell your boss if I don't get a copy of your interrogation transcript of those two Reds, I'm letting the White House know what the Bureau did, including the beat-down you gave Voigt while he was undercover."

Slater glared but didn't answer. Paslett wasn't just posturing—word was, Truman hated Hoover, wanted to get rid of him, and the old toad didn't have any dirt on the new president. Reid said, "Let's go," and the two agents left.

"You can stay standing," Paslett ordered.

"Yessir."

"What happened to Himmel last night? Daley said you were gonna find him."

"I did, sir. Traced him back to the Wardman, where he lives."

"And?"

"He went to the Automat, on F Street, to meet with a contact. The doorman at the Wardman told me this, sir, so I was able to come here, to the Navy Building, to get Filbert Donniker before I went to the Automat."

"Why?"

"To see if he had any gear we could use to eavesdrop. Couldn't let Himmel see me, sir, obviously—"

"Why didn't you get Daley, someone with field experience, to listen in?"

"Filbert's been in the field, sir, he was perfect for the job. Looked like an old man, they never gave him a second glance, plus with the rig he brought, I could listen to every word they said."

"Where were you?"

"In the kitchen, sir."

"How do you know Himmel and his contact never suspected Filbert?"

"I looked through the service door window after he sat down."

"Describe Himmel's contact."

I did, right down to the color of the man's sweater.

"What did Himmel and his contact talk about?"

"Nothing important that I could tell, sir," I lied.

"Filbert's rig, did it record the conversation?"

"Nosir, it only has a microphone and a headset."

"Did you memorize the conversation?"

"A'course, sir."

"I'll need a transcript as soon as possible."

"Yessir."

"But you don't think they discussed anything important?"

"Well, sir, one thing they talked a lot about was the weather—my guess is, Himmel was telling him that he was folding up the clipping service, that it had been compromised."

"I don't want your guesses, lieutenant."

"No, sir."

"I want a verbatim copy of what they said, I don't want you telling me what it means."

"Yessir, I'll do it straight-off."

"Where did these two go, after they left the Automat?"

"I don't know about the contact, he left first. I posted myself outside, two blocks away, to wait for Himmel, but he never came out the front. Maybe he did think something was odd about Filbert, so he went out through the back."

"You lost him, you mean."

"Yessir. I lost him."

Paslett sighed, lit a cigarette, drummed his fingers on his desk. "I gotta file a spec, you know that, don't you?"

"Yessir." A "spec" was a specification of an offense, a disciplinary charge. Depending on how Paslett worked it, I faced reassignment, demotion, even discharge.

"Not for losing Himmel, for telegramming the girl and breaking cover."

"I understand, sir."

"You wanna tell me why you did it?"

"I thought I could lead two lives at the same time, sir. I was wrong—the case comes first, it always comes first, it's always fulltime."

He tapped ash from his cigarette. Jesus, I wanted a smoke, but I couldn't light up without permission.

Paslett said, "My bigger problem right now is what you brought in as the Reds' courier, that schematic and the postcard."

"They're both fake, aren't they, sir?"

"How'd you know?" Surprised, leaning forward, looking straight at me.

I thought of exactly what I could tell the commander. *Because Himmel, a.k.a. Pavel Nevelskoi, plotted all of this out from the moment he discovered Skerrill had gone to the Bureau, sir. He knew his espionage ring was done, the best he could do was hold on until he got the last delivery from his source in New Mexico. That's why he had me kill Skerrill instead of having the N.K.V.D. do it, that's why he picked a location that would allow O.N.I. to take the case from the locals. He wanted me to draw the case, he expected it. Because he knows of your fixation with Reds—I've given them lots of reports about you, sir—and he was betting that you'd send me in under cover. Then he arranged for me, as Ted Barston, to courier hoax espionage material to throw O.N.I., and the Bureau, off the real trail. The trail that led to the Automat, that led to the final delivery, that led to the message and schematic on how to diffuse Uranium 235.*

But I didn't say any of this to Paslett. Instead, "Because it was too easy, sir. To waltz into the clipping service, even with the cover story of being that commie union man's son, and get a job that important. I thought I was doing a good job, but Himmel musta seen through me right away."

He shook his head wearily. "These goddamned Reds, they're devious bastards, aren't they?"

"Yessir, they are."

CHAPTER 41

TYPED UP A FICTITIOUS TRANSCRIPT OF THE CONVERSATION BETWEEN Himmel and his New Mexico source, making sure it sounded authentic. What I was going to do with the message about uranium and the schematic hidden in my flat, I had no idea—but instinct told me to keep them to myself. Paslett accepted the typed sheets with barely a word and dismissed me, told me to go home and return in the morning to find out about my spec.

But I didn't go home, I went straight to Liv's rooming house at Tenth and M Streets.

"Yeah?" The woman answering my knock was on the buxom side of fat, right hand propped on her hip.

"M'looking for Liv, Lavinia Burling. Is she here or at work?"

"She moved."

"What? When?"

"Today, right, Eunice?" she yelled into the parlor. In the dim hallway two women paused to listen, whispering shadows. I couldn't hear the answer from the parlor.

The big woman turned back and said, "She left an hour ago. Had her bags, trunk, too."

"Where'd she go?"

"Dunno."

"Could you ask?" Checking the urge to shove past her.

This time I caught the answer: "Union Station."

I ran off the porch and sprinted across the yard. Trotted east on M, looking around for a hack—none to be seen for a long block. Finally hailed one and told him I was in a hurry, gasping for breath.

"Everybody's in a hurry, Mac," he replied, but he pushed it, dropped me off at the station's west side portal in two minutes. I burst through the doors. Sunlight brightened the latticed skylights of the barrel vault roof and left a sheen on the smooth tiled floor. A wooden colonnade separated the concourse from the massive central lobby, queues of passengers funneling out from gates. I skidded to a stop at the departures board and scanned the westbound runs. Figured she was bound for California, that meant a transfer in Chicago. Shoved my way through the first line, waved my O.N.I. identification card at the startled gate agent.

"Capitol Limited—which track?" I shouted.

"Seventeen. But they already made last—"

I was at Track Four. I hurtled down the concourse, dodging luggage carts, porters, and passengers. The Capitol Limited's locomotive faced front, a gigantic black cylinder with a Cyclops-like headlight and a spotless brass bell. Faint smoke drifted from the stack as it idled. Athwart the spoked drivers, cylinders thrummed deeply, radio static crackled in the cab—this train was about to leave. I raced down the platform, past the tender, past the mail and baggage cars, past the gleaming riveted panels of the sleepers, toward the slim woman in a knee-length dress, a wide-brimmed hat atop black curls. She was talking to a Negro porter, who nodded and stepped sprightly aboard the train. She turned to board, reaching for the handrail—

"Liv!"

She whirled around. "El!" She stepped down to the platform and touched my cheek, damp with sweat. "You ran here?"

"Just about. From your boarding house." I tried to catch my breath. "Liv, listen, I'm so sorry for what happened. I shoulda told you they'd come to see you, but I didn't want you to worry, I was trying to keep you outta it."

"It's all right, it's okay."

"Did they—how bad was—"

"None of that matters, El, only what I make of it. When they threatened to have me fired, I realized what they were saying for real."

"I don't understand."

"It's like those agents were messengers, El, telling me it's time to go to the Pacific. So I quit, I packed up—I'm going to San Francisco, I can leave from there as soon as the war's over."

"I want to go with you," I said. "All the way."

"Are you sure?"

"Yes."

"Then come with me now."

"What?"

"To San Francisco."

"I don't have a ticket, I've got no money."

"We'll buy it onboard, I've got lots of money. The bank can wire your account when we get to California." Looking into my eyes, lips pursed, gripping my hand. *Live free, and the rest will follow.* Keeping true to those words meant I had to board that train with Liv and not look back. The whistle blew, two long blasts.

But I couldn't live free. I was a traitor, a coward, a murderer; a man without honor, friends, or allies. If I went with Liv, Paslett and Terrance would think I'd fled because I had something to hide, that I was afraid of what the specification of offenses might uncover. They'd start digging, they'd turn my life upside down, they'd search my flat—they'd find the schematic I'd taken off Himmel's body. And then they'd come get me, no place in the world was safe from Paslett's wrath and reach. Even if the O.N.I. couldn't find me, the Russians would. I'd go down, for good, dragging Liv with me. I had to stay behind, I had to clean up my mess, I had to make things right.

"I can't, Liv."

She said nothing.

"Ma'am, please." The porter spoke from the vestibule. "That was the last whistle."

Liv wrapped her arms around my shoulders and pressed close for a deep, long kiss, my flushed cheeks hot against her cool, smooth skin, our lips parting softly. The cars shuddered, couplers clanking as the engineer eased open the throttle. She dashed to the steps, the porter pulled her aboard. As the train glided away, she leaned out and shouted three words. And then she was gone.

I didn't answer until the locomotive had receded into the yard, just one train among many on countless tracks.

"And the rest will follow," I said to the empty platform.